By William Bernhardt
Published by The Ballantine Publishing Group:

PRIMARY JUSTICE
BLIND JUSTICE
DEADLY JUSTICE
PERFECT JUSTICE
CRUEL JUSTICE
NAKED JUSTICE

DOUBLE JEOPARDY

BLIND JUSTICE

William Bernhardt

BALLANTINE BOOKS • NEW YORK

A Ballantine Book
Published by The Ballantine Publishing Group
Copyright © 1992 by William Bernhardt
Excerpt from *Naked Justice* copyright © 1997 by William Bernhardt

http://www.randomhouse.com

ISBN 0-345-48326-X

Manufactured in the United States of America

BVG 01

For Michel, Valerie, and Karis

They say Justice is bloind. That she is.
And deef and doom and has a wooden leg,
as well.

Finley Peter Dunne's "Mister Dooley"

In law, what plea so tainted and corrupt,
But, being seasoned with a gracious voice
Obscure the show of evil?

William Shakespeare
The Merchant of Venice, Act III, scene ii

* Prologue *

He returned the gun to the end table drawer. That would be his last resort, he thought, as he closed the drawer, hands trembling. The absolute last.

There were all kinds of tricks he could try before it came to that. Options abounded. He strode into the kitchen, trying to buoy his spirits with false optimism. It didn't work.

He opened the refrigerator and removed the chilled carafe. He knew which one she would choose; it didn't take a genius. He removed a small bottle from his pocket, unscrewed the dropper, and carefully let eight drops fall into the carafe. That was the recommended dosage—more than enough, in all likelihood. Then again, he thought, better safe than sorry. He released six more drops into the carafe.

He returned the carafe to the refrigerator, almost dropping it in the process. He stared at his hands—they were covered with sweat. His whole body was soaked; a cold, clammy sensation radiated from his head to his toes. He wiped his brow, then dried his hands on a dish towel. He couldn't let this get to him. Options, he reminded himself. Abundant options. Everything would be fine. Well, except for her, of course.

He walked back into the living room, glancing through the patio windows on the north side. There were two cars parked on the ground level in the driveway, watching, ready to follow at a moment's notice. They had been there all day.

What were they waiting for? He felt his knees shaking, his respiration accelerating. Just don't panic, he told himself. There could be hundreds of reasons why two cars would be parked in the driveway. Perfectly innocent ones. It still wasn't hopeless. Options, abundant options.

Yeah, right. He couldn't just sit here and wait for them to come. He opened the end table drawer and reached for the gun—then stopped. Mother of God!—that wasn't the answer. At least not yet. He slammed the drawer closed, his heart palpitating violently in his chest.

He threw himself into an easy chair and tried to think through his plan, its intricate details and contingencies, but his eyes kept diverting to the window. Were they still there? And how much longer until—

He closed his eyes. This was pointless. He would just proceed according to plan; that was the only solution. Create a diversion, as it were—throw the heat off him. It would buy him sufficient time to get the hell out of town. At any rate, it was better than the alternative.

He inhaled deeply and felt his heartbeat slowly subside. That was the ticket—just stick to the plan, and watch everything work itself out. Oh!—he would have to call her and leave the appropriate message. But it was too early for that. The less time she had to think about it the better.

He smiled. This will work, he told himself. It really will. Let the bastards come; he would be ready for them. He fell back into his chair, at last confident that everything would work out, that the end table drawer would not have to be opened.

Until the phone rang.

PART ONE

* *

The Chicken Is in the Mail

* 1 *

There was something wrong with Ben's office, but he couldn't quite put his finger on what. Maybe it was the dozen or so chickens running amuck on the linoleum floor. Perhaps it was the toilet paper strewn throughout the lobby. Or possibly it was the man pointing a gun at Ben's face.

"Is there something I can do for you?" Ben asked, trying to appear calm.

"Not really," said the large, unshaven man holding the weapon. "I just come in to blow your head off."

"Oh," Ben said. It was hard to know what to say.

Jones, Ben's male secretary, stood up behind the small card table he called his secretarial station. "Is there something I should be doing, Boss?"

"Call 911," Ben said succinctly.

"Right away, Boss." Jones picked up the phone receiver and began to dial.

The intruder adjusted his aim slightly in Jones's direction. "You try it and I'll shoot the phone right out of your hand."

Jones hesitated. "Come on. You don't look like you're nearly that good a shot."

"You're right," the man replied. "I'll probably miss."

Jones hung up the phone.

"Look," Ben said, "at least tell me what this is all about. You know, grant the last wish of the condemned."

The man looked at Ben suspiciously. "Why should I?"

5

Ben thought for a moment. "So I can rue my fatal error in the hour of my doom?"

The man did not seem impressed.

"So I know what file to put the coroner's report in," Jones offered. "I hate it when the filing backs up."

Ben rolled his eyes. Thanks, Jones.

This line of reasoning, however, seemed to engage the man's attention. "Try the file labeled *Loving* versus *Loving*," he said bitterly.

Ben remembered the case. The surnames stuck in his mind; they were pretty ironic, given that it was a divorce case. "You must be Mr. Loving."

"Damn straight," Loving said, pushing the gun closer to Ben's face. "And you're the man who took my woman away from me."

"I'm the attorney who represented her in the divorce," Ben corrected. "Why didn't you show up at the hearing?"

Loving's broad, strong shoulders expanded. "Some things is between a man and a woman," he said. "I don't hold with airin' dirty laundry in public."

"When you didn't appear at the hearing or send a lawyer to represent you," Ben explained, "the matter became uncontested." He saw in the corner of his eye that Jones had quietly lifted the phone receiver again and was beginning to dial. He tried to keep Loving distracted. "The judge granted the divorce by default. She had no choice, really, under the circumstances."

Loving took a step closer. "I heard you told some disgusting, filthy lies about me in that courtroom."

Ben cleared his throat. "I . . . merely recited the allegations of my client."

"Like sayin' I liked to dress up in high heels and panty hose?"

"Uhh . . . I believe that was one of the reasons your ex wanted a divorce," Ben said weakly.

"And what was that stuff about barnyard animals?" Loving growled.

Ben stared at the ceiling. "Oh, was there something about barnyard animals? I don't recall exactly. . . ." He felt a bead of sweat trickling down his forehead. Couldn't Jones dial any faster?

"You made my life a living hell!" Loving shouted. He was waving the gun wildly back and forth. "You took away the best woman I ever knew. Now you're going to pay for it."

"I don't suppose it would make any difference if I told you today was my birthday?" Ben asked.

Loving cocked the hammer. "Consider this your present."

"If you really love your wife so much, why don't you try to win her back?"

"Win her back?"

"Yeah. Maybe you two could get remarried."

"It's too late for that."

"Of course it's not too late," Ben assured him. "Reconciliations happen all the time. Natalie Wood and Robert Wagner got married three times!"

Loving appeared to consider this. "I don't know. . . ."

"You've got to court her, that's all. Like when you were first dating. Bring her flowers, candy. Write her a poem. Hold hands in the moonlight."

"We never did any of that."

Ben frowned. "You must have done something romantic when you were courting."

"Courting?" Loving snorted. "I met Babs in a bar downtown. After a few drinks, we did the hokeypokey in the back of my semi. It wasn't no big deal. Damned if she didn't turn up pregnant, though. So we had to get married."

"Well then," Ben said, trying to salvage himself, "so much the better. This will all be new to her." He snapped his fingers. "I bet I have some old love poems I could loan you."

"You really think this could work?" Loving asked. He began to smile, however slightly.

"You'll never know until you try. But I think you two crazy kids could patch things up, assuming you don't make a tragic mistake that sends you to the penitentiary for the rest of your life."

"Babs might come back to me?"

"I think it's entirely possible."

"Well, I don't," Loving said. The last vestiges of a smile faded from his face. He leveled the gun at Ben's nose and fired.

Jones cracked the ice out of the tray. He wrapped the ice in a washcloth and tied it with a rubber band. After struggling with the person-proof bottle cap, he popped a few Tylenol tablets into his pocket. Just in case. He returned to Ben's tiny office and walked to the ratty sofa on the far wall.

He brushed Ben's hand aside and placed the ice pack on his forehead. "How does that feel?"

"Cold," Ben answered.

"Is it having a calming effect?"

"At the moment I don't think a hundred winged seraphs strumming Brahms's Lullaby on their harps would have a calming effect. I just got shot at, remember?"

"Well, yeah," Jones said, "by a man with a toy pistol containing a little flag with the word BOOM! on it. We're not exactly talking Lee Harvey Oswald here."

"Easy for you to say. The little flag didn't poke you in the eye. I nearly lost a contact." He read the expression on Jones's face. "I was startled, okay?"

"You don't have to tell me," Jones said. "I was there. I saw you swoon."

"I did not *swoon*. I lost my balance."

"If you say so." Jones tried not to smile.

"I can still hear that man's maniacal laughter. What was it he said? 'You put me through hell, Kincaid, so I decided to let you see what it was like.' What a sicko."

"Yeah. It was kind of funny, though." Jones glanced at Ben's somber expression. "In a sick sort of way, I mean."

"That's what I thought you meant." Ben covered his eyes with the ice pack. "Incidentally, Jones, this may be none of my business, but why are there chickens running all over my office?"

"Frank Brannon finally decided to pay his bill. He didn't have any money. But he has a surplus of hens."

"Great. This is what I get for taking a tractor repossession case."

"I wasn't aware you were in a position to choose."

"Yeah, well, nonetheless." Ben rubbed the ice pack up and down the sides of his face. "Chickens. Jeez, that'll help pay the rent. And think of the convenience, if a famine should suddenly strike Tulsa."

"Speaking of paying the rent, Boss—I don't like to be a nag, but my paycheck is overdue."

"That's true. Unfortunately, I'm fresh out of cash. But feel free to take all the chickens you want. By the way, is all that toilet paper still littering the lobby?"

"No. I cleaned that up right after the police hauled off Mr. Loving for assault with a practical joke."

"Jones," Ben said, pointedly ignoring the jibe, "may I ask who T.P.'d my office?"

"Who do you think?"

"Right." Ben stretched out on the sofa. "If you'll be so kind as to close the door on your way out, Jones, I'm going to lie here quietly for a few hours and see if I can bring my heart rate back down to the three-digit numbers."

Jones didn't move. "Boss?"

"Yes?"

"Was that true, what you said?"

"About my heart rate?"

"No. About Natalie Wood and Robert Wagner."

"Well . . . they divorced and remarried once."

"Oh. You lied."

"I did not lie. I . . . exaggerated." He touched the reddened skin around his eye gingerly. "Under the circumstances it was the best I could come up with."

Jones still hesitated.

"Yes?"

"Wasn't the Simmons trial scheduled to continue at ten o'clock today?"

Ben looked at his watch. "Ohmigosh. It's already ten till! Jones, you're supposed to keep me on time for my appointments!"

"Sorry, Boss. I was distracted by the gunplay."

Ben grabbed his briefcase and bolted out the door, still pressing the ice pack to his head. If he ran all the way to the courthouse, he just might make it.

* 2 *

Ben fought his way out of the crowded elevator and scrambled toward Judge Hart's courtroom on the fifth floor of the Tulsa County Courthouse. Christina was waiting for him just outside.

"What's the matter, Ben?" she asked, grinning from ear to ear. "Forget to set the alarm clock?"

He ran up to her, gasping for breath. "I've been awake for hours. It was the gunfight that slowed me down."

"*Gunfight?* What happened?"

"I'll tell you later. Where's Judge Hart?"

"She hasn't taken the bench yet. She had some arraignments she had to call before the trial resumes."

"Thank God for small miracles."

"Yeah. Your planets must be in alignment." Christina tossed her long strawberry blonde hair behind her shoulders. She was wearing a short leather skirt, hip boots, and yellow leotards. Standard Christina *accoutrements*. "Incidentally, Ben—happy birthday."

Ben gave her a quelling stare. "You promised you wouldn't tell anyone."

"Chill out already. I haven't told anyone. But I do have a little something for you. Will you be in your office later?"

"As soon as the trial ends."

"Mind if I drop by?"

"My door is always open to you, Christina. As long as you don't start snooping around for information your boss can use against me in court." He glanced at the courtroom doors. "Is Mrs. Simmons inside?"

"Yeah. I think you need to comfort her. She looks *les miserables*."

"In what way?"

"Oh, the usual. Sweaty palms, knocking knees."

Ben nodded. "Everybody gets the jitters before they take the stand. But thanks for the tip." If Christina said talk to the client, Ben talked to the client. She had first-rate instincts, in addition to being the best legal assistant he had ever known. Pity she was on the other side.

Ben and Christina met and first worked together during Ben's brief tenure as an associate at Raven, Tucker & Tubb, Tulsa's largest, swankiest law firm. After he got the boot, she quit in protest and started working for Swayze & Reynolds. The change seemed to be good for her; the managing partner, Quinn Reynolds, was giving her important assignments and access to their most prominent clients. As far as Ben could tell, she was very successful, although success hadn't improved her wardrobe or her penchant for abusing French clichés.

As they entered the courtroom together, Ben saw Reynolds shoot Christina a nasty look. She'd probably get chewed out later for fraternizing with the enemy. Although he was the managing partner at Swayze & Reynolds, Reynolds was, as a rule, arrogant, pretentious, and generally unlikable. Worst of all, he was a lousy lawyer—always obstreperous and unwilling to compromise. He liked to promote settlement by way of harassment and delaying tactics, both of which Ben had been fighting throughout this entire case. Reynolds would probably be ostracized by the majority of the legal community, but for one minor detail. His wife sat on the Oklahoma Supreme Court. Ben had heard people complain about Reynolds for months, but the stories always ended the same: "Hell, I'd like to tell the jerk what I really think of him, but what can you do? He sleeps with the judge."

Ben found his client, Amy Simmons, sitting at plaintiff's table by herself. She wore a tense, forlorn expression. Amy had been rear-ended in a car accident several months earlier. She brought a negligence action against the driver of the car that hit her, Tony Lombardi, seeking damages for her injuries. Reynolds was representing Lombardi and the insurance company that carried his policy.

"Morning, Amy. Sorry I'm late."

She smiled faintly. "It's all right. That legal assistant on the other side told me you were practicing your closing argument."

Another favor he owed Christina. "Do you feel secure about your testimony? Are there any other questions you wanted to ask me?"

Amy's face tightened. "Do I really have to go up there in front of the judge and everybody?"

"I'm afraid so." He patted her hand. "Don't worry about it, Amy. I'll be here the whole time. You'll do fine. Promise."

"I hope so," she said nervously. "I really do."

After Judge Helen Hart entered the courtroom, she reassembled the jury and resumed the trial. Judge Hart was in her mid-forties and had been on the bench long enough to approach her work with a sense of grace and humor Ben found extremely refreshing. A good judge could make a tense trial like this one much more bearable.

Ben's only remaining witness was Mrs. Simmons; she was the make-or-break witness for their case. The medical witnesses were perfectly convincing, but if Amy didn't persuade the jury she had been injured in the auto accident and was still suffering resultant damage, the jury would never enter a verdict in her favor.

After she took the stand, Ben steered Amy gently through the direct examination they had prepared and practiced countless times in advance of trial. She was extremely nervous, but her answers were solid, and she appeared sincere. She discussed her neck injury and the symptoms she experienced periodically: the sharp, stabbing pain, the uncontrollable spasms, the inability to hold her head erect. Her doctor said she had a severe soft tissue injury and, after performing some minor surgery, he prescribed medication and physical therapy for the rest of her life.

After they completed their prepared questions, Ben stepped away from the podium. Amy's testimony had been fine, but it hadn't really captured the jurors' heartstrings. It was a little too canned, too pat. Ben knew he needed to depart from the script and ask some zingers artfully designed to elicit jury sympathy.

"Amy, are you able to enjoy the same quality of life you had before the accident?"

Amy looked down at her hands. "Oh, you know. I do all right."

Hardly a stirring response. "Amy, are you still able to play tennis?"

"Well, you know, Mr. Kincaid, I never really enjoyed tennis that much."

"What about your golf game?"

"Well, now that I have grandchildren, I don't need to be out chasing a little ball all over the green."

Ben took a deep breath. "Amy, are you embarrassed when your neck starts to twitch in public?"

"Oh, my. You know, I don't give much thought to what other people think."

Sheesh. This called for drastic action. Ben approached the stand and leaned over the rail. "Amy. I know you're trying to be brave and uncomplaining, but you must be honest with the jury. I can see your neck trembling. It hurts, doesn't it? It hurts right now."

She pressed her hand against her neck. "Yes," she whispered.

Good girl. He was leading the witness, of course, but Reynolds was probably too dim to notice. "It hurts every day, doesn't it? So badly you can barely tolerate it?"

Her entire head was shaking. Her nod was barely perceptible.

"And if you can't afford to pay for the medication and the physical therapy, that pain is going to continue unabated for the rest of your life, isn't it?"

Her eyes were welling up with tears. "I-I guess so," she said.

"Thank you. No more questions, your honor."

Ben returned to plaintiff's table, pleased. It was a struggle, but Amy finally managed to tell the jury what they needed to know. Just let Reynolds try to take her apart on cross. If he got rough with her, the jury would hate his effete little guts.

Reynolds walked slowly to the podium. He obviously saw the dilemma as clearly as Ben, and as a result, wasn't sure how to begin. "Mrs. Simmons, my name is Quinn Reynolds." He stood for a moment, poised in thought. "I represent the defendant, Mr. Lombardi."

"And his insurance company," Amy added.

"Move to strike," Reynolds said, without missing a beat.

"Granted," Judge Hart said. "The jury will disregard the witness's last remark."

"And I move for a mistrial," Reynolds said.

"Don't you wish," the judge replied. "Proceed with your questions, counselor."

"Mrs. Simmons, you claim you have suffered a soft tissue injury to your neck. Is that correct?"

"That's what the doctor told me."

"But Mrs. Simmons, isn't what the doctor actually said—" Reynolds flipped through his notebook, then turned it over and flipped through it again. "Now where did I put that?" He walked back to defendant's table and began burrowing through his huge stash of documents.

Ben smiled. There was nothing better than seeing a sleaze-meister's dirty tricks backfire. Early in the case, Reynolds had issued a huge request for production of documents. Reynolds was obviously hoping to bury Ben, the sole practitioner, under a morass of paperwork, and to make the litigation as expensive for Amy as possible. Now Reynolds was unable to find the document he needed because it was lost somewhere in the morass of documents he brought into existence. Sweet irony.

Unfortunately, Christina, a far better legal assistant than Reynolds deserved, walked unobtrusively to the front of the courtroom, went directly to the proper file folder and retrieved the document he needed. Reynolds snatched it from her without so much as a nod and returned to the podium.

"As I was saying, Mrs. Simmons. Isn't it true your doctor referred to your injury as 'probably minor and easily removed'?"

"Easily removed?" A puzzled expression crossed her face. "May I see that?"

Reynolds didn't want to, but Judge Hart gestured at the witness stand, indicating she wanted the witness to examine the document. He passed it to the bailiff, who handed it to Amy.

"Probably minor and easily removed," Amy repeated, perusing the medical record. "Oh, I see now. This isn't about my neck injury. This is about a wart."

Reynolds blinked. "A wart?"

"Yes. See, at the top of the page, the doctor refers to my verruca vulgaris. That's a wart." She looked up at Reynolds. "You're right; that was minor and easily removed."

Ben covered his smile with his hands. This cross couldn't be better if he had scripted it himself. He could see the jury verdict crystalizing before his eyes; dollar signs were flashing like neon lights.

Reynolds flipped a few more pages in his notebook. At least he had the sense to know when to start over. "You say your neck causes you pain on a regular basis?"

"That's true."

"That you experience disorientation and dizziness."

"I'm afraid so."

"And that you are subject to sudden uncontrollable neck seizures."

"Yes. Particularly when I'm tired."

What softballs, Ben thought. Reynolds must've given up trying to win the case and decided just to act sympathetic and hope for the best.

"And you've testified that the neck spasms are interfering with your work."

"Well, as a nurse, I'm in contact with patients on a regular basis. A violent neck twitch doesn't make for good bedside manner."

"And these neck ailments began after the car accident?"

"Oh no," she said cheerily. "I've had this problem all my life."

Ben's jaw practically thudded against the table. *What?*

"Are you saying your injury was *not* caused by the car accident?" Reynolds asked.

Amy's mouth opened, but no words came out. Apparently it had dawned on her that she might have said something wrong. She looked at Ben, as if hoping he would answer for her.

Judge Hart glanced down from the bench. "The witness will answer the question."

Ben mentally envisioned the dollar signs slipping through his fingers. He jumped to his feet. "Your honor, I object. I can't see what possible relevance—"

"Save it," Judge Hart said, cutting him off. "Overruled. Not that I blame you for trying."

"I've had neck problems since I was a little girl," Amy answered. "I was about eight or nine when they started."

"Mrs. Simmons, when I took your deposition two months ago, you described in great detail the neck pains you experienced the day of the accident."

"That's true," she said. "I did have a bad attack that day."

"But it was not the first time you had the problem."

"Oh no. Not at all."

Reynolds grinned malevolently. If her neck ailment predated the accident, then it wasn't caused by the car accident, meaning the driver of the assaulting car wasn't liable. Nor was his insurance company. "No more questions, your honor."

"Any redirect?" Judge Hart asked.

Ben rose. "Yes, your honor."

The judge nodded. "Lotsa luck."

Ben hustled to the podium. He was going to have to rehabilitate this witness like he had never rehabilitated before.

"Amy. You did testify that your neck hurt shortly after the accident, didn't you?"

"Oh, yes. Terribly so."

"Was it just another spasm like the others you'd had before?" *Please, God, be with me now!*

"Oh no. It was much worse."

Yes! "So the pain after the accident was much worse."

"Much much more so. It had never really hurt before. After the accident, though, the pain was almost incapacitating."

"Do you know why?"

"According to Dr. Carter, the whiplash effect when Mr. Lombardi's car rammed into me caused a cervical disk between two cervical vertebrae to impinge upon a nerve."

"And that's a permanent injury, isn't it, Amy?"

"I'm afraid so. Although the medication, surgery, and therapy will help, the doctors say the condition will never entirely disappear."

"So even if the accident didn't instigate your neck problems, it would be fair to say it seriously aggravated the preexisting condition?"

"Oh yes. It's been much worse and more frequent since the accident."

Praise all that's holy. "Thank you, Amy. I have no more questions, your honor."

"Very well," the judge said. "Gentlemen, we'll resume at one o'clock. And incidentally, Mr. Kincaid," she added, "nice save."

* 3 *

Ben greeted Amy Simmons in his office lobby, carefully sidestepping the chickens. He hoped if he acted as if they weren't there, she wouldn't ask any questions.

"I just wanted to thank you again for taking my case, Mr. Kincaid," Amy said. "All the other lawyers I contacted turned me down flat."

"Well, soft tissue injuries are difficult to prove."

"You were wonderful in the courtroom today. Especially after my cross-examination."

"That was nothing special. I just had to adjust our theory of recovery to the eggshell skull doctrine. If the negligent party aggravates a preexisting injury, he can still be held liable for the increased pain and suffering. No big deal."

"I thought you were brilliant. I guess the jury thought so, too."

Ben shook his head. "I wouldn't say that. They only awarded you ten thousand dollars in damages. Fortunately, the other side settled, so you'll be spared an appeal, but you'll have to spend half the ten thou just to cover your preexisting medical bills, much less pay for future expenses."

"It isn't your fault I never told you I had neck problems before the accident. I just assumed everyone knew."

"Uh, no."

"Anyway, my brother-in-law is in law school at TU and he told me the verdict was excellent, given the circumstances. So before I do anything else, I want to pay your fee.''

Since Amy couldn't afford to pay an hourly rate or a flat fee, Ben had regretfully taken the case on a contingency fee, which meant he didn't get paid unless and until they recovered from the defendant. ''Amy, if you give me a third, you won't have enough for your own medical expenses.''

''That doesn't matter,'' she said. ''A deal is a deal. Here, I have the check already written out.''

She handed him a check for $3,333.

That would pay a great many overdue bills, Ben mused. But no. He folded the check and tore it into tiny pieces.

''Sorry, Amy,'' he said, ''but it's always the lawyer's prerogative to waive his fee, and that's what I'm doing.'' He let the check shreds fall to the floor. ''You keep your money and get the treatment you need.''

Amy gazed at Ben, her eyes sparkling. Wordlessly, she took his shoulders and kissed him on the cheek. Then she gathered her purse and left the office.

''Wow,'' Jones said, looking up from his card table. ''Whatta guy.''

''Yeah, yeah, yeah.''

''Point of order, though, Boss. Since you gave up your only prospect of recovering a fee anytime in the near future, how are you going to pay me?''

''With the milk of human kindness,'' Ben replied.

''Nothing personal, but I'd prefer a form of legal tender that's accepted at Kmart.''

The front door breezed open, and Christina bustled in carrying a package.

''A member of the opposition,'' Ben said. ''I hope you didn't come here to gloat.''

''Gloat? Hey, you got a jury verdict in your favor.''

Ben shrugged. ''For peanuts.''

"That was hardly your fault. Anyway, forget the trial. *Que será será.* I came to bring you a birthday present."

Jones straightened. "Birthday? You mean today really is your birthday?"

"Oops." Christina closed her eyes. *"Pardonnez-moi."*

"Boss, I can't believe you didn't tell me. How old are you?"

"Thirty," Ben replied, "which is exactly why I didn't tell you. I thought you might be tempted to indulge in black balloons or strippers or other such birthday shenanigans."

"I prefer those guys who dress up like gorillas and deliver pizza—"

"My point exactly." Ben examined Christina's package. "That's not my birthday present, is it?"

"Of course it is," she said, pushing it toward him. "What's your problem?"

"Well, I can't help but notice that the box appears to have air holes."

"Aren't you the amateur detective? C'mon, open it up."

Ben set the package on Jones's card table, pulled the bow loose, and removed the lid. Inside, he found a cat. A huge, black cat with a white ring around her nose.

"Don't you love her already?" Christina asked.

"Christina . . . I'm not really a cat person—"

"Oh, pish tosh. How would you know? You've never had a pet in your life."

"I like living alone."

"That's exactly my point," Christina said. "You've been living alone too long. It's not healthy."

"Are you afraid I'll have an arrested social development? Won't learn to play well with other children?"

"I just want you to get it through that thick skull of yours that you don't have to do everything all by yourself."

"In my experience, the less contact I have with other people, the better. For them and me."

"You're too old to be a lone wolf. It's time to start accepting help from others, to develop a family of friends."

"I've already had a family," Ben muttered. "It didn't work out."

"That's so wrong, Ben." She lifted the cat out of the box. "And that's what this little kitty is going to teach you."

"This little kitty? That monster must weigh twenty pounds!"

"She is a bit on the heavy side. She used to belong to my girlfriend, Sally Zacharias, but she's getting married and moving into a no-pets condo. She asked if I could find her a good home with a kind, nurturing master."

"So you're giving her to me?"

"I'm sure you could learn to be nurturing. In time." She passed the cat to Ben.

He took the cat awkwardly and held her like a science project. "What's her name?"

"Sally called her Giselle. I suppose you can call her anything you like."

"Giselle. That's a good name. Very classical music." He stroked her back timidly with one finger. Giselle purred happily.

"See?" Christina said. "You two are getting along famously already. Here's a couple of cans of cat food, just to get you through the night."

Ben read the labels. "What's Feline's Fancy?"

"Gourmet cat food. It's all she'll eat. I hate to break it to you, but it's the most expensive brand on the market, by far."

"If she's coming home with me, she'll have to develop more mundane tastes."

"Yeah, well, good luck. I have a food dish and litter box and various other cat essentials at my apartment. I'll bring them by tomorrow."

"Why don't you bring them by tonight? You can see how we're getting along."

"Sorry, pal. I have an appointment."

Ben cocked an eyebrow. "Oh? With whom?"

She hesitated. "Tony Lombardi."

"Dating a client? That doesn't seem smart."

"It's not a date. Exactly. I'm taking some settlement papers over for him to sign. Besides, the trial is over. Tony and I spent a lot of time together during the last two months. It was only natural for him to ask me out." She smoothed her silky red hair. "After all, I am devastatingly attractive."

"I thought Lombardi seemed very tense in court today. Totally stressed out. At the time, I assumed he was worried about the trial. Now I realize it was because he had a date with you."

"Ha, ha."

"Christina, this does not sound like a good idea to me."

Christina fluttered her eyelids. "Benjamin Kincaid. I believe you're jealous!"

"Oh, don't be ridiculous. I'm just concerned for your well-being. As I would be for any friend."

"Uh-huh."

"I am!"

She grinned. "If you say so."

"Anyway, it's none of my business. Just try to stay out of trouble."

"Don't worry about me, Ben. I can take care of myself." She headed toward the door. "Have fun with the cat. And happy birthday."

The second Christina left the office, Giselle began to mewl.

"Calm down," Ben said. "It looks like you're stuck with me. At least for a little while." He stared deeply into Giselle's marble green eyes. "I wonder if you would be any good at hunting chickens?"

* 4 *

Christina shoved another box of documents onto the top shelf. If Reynolds didn't insist on requesting every document generated during the last ten years by each of his adversaries in every case he had, there might actually be some wall space available for a poster—maybe even a photo or two. Instead, she was stuck with an office that looked more like a government storage depot. No windows, and temporary shelving lining all four walls. Oh, well, what did she expect, being a lowly legal assistant? She was permitted to save Reynolds's butt on a daily basis, but a decent office would be entirely out of the question.

She hoisted the last box of documents onto the shelf. There. Once she had Lombardi's signature on the dotted line, the Simmons case would be officially retired.

The after-hours receptionist, Candice, appeared in Christina's doorway. "Message for you."

"Thanks." Christina took the pink message slip. It was from Tony Lombardi: *Sorry—Emergency business meeting— A thousand apologies—How about meeting me at my apartment?—I may be late—Help yourself to a drink.* His address was written at the bottom.

Hmmph. Well, at least he wasn't standing her up. Not exactly. The address was about fifteen miles outside Tulsa, but she knew how to get there. It seemed a bit forward— inviting her to his apartment—but it would probably save

24

time. Heck, she was a modern, liberated woman; she could meet him anywhere she wanted. Even if her mother wouldn't approve.

She crumpled the message and tossed it into the trash can. You're being silly, she told herself. She grabbed her briefcase and left the office. I'll just do as he asks. After all, why shouldn't I? No harm in that.

Ben parked his Accord close to the corner, beneath the street lamp. It meant he would have to walk half the block to reach his rooming house, but it somewhat increased the chances that his tires would still be there in the morning.

He grabbed a large bag of groceries and cat food. After depositing Giselle in his room, he'd made a run to Petty's for supplies. Gourmet cat food—that was the stupidest Madison Avenue marketing ploy he'd heard of yet. He'd bought an assortment of reasonably priced cat foods. Giselle would just have to learn to like one of them—that was all there was to it.

He headed toward his house, past a row of faded yellow brick buildings, most of them dating back to WWII. Nothing ever seemed to change on the North Side.

The Singleton twins, Joni and Jami, were sitting on the steps outside, talking to two Hispanic boys wearing tight white T-shirts. Imagine—twins named Singleton. Ben had tried to discuss it with them once, but they didn't seem to grasp the irony.

"Hey, Benjamin," Joni said, fluffing her curly brown locks. "How go the wars?"

"Oh, about the same."

"Get any of my friends out of prison today?"

"Not yet," Ben replied, "but the day isn't over."

"True."

"Hey, Benjamin," Jami said, as he passed by. "I don't

want to catch you sneaking any women into your place tonight, understand?'' All four of them laughed uproariously.

"All right," Ben said, trying to be a good sport. "I promise not to let you catch me." He opened the torn screen door and stepped into the building.

There were only four rooms in the house. Mrs. Marmelstein, the landlady, took one ground floor flat, and Mr. Perry, whom Ben had never met, took the other. Ben had one of the upstairs flats; the Singleton twins and the rest of their family had the other.

Ben knocked on Mrs. Marmelstein's door. He heard *Wheel of Fortune* blaring inside, then her feet skittering toward the door.

"Oh, Ben," Mrs. Marmelstein said, opening the door. "I'm so glad you stopped by. I don't know what to do."

"What happened?"

"A man from PSO came by. A very nasty man. Terribly impolite. Told me I hadn't paid the electric bill yet."

Uh-oh.

"Of course, I told him that just wasn't possible. I have a professional attorney on retainer to supervise my business affairs, and I'm quite sure he wouldn't neglect paying a trivial little utility bill."

"Of course not," Ben said. "Why don't I take a look at your books, though, so I can try to figure out what their problem is?"

"Well, if you wouldn't mind." She pointed to her kitchen table. She already had the records waiting for him.

Ben examined the collection of shoeboxes and loose-leaf notebooks that constituted Mrs. Marmelstein's *books*. Since he'd moved into the room upstairs, Ben had tried to help her with varying degrees of success. Mrs. Marmelstein had moved to Tulsa in the 1940s (when the North Side was a swank neighborhood) with her husband, one of the oil barons of the early days. The Marmelsteins had owned properties throughout Tulsa, had been members of Tulsa high society, and had traveled all over the world. Mr. Marmelstein died in the late Seventies, and the oil boom died soon after that. Mrs. Marmelstein's holdings dwindled to next to nothing. She still owned this building, a low-rent four-room house in the Bad Part of Town, but that was about it. Her only regular income of any significance came from rent payments. Unfortunately, Mrs. Marmelstein still thought she was as rich as ever. Ben did the best he could to stretch, save, delay, and otherwise make her limited income satisfy her creditors.

To make matters worse, Mrs. Marmelstein was a notoriously soft touch, empathizing with every hard luck story she heard, often permitting late payments or forgiving them altogether. Just as Ben might get the bank to accept a payment plan so he could make ends meet for the month, he would learn that Mrs. Marmelstein had pledged $200 to a telephone solicitor for the Fraternal Order of Police.

Why not? she would say. It was her God-given duty to aid those less fortunate. So true, Ben would say, pulling out his calculator and starting over again.

This time, the problem was much simpler. She just didn't have enough money to pay the electric bill last month, so he'd set the bill aside, hoping the coming month would be more bountiful. He checked the envelope where Mrs. Marmelstein kept her petty cash. (Sometimes, for a variety of reasons, most of them illegal, her tenants preferred to pay in cash.) He found six bucks, hardly enough.

He glanced over his shoulder. Mrs. Marmelstein was sitting in the La-Z-Boy recliner beside her bookshelves, lined with Readers' Digest Condensed Books and every volume of the Warren Report. She was absorbed by the television, trying to come up with the name of a Fictional Character that fit SNO_ _HIT_. Ben withdrew his wallet, removed three twenties, and slid them into the envelope.

He walked back to the living room. "I don't know how I

overlooked that electricity bill," he told her, "but it's hardly worth worrying about. You can pay it out of the petty cash envelope. Since this man is in such a hurry, why don't you walk it over to the PSO office tomorrow?" He smiled. "You've been saying you need to get more exercise."

"I guess I have time to do that," she said, as if mentally checking her calendar.

"Good."

"Anything else in the mail of interest? A . . . party invitation perhaps?"

"I'm afraid not."

"Oh." Her hand fluttered against her cheek. She never quite understood that Tulsa high society had passed her by. Or perhaps she did.

"It's really too early in the year for the big social events," Ben said. "Perhaps next month, when it's cooler."

"Perhaps so."

"I'll stop in and see you again tomorrow."

"Oh, Ben—"

"Yes?"

Mrs. Marmelstein took a small plastic vase from the table beside her door. The vase was filled with fresh-cut flowers, mostly peonies and daisies, obviously from her garden.

"These are for you." She put the vase in his hands. "Happy birthday."

"Thank you, Mrs. Marmelstein." He brought the flowers to his face and inhaled deeply. "That was very thoughtful of you."

"Oh, well," she said, patting her bodice. "I had some extras."

The last thing Christina remembered clearly was the scent of her mother's perfume.

How strange, she thought. It made her feel like a little girl again, watching her mother plant her begonias and hyacinth, listening to her hum "Annie Laurie" over and over, seeing her agonized expression when asked for the millionth time when Daddy was coming home. It was Mother's perfume, all right. She never knew what it was called, but that's definitely what it was; the aroma was unmistakable. And then she could smell . . . nothing.

Then she was asleep. No, not asleep; she couldn't be asleep because she could still *see*—blurred, sketchy images, bathed in the blue glow of the flickering television screen. Someone was there, but hard as she tried, she couldn't focus, couldn't tell who it was. Her eyelids closed, and she was back in her mother's garden. They were smiling and laughing, planting tulip bulbs for the following spring, until suddenly, there was a tremendous explosion. Her eyelids struggled to open, to see what was happening.

She had no idea how long it took. It was the whiteness that finally parted her eyelids a little. She tried to comprehend the indistinct figure before her. It was—Frosty the Snowman? It was, but it wasn't, too. There was something wrong with him, something bitter, something malignant. Another violent explosion rocked the room, then another, again and again. His face began to melt, to change to something else, something horribly different. Christina closed her eyes and saw herself running, as far and as fast as she possibly could. And then she was swimming, drowning in his melted remains. The waves were crashing all around her, but then she remembered she couldn't swim, and she was sinking. . . .

She opened her eyes. Where was she now? She wasn't sure, but at least she seemed to be on dry ground. The scent of perfume was fading; in its place, she detected a new odor, a nauseating, putrid smell. The room seemed altered, strange.

With considerable effort, she pushed herself to her feet, then congratulated herself on this supreme accomplishment.

And then she saw his body sprawled on the floor, just a few feet away. Who was that—*Tony?* She kneeled beside him and put her hand over his. It was still warm.

It was then she noticed his head, or more accurately, the place where his head should have been. She tried to suppress her gag reflex; she had to stay in control, to find out what had happened. A large star-shaped crater replaced the right side of his head; she could almost see straight through. A puddle of blood formed a grotesque halo around what was left; bits of skull and brain tissue were splattered on the floor.

She saw a gun nearby. She picked it up and held it close to her face. It was still warm, too, or so she imagined.

The sound of the door slamming open was like a thunderbolt crashing in her head. She jumped, startled, and screamed. The gun fell to the floor.

Several men rushed into the room. Was it three? Four? It was too hard to focus, too hard to *see.*

"Freeze!" one of the men shouted. "Put your hands in the air."

What? Everything seemed shadowy, unreal. What is going on? Why are they pointing at me? I can't under*stand* you. . . .

"I said, put your hands in the air," the man yelled, even louder than before. "Jim. Go."

A second man rushed forward. He forced his hands under her shoulders, pressing the heel of his palms against her breasts. He jerked her to her feet and slammed her face first against the wall.

She began to cry. She felt his hands slapping her body. Why is he hurting me? Why is he here? *Why can't I understand anything?*

"My God," she heard the man say, "look at this!" There was a short silence, and then the man was back, pressing his face next to hers. "You killed him!"

She stared at him, barely comprehending. "I killed him. . . ."

"God Almighty!" the man shouted. She could feel the spray of his spittle against her face. "What kind of monster *are* you?"

He grabbed her long hair at the neck and shoved her across the room. But I can't go yet, she thought. I'm not finished here; I'm not finished! But the man kept on pushing. It was no use. It was too late. It was much too late.

* 5 *

Ben awoke to an unusual sensation—scratchy and suffocating and . . . *furry?* His eyes opened. And all he could see was a vast expanse of cat hair.

He shot upright in his bed, coughing and sputtering and wiping cat hair out of his mouth. It was Giselle, snuggling against his face. She jumped into his lap and purred, obviously glad he was finally awake.

"Look, Giselle," Ben said, "we're going to have a few rules around here. Number one, my bed is off limits." He picked her up and tossed her out the door. After a quick stop in the bathroom, he went into the kitchen and hunted for the cat food he'd bought the night before. She hadn't eaten any of it last night, but he figured by now she would be hungry enough to come down off her pedestal and eat ordinary food like the rest of the household.

He poured the food onto a plate on the floor. Giselle scampered up to it, sniffed for a moment, then stalked away with a sour expression on her face.

"Look, cat," Ben said, "I'm not giving in here. If I start giving you that expensive gourmet food, you'll want it for the rest of your life."

She pattered into the living room, not deigning to look back at him.

"You might as well give it up now, Giselle. I'm not going to let some cat run my life. This food is every bit as tasty as that expensive stuff, and much better for you."

Giselle settled into Ben's only easy chair without so much as looking back at him. If it was possible to get the cold shoulder treatment from a cat, Ben suspected this was pretty much what it would be like.

Fine. He wasn't going hungry just because his cat wouldn't eat. He opened the refrigerator and scanned the contents. Nothing there that would traditionally be called breakfast, but there was an unfinished carton of Vietnamese. Why not? Ri Le's was the best carryout in Tulsa, even three days after purchase.

Just as he got the double-delight cashew chicken in the microwave, the phone rang. "Yeah?"

"Boss, this is Jones. Have you read the newspaper yet?"

"Not yet. You think I could train Giselle to bring the paper to me in the morning?"

"Boy, do you have a lot to learn about cats. Check out the front page, Boss. The FBI picked up a woman on a murder rap last night."

"What do you expect me to do? Run over to the jailhouse and give her my business card? Look, Jones, I know you're anxious to be paid—"

"This isn't just any woman," Jones said. "Take a look at the paper."

Ben felt the short hairs on the back of his neck rise. Surely . . .

He put the phone down, walked to the front door, and

retrieved the morning edition of the *Tulsa World*. There it was, right on the front page. The woman was arrested at the scene of the crime, crouched beside the corpse, and charged with the murder of a man the paper linked to organized crime and South American drugs.

The photograph accompanying the article removed all doubt. Red hair, freckled face, yellow leotards.

It was Christina.

Ben knew the way from the Federal Courthouse on Fourth and Denver to the holding cells so well he could walk it with his eyes closed. He'd been a frequent visitor during the past year, since he was unceremoniously dismissed from the world of high-tone, blue-chip corporate litigation at Raven, Tucker & Tubb. Unable to find a job with anyone else, Ben opened his own office, but he soon found that building a practice from scratch was hard work, especially since he had no contacts, no connections, and worst of all, no money. Ben refused to advertise; he considered that bad form—low class and lousy lawyering. He'd build his practice the proper way or not at all.

Ben had rented a small office on the North Side of downtown—not a great location, but the best he could afford. He put a listing in the Yellow Pages and opened shop. His practice consisted principally of debt collection, divorce, and penny-ante felonies. His clientele was increasing somewhat—word of mouth was spreading—but customarily one drunk driving case led only to another drunk driving case. His chances of breaking into the big time, of working for rich corporate entities that could be billed out the kazoo, seemed pretty slim.

Ben pushed open the bullet-proof glass door that led to the holding cells. Lester Boggs was standing guard in the outer office. Lester had thinning black hair and was more than a little overweight—too many years at desk jobs like this one. He looked silly in his extra-large sheriff's uniform, with the slick black leather belt and holster. There really should be restrictions, Ben thought, on the people permitted to pack guns. He wondered if Lester had ever even held it, much less fired it.

Lester looked up from the black-and-white Watchman on his desk. "Morning, Kincaid."

"Morning, Les."

"You must be bailing out those two drunks we picked up on Osage territory last night."

Ben steeled himself and tried to seem convincing. He hated lying, and he wasn't particularly adept at it. "No. I'm here to see Christina McCall. I'm representing her."

Lester's eyebrows rose. "Really? I'm impressed." He fumbled around in a desk drawer for his keys. "A drug-related homicide. You are coming up in the world."

"She's a friend. Any chance they'll O.R. her? I brought my Bar card."

" 'Fraid not. You'll have to make bail."

Lester opened the clanging barred gate separating them from the holding cells. He led Ben down a long concrete corridor; his footsteps echoed as Lester brought his considerable weight down on his patent leather shoes. The derelicts and assorted sleazebags in the cells called out to Ben as he passed by; he tried to ignore them. As always, the cells were atrocious, nauseating. They reeked of booze, vomit, and human waste. Ben held his breath and tried not to be sick.

Lester stopped in front of the last cell on the left and opened the door. "Fifteen minutes."

"I know the drill," Ben replied.

"Hey, I'm not supposed to do this, but if you want, I could slip your card to those two drunks."

"Thanks just the same. I'm kind of busy right now." Ben stepped into the cell. The iron door clanged shut behind him.

She was lying on the bottom level of the metal bunk bed in the tiny six-by-eight-foot cell, beside the exposed sink and lidless toilet, the only decorative fixtures. Her eyes were shut; Ben couldn't tell if she was asleep.

Gradually, her eyes opened. "Ben?" She sat upright and rubbed the sleep from her eyes. "That you?"

"It's me," he said softly.

"Thank heaven." She stood slowly, hobbled unevenly to the sink and splashed water onto her face.

She looked awful. She was still wearing the clothes she had been picked up in. Her yellow leotards had a huge run. Her long red hair was sticking out in every direction at once. Mascara was smeared all over the side of her face.

Ben sat on the edge of the lower bunk. "So, what have you been up to?"

Christina sat down on the opposite end of the bed. "Well, I haven't killed anybody, if that's what you want to know."

"I assumed that much. How did you get into this mess?"

"It's hard to explain. I told you I was going to meet Tony Lombardi. He was delayed by a business meeting."

"And his business was running drugs."

"That's what they tell me."

"Did you ever see anything suspicious?"

"No. Never. Tony told me he was in the import-export business."

"At least he wasn't a liar. Did you ever see any of his imported goods?"

"Yeah. Parrots."

"Parrots?"

"Rare South American parrots. Supposed to be very valuable."

"South America, huh? That figures." Ben batted his lips with his pencil. "What happened last night?"

Christina pressed her fingers against her temples. "To be perfectly honest, Ben, I'm a little fuzzy on last night. I got a message telling me to meet Tony at his place. I did, but he wasn't home yet. I turned on the TV, poured myself a drink, and waited. I must've fallen asleep. When I woke up, it was two o'clock in the morning, and Tony was lying on the floor with a huge chunk of his head missing."

"That must've been a shock."

"It . . . was." She laughed softly. "And like the genius I am, I got up to investigate, rubbed my fingerprints all over everything, crouched over the body, and a nanosecond later the FBI showed up."

"I don't suppose you saved the message?"

"Nope. Tossed it in the trash. It's long gone by now."

"And the message was from Lombardi?"

"That's what the receptionist said. But anyone could've called in and claimed to be him. She wouldn't know."

"I suppose they remembered to read you your rights."

"Alas, yes." Christina wiped her face with her sleeve. "Thanks for asking."

"Were they . . . rough on you? I mean . . ."

Christina nodded. "They were okay. Under the circumstances. These guys were FBI, after all. They weren't going to let some loose cannon get their case thrown out." She paused; her eyes seemed to withdraw. "Didn't care much for the strip search, though. And the delousing spray definitely did not make me feel minty fresh."

Ben tried not to wince.

"So, counselor," Christina said, "are you going to take my case?"

"What, *me*? You don't want me to represent you."

"*Au contraire, mon ami.* I do."

"Christina, this is really . . . *serious*. I'm no criminal trial expert. Get Pat Williams. He's the best."

"I don't want Pat Williams. I can't afford Pat Williams. I want you." Her voice quieted. "You're the best. You just don't know it yet."

"Christina, I don't think this is wise."

"Are you saying you won't do this one little thing for me?"

"Christina, these accusations—this case could be really . . . important."

"If that's your articulate way of reminding me that the death penalty is a possibility, believe me, Ben, I know." She looked him square in the eyes. "I think it's essential that my attorney believe I'm innocent. You know I didn't kill Tony. I want *you*, Ben."

"There are any number of experienced trial attorneys who would realize you're innocent."

Christina leaned forward and placed her hand on Ben's shoulder. "I want more than that, Ben. I want to find out who really killed Tony. I want the SOB who set me up."

Ben scrutinized her face. "All right," he said finally. He stood up. "But I reserve the right to affiliate co-counsel if I get in over my head."

"Fine." She placed her hands behind her head and stretched out on the bed.

"I'll try to get you out of this rathole as soon as possible. In the meantime, I'll go by your apartment and pick up a change of clothes. Have you got a key?"

She looked at him pointedly. "I haven't changed my locks, Ben."

"Oh. Well. Fine then. I'll also talk to Mike and see what he knows."

"Good plan."

"If you need anything, just send word through Lester. I'll stay in touch."

"Ben?"

"Yes?"

Christina sat up. She opened her mouth, started to say something, then said something else. *"Merci beaucoup."*

* 6 *

Ben felt like a laboratory rat trying to find the path to the cheese in a gigantic maze. The plaza was easy enough. Wind your way through the roller bladers, the street preachers, and the panhandlers—and you find Tulsa's municipal offices. But how long had they been renovating the interior—six, maybe eight months? At least that long. And every day, the barricades and ropes changed, and Ben had to rediscover his way around. Usually, of course, he was only trying to get to traffic court. Today he had an even more difficult chore—plowing through the jumbled, poorly marked offices of the Law Enforcement Division.

Eventually, Ben spotted the glass door marked TULSA PO-LICE DEPARTMENT-CENTRAL. He walked inside. It was still early; no one was at the reception desk. In the most remote corner of the department HQ, Ben located the cubicle labeled LT. M. MORELLI. Ben and Mike Morelli had been friends since college days, when they were roommates and fellow Liberal Arts majors, reading Faulkner by day and making music in pizza parlors by night. Then Mike married Ben's younger sister, Julia. Everybody knew it was a bad match—everybody but Mike and Julia. Mike worked his butt off for three years, but still the result was an intensely nasty divorce, which strained Ben and Mike's friendship to the breaking point. Since Ben moved to Tulsa last year, he'd been trying to revive their friendship. But the effort was slow work—like a gigantic jigsaw puzzle that came together one piece at a time.

Mike's cubicle was as bland as they come. The only feature Ben could call a decoration was a coat rack bearing a stained overcoat and a loaded gun holster. Mike was on the phone, but as soon as he saw Ben, he said, "I'll have to get back to you later, Ellie."

He swiveled his chair around. "It's Benjamin Kincaid, counselor-at-law."

"And Lieutenant Michelangelo Morelli, homicide investigator," Ben replied. "Why do I feel we should now execute the secret handshake?"

"Must be a throwback to our wicked college days."

"Yeah. So give me the straight scoop, Mike. What are the charges against Christina?"

Mike looked at him gravely. "Murder one, I'm afraid."

"Why murder one?"

"Well . . . it doesn't look very accidental."

"Maybe it was self-defense."

"No signs of a struggle."

"Maybe Lombardi shot himself."

"Four times? In the head?"

"Oh." Ben fell into one of Mike's chairs. "Are you handling the case?"

"Nope. Outside my jurisdiction."

"Can't you make it your jurisdiction?"

"No." Mike fingered a manila folder on his desk. "I've got bad news for you. And Christina. What do you know about jurisdiction over crimes committed on tribal lands?"

"I know it's incredibly complicated. Why?"

Mike opened the file and read an address aloud. "That lodge where Lombardi was killed is on tribal land. Creek Nation. With a name like Lombardi, I would've sworn he was all-Italian, but it turns out he was part-Creek."

"Are we talking about tribal courts?"

Mike shook his head. "Christina was arrested by FBI agents in the course of an ongoing narcotics investigation. They're planning to charge her with drug-related homicide under the new 'continuing criminal enterprise' statute—which, I might remind you, is the only death penalty statute in the entire federal criminal code."

Ben felt a dryness in his throat. "Give me the bottom line, Mike."

"This one's going to be tried in federal court."

"Oh, great. A murder trial in federal court. With the death penalty." He pressed his fingers against his temples. "She was in the county jail."

"That's where the feds keep their prisoners. They don't have cells of their own, so they rent space from us."

"Will the feds push this?"

"They will," Mike said grimly. "This isn't a grounder, Ben. It could be a grand slam for them. With all the connections Lombardi had to organized crime and South American drugs, the case takes on a larger significance."

"What do you mean?"

"This is the kind of case a guy like Alexander Moltke can really make pay off for him."

Alexander Moltke, the U.S. Attorney. Sailing through life with one eye on his press clippings and the other eye on a soon-to-be-available Senate seat. "You think he'll use this case for a publicity play?"

"That's what prosecutors do, isn't it? Stay away from controversy, wait for the right case, and run for election in the courtroom."

"Damn. And the FBI is involved?"

"Like you wouldn't believe. The white shirts have been trying to get the goods on Lombardi and his druglord bosses for over a year. And they're still trying."

"So Christina ends up as shark bait. Let some blood and

try to attract the big fish. This stinks, Mike. How long till the grand jury sits?''

''Not long. The feds have filed a complaint so they can detain her in the meantime. And as you well know, the grand jury is just a formality. The government can get any indictment it wants.''

Ben took a deep breath. ''Mike, I need—''

''Let me stop you right there. What I've told you so far is already a matter of public record. Beyond that, I can't help you.''

Ben stared at him, stunned. ''What do you mean, you can't help?''

''Just that.''

''You know damn well Christina wouldn't kill anybody.''

''On the contrary, Ben, if I've learned anything during my time as a police officer, it's that anyone is capable of doing anything, under the right circumstances.''

Ben could see Mike was falling into his tough-guy routine again. That was Mike: the shell of Hammett, the heart of Rimbaud.

''How do I know what happened this morning?'' Mike continued. ''Maybe Lombardi was two-timing her. Maybe she decided to join the war on drugs. Maybe he tried to molest her. Anything could have happened. Anyway, I can't help you.''

''Not even for old times' sake?''

''*Before* we were both working together to accomplish the same goal. This is different. This time we're on opposite sides.''

Ben couldn't believe what he was hearing. ''I didn't realize we were on *sides*. I thought we were both trying to discover the *truth*. What really happened.''

''Well, you've been needing to grow up for a long time now.'' Mike took his pipe and tamper out of his desk drawer. ''Frankly, Ben, most of the guys in this office couldn't be less interested in convicting Christina; we consider this a community service homicide. But the feds are going forward gung-ho, and we've been told to assist whenever possible and otherwise stay out of the way. And I intend to do just that.''

There was a long silence, as if they had forgotten their lines. Both men avoided eye contact.

"Can you at least tell me what happened?" Ben asked.

"I can tell you what I know. You could get that through pretrial discovery anyway." He pressed the stamper deep into the bowl of his pipe. "The FBI, in association with our office, has been stalking Tony Lombardi for some time. They believe he's a smuggler for Albert DeCarlo.''

Ben whistled. Yet more bad news. DeCarlo had been the subject of more investigations than the Loch Ness monster, but no one had ever made anything stick. If Tulsa had a crime boss, he was it.

"The feds think DeCarlo is big with the Cali cartel, running drugs up from Colombia. Since the Medellin cartel bit the bullet with Noriega and got out of the business, the Cali goons are the feds' number-one target. They say DeCarlo's involved in every aspect of the drug pipeline—handling, warehousing, airstrips, planes, boats, bribery—the whole works. And having successfully put the alleged number-four man in the Medellin cartel away a few years ago—"

"José Abello." Ben remembered the trial well. It was probably the biggest criminal trial Tulsa had ever had.

"Right. Having done that, the feds now hope to snag someone even bigger. You know, to exemplify the escalating war on drugs. And they hope to shut down the Tulsa connection in the process.''

"The *Tulsa* connection? Sounds like a TV movie.''

Mike thumped his pipe against his desk and searched for a match. "It's serious stuff, believe me. Sickening as it may be, our little town has become a distribution center for South American drugs. Getting them into Mexico is easy, and from there, it's just a short hop over the border to us. Texas has been cracking down, making life miserable for drug runners, so they've been skipping the Lone Star State and coming straight to Oklahoma. And from Tulsa, it's just a drive down the interstate to anywhere else in the country."

What the hell had Christina gotten herself into? "That explains why the feds are involved," Ben said, "but what's all this drug business got to do with the murder?"

"A major shipment of cocaine was delivered last night, or so the feds believe. Anyway, four federal agents with a warrant burst into Lombardi's apartment around two o'clock this morning, hoping to find the drugs. Instead, they found Tony Lombardi lying on the floor with four bullet holes in his head." He paused. "And Christina hovering over the body."

"That hardly proves she killed him."

"Her prints are all over the place."

"So? We know she was at the apartment. There could be a million explanations for that."

"We're only interested in one."

"Can you get me in to see the scene of the crime?"

Mike shrugged. "You have that right under the law. I don't see any reason to make you file a lot of paperwork."

"I assume you'll have access to the forensic tests."

"True."

"Will you copy me on all the test results?"

"You mean, will I allow you to inspect any clearly exculpatory evidence we obtain?"

"No. I want to see everything, Mike."

"The toxicology and microscopy reports won't be completed for days," Mike hedged.

"The autopsy is probably already finished."

"Ben, you know goddamn well we're not required to produce every shred of evidence we turn up!"

Ben waited until Mike's eyes met his. "I'm not asking you as a police officer, Mike."

Mike looked away. He swiveled his chair around and stared

at the back wall of his cubicle. "I'll see what I can do," he
said quietly.

"Thanks, pal."

"But don't be hanging around here a lot, okay? Bad for
my reputation." His voice took on a somber tone. "You
need to be careful this time, Ben. Very careful."

"What do you mean?"

"You're playing with the big boys. Organized crime. South
American drug cartels. And worst of all, the FBI. If you get
in their way, they will not be kind."

"They may call in my unpaid parking tickets?"

"They may blow your fucking head off, Ben."

"Oh." The air around them seemed to go flat. "I'm not
dropping this, Mike."

"Then watch your backside, chum. At all times."

Ben rose. If this talk was intended to scare him, it was
working. "Well, I have about a million things to do. . . ."

"Ben?"

"Yes?"

"Are you interested in this case because Christina is your
friend, or . . . ?"

"She's asked me to represent her."

"I was afraid of that. You may want to reconsider."

"Look, Morelli, I may not be the best attorney in the
world, but I hardly think—"

"Do you know who this case has been assigned to?"

"The district court judge won't be assigned until after the
indictment."

"Technically, that's true. But consider—Judge Collins is
practically retired, and Judge Schmidt is up to his eyeballs
in that huge Sand Springs RICO class action. Who do you
think is going to get this case?"

A cold chill spread through Ben's body. *"No."*

"I'm afraid so."

Ben slapped his forehead. "I can't believe it. What *else* could go wrong?"

"I don't think it gets much worse than this. Not for you, anyway."

"He'll have to recuse himself. He knows her—he used to work with her."

"Says he doesn't remember her from Adam."

"Well, he sure as hell remembers me."

"True enough," Mike said. "Unfortunately, contacts with counsel generally are not grounds for recusal, as well you know. I don't see him stepping down from a high-profile case like this one promises to be."

Ben tried to reply, but found he was only able to produce a hoarse, choking sound. He stumbled toward the door, contemplating this hideous prospect.

The United States versus Christina McCall—with the Honorable Judge Richard O. Derek presiding.

Judge Derek, the newest member of the federal judiciary in the Northern District of Oklahoma, formerly in private practice at the firm of Raven, Tucker & Tubb.

Ben's old boss. The one who hated him.

* 7 *

As Ben drove to the Creek Estates Lodge, he tried to imagine what could possibly be worse than Richard Derek getting Christina's case. All things considered, Jack the Ripper would've been a more agreeable judicial assignment. It had been almost eight months since Derek had been appointed to the federal judiciary, and Ben had scrupulously managed to avoid being before His Honor. This time, unfortunately, it appeared there was no way out. Not without abandoning Christina.

Derek had been Ben's supervising attorney back at Raven, Tucker & Tubb. Just recalling the experience gave Ben shivers. Every single day he had been required to put up with Derek's egomaniacal, hypochondriacal ravings. Ben had suffered through as best he could. But when Ben started personally investigating the strange mutilation-murder of a client, Derek went through the roof. As a result of Ben's investigation, the firm ended up losing a major corporate client—a client that, as Ben discovered, was suppressing evidence and embezzling large sums of money from its shareholders to create a private slush fund. But Derek didn't care about any of that. Derek lost one of his drawing cards, and he blamed Ben. In a particularly nasty fit of pique, Derek trumped up some false charges and got Ben fired.

About four months later, Ben heard that Derek had been appointed to the federal bench. It seemed an odd move for someone who considered himself the Prince of Litigators, but it wouldn't be the first time the prestige and godlike power associated with a lifetime appointment to the federal judiciary had lured someone away from a lucrative practice.

Ben pulled his Honda Accord into the parking lot. It had taken him ten minutes to get the car started, and once he had, it shuddered, sputtered, coughed, and emitted several other noises Ben knew weren't described in the owner's manual. He needed to take the car in for a checkup, but luxuries like that didn't fit into his current budget. Maybe next month.

He opened his car door and pushed himself out. Might as well stop stalling.

Ben hated crime scenes. Maybe not worse than the prospect of being in court before Judge Derek, but certainly worse than anything else, including fingernails on chalkboard, teeth on aluminum foil, street mimes, and tax auditors. At least the corpse was gone—that provided some measure of relief—although a dark black stain on the carpet provided a grisly reminder of what had occurred earlier that morning.

Ben had an aching, hollow feeling, as if someone had carved out his internal organs and left him an empty shell, a transparent voyeur at this place of horrible violence. He had hoped the crime scene would give him some insight as to what had happened. So far, no insight. Just revulsion.

Ben didn't have any illusions that he could disturb anything; he knew Mike's men had already been over every inch of the place—the photographers with their cameras, the print boys with their dusters, the fiber boys with their tweezers. They would have tested and probed and sampled every stain, smudge, or tissue they could find. Mike undoubtedly had the room photographed and videotaped from every angle. Mike was always thorough. Ben had considered that an asset. Until now, anyway.

Except for the ghastly bloodstain, the room seemed to be an ordinary living room in a spacious, but otherwise ordinary, apartment suite. Ben had expected something grander from a room billed as the penthouse—a sunken Jacuzzi perhaps, beside a well-stocked wet bar. Everything was in place; there was no sign of a struggle, no scrapes or scratches, nothing overturned. Ben saw the TV and, next to it, the overstuffed chair Christina must have fallen asleep in. On the table beside the chair, he saw the wine carafe from which she must have poured her drink. And on the floor, not four feet away, the telltale stain. How could he possibly have been killed so near without waking Christina? It seemed incredible, and yet, he saw no evidence that the body had been moved. There was very little splattering—just a sickening mound of congealed blood where Lombardi's head would have been.

There was an unpleasant odor in the room; Ben couldn't quite identify it. Death, he supposed. He used to read about the smell of death and think, how banal, how melodramatic. But now he realized there was some undefinable odor that lingered at the site of a murder, even after all the technicians and forensic experts had scrubbed and tested and Lysoled the room from top to bottom.

Ben suddenly realized he had to leave. He wasn't accomplishing anything for Christina, and he certainly wasn't doing himself any good. And Mike would probably be pretty grumpy if he vomited on the crime scene.

Ben took a last look, then ducked back under the yellow tape. He signed out and searched for the men's room. He needed to splash some cold water on his face, wash his hands. Try to get rid of the smell of death.

Unlike most murder witnesses, the security guard actually seemed to enjoy being interrogated. Ben had expected another dazed testimonial from an unsuspecting innocent who suddenly found himself on the sidelines of murder, or perhaps a frightened paranoid who didn't want to get involved. Instead, he found an amiable man in his early sixties named Holden Hatfield, eager to be of service.

"Just call me Spud," Spud said. "Everybody does."

"All right," Ben said, ". . . Spud." He refused to let himself get sidetracked into asking how everybody got Spud out of Holden Hatfield. "Did Mr. Lombardi have any visitors last night?"

"Yup. Four. You want their names?"

Ben marveled at his exuberance. He must've told this story at least twice already to the police—probably some reporters as well. Then again, why shouldn't he be enthusiastic? Spud wasn't a suspect; no one was even suggesting he had done something wrong. This was probably a rare opportunity for him to shine in a job that normally seemed about as dull as counting cars on the turnpike.

"How can you be sure there were only four visitors?" Ben asked.

Spud pointed his thumb toward his chest. "Because they all have to go through me. I have to let them inside." He demonstrated the procedure of pushing the button on his control panel to release the front door. "And I have to activate the elevator with a key and push the floor button. I keep a list of everyone who comes in and where they're going." He tapped a clipboard on his desk.

Ben stepped closer and read over Spud's shoulder.

"Like it says right here," Spud continued. He brought the clipboard up about an inch from his eyes. "Only four people took the elevator to the top floor last night."

Ben took a giant step away from Spud. The stench of alcohol was so thick on the guard's breath he might as well have been wearing it as cologne. Perhaps this was the lodge's unique way of discouraging intruders. "How do you know someone didn't, say, ride the elevator up to the ninth floor, then walk up to the tenth?"

" 'Cause it ain't possible," Spud answered. "The doors are locked from the outside. We have to maintain access to the stairwell—fire codes, you know. But once you're in, you're in for good. You can't exit the stairwell until you get all the way down to the first floor."

"How do you know these four people weren't going to see some other tenant on the top floor?"

" 'Cause there ain't no other tenants on the top floor. Mr. Lombardi's suite takes up the whole floor."

Good answer, Ben thought.

"That's why they call it a penthouse, son."

"Does your list also record the times these four persons left the building?"

"No can do, son. See, there's only one way into the building, but there's a couple'a ways out. There's two back doors that are locked from the inside. You can't use them to get in, but you can sure use them to get out. Most folks do, since those doors are closer to the parking lot."

"Ah," Ben said, spotting an escape hatch. "Then someone could open a back door from the inside and let someone else in."

"Possibly," Spud admitted, "but the intruder still couldn't get nowhere. He couldn't ride the elevator unless I activated it for him. He couldn't enter the stairwell without my seein' him, and even if he could, he couldn't open the stairwell doors on any of the upper floors."

"Right. Locked from the outside."

"Absolutely correct," Spud said. "You're a pretty quick study, son."

"They teach that in law school," Ben replied. "I don't suppose you might've fallen asleep last night?"

Spud shook his head vigorously. "Not a chance. But what if I did? Unless I open the front door or activate the elevator, nobody gets in."

So it seemed, Ben had to admit.

"Doesn't matter anyway. It didn't happen. Let me tell you, son—I've been workin' this job over three years now, and I ain't fallen asleep once yet." He lowered his voice a notch. "Just between you and me, every now and then, when I feel myself gettin' a mite drowsy, I just whip out Jackie D here and take a good hard swig." He withdrew a silver flask strapped to his leg and waved it under Ben's nose. "Just a quick snort, and I'm wide awake again."

Not exactly the way they described it in driver's ed class, Ben thought, but whatever works. "Tell me, Spud, did you recognize any of these four visitors?"

"Recognized all of them."

"Who were they?"

"Well," Spud said, a bit awkwardly, "first of all, there was that cute redhead you're representin'."

Right. Wouldn't want to leave her out. "You saw Christina McCall come in?"

"Oh, yeah," Spud answered. "Couldn't have missed her. She seemed kinda angry." He leaned closer to Ben and whispered. "I think she was mad at Mr. Lombardi about something."

That's wonderful. Just feed them a motive, why don't you? "Who else?"

"There was Mr. Lombardi's lawyer, Quinn Reynolds."

Ben's eyebrows rose. "Is that a fact? Any idea why he was here?"

"Sorry. Can't help you there. T'wern't unusual, though. He came to see Mr. Lombardi all the time."

"Who else was here last night?"

"That animal nut, Clayton Langdell."

The name was familiar. "Doesn't he run some kind of society for animals?"

"That's the guy."

"What would he be doing with Lombardi?"

"He came callin' from time to time. Don't know what about. Don't think they were particularly friendly."

Ben made a notation on his legal pad. "And the other visitor to see Lombardi?"

Spud seemed to be prolonging the moment. Must be something good coming, Ben realized.

"Albert DeCarlo."

If Spud was waiting for a reaction (and he was), he must have been disappointed. Mike had already prepared Ben for this revelation. "How did you know it was DeCarlo?"

"Seen him here before. Seen him several times. Always the same. Dark sunglasses. Dark muffler. Big white overcoat. I'd recognize him a mile away."

"Any idea what business DeCarlo would have with Lombardi?"

Spud cleared his throat. "Well," he said *sotto voce*, "I wouldn't want to speculate. . . ."

What a perfect security guard. The soul of discretion, even about mob kingpins.

"Did DeCarlo say anything to you?"

"Heck, no. I just waved him through. You don't mess around with someone like Albert DeCarlo."

"How much do you know about Lombardi's . . . business activities?"

"Next to nothing. Some kind of import business, so I've heard. Every now and then Lennie will say a little something about it."

"Lennie?"

"Lombardi's assistant. Thin, wiry guy. Does the work Lombardi doesn't—excuse me—*didn't* want to do. You know, detail stuff. Making deliveries. Paying the bills. Taking the missus her money."

Ben looked up. "The *missus*?"

"Oh yeah. Lombardi was married. Thin, blonde-haired lady. You didn't know that?"

Ben felt his heart sink into the vicinity of his intestinal tract. "No. Did she come here often?"

"No way. Last time I let her in, Lombardi showed up with some floozy he'd picked up on Eleventh Street. Mrs. Lombardi went nuts. She started screaming and crying, calling names, slapping the woman around, making a major-league scene. She was like a madwoman. Crazy jealous. Ever since then, I've had strict instructions from Mr. Lombardi not to admit her under any circumstances."

"But they were still married?"

"Oh, yeah. They've been apart for several months now. I don't think they're divorced—just separated or something. I've heard Lennie gripe about having to take money over to her. I guess she could be pretty unpleasant about it."

A wife. Christina had a date with a married man. Ben's

eyes started to glaze over; the hollow feeling inside him increased a thousandfold. Ben expected the prosecution to try to paint Christina as some sort of tramp—the unmarried consort (wink, wink) of the perverted druglord. But this was worse. Now they would be talking (in hushed tones) about . . . *adultery*. Now they would take every opportunity to remind the jury she went to that penthouse apartment for a (dramatic pause) *liaison* with a married man.

What would the jury think? Ben knew all too well. They would loathe her. Before the government had even finished its opening statement.

The phone rang just seconds after Ben's Honda pulled out of the parking lot.

"Hello," Spud said. And a few seconds after that, "Yeah, Kincaid, that was his name. Why?"

Spud glided into the chair behind his station. His brow creased. "Sure, I told him. What, should I have clammed up?"

A burst of static from the phone. "Look, I'm sorry, I didn't know. If that's the way you want it, from now on, that's the way it'll be. Promise."

The tension in his face intensified. "Sure, whatever you want. No, he didn't say where he was going. Oh, wait, he did say he was going back to the police station later on. No, he doesn't know anything. Well, I don't see any cause for that. Yeah, I know, you're in charge, not me. Of course I will. You can count on it. I'll call you first thing. Right."

Spud wanted to hang up, but the voice on the other end would not release him. Another burst of staccato noise, finally followed by an abrupt disconnection.

Spud hung up the phone.

* 8 *

It took Ben over half an hour to return to his office. Most of Tulsa's law firms, courthouses, government facilities, and business offices were in the central downtown area. The outer border of downtown was First Street, and north of First Street, there was nothing. Nothing reputable, anyway. Bars, junkyards, strip joints. And Ben's office. Conveniently wedged between Ernie's Pool Hall and the B & J Pawn Shop, Ben's office was still within walking distance of the courthouses. It was just in a neighborhood through which no rational person would ever walk.

When Ben finally made it to his office, he found the front doors and windows splattered with dried egg yolks. Enough is enough, he swore silently. First T.P.'d, now egged. It was like high school all over again. He was going to have to put an end to this.

Jones was sitting at his card table in the small front lobby.

"I see you haven't gotten rid of the chickens yet," Ben noted. They seemed to be in constant motion, skittering frenetically from one side of the lobby to the other.

"What did you expect me to do?" Jones asked. "Sell them to the Colonel?"

"Not a bad idea, actually. I thought they were only supposed to run around like this when their heads were cut off."

Jones smiled. "I can tell you're a city boy."

"Yeah. Hey, guess what?"

"You're representing Christina on that murder rap."

Spoil sport. "How did you know?"

"My friend Didi called. You know, the court clerk. Must've gotten your name and phone number off your entry of appearance. Your client's preliminary hearing has been set for Friday."

"Friday? Why not sooner?"

"Didi was a little vague on that. Perhaps the magistrate has other plans."

"That's unacceptable. The magistrate has already denied bail. Draft an emergency appeal to the district court, Jones, pending the preliminary hearing. I don't want Christina spending any longer than necessary with the hookers and drug addicts."

"Derek won't like it."

"All the more reason. Call the U.S. Attorney's Office and get them to consent to the motion. Christina was arrested without a warrant. Under the *Riverside County* case, if the preliminary hearing isn't held within forty-eight hours, the burden shifts to the government to prove the delay wasn't unreasonable. Moltke won't want to risk having his case dismissed on a due process violation. Tell him I won't challenge the preliminary hearing date if he won't oppose an emergency bail appeal. He'll play along. Then Derek won't have any choice."

Jones searched the file cabinet beneath his table. "Application for emergency appeal," he repeated. "Do we have a form for that?"

Ben removed the proper file folder. "Just fill in the blanks. I'll review it later and make any necessary changes or additions. I want the hearing tomorrow morning."

Jones scribbled a note on his desk calendar. "Got it."

"While you're at it, Jones, see if you can work up a motion to dismiss for lack of subject matter jurisdiction. Find out whatever you can about this new death penalty statute. Let's see if we can get this case transferred somewhere else—state court, tribal court, the moon—just so it's away from Derek."

"Boss . . . do you think this is wise?"

"What? Bringing a motion to dismiss?"

"No. Representing Christina."

"Why does everyone in town think I'm such an incompetent attorney?"

"It's not that. It's just . . . well, I don't want to be indiscreet. . . ."

"She let me stay at her apartment for a short period after I got fired at Raven, till I got back on my feet." Ben placed one hand on his hip. "There was nothing romantic about it. We're just good friends. Totally platonic."

"Uh-huh. Whatever you say, Boss."

"Besides, this has nothing to do with personal feelings. This is a murder case, pure and simple. I can be perfectly objective about this."

"If you say so."

"You don't seem convinced."

Jones pressed his hand against his chest. "Who cares what I think? I am but a secretary, a vassal, a servant. You're the boss, Boss."

"Hmmph."

"By the by, I read the article in the *World*. The feds think they have her dead to rights."

Ben nodded. "They're like a terrier with a bone—once they bite into someone, they never let go. If I'm going to convince anybody that Christina didn't kill Lombardi, I'm going to have to be able to tell them who did."

"Good luck."

"Yeah."

"Anything else I can do?"

"As a matter of fact, yes." He opened his briefcase and tore off a sheet of legal paper. "I have the names of three people other than Christina who were at Lombardi's apartment last night.''

"All *right!*" Jones said, snatching the paper. "Suspects! You want me to investigate these guys?''

Ben rolled his eyes. "No, I definitely do *not* want you to investigate these guys.''

"Where did you get these names, anyway?''

"From the security guard at the lodge where Lombardi lived.''

"You went to the scene of the crime!''

"So to speak.''

"Without me?''

"Of course I went without you. You're a secretary, remember? A vassal, a servant. Not Paul Drake. Not Magnum, P.I.''

"I've been wanting to expand my horizons," Jones said, gazing at the list. "Albert DeCarlo! This is the big time.''

"Don't let it go to your head.''

"You really think one of these guys is the murderer?''

"Assuming the guard is telling the truth, it has to be one of them.''

"And assuming it wasn't Christina," Jones added.

Ben looked at him stiffly. "That's my job. Anyway, if you'll stop drooling over the list of suspects, I'll tell you what else I need.''

Properly scolded, Jones put the paper down on his table. "Shoot.''

"I want you to get me appointments to see these three people, sometime in the next day or two. Before the preliminary hearing, if possible.''

"You want an appointment with Albert DeCarlo? Before Friday? How am I going to get you an appointment with the Don Corleone of eastern Oklahoma?''

"You'll think of something. Try to line up Quinn Reynolds

first. There's no reason why he should deny an appointment to a fellow member of the bar.''

''I'll do my best.''

''Good. Also, I want you to drive over to Christina's apartment and get her a change of clothes, a toothbrush, and assorted other necessaries.''

''You got a key? From your totally platonic temporary residence there?''

Ben reached inside his jacket pocket and passed Jones the key.

''Anything else?''

''Yeah,'' Ben said, scanning the lobby. ''Do something with these chickens.'' He snapped his briefcase closed and headed out the door.

＊ 9 ＊

Ben managed to find Mike more quickly this time. Not that he had acquired any knowledge of the Law Enforcement Division floor plan—the barriers and detours had all been changed since morning—but at least now there was a receptionist on duty who could tell him whether he was hot or cold.

''I thought you weren't going to hang around,'' Mike said, as Ben entered his cubicle.

''Hey, I haven't been here since this morning,'' Ben replied. ''I thought I was showing restraint.''

Mike closed the book he was reading. ''Your restraint will probably get me fired.''

"Don't be a grump. I won't be long. I just wanted to learn if you had any forensic reports yet."

"Yeah, some. Remember, this is the feds' case. They don't share anything without a reason."

Ben noticed that the file folder on Mike's desk labeled *Lombardi* was thicker than it had been this morning. He also noticed the book Mike had just closed. "You're reading *The Complete Plays of William Shakespeare*?"

"Yeah. *Merchant of Venice*. What of it?"

"Oh, I don't know," Ben said. "It's just not what I expected from a hardboiled guy like you. Dashiell Hammett or Raymond Chandler, maybe. Sherlock Holmes, on the outside. But Shakespeare? What if someone found out? Your whole image could be destroyed."

"I try to keep it out of sight when I have company." Mike scooted the book to the side of his desk. "I love that trial scene toward the end of the play when Portia disguises herself as the judge and twists the law around to cheat Shylock out of his pound of flesh, not to mention half his property."

"A disguised judge? Probably grounds for appeal."

"No doubt. So, do you want this file, or do you want to give me grief about my literary taste?"

"Tough choice, but let's have a gander at the file."

Mike and Ben sat down at the table in the corner of Mike's cubicle. "This is the preliminary report from the hair and fiber boys. The most relevant discovery was the long curly red hairs they found all over the room. We've taken an exemplar from Christina. They match."

"So what? It's not as if she's claiming she wasn't there."

"It doesn't look good."

"What does? Anything else?"

"Lots of fibers from Lombardi's clothing. He seemed to favor tweeds and other sheddable fabrics. And a few other fibers we haven't been able to identify."

"I assume you're going to try."

"We'll check the carpets and clothes closets of Christina and the three men who came to Lombardi's place last night, if that's what you mean. But frankly, even if we find something, so what? All it will prove is that they've been to Lombardi's penthouse at one time or another, something they're not likely to deny in the first place."

"You should still make the attempt."

"We will, Ben, we will." He turned to another document in the folder. "There's absolutely no sign of a struggle. Nothing broken or dented, scraped or scratched. No stray bullets. Slight residual indentation in the carpet where the body fell, but that's to be expected."

"What about serology?"

"We found no blood or other trace evidence that appears to have come from the murderer. Nothing on Lombardi's skin or under his fingernails. Which is understandable, since there was apparently no struggle."

"There must be something in there that's helpful. What else have you got?"

"We've got the gun. A Bulldog .44 Special. The Son of Sam gun. Ballistics confirms that it's the gun that put four bullets in Lombardi's head."

"Trajectory?"

"Lombardi had contact wounds, from the barrel of the gun being pressed against his head. That's why the entry wound was star-shaped. Expanding gases from the exploding gunpowder tear the skin."

"Meaning?"

"Meaning the murderer was very close to Lombardi, which of course suggests that he . . . or she . . . was someone Lombardi knew. And trusted."

"Which could have been any of a number of people."

"Don't bother pleading your case to me, counselor. I won't be on the jury."

Mike passed another page of the report to Ben. "We searched Lombardi's suite from top to bottom, but we didn't find anything else of particular significance. Look for yourself."

Ben scanned the report. It itemized and detailed everything found in the penthouse. Dirty laundry—hardly unusual for a man living alone. An open carafe of rosé on the end table beside the chair. The TV was on. The phone was off the hook.

"What about the medical examiner's report?" Ben asked.

Mike rifled through his folder, then retrieved a three-page document. "The preliminary report is pretty much as expected. Lombardi died as a result of bullet wounds to the head. Koregai's having trouble confirming the time of death from the body heat of the liver. He's promised a supplemental report. Oh, one other thing. Koregai is absolutely positive about this. He's a D.R.T.—dead right there."

"Well, that hardly proves Christina killed him."

"Ben," Mike said, "think about it for a minute. Her story is that she fell asleep in that chair, not four feet from the body. Four feet from where Lombardi was killed, where that gun was fired four times. How could she possibly have slept through that?"

"Maybe the killer used a silencer."

"Not with a revolver."

Ben snapped his fingers. "She must've been drugged."

"Drugged?"

"Yeah. She said she drank something, almost immediately fell asleep, and didn't wake up until hours later. It all fits. Mike, I need you to get a lab tech in to do a blood test on Christina."

A third voice suddenly boomed through the cubicle. *"What the fucking hell is going on here?"*

Ben whirled around. There was a man hovering over him—tall, young, dark-haired, and bearing a disgusted expression.

Mike stood up. "Jim, this is—"

"I know goddamn well who this is," the man shouted. "I want to know what the hell is going on!"

Mike's face tightened. "We were reviewing some of the preliminary evidence—"

"Shit! This is the goddamn adversary you're talking to. Adversary, remember that? That's why they call it an adversarial system."

Ben watched Mike clench and reclench his fists. "The defense will be entitled to see our evidence—"

"In time—*maybe*." The man scooped the file off the table and cradled it in his arms, as if to protect it from Ben's corrupting influence. "After Mr. Defense Attorney files his paperwork, he *may* be entitled to see anything we deem exculpatory or intend to use at trial. Not the whole fucking file!"

"Jim, there's really no need—"

"Jesus Christ! We've got a goddamn slam dunk, and you're already trying to screw it up!"

"Mike," Ben said evenly, "who *is* this asshole?"

Mike stifled a smile. "This is Jim Abshire of the FBI. He's one of the FBI agents working this case."

"I'm the man who made this case fucking happen," Abshire said.

With some reluctance, Ben extended his hand. "I'm Ben Kincaid, the attorn—"

"I know who you are." He waved Ben's hand away. "Nothing personal, Kincaid, but my years of experience have taught me that it's bad policy to get too close to the opposition. Clouds your judgment."

Ben frowned. Years of experience? "You can't be much older than I am."

"How old are you?"

"I'm thirty."

"Well, I'm thirty-two."

Ahh, Ben thought. That explains your heightened maturity. "Look, Mike didn't really want to show me these reports. I sort of twisted his arm—"

"Don't give me that crap," Abshire said. "I know all about you two. You're college buddies formerly related by marriage. And I don't want any of that nostalgic bullshit polluting my case."

"*Your* case?"

"Damn straight, my case. I've been setting up this sting for over a year. This is going to take us straight to the big boys. And I put it together."

"Under the supervision of his boss," Mike said. "Roger Stanford."

Abshire smirked. "Well, I'm sure you know how that kind of arrangement works, Kincaid, and who ends up doing all the work. I understand you worked as an associate in a big firm. For about fifteen minutes." Abshire shouted out the door. "Hey, Roger, get in here!"

An older man wearing a white shirt and half glasses on the end of his nose walked into the cubicle. "Yes?"

"Check this out," Abshire said. "I caught Morelli here opening our files to counsel for the defendant."

Stanford pursed his lips. "The defense is entitled to review exculpatory evidence."

"Then, Christ, let him file a motion," Abshire said. "That's why we have procedures."

Stanford gave his protégé a long look. Ben got the impression he had been down this road with Abshire before. "I see little harm in cooperating to the extent of sharing evidence we will probably be required to produce at a later date."

"Yeah?" Abshire said, a bit stung. "Maybe that's why you're still a middle-level paper pusher."

Ben shook his head back and forth, trying to confirm that his ears were still working properly. This guy really knew how to win friends and influence people.

"FBI directors aren't interested in cooperation," Abshire

continued. "They're interested in results. And that's what I plan to give them. This case is a reputation-maker."

He took a step toward Ben, poking a finger into his chest. "So watch your step, Kincaid. If you screw up my case, I'll take you apart like a Tinker Toy. That's a promise."

Ben cast his eyes toward Mike. He had hoped, in fact, *expected* Mike to intercede, to tell this pompous FBI twit to back off. But Mike just stood there, stone-faced.

"Well," Ben said, stepping away from Abshire's finger, "I think I might as well be going."

"Agreed," Abshire said. "And nothing personal, Kincaid, but I don't want to catch you around here anymore. Cards-on-the-table time? If we have something to give you, we'll do it in court."

"Be seeing you," Ben said. He walked out of the cubicle.

Ben felt a bitter taste rising in his mouth. He needed to disappear before he said or did something he would regret, before his frustration overwhelmed him. Everything seemed increasingly hopeless. Everyone seemed determined to sign Christina up for a lethal injection, the sooner the better, and for all the wrong reasons. Abshire was the scariest one yet. He was determined to make his mark. He had to get a conviction, whatever the cost.

Which, in this case, was Christina.

* 10 *

Ben tapped himself on the chest again. "C'mon, Giselle. Listen to me. Jump."

Giselle was sprawled across the easy chair in the living room, peacefully licking herself clean. She glanced up at him, wriggled her nose, then returned to her bath.

"Giselle, this book Jones gave me says cats can be trained, just like dogs or dolphins or other smart animals. When I tap myself on the chest, I want you to jump into my arms and act like you're glad to see me. Got it?"

Giselle didn't even look up.

"C'mon, cat. I don't have all day. I have to get ready for tomorrow's hearing. So jump already."

Giselle shifted herself languorously to the other side of the chair. She stretched, meowed, and otherwise went about her business, totally snubbing him.

"Giselle, pay attention. I'm talking to you. I'd like to see some cooperation."

Giselle jumped down from her chair, strode into the kitchen, perched herself beside her food bowl, and stared at Ben.

"Forget it, Giselle. It's not going to work that way."

Giselle shook in a manner that Ben thought looked much like shoulder shrugging, except of course that cats don't have shoulders. She plopped down beside her bowl and waited.

"I'm not kidding, Giselle. I'm not going to let some over-stuffed feline boss me around."

Giselle absently resumed her bath.

"All right already! I give in!" Ben threw down the book and stomped into the kitchen. "I'll get the Feline's Fancy."

Giselle followed close on his heels. He opened a can of the gourmet cat food and set it on the floor. Giselle dove in nose first, acting as if she hadn't eaten in days. Come to think of it, Ben thought, she hadn't, although she appeared to have sufficient fat reserves to carry her through several lean periods.

"But don't get the idea that this is your permanent entrée," Ben said, trying to reassert his tenuous role as master of the house. "Once this can is gone, it's back to the cheap stuff."

Giselle nibbled happily and ignored him entirely.

Ben heated a Pizza Pocket in the microwave and took it into his living room. There was not much there in the way of furnishings—a TV, an old piano, and pizza delivery boxes stacked practically to the ceiling. His only indulgence was the stereo system: Mitsubishi receiver, Sony CD player, Boston Acoustic speakers. A throwback to his days as a music major, no doubt, and his dreams of glory.

Ben thought about playing the piano, but he knew he couldn't compete with Joni and Jami's Guns-N-Roses records reverberating on the other side of the paper-thin walls. He channel-surfed the TV—there was nothing worth watching. He listened to his CD of *Judy Garland—Live at Carnegie Hall*. An amazing recording, but he couldn't focus.

He decided to turn in early. He would have to get up around six to prepare for the hearing anyway. He performed his nightly ablutions, pulled on some old gym shorts, and crawled into bed. He tried to clear his mind, to drop off to sleep, but found it impossible. Everything was racing through his head at once, demanding his attention. Mike, and Spud, and Abshire, the FBI agent from hell. The chickens. Derek. And Christina, her face smeared with black.

He couldn't help but worry. Christina's life was on the

line. Even if she managed to avoid the Big Needle, this incident could destroy her life. He had to be thorough, had to consider every angle. If he let anything slip, the results could be tragic, even fatal. He would not let her down. The way he had Ellen.

There was a sharp stinging in his eyes. He couldn't sleep, couldn't relax, couldn't let go. His head was throbbing. He closed his eyes and tried to force the demons out of his head. It was no use. He rolled over and pulled the covers close.

He felt something wet and ticklish brush against his nose. He opened his eyes. It was Giselle.

Ben raised the covers, and she crawled inside. She did her push-paw routine for a little while, then she settled into a nice warm spot in the small of his back and fell asleep.

So did Ben.

* 11 *

Wolf almost stepped into the trap.

He shone his flashlight down toward the ground. There, partially hidden by leaves and brush, was a steel rabbit trap. He would have to be more careful. Even a rabbit trap could take off a toe or paralyze an ankle.

He poked a stick between the teethed blades and disarmed the mechanism. The drag chain was tied to a loose log—so the trapped animal couldn't get any leverage and escape. Wolf untied the chain and slipped the trap free. He noted the number engraved on the upper blade indicating its tensile strength, a matter of great importance to trappers. If the trap was too strong, it would snap off the animal's leg, or cut so deeply that the animal could (and would) chew his own leg off. Either way, the animal would escape, maimed but free. Until the next trapper came along.

Wolf tossed the disarmed trap into his backpack. Trapping wasn't allowed, at least not in his forest. He realized that some people were poor and hungry, especially around here. It didn't matter. They would have to think of something else. He managed to get by without killing anything. They could, too.

He completed his rounds, then headed back to the shack. The shack was probably originally built as a blind for hunters, but no hunter had used it for years, and none was likely to now. Wolf had posted a fake notice on the door alleging that the shack was the PRIVATE PROPERTY OF THE BUREAU OF ALCOHOL, TOBACCO, AND FIREARMS—KEEP OUT! He had designed the notice on the computer at the Creek Nation bingo parlor, and it looked pretty official, if he did say so himself. Not bad for a twelve-year-old.

He dialed the combination on the bicycle lock he used to secure the door, then stepped inside. The birds were still there. He kept them in cages he had fashioned from cardboard box lids and straightened coat hangers, both of which he found in the Dumpster behind Phoenix Cleaners. The birds beat their wings upon his arrival—glad to see him. Such excellent birds, he thought. Did you miss me?

The hawk, whom he called Katar, pressed his beak against the coat hanger barrier. If you really wanted to, you could get out of there. But why would you want to? It's too soon. When it's time, I'll let you out. You know I will.

Gently, Wolf examined the bird's bandage. The wound seemed to be healing nicely. He'd be well in no time, and back sailing the skies, hunting his prey.

The raven, whom he called Edgar, seemed equally pleased

to see him. His makeshift splint was still in place, and he seemed stronger than he had during Wolf's last visit. They said there was nothing they could do for a bird your size, Wolf remembered. They said you couldn't take a splint. Said even if they put one on, you'd pick at it till it was useless. They were wrong. As they and people like them had been wrong on so many other occasions.

He peered through a small slit between two warped wallboards. It was late, he realized, much later than he was supposed to be out. His mother would be furious. Assuming she noticed. Assuming she hadn't stayed late at the bingo parlor, or gone home with that Cherokee badass from Tahlequah again. Still, he couldn't risk one of her infrequent blasts of parental discipline. He had to remain free; the birds depended upon him.

He checked the other birds, made sure everyone had plenty to eat and drink, and locked the door behind him. He jogged toward the main road where he could pick up a ride. After a few minutes, though, he heard something—something that shouldn't be there. The same noise he had heard a week ago last Tuesday. It was the sound of an engine, but not a car or a truck or a motorcycle.

The noise grew louder. It was coming closer. Wolf saw a moonshadow swoop across the ground and realized what it was and where it must be going. He ran as fast as he could, through the trees, kicking up leaves in every direction. He reached the main clearing, a large area where the trees had been burned away. It was the only place in the forest a plane could land.

He watched as a small black plane positioned itself for final descent. Wolf knew about planes. He knew almost everything about anything that flew. Even as dark as it was, he recognized the aircraft as a Cessna 210—small, light, quick, quiet—perfect for long-range flights. It was painted black for invisibility and for flying at a low altitude (under radar) with its navigation and identification lights turned off.

He watched as the plane soared into the clearing and eased itself to the ground. After a few moments, the pilot hopped out of the cockpit, a thick, well-muscled man in jeans and a windbreaker. He was packing; Wolf could tell. A few seconds later, another man rode up on a dirt bike, his long blond hair streaming behind him. There were rifles strapped to both sides of the bike, just below the seat. The two men spoke briefly. Wolf saw a sudden glint of light, then packages changed hands. He couldn't tell what was being exchanged. To tell the truth, he didn't care. As long as they weren't hunters, they were outside his jurisdiction.

Wolf watched and waited. The man on the dirt bike rode away, and the pilot climbed back into his cockpit and took to the skies. After he was sure both were gone, Wolf jogged out to the place where the plane had landed. He thought he'd seen the pilot drop something.

He was right. On the ground, near one of the indentations in the grass left by the landing gear, he found a small glassy pouch with a powdery substance glistening inside.

Wolf shoved the package into his pocket. He thought he knew what the stuff was, and if he was right, it would buy him a lot of birdseed. Maybe some of that expensive scientific food the veterinarians used. Maybe he could even afford to take his birds to the veterinarian regularly, as soon as they were hurt, instead of having to make do on his own.

If the money was good enough. And if not, who knows? Maybe the men would come to the clearing again.

It was possible.

He would watch for them.

* 12 *

"What do you mean, you can't *find* her?"

The young officer from the federal marshal's office wiped his brow. He looked miserable. "We got the paperwork confused. They weren't sure whether to file McCall with the MCs or the MAs. Without the paperwork we couldn't find her."

Ben's neck muscles tightened. "It's not as if she could have gone out for a stroll. She's been behind bars, for God's sake."

"She's not in her cell. She must've been moved."

"Ask Lester. He'll know where she is."

"We can't. He doesn't come in till noon on Wednesdays."

"Call him at home."

"Can't. He doesn't have a phone."

Ben could feel his blood pressure rising. "This is the twentieth century. Everyone has a phone."

"Not Lester."

"The judge can't set bail unless the defendant is present."

"I'm sorry."

Ben placed his hands firmly on the officer's shoulders. "Look. Judge Derek didn't want to have this hearing in the first place; he's not going to be amused when he learns the defendant is absent."

"There's nothing I can do."

"You can search every holding cell personally. One at a time."

71

"I've already done that. She isn't there. She must've gotten lost somewhere in the processing—"

"All rise."

Ben whirled around. Derek was entering the courtroom. He hadn't changed much in the past year. Same blond hair (which Ben knew for unfortunate reasons to be largely toupee), same trim build, same generally handsome face. He wore the black robe well.

Derek sat down in his large burgundy chair. "Be seated. Counsel, approach the bench."

Like a convict on a forced march, Ben approached the bench. A woman from the prosecution table did the same.

"Well, Mr. Kincaid," Derek said, "it's been a while."

"So it has, your honor."

"Don't think for a moment you'll get any special treatment because we used to work together. You won't."

"Really? This upsets my entire case strategy."

Derek grimaced. "I am in great agony this morning. Wrenched my back last night during a . . . conversation with my wife. Threw it out completely." He touched the small of his back. "I would appreciate your keeping this as brief as possible."

"Understood, your honor."

"I had intended to spend the day lying in bed, attempting to heal my withered self, but Mr. Kincaid here thought it necessary we have this emergency hearing."

"My client has never been in jail before, your honor. And she's not enjoying it."

Derek ignored him. "Enter your appearances."

"Myra Mandell for the United States of America."

Ben examined Myra Mandell unobtrusively out of the corner of his eye. He thought he'd met most of the lawyers at the U.S. Attorney's Office, but he'd never seen Myra before. She was young and obviously nervous. Blonde, anorexically thin, with large wire-frame glasses. A bit of a squid. Must be tough to be so low on the totem pole you get sent to 8:30 bail hearings. Obviously this hearing wasn't of sufficient import to merit the personal attention of Alexander Moltke himself.

"Benjamin Kincaid for the defendant."

"Speaking of whom," Derek said, "where is she?"

Ben cleared his throat. "Ms. McCall seems to have been . . . misplaced."

"Misplaced?"

"Right. Somewhere in the bowels of the criminal justice system."

"I might've expected something like this from you, Kincaid."

"Don't blame me, your honor. I'm not in charge of prisoner processing."

"You're responsible for your client, and furthermore—"

At that moment, the courtroom doors opened. A large, strapping federal marshal entered, with Christina close at his side. She was wearing loose-fitting orange coveralls—standard issue for federal prisoners—that made it impossible to escape and blend into a crowd.

"Excuse me, your honor," Ben said. Without waiting for a reply, he strode to the back of the courtroom.

"Glad you could make it," Ben said.

Christina nodded. "That makes two of us."

Ben noticed she was handcuffed. "Is that necessary?"

"Standard procedure," the marshal said matter-of-factly.

"Just as well. She might overpower you." Ben took Christina's arm and led her to the defendant's table. "What happened to you?"

"I was delayed. There was a disturbance in the pat-down chamber."

"Can you be more specific?"

Christina shrugged. "I happened to tell this beef-brained three-hundred-pound matron that her strip-search technique lacked finesse. She then threatened to pound me into the pavement.''

Ben covered his eyes.

''Prisoner or not, I don't have to take that kind of guff from anyone. There was a scuffle. Marshals came running. Someone set off an alarm. There were reporters nearby. Everything got confused.''

''I get the general picture.''

''Like I said, I was delayed.''

''Just sit down, Christina.''

''*Tout de suite.*''

There was a sound of thunder from the bench. ''Mr. Kincaid, do you suppose we could get on with this?''

''Of course. Your honor, we're asking the court to set bail and release Ms. McCall, pending trial. Ms. McCall is a longtime Tulsa resident, she's employed here, and she has numerous local ties. She has no prior criminal record. There's no indication that she poses a threat to society or that she is likely to repeat the crime of which she is accused.''

''We oppose this motion, your honor, and seek detention,'' Myra Mandell said. ''Ms. McCall shot a man four times in the head at point-blank range—''

''That's yet to be determined,'' Ben interjected.

''*Accused* of shooting a man.'' Myra pushed her glasses up her nose. ''This is a drug-related homicide, your honor, and narcotics offenders have a very high jump-bail rate. Ms. McCall could be on a plane to an extradition-free South American hideaway before we can hold the preliminary hearing.''

''That's prejudicial and inflammatory,'' Ben said. ''My client shouldn't be detained on the basis of statistics.''

''We're not dealing in certainties here,'' Myra said. ''We're just trying to save this court the embarrassment of being deemed a weak soldier in the war on drugs.''

Ben threw his legal pad down on the table. ''That's grossly improper!''

Derek banged his gavel. "Please stop whining, Mr. Kincaid. The court is capable of recognizing an improper argument without your simpering objections. Give us some credit."

He shifted his attention to Myra. "Despite your noble sentiments, Ms. Mandell, I don't think I can justify not setting bail in this case. Much as I might like to."

Thank God, Ben thought. He had worried that Derek might refuse to set bail out of spite, because of his deep-seated animosity toward Ben.

Derek continued. "Bail will be set in the amount of five hundred thousand dollars."

"Thank you, your honor," Myra said, smiling.

"Five hundred thousand dollars!" Ben exclaimed. "Your honor, that's impossible!"

"Mr. Kincaid, do you want me to set bail or not?"

"Your honor, she's a legal assistant. She can't possibly raise enough to get a bond—"

"Do you want me to set bail or not?" Derek repeated, emphasizing each word.

Ben held his tongue.

"Very well. If there's nothing else—"

"There is one other matter," Ben said. "I have another motion."

"Yes?"

Ben hesitated. He glanced at the people sitting in the gallery. "Could we step into chambers, your honor?"

"No. If you have a motion, you can make it in open court."

"May we at least approach the bench?"

"No, counsel, you may not," Derek said, his voice rising, "and this is your last chance. Do you have a motion?"

"Yes, your honor. We move for recusal, pursuant to Title 28 of the United States Code, section 455. We want you to step down from this case."

Derek's eyes flared. "On what grounds?"

"On grounds of your extreme prejudice, your honor. Your inability to decide this case in an impartial manner."

"Your honor," Myra said, "we oppose—"

Derek cut her off with a flip of his hand. "Explain yourself, Mr. Kincaid."

"Your honor, I used to work at the same firm you did."

"For a mercifully brief period of time."

"In fact, I worked directly under your supervision."

"As you may be aware," Derek said, "conflicts of counsel are not grounds for recusal. If you feel your presence will prejudice your client's case, you should step down."

"Furthermore, you used to work at the same firm as the defendant, Ms. McCall. In fact, the two of you worked together on more than one occasion."

Derek squinted, peering across the bench at Christina. "I don't remember a Ms. McCall."

"Nonetheless, she was there."

"Well, I can hardly be expected to favor a person I can't remember."

"That wasn't exactly my concern," Ben murmured.

"Are you suggesting that when I was in private practice I or my firm served in any capacity with regard to the matter now before the court?"

"No, sir."

"Then your motion is denied, Mr. Kincaid. What's more, the court finds your motion offensive in the extreme. In fact, the court would probably issue sanctions; such action, however, would undoubtedly prejudice your client"—he paused significantly—"especially given the extremely early trial date I anticipate. So I will not issue sanctions. But neither will I forget."

He slammed his gavel on the desk. "This hearing is adjourned." He shambled out of the courtroom, rubbing his back.

Ben flopped down into the chair beside Christina.

"Did you have to bring that recusal motion now?" she asked. "In front of everybody?"

"If I'd waited, he would've said I waived it by not raising it at my first opportunity. I encouraged him to take the matter into chambers, but he insisted on playing to the peanut gallery."

"How much to get a bond for half a million?"

Ben sighed. "At least fifty thousand."

"In case you've forgotten, Ben, I'm not independently wealthy." Her voice wavered. "And my credit stinks."

"I know."

"Ben," she whispered, "I don't want to spend another night in there. It's not . . . they're not . . ." She couldn't finish her sentence.

Ben put his arm around her shoulder and pulled her close. "I know," he said quietly. "I'll think of something. I'll have to."

* 13 *

Everything had been changed. Since Ben's last visit the grand piano had been moved away from the bay window to the center of the room; evidently, the sunlight was causing the wood to crack. The entertainment center had been replaced by a white pine armoire. There were new curtains, new chairs, and new upholstery on the matching sofas.

"You've redecorated since I was here last," Ben said.

Ben's mother nodded slightly. "I have to do something to

pass the time. It's not as if I'm inundated with the attentions of my children.''

So soon? He had hoped for at least a minute or two of guilt-free small talk. "I've been swamped the last few weeks."

Mrs. Kincaid smoothed the lines of her pleated skirt. "And for the six months before that?"

"Now wait a minute, Mother. We talked . . . not too long ago. I remember. I phoned you."

"You telephoned on Christmas Day, if that's what you're referring to. I hardly think that qualifies you for Offspring of the Year."

"Mother, it takes constant effort to get a solo practice off the ground."

"I'm sure. Undoubtedly you had some holiday tipplers or gift snatchers who prevented you from appearing in person. It does, after all, take two entire hours to drive from Tulsa to Nichols Hills."

"It's a difficult drive—"

"I've driven it."

"You've driven to Tulsa?"

"Oh yes." She poured a cup of herbal tea from her porcelain oriental teapot. "Just after New Year's. When it became apparent you were not planning to visit at any time during the holiday season. I decided to see for myself what so occupied your time."

"Where did you go?"

"You had never given me the address of your apartment, and, of course, I had no letters bearing a return address. I was able to find your office address in the Yellow Pages."

Ben contemplated the carpet.

"It took me over an hour to locate your office. Actually, I kept driving past it, assuming I must be on the wrong street. At last, I realized that really *was* your office, right there between the pool hall and the arms dealer."

"That's a pawn shop."

"Whatever. I just remember the enormous neon sign flashing GUNS—AMMO in large red letters."

"Why didn't you come in?"

"I did plan to, but there was a skirmish of sorts outside your front door. Two bleached blondes in short leather skirts and pumps were clawing at one another."

That would be Honey Chile and Lamb Chop, engaged in their never-ending battle for territory, Ben realized. Unfortunate timing.

"Even then, I steeled myself and parked my car, determined to see your place of business." She hesitated. "I have nothing against the occasional well-tempered indulgence in alcohol, but when that man in the dirty raincoat vomited all over the parking meter . . ." She lifted her teacup and gently blew away the steam. "Well, I thought perhaps a visit at another time would be best."

"It's just as well," Ben said. "Your Mercedes would have been stripped clean sixty seconds after you got out."

"The thought did occur to me," she said. "Really, Benjamin, there must be a less disagreeable neighborhood somewhere in Tulsa. It is a large city."

"You don't start your practice working for the major corporations, Mother. At least not when you're on your own. You have to start on the ground floor. Build a strong client base over time."

"Being a solo practioner must be difficult."

"You don't know the half of it. Big firms use their large staff and resources for leverage. Bury their opposition with motions and discovery requests, then stand back and watch the solo guy crumble. They don't return your phone calls; in fact, they won't talk to you at all, unless it's to refer some scumbag client who's too dirty for them to touch. Judges don't trust you—they know you can't choose your clients. You never have anyone to cover for you when you have conflicting court dates. It's tough."

"It doesn't have to be. I could accelerate your progress."

"No. Absolutely not."

"I've talked to Jim Gregory. He's interested in bringing you into his firm."

"The only reason he's interested is because you're a long-time client and major source of income for him. No."

Mrs. Kincaid leaned forward. "At least let me assist you financially."

"No. Never."

"It's not as if I have any shortage of money."

"If that money had been intended for me . . ." Ben shook his head, eyes closed. He couldn't finish the sentence.

"Please don't start misinterpreting your father's wishes again, Benjamin. Your father wanted his entire family to be well provided for."

"Bull."

"It's true, Benjamin. He—"

"Don't waste your breath, Mother. I've seen the will."

"You—" She stopped, obviously surprised. "I didn't know that."

"Now you do. So don't bother."

Mrs. Kincaid fell back against the sofa. "Very well then. What is it you want?"

Ben suddenly wished he could shrink to the size of a microbe. "I . . . need to borrow some money."

"Is that all?" She reached into her purse and withdrew her checkbook. "It's about time you saw the light of day. How much do you want?"

"Fifty thousand dollars."

"Fifty—" She closed her checkbook. "Benjamin, what have you done?"

"It's not for me."

"Is this something to do with a woman?"

"Mother, I'm thirty years old. I think my private life is my own business."

"That's what you said before. And you haven't been the same since that horrible business in Toronto—"

"Mother!" He inhaled deeply, then lowered his voice. "It's for . . . a client."

"You're covering a client's gambling debts?"

"No. Helping my client make bail."

"Make bail? Is it . . . traditional for an attorney to advance bail money to a client?"

Well, you can't lie to your own mother. "No."

"Then I don't see why—"

"Mother, please. It's important."

Mrs. Kincaid gazed at her son for a long time. "Very well. I'll have Jim Gregory transfer the funds."

"Thank you. I . . . appreciate it." He took a piece of paper out of his wallet and scribbled a few lines. "Here's my home address. Next time you're in Tulsa, don't stay in your car the whole time. Okay?"

Mrs. Kincaid accepted the scrap of paper. "How delightful," she said. "This is a first. I trust your apartment is in a more respectable neighborhood than your office. Right?"

Ben smiled. "I don't want to spoil the surprise."

* 14 *

Christina closed the car door. "Let's get the hell out of here."

Ben turned the ignition. "There's no hurry, Christina. You're out on bail; you're not on the lam."

"The more distance between that jail cell and me, the better. Go."

Ben pulled out of the parking lot onto Denver. "I'm taking you to the Health Department for a blood test."

"Wrong. You're taking me to my apartment."

"This will only take a few minutes."

"Home, Ben."

"It's vital that we have the test done as soon as possible—"

"Ben, look at me. I'm a wreck. Physically, mentally, hygienically. I've spent the last day and a half with the sleaziest people I've ever met in my life. I'm talking total human refuse."

"Christina—"

"I haven't showered in days, unless you count being sprayed with that sticky disinfectant foam. I reek of lice spray. I have a deep and overpowering *tristesse* that reaches to the core of my being." She leaned forward, practically nose to nose. "I want to go home. *Now.*"

"Well, if you put it that way . . ."

"I do."

"Home it is." He changed lanes and turned onto Southwest Boulevard, then glanced at his rear-view mirror.

"Christina, did you see a black four-door sedan—a Cutlass, I think, with smoked glass windows—when I picked you up?"

"No."

"Well, I did."

"So?"

"So, it's following us. It's been following us since we left the municipal complex."

Christina looked puzzled. "Who would be following us?"

He wheeled into the parking lot of the Riverview apartment complex. "I wish I knew."

* * *

Ben and Christina walked toward her second-level apartment facing the Arkansas River.

"Who was that guy who brought my clothes to the jail?" she asked.

"That was Jones. He's my secretary."

"I never saw you as the male-secretary type."

"What did you see me as?"

"More the Donna Reed type. Some motherly secretary who brings you cookies during trial recesses and lays out your clothes in the morning."

"Jones was a client," Ben explained. "I helped bail him out of some trumped-up embezzlement charges brought by his former employer. Basically, Jones borrowed ten bucks from the till for lunch one day and forgot to replace it. The boss decided to make an example of him."

"A great humanitarian."

"I got Jones off, but he didn't have any way of paying my bill. I didn't have a secretary—Kathy having left me for the third time—so he filled in. It was his idea. I pay him when I can, and he's slowly paying off his bill."

"Is he any good?"

"Well, he only types about twenty words a minute, loses things, can't spell, and can't use a Dictaphone without erasing half the tape. But his attitude is exemplary."

"So he's better than Maggie?"

"By light years. He's handy with computers, too."

"Pity you can't afford one."

"Yeah. If there's a problem, it's that he's got Sherlock Holmes fever. Always wants to investigate the scene of the crime."

"You'll contain him."

"Oh? I was never able to contain you."

They arrived at apartment 210.

Christina inserted her key into the lock. "I hope the place wasn't too much of a mess when Jones came by. How embarrassing. I probably left my underwear lying all over the floor."

She turned the lock and pushed open the door.

Ben was reminded of the *Time* magazine photographs of the aftermath of Hurricane Bob. Everything in the apartment had been turned upside down, spilled, tossed, shattered. Sofa cushions lay on the floor, tossed in a heap with books, magazines, desk drawers, and upended chairs. Posters had been ripped off the walls; plants had been turned on their sides.

"Well," Ben said slowly, "I don't see any underwear."

"Is this Jones guy what you would call a messy person?" Christina asked.

"Not like this."

"Then I've had another visitor?"

"I'm afraid so."

They both heard the noise at the same time. Ben whipped around just in time to be body blocked by the man running out of the back bedroom. Ben fell back and crashed against the fireplace. Christina screamed; the fireplace tools clattered to the floor. The man bolted through the still-open door.

Ben pulled himself to his feet and started after him.

"Let him go," Christina yelled. "It's too dangerous."

Ben ignored her. He raced out the door and down the sidewalk to the parking lot. The intruder was already astride his motorcycle, kicking the starter. Ben grabbed him around the waist and pulled him to the ground. The man struggled, but Ben pinned him down with his knees, then tried to remove the man's black opaque motorcycle helmet.

Suddenly, the man lurched forward, bashing his helmet against Ben's forehead. Ben fell backward, clutching his head in pain. The man jumped onto his cycle and restarted it. Ben struggled to his feet just in time to see the man zooming away, his long blond hair trailing beneath his helmet.

Ben loped back to Christina's apartment, his head throbbing. "Got away," he said, panting heavily.

"You shouldn't have gone after him in the first place. You're a lawyer, not a cop."

"Obviously." Disgusted with himself, he walked across the room. "At least he didn't take the French collection," Ben said, trying to sound upbeat. He examined the evidence of Christina's Francophilia on her mantel. Travel posters of the Sorbonne, an Eiffel Tower paperweight, matching *chien* and *chat* potholders, Lautrec reproductions. A plastic bubble that, turned upside down, caused snow to fall on Notre Dame.

Ben picked up a thick paperback book and examined the spine. *The Trial of Joan of Arc.* "I didn't know you were a fan of the Maid of Orleans," Ben said.

"Now more than ever," Christina answered. "I feel we have a lot in common."

"I hope that's because you've both been wrongly accused. Not because you hear voices."

"Well, actually . . ." Christina picked up her Garfield phone and put the receiver back in the cradle. "You think we should call the police?"

"Definitely. I think this is the murderer's work. Any idea what he might have been looking for?"

"I can't imagine."

"Maybe we'll figure it out if we take note of what was searched."

"Ben!"

Ben whirled. "What?"

"My animals! They've been drilled!"

Ben surveyed the twenty or so stuffed animals that normally occupied most of the sitting space on her sofa. They were tossed haphazardly onto the floor on the opposite side of the room. Every one had a hand-size hole cut in its belly, with its stuffings falling out.

"I'm sorry, Christina," Ben said. "I've heard smugglers

sometimes hide contraband in dolls and stuffed animals. I guess your visitor was checking."

"What else could they possibly . . ." A horrified expression suddenly came upon her face. She walked quickly into the kitchen. Everything was silent for a moment, then, suddenly, she cried out.

Ben raced into the kitchen. "Is someone—" He stopped. Christina was kneeling on the floor. "What's wrong?"

Christina's hands were pressed against her eyes. "They got my babies."

Ben saw Christina's countless ceramic and porcelain pig figurines shattered into pieces on the floor.

"Those . . . dirty . . . It took me years to collect all these." She picked up a small pig shard with the word *cochon* in bold black letters. "They even got my little French piggy! He was my favorite!" Her damp eyes began to swell.

Ben patted her on the shoulder. "I'm sorry, Christina. There'll be other pigs. Really." He didn't know what to do. Murders he could deal with; on ceramic French piggies, he was helpless.

"Hey, look at this," Ben said, hoping to distract her. He pointed toward a muddy smudge on the kitchen linoleum. The mud retained the clear imprint of the heel of a shoe. "Was this here when you were home last?"

"Of course not. I'm not a total slob, you know." She wiped her eyes and studied the footprint. "Ben, it's a clue!"

"Not a very helpful one."

"If you were Sherlock Holmes, you'd run tests and discover that that particular type of mud is only found in one place in all of Tulsa."

"Indubitably. But I'm not Sherlock Holmes, and that's not bloody likely." He saw Christina's face droop. "Still, we have nothing to lose. Have you got a paper bag I can borrow?"

Christina seemed to recover a bit from her pig-induced melancholia. The thrill of the hunt, Ben supposed. "I'll give you a baggie,'' she said. "The pros always put evidence into little plastic bags."

"Wrong. The pros avoid little plastic bags because they retain moisture that can taint the evidence. Pros use paper bags and then transfer the evidence to plastic before trial so it can be viewed more easily by the jury."

"Is that so?" She opened the cabinet beneath the sink and withdrew a small paper bag. "I guess I could be Mister Know-It-All too if my brother-in-law was a cop."

"*Ex*-brother-in-law." Using his forefinger, Ben brushed the mud into the bag. Inside the mud, he discovered a small leaf fragment about the size of his thumb. "This give you any ideas?"

Christina shook her head. "Sorry. Trees aren't my forte."

"Probably a rare leaf only found in one place in all of Tulsa," Ben said. "I'm going to call the police and report this break-in. You take your shower. You're already late for a very important date with a lab tech."

As soon as she was out of sight, Ben took another paper bag from beneath the sink and methodically retrieved every broken piece of the ceramic *cochon*. You never know, he thought. I always was good at jigsaw puzzles.

* 15 *

Christina admired the latest additions to Ben's office decor. "Are these eating chickens or laying chickens?"

"Is there a difference?" Ben asked.

"He's a city boy," Jones explained.

"Obviously."

The three of them sat in Ben's tiny private office, Ben and Christina on the sofa, Jones in the chair behind the desk. Jones held his steno pad at the ready, just in case something important was said.

Ben passed Christina his list of suspects. "Tell me everything you know about these three men."

Christina examined the list. "Do you really think the murderer is one of these three?"

"Has to be. If Spud is telling the truth."

"Spud?"

"Lombardi's dipsomaniacal doorman."

Christina appeared puzzled. "His desk plate says Holden Hatfield. How does he get—"

"Don't ask." He redirected her attention to the list.

"Well, of course I know Reynolds. And I've heard of DeCarlo—never met him though. Tony mentioned him a few times. They had some kind of business arrangement."

"Did Lombardi like him?"

"Far from it. He was scared to death of him. Normally, Tony thought he was king of the world—serious *folie de grandeur*. But when it came to DeCarlo, Tony became a Nervous Nellie. DeCarlo sent him into fits of abject apoplexy."

A not altogether unreasonable response, Ben thought. "But you don't know what their business activities were?"

"Something to do with parrots, I assumed."

"What about Clayton Langdell?"

"That's the animal guy, right? I've seen him on television." She searched her memory. "I know he was hassling Tony about the parrots. Thought Tony's employees were trapping endangered species. Tony wasn't too worried about it. 'A bird is a bird is a bird.' That's what Tony used to say."

"Very literary," Ben replied. "I can see what attracted you to him."

"So he wasn't a philosophy major. Tony was a courteous, harmless man."

"So you thought, anyway. I'm going to interview your boss and the other two as soon as possible."

"What about Mrs. Lombardi, Tony's widow?"

"What about her?"

"You need to check her out, too."

"Why?"

"Just a hunch. *Cherchez la femme.*"

"Yeah—as long as you're not the *femme.*"

The phone rang. Jones picked it up. "It's the lab."

Ben took the call. After a few minutes, he thanked the person on the other end and hung up. "Totally inconclusive," he announced. "We waited too long to have the blood sample taken. Damn. Now I'm going to have to try to get access to the government's test results."

"The lab found nothing at all?"

"There were strong residual traces of alcohol in your bloodstream that could indicate you were drugged, perhaps with chloral hydrate, a sedative-hypnotic. It has an elimination half-life of four to twelve hours, depending upon the dosage, so it could easily put you out for six hours. On the other hand, the residual alcohol could just indicate that you were drinking. Which you were."

"Not that much," Christina insisted. "I hadn't had more than a few sips before I was out."

"But how do we prove that to the jury?" Ben glanced at his notes. "Chloral hydrate is a relatively common drug, something anyone with criminal connections could lay their hands on. It has a sickening sweet taste, but that would probably be masked by the rosé you were drinking. Oh, and it smells like perfume."

Christina blinked. An errant thought skipped through her head, but it was gone before she could capture it.

"They did a urine test with a barbiturate screen, but it was inconclusive. Again, it came too late."

"I know I didn't drink enough to have alcohol show up in my blood almost forty-eight hours later," Christina said.

"You know it and I know it, but so what? The bottom line is: the test doesn't prove anything. We have no evidence." He threw himself back on the sofa. "Are you sure you don't remember anything else that happened Monday night?"

"My memory's fuzzy. I went over to see Tony. He wasn't home. I waited for him."

"Spud says you seemed upset with Tony."

"Well, I was a little put out about having to meet him at his apartment. It's not even within the Tulsa city limits."

"I see. Did you eat or drink anything in his apartment? Other than the rosé?"

"I don't think so."

"Okay. Jones, draft another motion. I want that rosé *and* the carafe tested."

"Got it, Boss."

"What else can you remember, Christina?"

"That's about it. I watched TV awhile, drank, then conked out. I mean totally. And I had the weirdest dream. Really bizarro. Something about swimming and . . . Frosty the Snowman."

"I beg your pardon?"

"You heard me. Frosty the Snowman. You know"—she began to sing—"with a corncob pipe and two eyes made out of coal."

"You're lucky I'm a lawyer, not a psychiatrist."

"Yeah. Anyway, you know the rest. I woke up and poked around like an idiot. The FBI goons came in, roughed me up, and hauled me off to the slammer."

"Got all that, Jones?"

Jones nodded.

"If you think of anything else, write it down immediately, or tell Jones or me."

"Okay."

"I need some hard evidence before the hearing on Friday. With any luck, we can shut down this dog-and-pony show before it goes to trial."

"Sounds good to me," Christina said. "What should I do in the meantime?"

Ben considered her question. "I think you should either fry them, or collect their eggs, depending on which they are. Jones will know. He's a country boy."

Ben held the small brown package about a foot away from him. Although it was somewhat heavy, he preferred not to brace the weight against his body. The further away, the better.

He walked next door to the B & J Pawn Shop and peered through the iron bars. Excellent. Burris was in.

He pushed open the door, ringing the cowbell. The proprietor, Burris Judd (he was both the B and the J), was standing behind the counter.

Burris looked up. His face seemed to contract; his eyes became narrow slits. "What do you want?" The hostility was unmistakable.

Ben plopped his package down on the counter. "You'll never guess what I got in the mail today, Burris."

Burris scratched his stubbled chin. "How the hell would I know what you got in the mail?"

"Like I said, you'll never guess." Ben started to open the box.

Burris's eyes lit up. "Now wait just a cotton pickin' minute. What do you think you're doin'?"

"You don't want me to open this in your shop, do you? Kind of odd, since you don't know what's in it."

"I've got customers to attend to, shyster. If you'll excuse me."

Ben scanned the small, otherwise empty pawn shop. "Looks like it's just you and me from where I'm standing, Burris." He pointed at the box and whispered. "It's a gopher."

"That a fact."

"Yup. What's worse, it's a *dead* gopher."

"Do tell."

"Yup. Somebody shot it dead. With a Smith and Wesson .44. Can you imagine?"

"Nope."

"What I really liked, Burris, was that it was sent Fourth Class—Book Rate, so it could decompose for at least two weeks before it arrived."

"Don't know what you're botherin' me for, Kincaid. Probably a gift from one of your low-life clients."

"I have some strange clients, Burris, but I'm not aware of one with a gopher fetish. And I can't imagine why a client would want to kill a gopher, much less send it to me."

Burris rolled his tongue around in his mouth. "Them gophers is a pernicious breed. They've been raisin' hell in my backyard."

"So I've been informed. And that, coupled with your access to about five hundred or so Smith and Wessons right here in your shop and your predilection for juvenile terrorism, made me think it was just possible you were my mystery correspondent."

"And what if I am?"

"Transporting dead gophers through the U.S. Mail is against federal law."

"What law?"

"I don't exactly know, but I'm confident that if I spent an hour or so in the library I could find one."

"Wouldn't be surprised if you did take me to court. You

ain't shown much judgment about selecting your cases in the past."

Ah, the truth at last. About three months earlier Ben had represented a deadbeat named Hal Utley who was being sued by Burris. Utley bought a used black-and-white television from Burris on credit, sold it, then stopped making his payments. Burris sued in Small Claims to collect the debt. Ben managed to salvage Utley's case, principally because Burris had lost the paperwork and was charging a legally unconscionable rate of interest. It was his own fault, but of course Burris didn't see it that way.

Ever since the day of the trial, Ben had been the victim of Burris's adolescent assaults. Toilet paper, eggs. Shoe polish on Ben's car. One day a confused handyman showed up to install a Jacuzzi in Ben's office; another day eighteen pizzas were delivered within half an hour. The gopher gambit was the most creative stroke yet.

"Tell you what, Burris," Ben said. "You answer some questions for me, and I'll forget about this incident."

"I don't know nothin' about nothin'."

"Ah, but this question falls squarely within your field of expertise."

"And what might that be?"

"Smuggling."

Burris pointed toward the door. "Git out of here, Kincaid."

"Now calm down, Burris. I'm not suggesting that you'd be involved in anything illegal yourself. It's just that a man in your profession, a man who deals in . . . valuable goods, is bound to hear about certain nefarious activities. Even if he doesn't want to."

"Like what?"

"Like Tony Lombardi's smuggling pipeline."

Burris didn't reply.

"And Albert DeCarlo's connection to Lombardi's connection, whatever that was. What do you know about Lombardi?"

Burris gave him a long, stony stare. "And if I help you, you'll forget about the gopher?" He paused. "Whoever did it."

"Scout's honor."

Burris took a step back from the counter. "I do know that a lot of the boys who worked for Lombardi from time to time used to head out for Creek territory every other Monday night or so. Some of 'em'd come by here beforehand to gun up."

"And you never asked what they needed guns for?"

Burris examined his fingernails. "Figgered they was goin' rabbit huntin'."

I'll just bet you did. "When you say Creek territory, do you mean the tribal lands where Lombardi was killed?"

"No. Further north." He unfolded a map of Oklahoma and pointed. "Out in the wild country. No roads, no houses. No witnesses."

"Have any idea what they were doing out there?"

"Nope. Nor would I care to speculate."

Ben realized he had extracted as much information as he was likely to get. "Burris, I appreciate your assistance. It was right neighborly of you." He turned toward the door.

"Wait a goldarned minute," Burris shouted behind him. "You forgot your package."

Ben didn't stop. "Gophers are like pigeons, Burris. They always come home to roost."

* 16 *

Ben entered the office lobby of Swayze & Reynolds on the tenth floor of the Oneok Building at two o' clock sharp and introduced himself to the receptionist, an attractive young woman seated behind a large word-processing terminal.

"Please have a seat," she said, smiling. "I'll tell Mr. Reynolds you're here."

Ben sat. He watched the receptionist whisper into her intercom. Then she said aloud, "Mr. Reynolds is in conference at the moment, but he'll be out as soon as he can."

Liar, Ben thought. He's going to make me wait just to show what a bigshot he is. Oh well, it's not the receptionist's fault. He smiled back.

He scrutinized the exquisitely color-coordinated office. The walls were covered with an ornate burnished wallpaper, muted red with gold flecks, and waist-high wainscotting. Heavy curtains on the windows. Every little expensive doodad and geegaw seemed to be exactly placed. Against the far wall, Ben saw a cabinet displaying several eye-catching *objets d'art*. He noticed a particularly striking crystal vase, probably Lalique, beside a Baccarat shell sculpture. No doubt about it—this office reeked of money.

Ben continued scanning the room. After a moment, his eyes alighted on the receptionist. She's looking at me! Ben suddenly realized.

"Can I get you something?" the receptionist asked, still smiling.

"Uh, no," Ben said.

"All right. But if there's anything I can do to make you more comfortable, just let me know." She reached forward for a pencil on the far end of her desk, giving Ben a generous view of her generous cleavage.

This woman is coming on to me! Ben thought, with a sudden flash of happiness and horror. He forced himself to his feet and walked to her desk. He felt his face flushing red. "So . . . have you been working for Mr. Reynolds long?" Ben could have kicked himself. What lame small talk!

"I just started today," she said. She had a luminous smile. "Mr. Reynolds was kind enough to give me a job when I needed one."

"I see. Tell me . . ." He searched her desk for a name plate.

"Marjorie," she said.

"Marjorie. Of course. Tell me, Marjorie, do you ever . . . go to movies or anything like that?"

A tiny wrinkle appeared between her eyebrows. "Sure." She giggled. "I love movies. Why?"

"Well, I just . . ." He cleared his throat. "I thought that perhaps you and I—"

A deep voice interrupted Ben's badinage. "Mr. Kincaid."

Ben turned and saw Quinn Reynolds standing in the hallway.

"Mr. Reynolds," Marjorie said, "he's your two o' clock." She rose to her full height.

Ben almost gasped. Marjorie was pregnant, very pregnant. He would've guessed ten months, if he hadn't known that was biologically impossible. She looked perfectly normal from the cleavage up, but once she stood . . .

"Is something wrong, Mr. Kincaid?" Reynolds asked.

"No, no, no," Ben said, trying to bring some coherency

to his whalelike sputtering. "I just—it was—" He took a deep breath. "Could we go somewhere and talk?"

"Certainly." Reynolds gestured for Ben to follow him down the long wainscotted hallway.

"I . . . assume your visit concerns the Simmons case." Reynolds spoke in a slow, pained manner. Perhaps it was just too terribly hard for him to commune with the commonfolk. "Was there a . . . problem with the settlement agreement?"

"No. I came to ask you a few questions."

Reynolds looked at him expressionlessly. "Questions? Hmm." Listening to Reynolds was like being stuck in traffic. "What . . . kind of questions?"

"I was curious why you went to Tony Lombardi's apartment Monday night."

Even given his slow-as-molasses delivery, Reynolds's surprise was evident. "I—mmm." He folded his arms across his chest, flashing his French cuffs, studded links, and Rolex watch.

"You're not denying it, are you?"

"No. Why should I? I was just . . . surprised that you were aware of the fact. My wife suggested that something like this could happen. I should have listened to her; she's the judge."

Ben wondered how many times in the course of the average conversation Reynolds managed to mention that his wife sat on the Supreme Court. "You are aware that Mr. Lombardi was killed Monday night, aren't you?"

"Oh yes." Reynolds unfolded his arms and pressed a finger against his long, thin face. "But why does that concern you, Mr. Kincaid?"

"Didn't Marjorie tell you? I'm representing your employee, Christina McCall."

"I see." Now that Reynolds had the key information, that

Ben was handling one of those nasty criminal things, he was able to put Ben into perspective.

Ben glanced at the chairs surrounding a round conference table. "Do you mind if I sit down?"

"How inhospitable of me," Reynolds said, without much conviction. "Please." He gestured toward the table.

Reynolds apparently eschewed the traditional desk, with its hierarchal I'm-behind-the-desk, you're-not implications. He favored the open forum feel of a large round table. How very modern of him, Ben mused. The table was bare, except for a stained glass–paneled lamp and an art deco clock. As he sat, Ben glanced at the feet of the mahogany chairs. He had read somewhere that clawed feet were the indicia of high-quality antique furniture. These chairs qualified.

"I see you've noticed the chairs," Reynolds said. "They're Chippendale, nineteenth century." He sighed. "Many people think they're Louis the Fourteenths, not that the two are at all alike. I much prefer these. French furniture is so . . ." He waved his hand limply in the air, then shrugged his shoulders. "Well, you know."

Ben didn't, but he wasn't about to admit it. "Is that a Tiffany lamp?"

"Oh yes," Reynolds said wearily. "Almost required, isn't it? The clock is an Erte design. My wife commutes to Oklahoma City on a regular basis . . . when the Court is in session . . . and she always takes the opportunity to shop the antique dealers."

That's two, Ben thought. "Can you tell me what your relationship with Mr. Lombardi is?"

"Was, don't you mean?"

"Was," Ben corrected.

"I acted as his attorney."

"I know you handled that automobile accident litigation. Did you draft his will?"

Reynolds nodded.

"Care to tell me what's in it?"

"I'm afraid I can't disclose that."

"Not even a hint?"

"I can tell you this. I'm the executor of his estate."

"That means you'll be receiving all his financial and business records."

"I already have them. I acted as his . . . business adviser in many respects. When he was alive."

"What can you tell me about Lombardi's business?"

"What . . . would you like to know?"

"Almost anything would be helpful. I understand he imported parrots?"

"Not exclusively parrots. Many exotic birds."

"Doesn't seem like much of a business."

"How naïve of you. The retail bird business is worth $300 million in gross sales per year, with a sixty percent profit margin at every level. Tony did handsomely by it. There's quite a demand for rare birds."

"Did you ever see any of these alleged parrots?"

Reynolds stared at Ben as if he were utterly brainless. "Did you not notice?"

"Notice what?"

"My bird, of course. Behind you."

Ben glanced over his shoulder. There were several more antiques in that corner of the office, but even more noticeable was the large blue-and-green parrot in a small cage.

"You have a parrot," Ben said.

"Obviously. It was a gift from Tony. An Imperial Amazon. *A. imperialis*. The emperor of parrots. Very rare." Reynolds almost smiled. "He said that nothing but the rarest of birds could possibly fit in my office."

Ben took a closer look. The parrot's head, neck, and abdomen were purplish blue; its crown feathers were dark green with black edges. Its tail was a deep reddish brown; the irises of its eyes were orange. The parrot was at least nineteen or twenty inches in length. "What's his name?"

Reynolds's eyes tossed about in their sockets. "It's a her."

"Okay, what's *her* name?"

"I—" He sighed. "It was my wife's idea. She insisted. She named her for a fellow member of the court. Polly." He frowned.

"Polly?"

Reynolds appeared embarrassed. "I'm afraid so."

Ben smiled, pleased by this breathtaking lack of creativity. "Does Polly speak?"

"Only when spoken to," Reynolds answered. "The ideal pet."

"Make her say something."

"I prefer not to. We don't do tricks."

"Just once?"

"Oh, very well." He turned toward the parrot. "Polly, introduce me."

The parrot spoke in a sharp nasal tone. "Quinn Reynolds," it squawked. "Attorney-at-law."

How unbearably egocentric. Reynolds had turned his pet into the doorman. "Does she ever get out of the cage?"

"Heavens, no." Reynolds shuddered. "Letting a bird fly around the office. What a mess. You know, parrots, like all birds . . ." He cleared his throat. "Are incontinent."

Lawyers learn the most fascinating things. "You never let her out of the cage?"

Reynolds shifted his weight. "If there's nothing else, Mr. Kincaid, I have several legal matters that require my attention. . . ."

"Just one more question. What happened at Lombardi's apartment Monday night?"

Reynolds shrugged listlessly. "Absolutely nothing. The doorman let me in; I rode the elevator to Tony's apartment;

I knocked on the door. After a few moments, I surmised that he was not in. So I left.''

"And that's it?"

"That's it."

"Why did you go?"

"I had a business matter to discuss."

"What kind of business matter?"

"I'm afraid that's confidential."

"The police will ask you the same question."

"Then I shall answer it," Reynolds replied. "But you are not the police, are you?"

Ben felt his fists tighten. Reynolds's air of passive serenity was making his skin crawl. "I'd like to look at Lombardi's business records."

"I'm afraid that is impossible."

"Mr. Reynolds, it may be very important to Christina's case."

"I'm afraid I can't help you."

"Mr. Reynolds, I have a responsibility to my client—"

"As do I, Mr. Kincaid." For the first time, Reynolds's voice increased minutely, both in volume and speed. "Those documents are strictly confidential. At least until we've completed probate. Then you may take the matter up with Tony's heirs."

"That could take months!"

"I'm afraid that will likely be the case. I'm sorry."

His voice, Ben thought, gave little indication of either fear or sorrow. "Mr. Reynolds, think about Christina, your own legal assistant. This could be a matter of life or death for her."

"Mr. Kincaid," Reynolds said, "there's nothing you can do to change my mind."

"I can subpoena those records."

"You can try. But you will have to convince the judge that the business records are somehow relevant to your murder case, and that may be rather difficult."

Yeah. Especially with the judge I drew.

"And of course," Reynolds continued, "your subpoena will put the federal district court judge in conflict with the state probate court judge. Those interjudicial disputes are always messy . . . and extremely time consuming."

I get the message, jerk. I might as well lay off, because I don't have that much time. The government has already filed a complaint and the date for the preliminary hearing was set; under the Speedy Trial Act, the countdown to Christina's trial had already begun. A lawyer of Reynolds's ilk could file motions and countersuits and cause all manner of delays for a good deal longer than it would take Moltke to get Christina into the courtroom. While Reynolds sat around playing lawyer games, Christina would go to trial, on schedule.

Whether she had any defense or not.

Christina sat in her office staring at the walls. The cardboard boxes had multiplied while she was gone—whether by spontaneous generation or inbreeding, she wasn't sure. But they totally covered all four walls now; there wasn't even a space where she could pretend there was a window. She had never liked this claustrophobic decor, but now it provided a distinct reminder of a certain six-by-eight-foot cell she had no desire to ever see again in her life.

She was distracted from her interior decorating reverie by a timid knock. Alf Robins was standing in the doorway. "What's up, Alf? Come by to see if the slammer changed me?"

Alf stepped cautiously into the office. "I . . . er . . . need to discuss something with you."

"Well, don't be shy. I live to serve. Have a seat."

Alf sat in the chair opposite her desk. He was one of five attorneys in the firm for whom Christina worked. Alf was the youngest of them by far; he had just graduated from TU law school the previous May. "I've been asked to . . . well, to deliver a message."

"Oh?"

Alf fiddled with his fingers. "I want you to know this isn't my idea. I'm just the messenger."

Christina definitely didn't like the sound of that. "What's it all about, Alfie? Are you here to tell me the firm isn't going to pay me for the time I was in jail? If so, don't sweat it—I think that's fair. The firm's disability policy probably doesn't cover incarceration."

"I'm afraid it's a bit . . . more than that," Alf said. He was beginning to stutter, and he looked as if he sincerely wished he was anywhere other than where he was. "It seems the firm has decided to let you go."

Christina stared back at him. "*Me?* You're kidding."

"I wouldn't kid about something like that."

"But why? I've kept my billable hours up. I'm the most experienced legal assistant in the firm. Every litigator here has been trying to get me on his team."

"I know," Alf said, hugging his knees. "I know."

"Then why the hell am I being fired?"

"I believe the firm feels there could be adverse publicity resulting from having—" He looked down at the floor. "—an accused murderess on the payroll."

Christina leaped out of her chair. "But I didn't do it!"

Alf held his hands in front of himself, as if to hold her back. "I'm sure . . . I mean, I know—"

Christina slapped his hands away. "Don't be such a wimp, Alf. I'm not going to hurt you." She widened her eyes and held her hands like claws. "We murderesses only strike at night, when the moon is full."

"It wasn't my idea," Alf said hastily. "The decision was made by the Executive Committee by consensus."

"And they sent you, the lowest man on the totem pole, to give me the bad news. What a bunch of cowards."

"Believe me, Christina, I didn't want to do this."

"Yeah, yeah, yeah. But you didn't want to lose your job either, huh? Who gave the order? Reynolds?"

Alf cleared his throat. "I'm . . . er, not altogether sure I should say."

"As I thought. Reynolds." She strode toward the door. "Well, by God, I'm not leaving without giving him a piece of my mind!"

"Christina, wait!"

It was too late. Christina was already down the hall and around the corridor. She arrived at Reynolds's office just as he was escorting Ben out.

"Ben!" she said. "What are you doing here?"

"Mr. Reynolds and I were having a little chat," Ben said succinctly.

"Yeah?" She glared at Reynolds. "Well, I'm going to have a little chat with you too, you miserable pantywaist."

Reynolds fingered his shirt collar. "I believe you should, uh, be speaking to Mr. Robins."

"I'm not going to waste my time with your toadies, Reynolds. I'm going straight to the horse's butt!"

"What's this all about?" Ben asked.

"This miserable SOB fired me! Can you believe it?"

Ben faced Reynolds. "Is this true?"

Reynolds shrugged uncomfortably. "The economy being what it is . . . Cutbacks became necessary. . . ."

"Bull," Christina said. "He's cutting me loose because he's afraid of adverse publicity. He's convicting me before the trial begins!"

"I assure you the firm will provide a full two-week severance package—"

"I ought to sever you from your head!" Christina shouted. "I'm the best legal assistant you ever had!"

Reynolds glanced up and down the hallway. A crowd was beginning to gather. "Perhaps we should step into my office—"

"I'd sooner die, you miserable worm," Christina said. "How can you live with yourself, anyway?"

Ben grabbed Christina's arm. "Christina, perhaps you should calm down. . . ."

"Why should I? I've never been fired in my entire life. And now this cretin puts a permanent stain on my record!"

Ben stepped between Christina and Reynolds. "Mr. Reynolds, I would ask you, as one attorney to another, to reconsider your decision. The prosecuting attorney will almost certainly use this against us. He'll make sure the jury knows Christina is unemployed and will either suggest that she is a shiftless loser or that the people who know her best believe she is guilty."

"The decision is out of my hands."

"Perhaps you could retain her temporarily on a contract basis. After all, this incident did arise to some degree as a result of Christina's work for your firm."

"That's just the difficulty," Reynolds said. "She's been accused of killing a client, someone the firm owes a duty of zealous loyalty. It was an unpleasant decision, but the members of the Executive Committee have spoken."

"The members of the Executive Committee are puppets," Christina said. "They do what you tell them to do."

Reynolds stiffened. "I'm going to have to ask you both to leave."

Christina grabbed his lapel. "Not until you explain to me—"

"If you don't," Reynolds continued, "I will call security. Would you like charges for trespassing and assault to add to your collection?"

"Come on, Christina," Ben said, tugging her arm. "This isn't doing you any good. Let's get out of here."

"Fine." Christina stomped toward the lobby. "Make sure my check gets sent to my home address," she shouted back at Reynolds. "If it isn't, I'll come back for one of your Louis the Fourteenths!"

Happily, Ben managed to prevent her from kicking any priceless antiques on her way out.

Shortly after Ben and Christina left, Reynolds punched the button on his intercom phone.

"Marjorie?"

"Yes, Mr. Reynolds."

"Can you requisition some office equipment from Central Supply? Without filling out the usual dreary forms?"

"Well . . ." She thought for a moment. "I can try."

"I would appreciate it. I don't wish to leave a written record if I can avoid it. It might, um, be accidentally produced during discovery."

"I can probably bring it off," she said cheerily. "Those guys in Central Supply can't resist a pregnant woman. What do you need?"

"A paper shredder," he said, slowly and carefully. "A large one. Industrial strength."

* 17 *

Ben and Christina approached a small booth in the front plaza of the Tulsa Zoo. A banner stretched across the booth identified it as belonging to the Oklahoma Society for the Protection of Other-Than-Human Lives.

"May I help you?" the woman behind the booth asked.

"We're here to see Clayton Langdell," Ben said. "We have an appointment."

"He's in the aviary at the moment. Can I interest you in a bumper sticker?"

She had two different stacks of bumper stickers; one read SAVE A SEAGULL—CLIP SIX-PACK RINGS, while the other explained that FUR ISN'T FASHIONABLE, with a bloody raccoon draped around a woman's neck.

Ben took one of the brochures and began to read.

In 1980, the population of Spaceship Earth was 4.4 billion. In 1990, the population was 5.2 billion. Every single day, human beings move into rain forests, oceans, ice caps and prairies where once only plants and animals lived.

I get the message, Ben thought. He skipped to the last page.

Extinctions are accelerating on an exponential basis. Spaceship Earth loses as many as three species per day. By 1995, we may lose three species per hour. By 2000, twenty percent of all species currently living on this planet may be gone.

"Got anything lighter?" Ben asked.

"I don't know what you mean," the woman replied.

"I'm not surprised." He put the brochure back on the desk.

"They're free. Take as many as you want."

"No thanks. Just point me to the aviary."

The aviary was a huge sunlit building surrounded by transparent glass walls. The interior replicated a natural woodland area; it was filled with tall trees and plants and brush. Perches disguised as branches provided numerous places to rest. Exotic birds of every color and variety fluttered across the aviary, nesting, swooping, or making the proverbial lazy circles in the sky.

Ben and Christina stepped inside. "Have you ever seen that Hitchcock movie?" she asked.

"Which? *North by Northwest?*"

"No, stupid. *The Birds.*" She looked around uneasily. "They kind of give me the creeps."

"Don't be ridiculous. We're in a zoo. What could be more harmless?" Ben spotted a short, pudgy man with a bird perched on each shoulder. "That must be Langdell."

"You go chat with him," Christina said. "He might be inhibited if I'm around. I'll just stay here and try not to look like carrion."

Ben approached the man with the birds, his arm extended, and introduced himself. "Thank you for taking the time to see me."

"Not at all." Langdell had improbable orange hair and a speckled turnip of a nose. He seemed born to seriousness, his face set in stern lines. "Your secretary indicated you had some vital information about cruelty to animals."

Oh great, Ben thought. This was going to get them off to a fine start. "Well, he may have been a bit misleading."

"You're not here to discuss cruelty to animals?"

"Well, I am, but the animal suffering cruelty was a human animal. I'm here about Tony Lombardi."

Langdell's movements slowed. He shrugged slightly and the two birds on his shoulders flew off.

"I'm representing the woman accused of murdering him," Ben added.

A tiny light flickered in Langdell's eyes. "There's no question about her guilt, is there?"

"There's a supremely big question. I'm convinced she didn't murder Tony Lombardi, and I'm trying to find out who did."

"Very well then. What do you want to know?"

"Why did you go to Lombardi's apartment the night he was killed?"

To Ben's relief, Langdell didn't try to deny it. "I wanted to talk to him privately."

"Why?"

"I'd been writing letters to him for months. And attempting to reach him by telephone. He never answered, and he never returned my calls. So I decided to confront him face-to-face."

"About what?"

"About his despicable parrot trade."

"Despicable? Because he was using parrots as a front to smuggle drugs?"

"Is that true? I knew nothing about that, although I'm not surprised. I just wanted Lombardi to terminate his cruelty to fellow members of the animal kingdom."

"Lombardi was cruel to the parrots he imported?"

"The practice of importing parrots is cruel in and of itself, and it ought to be abolished. Do you know how parrots are caught? Lombardi's men, like all parrot trappers, will do anything, so long as it's quick, efficient, and heartless. They invade the birds' South American habitat and wantonly cut down trees so they can rob the nests. Or they trap the birds with leg snares from which the birds dangle helplessly for extended periods. Or they ignite a sulfur smudge to create a dense cloud of smoke, until the birds fall out of the trees unconscious. Then they can be plucked off the ground like ripe fruit.

"Or they simply shoot the birds' wings with pellets to wound them so they can't fly and can be captured easily. Of course, since wing-shooting requires good aim, which most of the trappers don't have, more birds are killed than crippled." Langdell's lips tightened. "Some poor birds never have the opportunity to fly free; thanks to Lombardi and his ilk, their life begins in captivity. And ends in death."

"Mr. Langdell, I like animals as much as the next man, but that's not why I came here."

Langdell glared at him. "Thirty million wild birds world-wide are caught each year for resale as pets, Kincaid."

Ben was stunned. "Thirty *million*?"

"That's right."

"There must be some restrictions . . . something at Customs."

"A routine examination by the woefully understaffed Department of Agriculture, followed by a cursory thirty-day quarantine. It accomplishes nothing. Especially for the birds that are smuggled illegally into the country."

"Smuggled?"

"You got it, counselor. About a quarter of a million parrots and other exotic birds are smuggled into the United States every year—often with drugs—for sale to pet shops and private dealers."

"How are the birds smuggled?"

"You name it; it's probably been done. Parrots are sewn into the lining of coats, crammed into false-bottomed suitcases, or stuffed into machinery, pipes, or gutted auto parts. Hundreds of birds are often packed in tiny crates meant for two dozen and left with no food or water. For days. Of course, their beaks are taped shut. The beak of an angry parrot can be a dangerous weapon."

"I can see where they might be angry."

"You don't know the half of it. The mortality rate for smuggled birds is between fifty and seventy-five percent."

Ben felt the need to sit down. "That's incredible."

"But true. Of the thirty million birds captured each year, only seven and a half million survive importation. And ninety percent of those will be dead within two years."

"That does seem rather . . . inefficient."

"You don't know the half of it. Do you realize some studies indicate parrots are intelligent?"

Ben didn't.

"A recent Purdue University study indicated that to some degree parrots may actually understand the meaning of the phrases they are taught to say. They may be able to deduce and reason in response to their environmental conditions. And I'll tell you something else. Parrots mate for life. As a result, they suffer even more from the loss of their mates."

"Amazing. Is there much money in parrot smuggling?"

"Like you wouldn't believe. And the rarer the bird, the higher the price. Some go for as much as a hundred thousand dollars."

Ben whistled. "How much could a guy get for an Imperial Amazon?"

Langdell smiled bitterly. "You've been to see Quinn Reynolds."

"Yeah. Nice bird."

"It's a revolting situation. Quinn Reynolds is an ethical toxic waste dump."

"You don't approve?"

"Damn right I don't approve. He keeps that bird in a cage every second of its life. It never gets a chance to fly free. If you must keep a bird in captivity, particularly one that size, you have a moral obligation to keep it in an aviary."

"Wouldn't that be expensive?"

"Reynolds can afford it. And if he can't, he can send the bird here. The Tulsa Zoo takes exceptional care of its animals. That's where the bird should be, assuming it has to be in captivity."

"You think it should be set free?"

"At the very least, I think it should be set free of Reynolds. He doesn't care for it worth a damn. Parrots need attention, care, grooming. Reynolds doesn't provide any of that. That bird gets the same oilseed to eat every day, and virtually no attention. The last time I was in his office, the poor thing had started feather-plucking."

"Feather-plucking?"

"Sounds horrible, doesn't it? It is. It's an aberrant behavior pattern brought on by monotony of diet, lack of companionship, and inability to bathe. In the tropics, parrots bathe themselves in the frequent rains. That never happens in Reynolds's eighteen-inch cage. So the bird begins yanking its own feathers out, trying to clean itself. Sometimes they bite off their own toes. Unless some change occurs, the bird will continue mutilating itself until it's plucked out every feather it has. And then it will die."

Ben felt a churning sensation in his stomach. "Aren't there any laws restricting traffic in rare birds?" he asked.

"Oh yes. The Imperial Amazon is an endangered species. We're not even sure they exist in the wild anymore."

"Can't you turn Reynolds in to the authorities?"

"He claims he hasn't done anything illegal. That's the problem with lawyers. They can talk their way out of anything. The 1973 Convention on International Trade in Endangered Species forbids trade in certain species, including *Amazona imperialis*. But, as Reynolds is quick to point out, he isn't engaged in the parrot trade and the Convention does not forbid ownership. Lombardi claims his bird was a gift. Damned expensive gift, if it was."

"If this bird is so controversial, why would Reynolds want one in his office?"

"Ego. The hotshot collector with his one-of-a-kind rare bird."

A sudden shriek pierced the aviary. Ben whirled back toward Christina.

"I'm under attack!" she cried.

Ben ran across the aviary, Langdell close behind. A large bird was hovering over her head, pulling Christina's long red hair with its beak.

"It's just like the movie!" Christina screamed. "What is that monster, a vulture?"

"A buzzard," Langdell said, smiling. "And it's not attacking you. It's trying to build a nest. Your hair looks like prime nesting material."

"I don't care if it's trying to save the universe," Christina said. "Make it let go of my hair!"

Langdell picked up a stick and gently inserted it into the buzzard's beak. The bird released Christina's hair and flew away.

"Bless you," Christina said. "I think you just saved my life."

"I doubt it," Langdell said. "But I may have saved you some hair. Did you have any other questions, Mr. Kincaid?"

"Yes. What happened when you went to see Lombardi the night he was killed?"

"Nothing. The security guard let me up. I knocked on the door. No one was home, or if they were, they didn't answer. After a few minutes, I left. The next morning, I read in the *World* that Lombardi was dead." He was silent for a moment. "My God, do you think Lombardi was already dead when I was there? Or"—he swallowed—"that the murderer was inside?"

"I couldn't tell you." Ben took a step toward Langdell. "You were determined to put an end to Lombardi's parrot trade, weren't you?"

"Now wait a minute, counselor. If you're trying to twist my concern for the rights of other living creatures into a motive for murder—"

"I'm just asking questions. I have to explore all the possibilities."

"It's true I wanted to shut down Lombardi's parrot operation," he said cautiously. "But I wouldn't kill the man. I knew his death wouldn't accomplish anything. Lombardi had an assistant who worked on everything with him. For all I know, he's going to follow in Lombardi's footsteps. No, it made no sense for me to try to kill Lombardi. I could be much more productive pursuing the tried-and-true paths of political activism to effect change.''

"I guess that's all I need to know at the moment,'' Ben said. "I might come by again later if I think of something else.''

"I have a lot more information about parrots.'' Langdell reached inside his coat pocket. "Here, take some brochures.''

"No thanks, I have other—'' On the top brochure, Ben saw a photograph of a beautiful Amazon parrot, with regal green wings and penetrating orange eyes. Langdell was right. They did look intelligent.

"Well, perhaps one or two,'' Ben muttered. He took a fistful of brochures and left the aviary.

* 18 *

Despite his technical incompetence at most fundamental secretarial chores, Jones still managed to impress Ben from time to time.

"How did you ever get me an appointment to see Albert DeCarlo?'' Ben asked.

Jones just smiled. "I made him an offer he couldn't refuse.''

There was no denying it. Ben was definitely nervous as he strode into the offices of Intercontinental Imports. The place looked legitimate enough—very high class, very corporate. It reminded Ben of the days when he visited Sanguine Enterprises, when he almost became their in-house counsel. Unfortunately, by the time Ben had finished investigating them, most of the officers were facing securities fraud charges, and the whole corporation went into receivership. Which might explain why Ben hadn't been getting those high-tone corporate clients lately.

Ben introduced himself to a gorgeous receptionist who directed him to the top of the building, the twentieth floor. He mentally noted the omnipresent security cameras in the lobby, the elevator, and the hallways. He wondered if the place was wired for sound as well. Probably.

When Ben arrived on the twentieth floor, he faced a comely woman announcing that she was DeCarlo's personal secretary.

"I'm Ben—"

"I know who you are," the woman interrupted, "Please go on in. Mr. DeCarlo just arrived himself."

The woman pushed a button, and the wood-paneled double doors swung open. Not bad.

Ben stepped into the inner office. He faced a huge bay window; practically the entire back wall was window. The adjoining walls were lined with bookshelves, and the shelves were thick with books of all kinds and sizes. The furnishings were contemporary and utilitarian. The one exception was the heavy oak desk in the center of the room, with Albert DeCarlo standing behind it.

DeCarlo extended his hand. "I'm Albert DeCarlo," he said. "My friends call me Trey. I hope you will, too."

Almost like a statue, Ben shook the proffered hand. DeCarlo was not at all what he'd expected. Among other things . . . he was *young*. He was Ben's age, maybe a few years older, but not many. He was tall and lean; his jet black hair was pulled straight back and tied in a ponytail. He was wearing his trademark outfit: dark sunglasses, dark muffler, and white overcoat.

He removed his scarf and coat. "Won't you have a seat, Mr. Kincaid?"

Ben took the indicated chair. DeCarlo returned to his nest

on the other side of the desk, and Ben immediately realized why. There were two large, dark-haired men positioned on either side of him, both with bad complexions and suspiciously bulging jackets.

"These are my vice presidents," DeCarlo said. "Johnny and Antonio. They're in charge of security."

I'll bet they are, Ben thought. He noticed an extremely large man with long blond hair standing in the corner. "Another of your vice presidents?"

"On the contrary," DeCarlo said. "Vinny is my executive officer. He makes sure everything gets done smoothly."

"No doubt." Ben examined Vinny carefully. "I had a scuffle with a big man with long blond hair outside Christina McCall's apartment the day she was released from jail."

"Is that a fact?" DeCarlo said. "Surely it wasn't my executive officer."

"The man was wearing a black motorcycle helmet," Ben said, "so I can't say for certain. Quite a coincidence, though, wouldn't you agree?"

DeCarlo raised an eyebrow. "That two men in all of Tulsa have long blond hair? Hardly. And you surely can't blame me for wanting to be surrounded by friendly faces. There have been some inexplicable threats against my company and myself. It's trying, but some extra precautions are required."

He placed his hands upon the green desk blotter. "Anyway, that's not why you're here. Your secretary indicated that you had a business proposition for me. Something that would turn Intercontinental Imports upside down, I believe he said."

Ben vowed to have a heart-to-heart with Jones about how big he lied—and to whom. "That may be somewhat inaccurate, Mr. DeCarlo."

"Trey. Call me Trey." He chuckled. "Let me see if I can help you out, Ben." He glanced down at a sheet of paper on his desk. "You're an attorney, graduate of the University of Oklahoma College of Law. Your office is at 462 North Abilene Drive; your home is at 2080 North Eleventh Street, second floor flat. The building is owned by a widow, a Mrs. Harriet Marmelstein. You have a mother living in Nichols Hills and a sister living in Edmond.'' He looked up. ''Am I right so far?''

Ben nodded slowly.

''You drive a Honda Accord, 1982 model, license tag XAU-208. Not in good shape; hard to start. You have a male secretary you call Jones. Somewhat eccentric, but who are we to judge? You were fired last year by Raven, Tucker & Tubb under unusual circumstances. Your solo practice is . . . not exactly flourishing.''

''I get the message,'' Ben said coldly. ''There's no need to show off.''

''Not at all,'' DeCarlo replied. ''You misunderstand my intentions. I'm trying to expedite matters. You're currently representing Christina McCall, the woman who has understandably been charged with the murder of my business associate and friend, Tony Lombardi. I assume that's the real reason you've come to see me today.''

''You assume correctly.''

''You realize I've already spoken to the FBI.''

''The FBI is not currently sharing their information with me.''

''I can sympathize. I, too, have found the law enforcement community less than cooperative on occasion.'' He pressed his fingers together, forming a steeple. ''So tell me, Mr. Kincaid. What would you like to know?''

There was no point in dillydallying. The man held all the aces. ''Why did you go to Lombardi's apartment the night he was killed?''

DeCarlo returned Ben's gaze calmly. ''I didn't.''

''Mr. DeCarlo . . .'' He saw DeCarlo about to interrupt. ''*Trey*. The security guard on duty has already said he let you up that night. He even made a contemporaneous written record."

"Spud is a nice old man, but he has a tendency to imbibe rather substantial quantities of alcohol while on duty. I wouldn't be surprised if he saw *pink* Albert DeCarlos."

"Spud seemed quite certain when he spoke with me."

"Nonetheless, Ben, he is mistaken. I have certainly been at Tony's apartment on other nights. Perhaps he was confused."

"I don't think so."

"Ben, I have numerous eyewitnesses who will testify that I was right here that entire night."

"Really. How many?"

DeCarlo smiled. "How many would you like?"

Ben thought a long time before he spoke again. There was no point in trying to pressure DeCarlo. The best Ben could do was take a step back and learn what he could about the subtext, if not the murder itself.

"All right. You say you've been to Lombardi's place on previous occasions. Why?"

DeCarlo looked at Ben as though he was explaining higher mathematics to an infant. "Tony and I were business partners."

"Meaning partners in his parrot business?"

"Exactly. Tony brought in the parrots, Intercontinental Imports handled distribution and retail sales."

"That seems an odd business for you to be involved in."

"Not at all. It's very profitable."

"I've been talking to Clayton Langdell about the parrot trade, and—"

"I know Mr. Langdell," DeCarlo said. "I donated ten thousand dollars to his organization last year."

Ben's mouth worked wordlessly for several seconds. "I'm . . . surprised."

"That he would accept money from a suspected mobster? Of course, the donations are all made in the name of Intercontinental Imports. It's possible he doesn't know who owns the company. Or more likely that he just prefers not to focus on that issue.''

"I've been told parrots are often used as a front for drug smuggling.''

The pleasantness drained away from DeCarlo's face. "Just what are you suggesting, Ben?''

"Well, I would hardly be the first person to link the DeCarlo family with illegal drugs.''

"Those allegations have never been proven.''

"Your name was mentioned repeatedly during the Abello trial.''

A small but detectable edge crept into DeCarlo's voice. "*That* was my father.''

Of course. Ben knew this guy was too young to be Tulsa's top crime boss.

"My father, God rest his soul, was Albert DeCarlo the second. I'm Albert DeCarlo the third. Hence the nickname Trey. I inherited this business from my father, just as he inherited it from his father.''

"A dynasty,'' Ben remarked.

"True enough. But I am not my father, Ben. Times change. I received my MBA at Princeton. I have a different approach to business. I've restructured the family operations into a more traditional corporate format. I've been attempting to redirect our activities into more legitimate enterprises.'' He paused. "Not that they weren't before. Only now, more so.''

"Sounds like the old mob with a new cover.''

"That's where you're wrong. Everything is changing. It always has. The organization you call the mob was originally a secret society formed to protect poor and oppressed Sicilians from the French Angevins in power. Did you know that?''

"No, I didn't.''

"Somewhere along the way, the focus changed. And now it will change again. The truth is, the old businesses are dying out. We needed a new profit center. In this ever-so-liberal society of ours, prostitution is becoming an increasingly unnecessary commerce. And a dangerous one. Gambling is an overcrowded market—even the governments are players now.

"Do you realize various companies make tiny computers a gambler can hide under his pant leg to help him count cards at the blackjack table? The readout appears on an LED screen disguised as a wristwatch!" DeCarlo shook his head with disgust. "Games of chance perverted for personal profit."

Ben found it hard to be sympathetic.

"And the drug trade, although lucrative—I've heard—has become too competitive. Now there's the Japanese Yakuza, the Chinese Triad, the Jamaican Posse, the Colombian Cali cartel—all squabbling over the same territory. Soon it will be impossible for anyone to make a profit."

"Seems like the most logical plan for a Princeton MBA is to work a joint venture with the South American cartels."

"You are not a stupid person, Ben." DeCarlo opened a desk drawer and removed several files. "But let me assure you that I intend to engage in entirely legal business activities. Feel free to examine our portfolios. Securities, banking, real estate, entertainment. These have been part of the family business for some time, perhaps more as a mask than a genuine pursuit. But that is changing."

"Well, if so, I wish you the best of luck."

"Thank you." DeCarlo's eyes became tiny embers. "Regardless of the nature of the activities in which we are engaged, however, I would take very seriously any threat to my business or to my personal liberty. That, too, is a family tradition."

Ben felt an involuntary shiver creep down his spine. He saw the bodyguards on either side of DeCarlo twitch, then take the tiniest step forward. Message received and understood.

DeCarlo rose to his feet. "But I like you, Ben, and I'm confident we won't have any problems." He walked around his desk. "Tell you what. My sister is getting married soon. Please accept my invitation to the wedding reception."

"No thanks," Ben said. "I've already seen *The Godfather*. I'd be bored."

DeCarlo laughed. "It's going to be a huge party, Ben. At the Twelve Oaks country club. There'll be music, dancing, food, drink—after all, it's not every day my baby sister is married. It might give you a better opportunity to see what Intercontinental Imports, and the new DeCarlo family, are all about."

"I don't think—"

"I'll send you an invitation, just in case."

He accompanied Ben to the door. "May I also send an invitation to a companion? A lady friend, perhaps?"

"No, I don't—" Ben thought for a moment. "This gala is going to be at the country club?"

"Oh yes. We've reserved it for the entire day."

"Pretty big bash?"

"The biggest Tulsa has ever seen. Or is ever likely to see."

"Okay then. Send an invitation to Harriet Marmelstein." Ben smiled. "I believe you have the address."

* 19 *

Jones left Ben a message on his answering machine: Alexander Moltke requested a meeting before the preliminary hearing, at 8:30 sharp, in the law library at the courthouse.

If Moltke wanted to talk, Ben reasoned, he must be plan-

ning to offer a deal. Thank goodness. Even if Ben didn't like
the offer, even if he turned Moltke down cold, the fact that
it was proposed indicated the prosecution perceived some
weakness in their case, some possibility of failure. That alone
would make Ben breathe a lot easier.

At 8:35, Ben pushed open the library door. Before he had
a chance to get his bearings, a stark white light blinded him.
He could hear Moltke's voice, reverberating through a microphone somewhere at the front of the room.

"Rest assured, ladies and gentlemen, that in this court of
law, this ingenious device by which we mortals achieve some
measure of earthly justice, the guilty will be punished."

Ben blinked his eyes, wiped away the tearing caused by
the stinging lights. His vision began to clear. He was surrounded by reporters, armed with microphones and minicams and plastic hairdos.

The realization dawned on Ben slowly but certainly. It was
a sucker play. This was a press conference, goddamn it. A
press conference!

"I see my worthy opponent has arrived," Moltke said, in
his bombastic oratorical voice. "I must say, I sometimes
despair of the direction our youth are taking. So much energy
is channeled into pursuits of such little moral value. My opponent formerly practiced with one of the most distinguished
firms in this city, but after that relationship was terminated,
Mr. Kincaid was forced by economic circumstances to take
cases such as this one, assisting certain liberal judges in their
quest to return the guilty to the streets."

"I resent that," Ben said. The reporters parted, letting
him move to the front. "The Constitution guarantee every
accused person the right to counsel."

"I'm not challenging the right of your client to counsel,
son. I'm just glad I don't have to be the one to do it. I don't
know how I'd live with myself, much less sleep at night."

Ben's face flushed with anger. "How can the court of law

be an effective device to achieve justice if cheap politicians like you try to pressure lawyers to not represent the accused?''

The reporters pressed forward, minicams whirring. Someone from Channel 2 shoved a microphone under Ben's nose. They were loving it—great fodder for the six o'clock news.

Moltke looked calmly into the cameras. "Now don't get all riled up, son. You do your job, and I'll do mine.'' He leaned forward, his eyes steely and determined. "But rest assured, ladies and gentlemen, that justice *will* be done in Tulsa. The pernicious taint of South American drugs, destroying our children and poisoning our society, will be eliminated. That's my promise to you.''

He straightened and smiled. "That's all for now. I'll answer questions after the hearing.''

Ben wasn't normally given to bouts of claustrophobia, but he could swear the walls of the magistrate's hearing room were closing in on him. The room was small to begin with, and was even more so now, with bailiffs, clerks, court reporters, newspaper reporters, and members of the U.S. Attorney's office all jockeying for position. Everyone was talking at once; the cacophony was giving Ben a headache. He was queasy, sweaty, and nervous. And Christina was late. Again.

The prosecution team, Moltke and two other men, no Myra, seemed supremely confident. They were whispering among themselves; periodically, one would glance at Ben, smirk, then look away. If that was supposed to be an intimidation tactic, it was working.

To Ben's surprise, Moltke walked over to his table. "Good morning, Mr. Kincaid.''

"You set me up, you son of a bitch.''

"Whatever do you mean?''

"You invited me to a plea bargain. Instead, it turned out to be an ambush.''

"My press conference ran a little longer than I antici-pated."

"Bullshit. You planned the whole thing, so you could score a few points at my expense on the six o'clock news."

"Well . . . I'm sorry if you were rattled, son. The people have a right to know."

"The Rules of Professional Conduct restrict press state-ments on pending criminal matters."

"Try explaining that to the press."

"Where's Myra?"

"Myra?" Moltke grinned. "Myra's a fine girl. A bit green, but she has potential. She can be an invaluable assis-tant, at times, if you know what I mean."

"I hope I don't."

"Under my tutelage she'll expand her talents. She's al-ready displayed an exceptional flare for . . . oral argument."

"You're disgusting, Moltke. Nothing personal. I wish you *had* sent Myra."

"Myra is perfectly adequate for an eight-thirty bail hear-ing, but this is the big time."

"You mean, there's press coverage galore, so you dis-missed the acolytes so you could soak up the glory yourself."

Moltke made a harrumphing noise. "A man learns to take advantage of his opportunities. If he hopes to make anything of himself. I'm sure you'll learn that in time. If you ever make anything of yourself."

Touché. "We probably shouldn't be conferring, Moltke. The reporters will assume you're offering me a deal."

"Actually, son, I am." He whipped his arm around Ben's neck and steered him away from the gallery. "I'm proposing an offer that will save us both considerable trouble."

Ben looked at him suspiciously. "Are you proposing a plea bargain?"

"No, son, this isn't a plea bargain. The press would hang

my carcass out to dry if I did that. I'm just suggesting that we . . . simplify this proceeding.''

"Simplify?''

"Tell you what. You promise me you won't move to dismiss after we put on our evidence, and I'll spare your client the ordeal of hearing a litany of nasty testimony against her.''

Tiny wrinkles appeared around Ben's eyes. "I'm not sure I understand.''

"It's like this. If we think you're going to try for a demurrer after we put on our evidence, we're going to have to haul out everything we've got. No reason your client should be put through that. We're here to search for the truth, not to put on a show. Just agree not to make the motion, and we'll save your little lady a lot of unnecessary hell. It's the humane approach. What do you think?''

"I think,'' Ben said, removing Moltke's arm, "I'm not nearly as green as you think.''

Moltke seemed taken aback. "What's that?''

"That's my way of saying, take your offer and get the hell out of my face. Nicely.''

"I thought it was a fair proposition—''

"You thought you could con me into being incredibly stupid. If I accepted your soft-soap appeal to my better nature, not only would I forfeit my chances of getting the charges dismissed today, I would also lose the opportunity to learn about your case—because you wouldn't put forward your best evidence. Given the lack of cooperation from your office so far, this may be the only discovery I get. I'm not going to throw that away.''

"I was just trying to spare your client—''

"I know exactly what you were trying, Moltke, and it had nothing to do with the search for truth or any of your other sanctimonious twaddle.''

Moltke's face became grave. "You're making a mistake, son. Our case is stronger than you think.''

"We'll see. If you'll excuse me, I'd like to review my notes."

Moltke walked away solemnly, shaking his head.

A few moments later, the bailiff cracked open the door. "All rise."

Magistrate Gould stepped into the courtroom. He was a relatively young man, probably in his mid-thirties. Ben had never been before him; Gould had only been appointed about eight months earlier, to work in conjunction with Judge Derek. Word on the street was that he had a bad case of judgeitis—carrying himself ponderously, pushing people around at hearings, wielding sanctions like a whipping stick. If true, Ben knew Gould wouldn't be the first person who had trouble adjusting to the immense power of his new position.

Gould hushed the bailiff before she could read the case file. "Where's the defendant?"

"I'm sure she'll be here soon," Ben said, fingering his collar. "Any minute."

"This hearing was scheduled to begin ten minutes ago. She's late."

Ben decided not to mention that His Eminence was also late. "I'm sure you've had parties arrive late before, sir."

Gould drummed his fingers on the bench. "True. The defendant at a detention hearing I held yesterday was ten minutes late."

"Well, there you go."

"I revoked his bail and sanctioned his attorney."

Ben craned his neck and adjusted his tie.

Suddenly, Gould leaned forward across the bench and boomed, "What *is* that you're wearing?"

Ben looked back over his shoulder, then front and forward. "Who, me?"

"Yes, of course, *you.*"

What was it? His shirt, his shoes, his fly? Ben quickly checked himself out. Everything seemed to be in order.

"I'm referring to your tie, counselor," Gould explained. "Is that . . . pink?"

Ben had to look. "Well, yes, sir. With little blue squiggles—"

"This is a courtroom, counselor. Not a discotheque."

"Of course it is, sir."

"I guess you think that because I'm just a magistrate rather than a full federal judge you can dress in this disrespectful manner?"

"Not at all, sir."

"I don't want to see that tie in my courtroom ever again, counsel. Do you understand me?"

"But my mother gave me this tie. . . ."

Gould pointed a finger at Ben. "You're—" He seemed to be hauling a memory out of some faraway corner of his brain. "You're the one who filed this pleading." He held up several stapled sheets of paper.

"Yes, your honor. That's our pretrial motion to—"

"It's on legal-size paper."

"Uh, yes, your honor. So it is."

"That's eight-by-fourteen-inch paper."

"I believe that's correct."

"This is *federal* court, counselor. We file our pleadings on eight-by-eleven-inch paper."

"I'm sorry, your honor, my secretary must've—"

"That's no excuse, counsel."

"No, of course not. I hope your honor will permit the pleading to be considered despite this grievous error. . . ."

"Of course I will." Gould reached into a drawer and withdrew a pair of scissors. In two quick snips, he cut off the bottom three inches of Ben's motion. "There. Now it can be considered by the court. I hope we didn't lose anything important."

"Me too, sir." Why did he have the feeling he was losing this hearing before it had begun?

Gould reached for his gavel. "Under the circumstances, with no defendant present—"

Ben heard a shuffling of feet behind him. It was Christina. Thank God. "Magistrate, may I have a minute to talk with my client before we begin?"

Gould glanced at his watch. "One minute."

Ben met Christina in the gallery.

"Did I miss anything?" Christina whispered.

"Nothing worth mentioning. Where have you been?"

"The police showed up this morning for a follow-up investigation of the break-in."

"Did they find any indication of who tore the place up?"

"Not as of half an hour ago. I had to leave them to get here. Is that all right? Mike was with them."

"If Mike was there, I'm sure it will be fine. Take a seat at defendant's table."

Christina walked briskly to the table, giving Ben a chance to inspect her more closely. She was wearing a thin V-necked dress with purple flowers. Her high-heeled sandals were laced up to her knees.

"Christina," he whispered, "I specifically told you to dress normal!"

"What's wrong with this?" she asked, astonished. "It has padded shoulders."

"I know. You look like Herman Munster."

"You told me to wear what I would wear to church. This is it."

Ben sighed. If this case went to trial, he would have to choose her clothes himself.

"Can you still get the charges dismissed?" Christina asked.

"There's a chance. As far as we know, all they've got is your presence in Lombardi's penthouse when the FBI found the body. That might look good in the papers, but Magistrate Gould is going to require something more concrete."

Ben heard a pronounced throat clearing from the bench. "Are we ready to proceed yet, counsel?"

"Yes, sir."

"Very well. Let's begin." Gould rushed efficiently through the preliminary rigamarole. "Call your first witness."

Moltke rose to his feet. "The United States calls James Abshire."

Abshire was sworn in. He gave a bit of personal background information, then described his activities the night of the murder. He'd rushed into Lombardi's suite expecting to find a drug deal in progress, but instead, he found Christina hovering over Lombardi's body. He'd searched her, then cuffed her.

"Harmless," Ben whispered to Christina. "Nothing in his testimony establishes sufficient cause to hold you over for trial."

Moltke continued his direct examination. "Did Ms. McCall say anything as you arrested her?"

"Yes." Abshire looked up at the magistrate. "She said, 'I killed him.' "

There was an unmistakable reaction from the gallery, audible for all its silence.

Ben pressed close to Christina's ear. "Is that true?"

"I'm not sure. I remember saying something, but it didn't happen like that."

"No more questions," Moltke said, stepping down.

"Very well." Gould turned toward Ben. "Any cross?"

Ben was trying to understand what Christina was whispering in his ear. "Just a moment, sir."

"It's now or never, counselor."

"Then I guess it's now." Ben went to the podium. "Agent Abshire, did you see Ms. McCall fire the gun?"

"No."

"Did you even see her holding the gun?"

"I'm not sure."

"Agent Abshire, can you swear under oath that you saw Ms. McCall holding the gun?"

He frowned. "No."

"You did not come into the apartment until after the crime was committed."

"True."

"When you searched Ms. McCall, did you find a gun on her person?"

"No."

"Or any other weapon?"

"No."

"Did you find any drugs or other illegal substances?"

"No." He glanced at Moltke. "*I* didn't."

What was that supposed to mean? "And that self-serving hearsay statement you repeated, what was the context of the statement?"

"I'm . . . not sure I understand you."

"Well, didn't you first accuse Ms. McCall of killing Lombardi?"

He shifted his weight slightly. "I may have said something to that effect."

"Did she seem to comprehend your question?"

"She sure as hell didn't deny it."

"Please answer my question."

"She confessed right there in my face."

"Isn't it true she merely repeated *your* words?"

"Look, if she wasn't guilty, all she had to do was say so."

"Please answer the question."

"But instead, she says 'I killed him.' Now if that isn't a confession, I don't know what is."

"Magistrate, please instruct the witness to answer my question."

"It's your job to control the witness on cross-examination, counselor. But I will instruct the witness to listen carefully to the question and try to be more responsive."

"I'm sorry, sir," Abshire said contritely.

"I'm sure you are. Proceed."

"Agent Abshire, would it be fair to say that your comment, whatever it was, provoked Ms. McCall's statement?"

"Cards-on-the-table time? No, I didn't make her say anything. Maybe her own guilt did—"

"Move to strike the last remark. Agent Abshire, she didn't just start babbling out of the blue, did she?"

"I don't exactly remember."

"She was responding to what you said."

"I suppose."

"In other words"—Ben paused—"you had begun questioning her."

Abshire drew back. He was beginning to see where they were headed. "I wouldn't say that."

"Had you read Ms. McCall her rights yet?"

"Well . . ." He licked his lips. "Not yet. We hadn't had time."

"You had time to initiate a conversation. One designed to elicit . . . what were your own words? . . . a *confession*. Sounds like a Miranda problem to me."

Moltke rose to his feet. "Magistrate, I object. If we're going to have legal argument, it should be addressed to the court, not a witness."

"That will be overruled, Mr. Prosecutor. He's entitled to explore the legalities surrounding this alleged confession, to determine the full extent of the taint created by this apparent Miranda violation. Unless," he added significantly, "you wish to withdraw that testimony."

Ben watched the magistrate stare down Moltke. The choice he was offering was clear. Withdraw the testimony, or risk a ruling that a custodial interrogation took place prior to reading Christina her rights, a violation that could conceivably make all their evidence to date inadmissible. No choice at all, really. Moltke would have to confer with Abshire later to determine the gravity of the problem and plan a course of action for the trial. But he couldn't run the risk now.

"We'll withdraw the testimony, sir. For the purpose of this hearing only, of course."

Why not? Having heard the testimony, the magistrate would remember it, withdrawn or not. He might not decide the case based upon it, but he couldn't possibly put it out of his mind.

Round one was a draw.

There was nothing duller than forensic testimony. Autopsies, fabrics, fibers, blood types. All sure-fire yawn inducers. Gould had been tapping his pen for ten minutes, a certain sign that this testimony had gone too long.

The investigating officer droned on. "We then proceeded to examine the room for dactylograms."

"I beg your pardon?" Moltke said.

"Fingerprints."

"Ah. And you didn't find the defendant's fingerprints on Lombardi's body, did you?"

"No, I did not."

"And you didn't find her fingerprints in the bloodstains?"

"No, I did not."

"Well, I guess that looks pretty good for the defendant."

Ben's head jerked up. Cheap theatrics were almost certainly a prelude to something Moltke thought was important.

"It seems like I'm forgetting something," Moltke said. He snapped his fingers. "Oh, yes. I know what it was. I wanted to ask you, Officer—did you find any fingerprints on the *gun*?"

"Yes, sir, I did."

"And whose fingerprints were they?"

"They were the defendant's."

"Are you sure?"

"Absolutely positive. We discovered two crystal clear latents. Thumb and forefinger."

Ben cupped his hand over Christina's ear. "Did you pick up the gun?"

" 'Fraid so, pal."

This was bad news. Although still circumstantial, eventually even circumstantial evidence could suggest only one reasonable conclusion.

Ben suddenly realized the magistrate was trying to get his attention. "I asked, will there be any cross-examination?"

"No, sir," Ben said. He glanced at Christina and shrugged. There was no point.

Round two went to the prosecution.

Ben hoped that was the end of it. The gun evidence wasn't helpful, but it was far from conclusive. There was still a chance he could get the charges dismissed.

"Any further witnesses?" Gould asked.

"No, sir. The prosecution—"

Moltke stopped mid-sentence. One of his junior assistants jabbed his arm, then pointed to the rear of the room, where a man in uniform stood.

"Magistrate," Moltke said, "may I have a brief recess to confer with a possible witness?"

"I'll give you two minutes," Gould said.

Moltke walked to the back and talked with the officer. Ben tried to read lips or pick up some hint of what they were discussing, but it was impossible.

Just before his time elapsed, Moltke returned to the podium. He seemed energized. Even worse, he was smiling.

"Magistrate Gould, the government wishes to call one more witness."

"Very well. Get on with it."

"The United States calls Officer John Tompkins."

Officer Tompkins, a ruddy, well-scrubbed officer in middle age and middle paunch, took the stand. Moltke made a cursory run through his credentials, principally his years on the Tulsa police force. Moltke appeared eager to move on.

"What was your first assignment when you reported to work this morning, Officer?"

"I was dispatched to an apartment on Southwest Boulevard to assist a follow-up investigation of a reported B and E." He looked up at the magistrate. "That's a breaking and entering, sir."

"Ah," Gould said. "Thank you for removing the scales from my eyes."

"And who is the tenant of the apartment in question?"

"That would be the defendant." He nodded in Christina's direction.

Ben leaped to his feet. "Objection. Magistrate, I fail to see the relevance of this line of questioning."

Gould squinted at Moltke. "I'm afraid I share defense counsel's mystification, Mr. Prosecutor. Care to elucidate?"

"I'll cut straight to the point, sir." Moltke addressed his witness. "Did you discover anything during your investigation of the breaking and entering that pertains to this case?"

"Yes, I did."

"And what would that be?"

"Well . . ." He leaned forward, as if preparing to tell a ripsnorting story. "The defendant has a number of stuffed animals."

The magistrate blinked. "Stuffed animals?"

"Yes, sir. Well, animals, dolls, teddy bears—that sort of thing. Most of them had been torn apart and had their stuffings ripped out."

"The court is undoubtedly grieved to learn of their disembowelment," Moltke said. "Did you search the dolls?"

"Well, I picked up this one, a Betty Boop doll—"

The magistrate peered down at the witness. "Excuse me? A what?"

"A Betty Boop doll. You know, the cartoon character."

Gould took up his pen. "Is that B-e-t-t-y B-o-o-p?"

Oh, give me a break, Ben thought. You can be dignified without acting as if you came from another planet.

"Yes, sir," Tompkins said. "I believe that's correct."

Gould made a few more squiggles on his notepad. "I see. You may proceed."

"And inside the Betty Boop doll, I found several clear glassy packets containing a white powdery substance. A tongue test confirmed my initial suspicion. It was about six hundred grams of cocaine."

The buzz from the gallery was instantaneous. The reporters' pencils flew into action.

"And were there any identifying markings on these glassy packages?"

"Yes." Tompkins allowed a pregnant pause, then said, "Stapled to the first package was a small scrap of paper bearing the word *Monster*. That is what drug dealers refer to as a brand name, a mark identifying a particular dealer's product and distinguishing it from those of competitors. And beneath the brand name, someone had written the word *Lombardi*. We believe this is part of the drug shipment that was delivered to Tony Lombardi the night he was killed. She must have taken it after she killed him."

Ben screamed out an objection, but it was no use. The dull buzz in the courtroom became a full-fledged roar. Reporters began running toward the back door. They didn't need to hear any more. They could confidently predict the outcome now.

The magistrate pounded his gavel to little effect. The world seemed to be swirling around Ben, everything happening at once, everything happening much too quickly. He was conscious of mumbling that he had no questions, and then of a continuous, indistinct chatter, till he picked up the phrase *held to answer in the district court before a jury of her peers*.

"Held to answer," Ben echoed.

Gould pounded his gavel again. "Trial is set for May fifteenth."

"May fifteenth! That's too soon!"

"Too soon?" Gould tossed down his gavel in disgust. "Given what we've heard today, I wonder if it's soon enough."

"Your honor, I move for a continuance."

"Premature. Make your motion to the district court judge."

"We'll waive the Speedy Trial Act."

"I won't."

"Sir, I have potential witnesses to interview."

"Then you had better get started, counsel." Gould rose to his feet. "This hearing is adjourned."

Gould slipped away into chambers; those few still remaining in the gallery raced toward the door. Moltke waltzed past Ben, a smug expression plastered on his face.

Ben felt as if his veins were filled with poison. His vision blurred until he could see nothing at all, nothing but Christina, sitting at defendant's table by herself.

Christina, all alone. And soon to be on trial for her life.

PART TWO

*   *

Bloind and Deef and Doom

* 20 *

The full moon shone down on the forest, casting shadows between the trees, glistening against the moist grass. Despite the moonlight, the forest was dark, and almost unbearably quiet. The occasional fluttering of birds or chirping of insects was all that relieved the damnable tranquility.

Ben and Christina crept from one tree to the next, trying to be as inconspicuous as possible. The fragrance of pine needles and damp leaves was sweet and strong, but it gave Ben no comfort. The forest was immaculate, seemingly untouched by human hand. Under other circumstances, Ben might've enjoyed this. Under any other circumstances.

Their flashlights offered precious little illumination; it was too dark and the forest was too large. With each step, each crackle of twigs and brush, a cold shudder crept up Ben's spine. He hated risky activities and yet he always seemed to be doing them. And he always seemed to be doing them with Christina.

"Can't you be any quieter?" Ben asked.

"I don't see how," Christina said. "Unless you want me to swing from tree to tree like Tarzan."

"Just be more careful where you step. We don't want to attract any attention."

"Ben, we've been out here for over three hours, and we haven't seen any evidence that human beings have *ever* come here, much less that they're here now."

"Nonetheless, Burris told me this is where Lombardi sent his hired hoods on Monday nights. Combined with the information from Langdell, I get the definite impression they were here to receive contraband."

"Fine. I'll keep my eyes peeled for vicious parrot smugglers, *mon capitaine.*"

Despite her attempt at levity, Ben knew Christina had a severe case of the willies herself. They were both creeping along in dark shirts, blue jeans, and sneakers. Comfortable, lightweight, inconspicuous, but not ostentatiously incriminating. Actually, Ben thought Christina looked stunning; of course, any deviation from her usual wardrobe was an improvement.

"Did you hear something?" Ben asked.

Christina stopped and listened. "No. Why?"

"I thought I heard something."

"Ben, you're becoming paranoid. You think you're being followed every place you go."

"Just because I'm paranoid doesn't mean we're not being followed."

"The possibility of someone else being out here gives me the creeps."

"Me, too."

They both fell silent. The natural, intolerable stillness flooded their ears.

"Look at all these oak leaves on the ground," Christina whispered. "They're just like the piece you found in the mud in my apartment. I think that proves the guy who ransacked my apartment had been out here. Recently."

"Let's hope I don't have to go before the jury with evidence like that," Ben said. "I can't believe I let you talk me into this escapade."

"If you're such a fraidy cat, why didn't you just give your information to the police? Let Mike investigate."

A shadow passed across Ben's face. "After what happened

at the preliminary hearing? I never thought I'd say it . . . but we can't trust Mike. Not this time."

"Then why didn't you hire an investigator?"

"With what? I can't afford to hire an investigator, and you didn't exactly give me a munificent retainer when I took this case."

"True enough. Money's been tight, especially since I was fired. But I have a friend who might be able to get you some more chickens."

"Very funny."

She adopted a thick French accent. "The lee-tle *poulet*, they are *magnifique*—"

Ben froze and clenched her arm. "What was that?"

"Ben, will you give it a rest already?"

"Ssshh! I heard something behind us."

They listened. They heard the hooting of an owl. They heard the leaves rustling as they skittered across the ground. Nothing more.

"Ben," Christina whispered, "you're scaring me."

"I'm sorry. Let's move on."

Christina followed his lead, but with noticeably less enthusiasm than before.

The beam of Ben's flashlight shone upon something solid. "What's that?"

Ben and Christina moved forward cautiously. It seemed to be a small wooden building, a shack. Many of the wooden planks were warped and knotted, leaving gaping holes in the walls.

"Look at this." On the door, Christina found a notice bearing the emblem of the Bureau of Alcohol, Tobacco and Firearms.

Ben read the notice. "The feds again," he said. "The FBI often uses the BATF when they want agents from outside their own club."

"They wouldn't have an outpost here for no reason, Ben. We must be close to something."

"Agreed. Can we get in?"

Christina scanned the door with her flashlight. She found the handle and, just beneath it, a chain. "Ben," she said, "this is a bicycle lock."

"What?" The wire chain was covered with a thin yellow plastic. The lock itself consisted of three metal tumblers, each bearing numbers zero through six. "The BATF uses bicycle locks for security?"

"Must be experiencing serious cutbacks." She began turning the tumblers.

"What are you doing?"

"I'm picking the lock, of course. Didn't you ever do this when you were a kid?"

"I should say not."

"Of course. I expect they didn't have bicycle locks in Nichols Hills. The local kids probably just posted security guards."

She drew Ben's attention to the lock. "It's very simple. You try each number on the first tumbler, tugging the chain as you go. There are only seven choices. When you get the right number in place, you'll feel a slight give in the lock— the inner key has been released from the first third of the lock. You then move to the second tumbler. When you dial the right number, the chain will give even more. And when you've got the third number, you're home free."

"As usual, I'm amazed at your vast range of expertise."

A few moments later, the chain was unlocked. Ben gave the door a solid push; it swung open.

The interior was pitch black, even as Ben shone his flashlight around. He could hear something, though—an eerie brushing and scraping. He took a deep breath and stepped inside.

It took him a moment to identify the sounds: the beating of wings, the scraping of claws against metal. The beam of his flashlight lit on a long bench holding various birds, each in makeshift cages made from wire and cardboard.

"Look at these poor creatures," Christina said. "What kind of bastard would keep them locked up in cages?"

"I don't know," Ben said, "but I bet it wasn't the BATF."

"I don't care if it was. I'm setting them free."

"Freeze!"

Ben and Christina whirled. The voice came from behind them, somewhere in the darkness.

"I have a gun," the voice said. "Don't try anything. Move toward the door. Slowly."

Cautiously, Ben shone his flashlight in the general direction of the voice. The figure was so small . . . was this a dwarf? Someone on his knees? No—

"It's a boy."

"A very little boy," Christina confirmed.

"With a very big gun," the boy said.

"Yeaaaa!" Ben howled. "Be careful with that! It could go off!"

"That's right," the boy said evenly. He thrust the gun forward menacingly. "It could."

"Don't shoot!" Ben covered his head with his arms.

"What poise," Christina said. "What steely composure." She advanced toward the weapon.

The boy stepped back, waving his gun in the air. "Don't come any closer. I'll shoot!"

Christina stifled a yawn. "So shoot. I've been hit with rubber bands before. Stings a little, but it passes." She snatched the gun away from him, then handed the wooden weapon to Ben. "Now don't you feel just a little silly, cowering in the face of a rubber-band gun?"

Ben wiped his brow. "You'd be more sympathetic if a crazed madman had held you at gunpoint a few days ago."

"From what I hear, that gun was even less dangerous than

this one." She addressed the boy. "So what exactly is your problem, kid? Why the muscle tactics?"

The boy's face was fixed and determined. "I can't let you release my birds."

"And why not? It's cruel to keep these birds locked up."

The boy placed one hand against the hawk cage on the far left. The bird pressed his head gently against his hand. "They're all hurt," he said. "Shot up or worse. I clean 'em up and try to nurse them back to health. Then I set them free."

"Hunters?" Ben asked.

The boy nodded. "Or trappers. Lucky for you I combed the forest and collected all the traps today. The way you two were stumbling around, you'd have stepped in a dozen of them."

"Why don't you take them to an animal doctor?" Ben asked.

"Because animal doctors want money. Like everybody else."

Ben examined the birds more carefully. Clean dressed bandages, gauze patches—even splints. He realized their snap judgment had been mistaken. This boy was obviously dedicated to his birds.

"What's your name, kid?"

The boy hesitated. "I go by Wolf."

"Wolf?" Ben scrutinized his ruddy skin and his long, inky black hair. "You're a Native American."

"So?"

"Creek Nation?"

"Maybe. What's it to you?"

"What's your real name, Wolf?"

"Why should I tell you?"

"Because if you don't, I'll tell your parents you held us at rubber-band-point."

"Names are personal."

Christina stepped forward. "Mine's Christina. He's Ben. Now what's yours?"

He looked away. "Lemuel."

"Lemuel?" It was worse than Ben had imagined. "Not exactly an Indian name, huh?"

"It's no kind of name for a warrior," the boy said.

Ben couldn't dispute that. "We'll call you Wolf. What's your last name?"

"Natonobah."

"Great. Wolf Natonobah."

"So you're a warrior," Christina said. "Like in *Dances With Wolves*?"

He stared at her stonily.

"Didn't you see that movie?"

"Yeah," he said. "I snuck in the exit door after the lights went down. I hated it."

"Really?"

"I hate all that noble savage crap. Give me a movie where the Indians beat the hell out of the white men, that's what I like. White men ruin everything."

"Like this forest?" Ben asked.

"Yeah. And my birds."

"You must come here often."

"What of it?"

"Have you seen any . . . suspicious activity out here?"

"Tonight I saw two white fools creeping around with flashlights."

Ben had to smile. "You were tracking us, weren't you?"

"I followed you. Tracking wasn't required. A blind man could've followed your trail."

"What about before tonight?"

"I've seen other white people, if that's what you mean."

"On Monday nights?"

"Yeah. A week ago, last Monday night, I saw a small plane land in the clearing."

Bingo. "And what happened after the plane landed?"

"The pilot and a man on a dirt bike met. They traded packages."

"And what was in the packages?"

Instinctively, Wolf glanced down at his pocket. He caught himself, looked up quickly. "I don't know."

It was too late. "What's in your pocket?" Ben asked.

"None of your business."

Ben tilted his head. "Christina."

Christina stood behind Wolf and held his arms while Ben searched his pocket.

"Hey, where's your goddamn warrant?" Wolf squirmed beneath her grasp.

"Sorry," Ben said. "We're not cops. Far from it." He removed a small glassy package from Wolf's torn jeans and shone the beam of the flashlight on it. The white powder twinkled in the light.

"Holy smokes," Christina said. "Is that what I think it is?"

"I don't know," Ben replied.

"Well, taste it."

"Taste it? How would I know what cocaine tastes like?"

"You used to work for the D.A., didn't you?"

"Oh yeah. And on the first day of work he used to line us all up and make us taste cocaine. Give me a break." He placed the powder in his pocket for future examination. "Wolf, had you ever seen a rendezvous in the clearing before?"

"No. But two Mondays before, I heard a strange noise. I was too far away to follow it, but I think that was the plane coming in for a landing."

"That jibes with what Burris told me. Shipments every other Monday." Ben grasped Wolf by the shoulders. "Wolf, do you think you would recognize these men if you saw them again?"

"It was very dark. But my eyes are like Katar, the hawk's. I would recognize them."

"Christina, if we can learn who was running the drugs, we can prove you weren't involved. And maybe find out who the murderer was in the process. Wolf, can you show us this clearing you mentioned?"

Wolf folded his arms across his chest. "What's in it for me?"

Ben pulled two twenty dollar bills out of his wallet. "This would buy a lot of birdseed. Maybe some first aid supplies, too."

Wolf snatched the bills out of his hand. "Let's go."

He led them out of the shack, careful to rechain the bicycle lock behind him. They had gone only a few hundred yards before Ben clamped down on Christina and Wolf's shoulders. "Shhh!"

"Not again!" Christina said. "Are you still hearing things?"

"Yes. Behind us."

"That's what you said before."

"Yeah, and as it turns out, Wolf was following us. But since he's right here at the moment, who's following us now?"

Ben and Christina looked at one another, then out into the black forest. They spread their flashlight beams in a wide arc, but saw nothing.

The now familiar shiver crept up Ben's spine, then spread throughout his entire body. Was he losing his grip? Or *was* someone following them? The same person who followed them from the jailhouse, perhaps, or who ransacked Christina's apartment. And if so, what did he want now?

"Do you want to see the clearing or not?" Wolf asked impatiently.

"We do," Ben said. He turned his eyes to the path ahead and followed Wolf through the forest.

But he kept his ears focused behind him.

* 21 *

Ben drove up the curved driveway of Margot Lombardi's home in the South Livingston Park neighborhood near Southern Hills. Her house was French Provincial, painted white brick with a blue canopy over the front door. The flower beds were blooming with bright red tulips.

The glass front door was slightly ajar. Ben knocked.

A voice emerged from inside. "Please come in."

He pushed through the door. Although none of the foyer furnishings were Reynoldsesque showstoppers, they were attractive—delicate, tidy, and tasteful. He found Mrs. Lombardi in a sunken living room on a striped fabric sofa. She was wearing a long dark skirt that reflected her shoulder-length black hair and dark sad eyes. They introduced themselves.

"Thank you for seeing me," Ben said.

"You're the lawyer?" Her voice was like crystal—thin and fragile.

"That's right. Ben Kincaid."

"You seem young for a lawyer. Forgive me, but do you have a business card?"

"I'm sorry, no. I don't use them. They give me the heebie-jeebies."

Margot arched one thinly penciled eyebrow. "You're afraid of business cards?"

"It's a long story. Do you mind if I sit down?"

She motioned toward a chair separated from the sofa by a

cherrywood coffee table. Margot was tall and extremely slender. Possibly less than a hundred pounds. She seemed to favor loose-fitting, billowy clothes, probably because they gave her an imagined fullness nature didn't provide.

Ben passed his Oklahoma driver's license across the table, careful not to disturb any of the ornamental knickknacks and figurines. He had the feeling that if he breathed too hard the entire room would shatter and dissolve. Including the hostess.

She examined the license briefly. "Forgive me for being overcautious. I find I must restrict with whom I speak. Recent events are bad enough without fanning the flames of gossip."

She passed the license back. Ben noticed her fingernails were chewed to the quick. "First of all," Ben said, "let me convey my sincere condolences regarding your husband's death."

She waved her hand in a get-on-with-it motion.

"I'm following up several leads relating to your husband and his business."

"Frankly, I was never very knowledgeable about Tony's business," she said. "The FBI would know more. I understand they're investigating his holdings, hoping to seize our property under some federal foreclosure laws."

"I didn't know that."

"It seems it's not enough that I be widowed. I must be penniless as well." Frown lines outlined her mouth. "But if I can help you, I will."

"That's very generous of you."

"I just want to see that Tony's killer is caught. And I'm not at all convinced your client was the culprit."

Now that was a refreshing point of view. "Why do you say that?"

"She seems more a victim of circumstance than anything. Tony had a habit of turning the people in his life into victims."

Ben took a small notepad out of his pocket. "What exactly did your husband do?"

"He imported parrots. Found them in South America, brought them to the United States for sale to pet shops, collectors, zoos. As of late, he'd been using an Albert DeCarlo shell corporation as distributor."

"And how was that working out?"

"Horribly. I'm not privy to the details, but I know Tony considered linking with DeCarlo the worst mistake he'd ever made."

"Why did he do it?"

"It was DeCarlo's idea. He came to Tony. For some reason, he was very interested in Tony's business. Said it could be the basis for a profitable partnership. And as it turned out, he was right."

"Tony was making large sums of money?"

"More than he'd ever imagined. Tony told me it was due to the increased penetration of DeCarlo's distribution network, but of course, one couldn't help but wonder . . ." She brushed her hand against her face. "Tony obtained no pleasure from the arrangement, profitable or not. He was scared to death."

"Scared?"

"One morning I came downstairs and found Tony crying in his Rice Krispies. Out-and-out bawling like a baby. He told me something someone had told him. He said, 'Once you're in the mob, you're in for life.' "

The mob credo. Ben wondered what Lombardi had done— or attempted—that had brought that down on his head.

"I asked him for details, but he refused. Insisted it could be dangerous to talk. Both for him and me."

"The Omerta," Ben said. "The mob code of silence. They make everyone take their secrets very seriously."

"Tony was never stable under the best of circumstances," Margot continued. "DeCarlo just made matters worse. Tony was terrified. He was afraid his association with DeCarlo would land him in prison, and he had a horrible fear of prison. Absolutely pathological. He'd do anything to avoid that."

"Do you think he tried to sever relations with DeCarlo? And that might've led to his murder?"

"I think . . . that's possible. Of course I can't say with any certainty."

"When did you last see Tony?"

She searched her memory. "I can't recall the date. It's been several months. After my last visit, the doorman stopped letting me in."

"The doorman told me you were jealous—"

"Spud?" The corners of her mouth turned up. "I've had the pleasure of smelling the booze on his breath several times. I would advise you not to take anything he says too seriously."

"And you haven't seen your husband lately?"

"No. I did hear from him the night he died, however."

"You did? How?"

"He called me that evening. He was terribly distraught, panicked—almost irrational. He said he needed money immediately, but he wouldn't tell me why."

"Did you help him?"

"How could I? The only money I had was what he gave me, and that wasn't much." Her face lost all expression. "Of course I loved him, but the fact is Tony was not a strong man. Some might say he was . . . weak." She pressed the flats of her hands against the sofa. "He'd been in and out of mental hospitals. They told me he attempted suicide once, although he denied it. He was an acute manic-depressive, with considerably more depressive than manic."

"Just the sort of person DeCarlo could easily manipulate."

"I'm afraid that is precisely correct."

"Do you know anything about your husband's assistant? A man named Lennie?"

"Lennie?" Her laugh was brittle. "Of course. Lennie's been with Tony ever since he fell in with DeCarlo. Lennie was always ready and willing to do the dirty jobs Tony didn't want to handle himself."

"Do you know his full name?"

"Lucas Grundy." She saved Ben the trouble of asking. "Lennie wasn't his real name; that was just what Tony called him. After a character in a book. *Of Mice and Men,* I believe. Tony was quite well read." She ran her fingers slowly down the line of her neck. "It was not a compliment, if I'm not mistaken. Tony could be rather cruel at times."

"Do you know where I could find Lennie?"

"Not offhand. He always found me—to deliver the separate maintenance checks."

"You mentioned that you left Tony, ma'm." Ben hesitated. There was no graceful way to do this. "I know this is personal, but may I ask why?"

Her mouth trembled almost imperceptibly. Her fingers fluttered upward to cover it. "Of course, in part, I've already told you. The strain of working with Albert DeCarlo was beginning to tell on us both."

"And what was the other part?"

She opened her mouth, then closed it several times before she actually spoke. "Tony had some eccentric tastes."

"You mean . . . what he spent his money on?"

"No." She hesitated, then fell back against the sofa, resigned. "I mean . . . sexually."

"Oh. Can you . . ." He closed his eyes and swallowed. "Were there problems?"

She seemed to look through him. "Yes, there were problems. I didn't share some of Tony's interests. I was never able to . . . satisfy him. No matter what I tried. No matter what I was willing to do. After a while, he simply lost interest."

Ben waited as she struggled to regain her composure.

"Of course, that meant he began to look elsewhere. I knew what he was doing, but I didn't say anything. It seemed the least I could do. Clearly, I had failed him."

She closed her eyes. "At one point, Tony actually placed a personal ad in one of those swinging-singles tabloids. I'm sure you know what I mean—notices for couples who are willing to rendezvous at a secluded location and . . . swap." She pronounced the word as if it were a spider poised on the tip of her tongue.

"And did you . . ."

"No. I refused. Even after Tony had everything arranged. He was furious. That's when everything worsened."

"What did Tony do then?"

"It's difficult to know where to begin. Tony liked . . . to punish me."

"Punish?" Ben felt a warm flush creeping up his neck. "You mean he liked to . . . spank you?"

"Yes. With an electric cattle prod."

Ben stared at her—stunned and silent.

"It was part of his mania, I suppose, his unstable mental state. His temperament would change in a heartbeat. He would become frustrated, then enraged. He had to hit something, to hurt something, and of course, I was the only person around."

"Perhaps you should've bought him a cheap set of china."

"He wouldn't have liked that," she said matter-of-factly. "China wouldn't scream. China wouldn't cry."

The room fell quiet.

"I don't know how many times I had to resort to high collars, scarves, sunglasses, or just staying inside. Twice I was admitted to St. Francis." Ben could see no light in her eyes. "Of course, you tell them you fell down the stairs or tripped over a potted plant. But they don't believe you."

"That must've been horrible."

"It wasn't the worst. As a result of one of Tony's fits, we lost a baby." Her eyes met Ben's. "I won't be having any more."

"When did you leave?" he managed to ask.

"When he came home with a taser. Wouldn't you?"

"I hope," Ben said, choosing his words carefully, "I would have left a long time before that."

Margot's head began to shake. "Easy to say," she said. "Easy—" She choked, then covered her face with her hands. "I think you should go now, Mr. Kincaid."

As Ben drove back to his office, he replayed the conversation in his head. Strange—he had been looking for a killer, but instead, he found another victim. Another victim of cruelty, and greed, and organized crime.

Another victim of the murderer.

* 22 *

Ben sat in the conference room with Mike, Roger Stanford, and Myra. They were waiting for Abshire to appear so they could begin the discovery process.

Most people probably thought of criminal cases as being more glamorous and exciting than civil suits. Ben did not agree, and days like this reminded him why. Discovery was rarely as extensive and never as revealing in criminal cases. Of course, that heightened the drama, leaving the possibility of surprises at trial. But Ben wasn't interested in surprises. He wanted information that would get Christina off the hook. And so far, the government had been about as cooperative as an eight-year-old at the dentist's office.

Mike sat at the far end of the table, staring at the wall. He hadn't said a word to Ben.

At last, Abshire rushed into the room carrying a large

stack of files. "Busy, busy, busy," he said, thunking his load onto the conference table. "Sorry I'm late. Hope you all had a nice chat."

No one replied.

"Ready to throw in the towel yet, Kincaid?"

Ben tried not to curl his lip. "Let's just get on with it."

"Oooh, we're verrrrry touchy today." He opened the top file folder. "Let's see . . . the defendant has moved for the production of all exculpatory evidence in the possession of the government, both state and federal levels. Unfortunately, I don't believe we have any exculpatory evidence, do we, gentlemen?"

Stanford seemed embarrassed. Mike didn't even grunt.

Ben, however, exploded. "Goddamn it, Abshire, I'm sick and tired of your withholding evidence. I'm calling the judge."

"Feel free."

Stanford pushed his half glasses up his nose. "Perhaps we could be more helpful if you would ask specific questions, Mr. Kincaid."

"All right. I'll give it a try." Ben tried to read the notes he had scrawled that morning at breakfast. Unfortunately, there was a large chocolate-milk stain obscuring the top of the page. "What were the results of the blood test you performed on Christina?"

"We didn't do a blood test," Abshire said calmly.

Ben's eyes expanded to saucer-size. "You didn't—I specifically requested a blood test. In your presence."

"I don't feel obligated to do the opposition's work for them. You should have done it yourself."

"She was in custody!"

"You could have tested her when she was released."

"I did. It was too late. The results were inconclusive."

"Did it ever occur to you that might be because your client is guilty?"

Ben sprang out of his chair. "You son of a—" He gripped the edge of the table. "I'll take this up with the judge."

Abshire appeared indifferent. "Cards-on-the-table time? I don't care what you take up with the judge. He hasn't ruled in your favor yet, and he's hardly likely to start doing so now."

True enough, Ben thought, but he'd be damned if that would stop him from trying. "What about the time of death?"

"What about it?"

"When last I was permitted to discuss these matters, I was told Koregai was having trouble establishing the time of death. Koregai's too smart to have trouble with a fundamental like that, unless there's some unusual factor involved."

"The coroner has had trouble establishing a definite time of death. He says there's conflicting evidence. But none of it is exculpatory."

"Says you. Can I talk with Koregai? Alone?"

"Can I talk to your client? Alone?"

"Only if you can get the Fifth Amendment repealed."

Abshire folded his arms. "Then you'll see Dr. Koregai in my presence. If he isn't busy."

Ben had to keep reminding himself that an assault charge against Christina's attorney would not help her case. "Did you conduct a paraffin test?"

"Uh . . . yeah, we may have done that."

"And the results?"

"Were not necessarily exculpatory."

Stanford looked at his protégé sternly. "Tell him."

Abshire's face tightened. "But it's not exculpatory," he hissed.

"I believe I am still your supervisor, Agent Abshire," Stanford said. "Tell him."

"We did the test," he said bitterly, like a child forced to share his candy. "She was clean." He withdrew a file folder from his stack, then tossed it across the table to Ben.

Ben scanned the report. He knew from his days at the D.A.'s office that the discharge of a firearm automatically released gas and powder residue, including suspended nitrate particles, and that the particles would adhere to any skin touching the gun when fired. As best he could tell, the test had been performed properly—swabs moistened with dilute nitric acid, followed by neutron activation analysis. And they found no nitrate particles on Christina's hands.

"This is great." Ben shot Abshire a pointed look. "And you were of the opinion that this wasn't exculpatory?"

"We're required to produce exculpatory *evidence*. The *absence* of evidence is by definition not evidence."

"So you weren't going to produce this? Even though it proves Christina isn't the killer?"

"I hardly agree," Abshire said, snatching back the report. "Have you never heard of gloves?"

"I've heard of them. Did you find any?"

"Yes. We found three pair."

"Where?"

"In Lombardi's bedroom closet."

"In his closet? What are you saying? That she killed him, then folded the gloves neatly and put them away in the closet?"

"That's what I'd do," Abshire replied.

Ben's teeth ached from the pressure. Abshire obviously didn't give a damn about evidence. He had a thirst for conviction that was unquenchable. Ben glanced at Mike, but he was still staring at the wall.

"Talked to any witnesses?" Ben asked.

"Scads."

"Did you learn anything exculpatory?"

"Not by my definition. On the contrary, I think everyone I've spoken to is convinced your client offed Lombardi."

"Then what else have you got for me?"

"Absolutely nothing."

Ben put his notes back in his briefcase. "This is just as well, Abshire. It removes some confusion I was having. For a second, I thought I saw a glimmer of decency in you. Now I realize it must have been a trick of the light."

Stanford turned away and covered his mouth. Even Myra appeared to be suppressing a smile. And Mike—did he look up? Ben couldn't be sure.

"I'm moving to suppress your testimony at trial, Abshire," Ben added. "You're a hopelessly biased witness."

"You certainly are planning a lot of motions. I guess that's based on your record of success with the judge."

Bastard. "If you come up with anything new, I expect to be informed."

"Of course," Abshire said, grinning. "If it's exculpatory."

Ben hesitated beside his chair. He wanted to give Mike one last chance to say he wasn't in on this railroad, that he was appalled by Abshire and the way he and Moltke were handling this case.

Or just one last chance to acknowledge that he was listening. But Mike didn't move a muscle.

* 23 *

Ben's office was in chaos. Even more so than usual.

Outside, representatives of the Creek Nation were protest marching, insisting that the McCall case be referred to tribal courts. A large placard read: WHITE MAN'S LAW—WHITE MAN'S JUSTICE.

The protest was senseless; tribal courts don't have felony jurisdiction. Besides, didn't they know he tried to get the case out of federal court? Why protest here? Because they weren't allowed in the courtroom, Ben supposed, and besides, this was where the reporters were.

Inside, the front lobby of Ben's office was brimming with journalists of every variety. The blue beam of minicams crisscrossed the room. Reporters were huddled around Jones's table, trying to read the paper in his typewriter.

They spotted Ben before he had a chance to sneak into his private office. A tall, anorexic-looking female he thought he recognized from the Channel 8 news pressed herself in front of him.

"Mr. Kincaid!" the woman shouted, although she was less than a foot away. "Can you give us a statement?"

"No." He tried unsuccessfully to pass her.

"Can we take your reluctance to speak as an admission that you haven't got much of a case?" Her microphone was tickling his nose.

"No, you may not. Our case is rock-solid. The Rules of Professional Conduct prohibit me from making substantive comments regarding pending criminal actions."

"U.S. Attorney Moltke didn't have any problem talking to us."

"No comment."

Another reporter, a tall man with wavy blond hair, accosted Ben from the other direction.

"Is it true that a radical minority sect of the Creek Nation tribe is protesting your representation and requesting immediate custody of the murderess?"

"Christina McCall is not a murderess! She's innocent until proven guilty."

"Can you tell us what, if any, evidence you have uncovered to rebut the prosecutor's seemingly airtight case?"

Ben clenched his teeth. "No."

"Mr. Kincaid, with the scheduled trial date close at hand, the evidence against Christina McCall appears to be overwhelming—"

Ben grabbed the microphone and shoved it back in the man's face. He grabbed the reporter by the lapels of his double-breasted jacket. "Don't you have any sense of *decency*, you acerebral twit?"

The minicam operators scrambled, butting heads for the best angle.

"Don't you realize what you're doing?" Ben continued. "You're tainting the jury pool!"

"Can you explain that?" someone shouted.

"Those aren't just Neilson ratings sitting out there in television land. Those are prospective jurors! And if you tell your viewers the evidence against Christina McCall is overwhelming, most of them will believe you!"

Ben shoved the blond man away with disgust but found he had nowhere to go. The reporters pressed even closer. The bright white lights were everywhere, disorienting him. Beads of sweat trickled down his brow, his face, under his collar. He was trapped. And the cameras were rolling.

Suddenly a new voice emerged from the crowd. "Yo! Armed robbery at the pawn shop next door. They've got automatic weapons!"

As one body, the reporters scrambled toward the front door. After an unseemly scuffle, they managed to plunge through the narrow opening—leaving Jones standing just outside.

He smiled. "Hiya, Boss. Giving an interview?"

"Not very well," Ben replied. "I don't suppose there really *is* a robbery at the pawn shop."

"Nope," Jones said, locking the door behind him. "But wouldn't you like to see the look on Burris's face when he sees twenty or so reporters bashing their way into his shop? He's gonna think he's on *Sixty Minutes*."

Ben pictured the tableau next door. He would like to see it, at that.

"You got off easy," Jones continued. "I've been dealing with those news fiends all week. What vultures."

"They're not vultures. They're just doing their job."

"Easy for you to say. You haven't been around them, day in, day out, in addition to the hostile Native American protesters. It's making this place a pressure cooker. I feel like someone's watching every move I make."

"You and me both." Ben sighed. "We have the regrettable pleasure of being Tulsa's current headline news."

"Actually, we're the top story throughout the state," Jones said. He showed Ben the headline on the day's *Daily Oklahoman*. The bold black letters covered nearly half the front page: DRUG PRINCESS TRIAL NEARS.

"That's just great," Ben groaned.

"The shooting death of a linchpin in the Cali cartel—that's big news. The Texas papers are starting to pick up the story, too."

"Much as I've needed publicity, this wasn't what I had in mind. Pray for a natural disaster to divert everyone's attention. Or maybe a small war. By the way, heard anything from Mike?"

"No. He's dodging me. I keep calling, but he won't take my calls and he doesn't call back."

Ben shook his head. He couldn't believe Mike was avoiding him, that he was so determined to toe the line he'd let Christina fall through the cracks. Permanently.

"Keep trying," Ben said quietly. "Anything else we need to catch up on?"

"Yeah. How 'bout I run over and check out the crime scene?"

"How 'bout you stay here and man the telephone?"

"Boss, I want to do some legwork."

"I've been to the crime scene already. Trust me—it wasn't that enlightening."

"Easy for you to say. You get all the fun assignments. I have to stay here all day fending off creditors and drunks and reporters."

"Life is tough."

"Aw, c'mon, let me go. I can handle myself."

"I'm sure you can."

"I *can*. How can I prove myself to you?"

Ben glanced down at the floor, where he saw two chickens, each pecking a shoe. "Well," he said, "for starters . . ."

* 24 *

The white lights throbbed on and off at the Cowpoke Motor Inn on I-44, just before the Turner Turnpike tollgates. The marquee informed Ben that there were vacancies (no great surprise) and that a room could be obtained for twelve dollars. He wondered if that was for the night or the hour.

Two muscular men stood in the parking lot, leaning against the tailgate of a pickup truck. Looked like an illicit transaction was going down, but Ben didn't have time to investigate. He knocked on the door—room 13. How ironic.

The door parted, just the length of the chain. All Ben could see was a beak nose poking through the gap.

"Who izzit?" said the voice behind the door.

"My name is Ben Kincaid. I'm an attorney."

"I already got an attorney." He started to close the door.

"I didn't come here to solicit business." Ben wedged his foot into the door. "I'm representing Christina McCall."

"Oh yeah? Prove it."

"How can I prove it through a closed door? Look, if you won't talk to me voluntarily, I'll be forced to get a subpoena. Then the marshal will come out and drag you down to the courthouse, where all the cops hang out, and we'll all hear what you have to say."

The pressure on the door eased.

"Of course, while the marshal is here, he might want to take a look around your room. Just to see if he can turn up anything interesting."

With that, the man unfastened the chain and opened the door. "Ten minutes," he said. "I got an appointment."

I'll just bet you do, Ben thought. He walked inside. The room was a sewer. Dirty clothes, newspapers, and fast food containers were strewn across the floor and the unmade bed. The mirror over the dresser was cracked in several places. Ben didn't know if it was the clothes, the food, the bathroom, or some other horror, but the room stank abominably.

"Swell place," Ben said, sitting down in the chair closest to the door.

"It ain't great," the man said, "but it's the only motel room under fifteen bucks that gets the Playboy Channel. Just a buck extra."

"Sounds like a deal."

"You know it, pal."

"My secretary had a hell of a time finding you."

"Good. I'll give you a little clue, chump. You oughta make yourself scarce, too."

"Why is that?"

He leaned forward, spitting as he spoke. " 'Cause there's certain people, man, who do not want Lombardi's murder investigated. The kind of people who'd blow your brains out just to relieve a hangnail. And they know who you are."

Ben tried not to react. "Is that a fact?"

"Yeah, that's a fuckin' fact. The only thing worse than a fuckin' killer is a fuckin' *scared* killer. And these guys are scared."

"I take it you're referring to your former employers?"

He didn't answer.

"Can I call you Lennie? That's what people call you, isn't it?"

"My friends, yeah. Which you ain't."

Ben had heard of people being described as weasely before, but Lennie must've been the prototype. He had a pencil-thin mustache and long sideburns. There was something pervasively oily about his complexion and his manner.

"About your late employer, Tony Lombardi. I understand you acted as a . . . runner for him. On both personal and business matters."

"That's true," Lennie said, stretching. His sleeves were rolled up; Ben could see the tracks on his arms.

"Looks like you occasionally dipped into the inventory."

Lennie jerked his arms back. "I don't know what the hell you're talking about."

"Never mind. What can you tell me about Tony's business?"

"Which one?"

"The drugs one."

"Don't know shit about it. I can't believe Tony would do something illegal."

He was nothing if not loyal. Although there was probably a strong element of self-preservation involved as well. "All right, then. Tell me about the parrot business."

"What do you want to know?"

"It was a front for the drug smuggling, right?"

"I already told you—"

"Yeah, yeah. Forget I spoke." He tried a different tack. "Did you ever make any deliveries or pickups for Albert DeCarlo?"

"Yes. Both. So?"

"Any idea what was being delivered?"

"Money, sometimes. That always got counted in my presence. On both ends. Just so I didn't get any ideas, they said."

"And your belief is that this money being exchanged was for parrots?"

"I never asked what the money was for, and nobody ever told me. It don't pay to be too curious around Albert De-Carlo. He's a bastard."

"You sound as if you know him well."

"I do. Since he was a little shit. I worked for the DeCarlo family back when his father was in charge."

"DeCarlo told me he's making big changes in his daddy's business. Making it more wholesome."

Lennie laughed, then started to choke. "That's a laugh. He's changing the business, all right, but it has nothin' to do with being wholesome. I worked for his papa for twelve years and never had any problems. Albert Junior takes over, and within six months, this."

He held up his right hand, palm back. The tips of his two smallest fingers had been cut off at the second knuckle.

"What did you do to—"

"Forget it. I ain't gonna talk about it."

"Because of the Omerta?"

"You're goddamn right because of the Omerta! I won't make that mistake twice."

"I guess that's when you quit working for DeCarlo?"

"Quit? I got news for you, pal. You never quit working for DeCarlo. I was reassigned by him to Lombardi. DeCarlo had taken a strong interest in Lombardi, and I think he wanted one of his men on the inside."

It made sense. If nothing else, it explained Lombardi's apparent hostility toward his own henchman. Lennie was DeCarlo's pawn, not Lombardi's. "Do you know anything about Christina McCall?"

"Nah. What's to know? Just another dumb bitch."

Someone should set this man on fire, Ben thought. "Do you have any idea why he asked her to meet him at his apartment?"

Lennie shrugged. "Just dumb luck, I guess."

"Then you don't think she killed him?"

"I don't know. I wasn't there. It's possible. But when a guy has as many enemies as Tony had, there's no reason to jump to any conclusions. Hell, Tony was especially weird when it came to women."

"So I've heard."

"I saw Tony with his wife a hundred times, but if I hadn't already known, I never would've guessed they were married. Cold as ice."

Ben shifted positions in his chair. He couldn't get comfortable. He leaned to one side . . . and realized he was sitting on something. He yanked it out from under him. It was a pair of Lennie's underwear, soiled and rank. A wave of revulsion swept over him; he tossed it onto the floor.

"Sorry about that," Lennie said.

"Yeah." While leaning forward, Ben noticed a phone number scrawled on the cover of the motel room phone book. "That's the local FBI office, isn't it?"

Lennie grabbed the phone book and threw it to the other side of the room. "That's nobody's business but mine."

Ben's eyes narrowed. "Are you planning to turn state's evidence? Is that your ticket out of town?"

"I don't know what you're talking about. Your ten minutes is up."

Ben stood, but he did not leave. "What do you know that you haven't already told me?"

"I don't know nothin'. I told you to leave already."

Ben walked toward him, eyes like stone. "Goddamn it, you slimy worm. The feds wouldn't be interested in you if you didn't know something that helped their case. Tell me what you know!''

''Forget you, asshole.''

''Tell me now!''

In a heartbeat, Lennie reached under his pillow and withdrew a small caliber pistol. ''All right, you son of a bitch. I warned you! Now just get the hell out of here!''

''Not again!'' Ben slowly backed away. ''I am sick and tired of having guns pulled on me!''

''I tried to be Mr. Nice,'' Lennie said. His arms were shaking. ''But no, you had to push me around. Everyone pushes Lennie around. Well, a guy can only push so far!''

He fired the pistol. The gun flared and the bullet smashed into the wall just over Ben's head. This time it was the real thing.

''Now are you gettin' out of here or what?''

''I'm leaving, Lennie. See? I'm opening the door.''

''Count of five, man. One, two . . .''

By five, Ben was already back on the interstate.

* 25 *

He had hoped she wouldn't be there.

But of course, she was. Marjorie sat at the front desk in Swayze & Reynolds's office lobby, typing away. If she had been ten months pregnant before, she was at least twelve months pregnant now. She greeted him by name.

Well, it was encouraging that she remembered. Sort of. "Hello, Marjorie. I'm here to see Mr. Reynolds."

"I don't see you on his appointment schedule. Perhaps you called while I was at my Lamaze class?"

"No, I don't have an appointment. But it's urgent that I see him."

She frowned, then punched a button on her intercom and whispered into the box. After a few moments, she said, "I'm sorry, Mr. Kincaid. He says he's busy—"

"Tell him if he's not out in five minutes, I start smashing Lalique."

He was out in two.

"I'm sorry for the delay," Reynolds said, as he escorted Ben back to his office. "I was on the telephone with my wife. The judge."

No kidding. I thought maybe it was your other wife. Ben walked into Reynolds's office and, to his surprise, found Margot Lombardi sitting at the conference table.

Margot spared Reynolds the ordeal of a graceful introduction. "Mr. Kincaid and I have met," she explained. "And I behaved disgracefully. I had no right to burden you with my problems."

"Don't worry about it," Ben said.

"There's no excuse for such a public display. On the contrary, it's time for me to stop feeling sorry for myself and get on with my life. That's what Mr. Reynolds is helping me do. He's the executor of Tony's estate."

"So I've heard."

"The FBI is determined to link Tony's assets to drug smuggling," Reynolds said. "If they are successful, they can confiscate the assets. In the meantime, the estate is frozen."

"I don't know why they're doing this," Margot said. "What have I ever done to them?"

"Don't fret," Reynolds said, patting her on the shoulder.

For a moment, Ben thought, he almost sounded human. "Everything will work out in time."

"I didn't mean to interrupt. . . ." Ben said, suddenly regretting his door-smashing tactics.

"Not at all," Margot said. "I was on my way out."

Reynolds helped her out of her chair, then escorted her to the door. When he returned, he and Ben sat at the center table.

"How's Polly?" Ben asked.

"Oh, she's . . . as she always is."

Ben examined the parrot, almost motionless in her tiny cage. She was not as she always was. She was still a regal purplish blue, but the colors seemed faded since his last visit. Her reddish brown tail feathers were almost black. At the bottom of the cage, he saw a small bed of feathers.

"She's feather-plucking!" Ben cried.

"She's what?"

"Feather-plucking. Clayton Langdell was telling me about it."

"Clayton Langdell is . . . something of an extremist," Reynolds said, in his slow, pained manner.

"Maybe so, but he knows his parrots. Feather-plucking is an abnormal behavior pattern—the parrot goes crazy and starts mutilating itself."

"That hardly seems likely."

"That's exactly what's happening. You've got to set this bird free. Or turn her over to someone trained to care for birds."

"Mr. Kincaid. Do you have any idea how valuable that bird is?"

"I don't really care. This isn't Waterford crystal you've got locked up there. It's a living creature. A fellow animal."

Reynolds seemed vaguely amused. "Have you been spending an inordinate quantity of time with Mr. Langdell?"

"I've been reading his brochures."

"That explains a great deal. Now, were there any *legal*

matters you wished to discuss, or are you simply here to admire my parrot?''

''I've come to renew my request that you permit me to examine Lombardi's financial records.''

''Really, Mr. Kincaid . . .''

''Hear me out. I know you don't have to comply. But I'm hoping you will anyway. I need to learn more about Lombardi's business, especially his dealings with Albert De-Carlo. Those financial records may be the first step toward discovering who's behind Lombardi's murder. I can't believe you're so heartless you'd let your former employee be executed just to keep a dead client's confidences.''

''My position is not changed by your hyperbole, Mr. Kincaid. What if you in turn provided the documents to the FBI, and they used them to seize the assets that rightfully belong to Margot Lombardi? I simply can't risk it. And may I also say I resent your turning my compliance with established rules of ethics into a vast moral indictment.''

''Mr. Reynolds, you are somewhat responsible for Christina's plight. And so far, your only contribution has been firing her. Here's your chance to help.''

''You're wasting your time, Mr. Kincaid.''

''What's in those records that you don't want revealed?''

''I don't understand you.''

''You're not a stupid man, Reynolds. And I can't believe you're devoid of human kindness, much as you might pretend to be. Therefore, I have to assume there's information in those records you don't want me to see.''

''Assume what you like. However, if you do your assuming anywhere outside this office, you may find yourself in a court of law. Not as a counselor, but as a defendant.''

''At least allow me to see the documents in probate. The will, any prior wills, the property assignments. Let me see who else might've had a motive to kill Lombardi.''

''I can't do that.''

"Those documents are going to be public eventually."

"All the better for you. Perhaps you should move for a continuance."

"I already have. Several times. The motions were denied. I need those documents *now*."

"I am sorry."

"Are you a beneficiary of Lombardi's will?"

Reynolds stared at Ben as if his parents simply *had* to be first cousins. "As you should know, if I were a beneficiary, I couldn't act as executor."

"Did Lombardi create any charitable trusts? And appoint you as trustee?"

Reynolds stuttered for a moment. "I—he—"

"Yeah. I get it now. You're going to be the chairman of the Lombardi Memorial Fund for Widows and Orphans."

Reynolds wasn't pleased, but he wasn't denying, either.

"You must be looking forward to playing J. P. Morgan—doling out money to charitable groups as the whim strikes you. If they please your delicate sensibilities. If the fund is well endowed, this could make you almost as important as your wife."

"I think you should leave now, Mr. Kincaid."

No way. "Funny thing is, nothing I've heard about Lombardi suggests that he was the charitable type. I wonder if maybe *you* cooked up this trust yourself, then shredded all the prior wills and underlying documents to cover your trail. That would explain why you're refusing to cooperate. If I scrutinized the records too carefully, I just might figure out what you've done."

Reynolds rose to his feet. "Go."

"When I see the documents."

Reynolds walked to the credenza on the north wall. "Do you see this drawer, Mr. Kincaid? It is *filled* with the documents you so strongly desire. All the information you need to know. I'll tell you something else, too. The documents are loaded with information you would love to have. The references to Albert DeCarlo are legion.''

His voice rose. "And do you know what else, Mr. Kincaid? You will never see these documents. Absolutely *never!*''

He pointed toward the door. "Now leave, before I call the security guards.''

Ben stomped out of the office, smiling at Marjorie on his way through the lobby. All right, he thought. Have it your way. I'll go.

But I'll be back.

* 26 *

"Of all your lame ideas, this is the lamest!''

Christina sat on the sofa in Ben's office, stuffing a large pillow under her oversized blouse. "It is not lame! It could work!''

"Or it could get us both thrown in prison.''

"You supplied the idea," Christina insisted. "All I did was analyze it and figure out how we're going to get what we need: *c'est à dire,* Reynolds's files.'' She shoved the bulk of the pillow into the top part of the pillowcase, twisted the tail tight, and tucked it into her slacks. "You told me where the records are. And that Marjorie opens the office each morning and locks up at night. And most importantly, you told me she goes to a Lamaze class. All I did was come up with a plan for infiltration.''

"And a brilliant plan it is, too. Sets up our insanity defense nicely." Ben paced back and forth. Since the office was only about fourteen by fourteen, he did as much turning as pacing.

"I wish I had a key to the office," Christina said, "but I don't. I never did. Only Reynolds and the receptionist do."

"Are you certain her class is at St. Francis?" Ben asked.

"*Oui.* Besides, why would she go anywhere else? It's just down the road from the office."

Ben continued pacing and pondering. "Even if we do this, how will we get the records?"

"I can't think of everything, Ben. Let's just get in there, cuddle up to this woman, and see what happens." She fixed the pillow into place with masking tape. "We'll play it by ear."

"But won't Marjorie know you?"

"Nope. She started working at Swayze & Reynolds the day I was fired. I've barely even seen the woman."

"I can't believe you're resorting to that old pillow-under-the-shirt gag. You're not going to fool anyone."

"Just give me another minute." She adjusted the pillow, fluffed things up a bit, applied more tape, then let her blouse fall over the whole. "What do you think?"

Ben reconsidered. To tell the truth, she looked pregnant. "You'll make a lovely mother one day, Christina."

"Not at the rate I'm going. Help me with this scarf."

Christina rolled up her hair while Ben pulled the dark scarf over her head. "I'm going to add some thick makeup, too," she said. "Just to change my general look. Probably no one would recognize me anyway, but you never know. The Drug Princess has been in the papers lately."

"Christina, I have serious misgivings about this. We could jeopardize your whole case."

Christina didn't answer. She opened her compact, studied her face in the mirror, and busied herself with her disguise.

Ben realized he was being purposely ignored. He'd been so wrapped up in his own worries that he'd forgotten the defendant might have a few of her own. If this case went bad, she was the one who would be on the receiving end of a lethal syringe.

"Are you sure you want to do this?" Ben asked.

Christina nodded her head.

"Then do it we will." He smiled. "Finish putting on your disguise. But don't wear the fake glasses with the Groucho mustache."

Ben and Christina walked through the door marked LA-MAZE—SEPTEMBER DELIVERIES. The room was decorated like a grade-school classroom: construction paper cutouts and pseudo-inspirational posters (WHEN LIFE GIVES YOU LEM-ONS, MAKE LEMONADE). There were photographs of babies everywhere, and all of them looked identical to Ben. Like little General Schwarzkopfs.

"She's over there in the corner," Ben whispered to Christina. "The blonde. Next to the guy in the tweed jacket."

Christina nodded. "I can see why she caught your eye. Nursing should come naturally to her."

They strolled to the other side of the room.

"Mr. Kincaid!" Marjorie said. "What are you doing here?"

"Well . . ." He cleared his throat. Get the story straight. "Our usual class at St. John's was canceled. So we decided to sit in here."

"Oh, I know how you feel," Marjorie said. "I just hate to miss a session. I feel like I'm cheating the baby, you know?"

"Exactly."

"Our obligations begin at the moment of conception, right?"

Without even time out for a cigarette? "Right."

Marjorie gestured toward the gentleman standing behind her. "This is my husband, Rich."

They shook hands. "Nice to meet you," Ben said. Rich appeared to be about as happy to be here as Ben was.

"Conception is easy," Marjorie said, expanding upon her theme. "It's everything that comes afterward that's difficult. If you can't do something as simple as driving without a license, why should just anyone be permitted to have a baby? I think people should have to be licensed to have children. You know, a procreation license."

Rich's uneasy grin told Ben he dearly wished his wife would stop prattling on about conception and procreation.

"I didn't realize you were expecting," Marjorie continued. "I didn't even know you were married."

"Well, I'm not," Ben said.

"Ohhh." She glanced sideways at Christina's protuberant tummy. "Well, of course, I didn't mean to—"

"Ben's filling in for my husband tonight," Christina said. "We're old friends."

"I see," Marjorie said. "How thoughtful of you. Well, I see the instructor's here. We'd better get into position."

The couples sat in a semicircle on the floor, men seated behind the women. The instructor (Ben could tell because she was wearing a large construction paper name tag: VICKIE—INSTRUCTOR) walked into the center of the circle and squatted in the lotus position. She was a petite, auburn-haired woman wearing a pink sweater and a short skirt. To Ben, she looked more like a cheerleader than an instructor. Vickie, the Childbirth Cheerleader.

"All right, everybody," Vickie said perkily, "how do we feel today? Are we in love with our lives, our bodies, our babies, and most importantly, ourselves?"

There was a general chorus of assent. One disgruntled soul, however, mumbled that she was "sick of being fat."

Vickie pointed her finger at the offender. "That's the wrong feeling, Sarah—exactly the kind of negativism we want to stamp out. Remember, you're not fat—you're pregnant."

"What's the difference?" Ben whispered. Christina slapped his shoulder.

"I've got a special activity planned to break the ice for tonight's session," Vickie continued, "and to help us focus our positive energies on the new life that lies ahead." She passed a stack of purple paper around the circle. "I want each of you to take a piece of construction paper and tear it into some shape that represents your feelings right now about the baby."

"I am *not* an origami artist," Ben whispered.

"Oh, Ben, don't be such a stick-in-the-mud." Christina handed him several sheets of construction paper. "Let's see some *joie de vivre*."

Marjorie tapped Christina's leg. "Rich is balking, too," she said with a giggle. "Aren't men pathetic?"

"Truly," Christina agreed. "As if construction paper posed a threat to their virility." They laughed.

Ben began folding and ripping his paper. Aren't we having a jolly time?

When they were done, Vickie directed the participants to explain what they had made and what its significance was. There were numerous hearts, some beds (representing the sleep the parents wouldn't get anymore, or the act that had gotten them into this mess in the first place), and several houses (representing the family unit, or the second mortgage they were going to need to pay for this blessed event). Christina created a calendar because, she said, every single day from now on she would be grateful for this precious gift from God.

Good grief, Ben thought. She's more sentimental than the real mothers.

"And what did you make, Mr. Kincaid?" Vickie asked.

Ben held up his artwork. "A pillow."

Christina blanched. She whipped her head around and glared at him.

"Because I expect my kids to cushion me in my old age," he explained.

"Oh, of course." Everyone laughed. Except Christina.

"Well, that was fun," Vickie said when they were through. "I learned a lot from that exercise, and I hope you did, too. I feel a lot of love in this room."

How could she be so perky? Someone needed to turn a fire hose on the woman.

"Let's start with our breathing exercises. Assume you're experiencing a contraction peak. Remember, short, shallow breaths, then blow. You don't want to hyperventilate in the middle of labor."

Ben watched as all the women in the circle huffed and puffed in unison. They puffed up their cheeks like chipmunks. Short, short, short, long. Short, short, short, long.

"Pssst!" Christina was pushing her hand toward him. "You're supposed to hold my hand."

"Why? Surely you can breathe by yourself."

"It's how it's done, you dweeb. Here!" She thrust her hand into his.

Her hand felt warm and soft; he could feel her pulse as she inhaled and exhaled.

"Mr. Kincaid, where's your focal point?"

He looked up. Vickie appeared to be displeased with him, in a perky sort of way. "Excuse me?"

"You're her partner, Mr. Kincaid. You're in charge of bringing the focal point."

"The focal point?"

"Yes. Some familiar object your partner responds positively to and can concentrate on, to focus her breathing energies. Don't they do that at St. John's? It's a widely recognized technique."

"Uh, gee," Ben said. "I guess I left that at home."

"Hmmph." Vickie strode sullenly away. Wonderful, Ben thought, now the Childbirth Cheerleader is mad at me.

She returned carrying a small teddy bear. "You can use this as a substitute, dear. Let's hope your regular partner will be a bit more conscientious."

"I don't mean to complain," Christina said, "but can I request a different focal point? I've had bad luck with stuffed animals lately."

Vickie's lips pursed tightly together. For a perky woman she was becoming decidedly grumpy. She returned a few moments later with a framed photo of a lumpish newborn and plunked it in front of Christina without discussion.

Ben waited patiently for about ten minutes as the class ran through their breathing exercises. Personally, he thought he did a commendable job of hand-holding.

"All right," Vickie announced. "Time for the abdominal massage."

"No," Ben whispered. "I absolutely refuse."

"Ben," Christina hissed, "stop being a pain."

"I am not going to sit here massaging a pillow!"

"Hurry along," Vickie said, staring at Ben. "Put your body bolsters in place."

Ben looked puzzled. "Body bolsters?"

Vickie rolled her eyes and turned away. Apparently he was beyond help.

Marjorie tried to explain. "A firm pillow. Something your friend can rest her tummy on."

"Darn," Christina said. "I think we left mine at home."

Marjorie commiserated with her. "Oh, that's awful, dear. You'll never make it through the rest of the session without one."

"I guess I'll have to try," Christina said, looking sorrowful. "Unless someone has an extra."

"I have a spare that I use in the office," Marjorie said. "It's just down the street."

"That's generous of you," Ben said, quick on the uptake, "but I'd hate for you to miss any more of the class."

"Me, too," Marjorie replied. "You think you'd mind getting it?"

"Me?"

"Well, I don't want your friend to miss anything. And you don't seem terribly . . . occupied at the moment."

"You're right," Ben said, trying to contain himself. "I'll go."

Marjorie groped around in her purse. "Here's the key," she said. "You shouldn't have any problem. The security guard doesn't start taking names until eight."

"This is awfully nice of you," Christina said. "I really appreciate it."

"Don't be silly. It's just a pillow."

True in more ways than one tonight, Ben thought. "I'll be back in a flash."

And he was.

But he made a stop at the locksmith's first.

* 27 *

Ben hoisted the heavy document boxes out of the back of his Accord and onto the sidewalk in front of the Oneok Building. "I thought we swore we were never, *ever* going to do something like this again."

"This is different," Christina said. She pushed the boxes onto the flat of the dolly. "This isn't nearly as dangerous."

"I'm not sure I see the distinction. It's late at night, we're breaking into someone's office, there are guards, possibly alarms, and a high likelihood of getting caught."

"Ah," Christina said, recalling their earlier breaking and entering, "but there are no Dobermans."

"You're right. I feel much better now." He tilted the loaded dolly back and pushed it toward the front doors of the office building. He was wearing blue jeans and a blue work shirt. Christina was wearing cling-tight black leggings, a black shirt, and a sequinned black jacket with a gold lame collar.

"By the way," Ben said, "if you were trying to dress inconspicuously, you failed."

"I'm not trying to be invisible," she replied huffily. She held open the door while Ben wheeled the dolly through.

The security guard, sitting behind a large oval station, waited for them to arrive. "Can I help you?" he asked.

"Got a delivery for Quinn Reynolds," Ben said.

"Awfully late to be making deliveries."

"We did the best we could. We had to bring these documents all the way from Amarillo."

The guard nodded toward Christina. "You with him?"

"Oh yes. Haven't you seen me before? I'm a legal assistant working for Mr. Reynolds. I've got to organize these documents."

"We've got a trial first thing in the morning before Judge Schmidt. Mr. Reynolds is going to be furious if we're not ready."

At the mention of the judge's name, the guard's resistance dissolved. "You got a key?"

"Of course," she said. "How else would we get in?"

"Okay. I'll let you up." He led them to the main bank of elevators. Christina and Ben followed with the dolly. After the elevator doors opened, the guard inserted a card into the metal slot just beneath the floor buttons.

"If you have any problems, call my desk," the guard said. "Extension 4571."

"Got it." The door closed between them.

Ben and Christina exhaled. "See," Christina said. "I told

you it would be easy. You just needed to get the old testosterone pumping, Ben.''

''We're not home free yet.''

They exited the elevator on the seventh floor and wheeled the document boxes to the front door of Swayze & Reynolds. Ben inserted the key and pushed. No alarm sounded. That was one point in their favor, anyway. Assuming it wasn't a silent alarm.

They scrambled through the lobby and into Reynolds's interior office. Ben saw Polly perched in her usual spot in the corner. ''Hello, Polly.''

Polly did not respond. She looked even worse than she had on Ben's last visit. Her eyes were hazy; her plumage had faded. The pile of plucked feathers on the bottom of the cage had grown taller.

Ben pointed to the large credenza. ''The documents are in there.''

Christina scrutinized the lock. ''Piece of cake. I used to pick locks like this regularly at Raven, Tucker & Tubb. So I could read my quarterly evaluations.''

She took a paper clip from Reynolds's tabletop, straightened the outer prong, and inserted the rounded center into the lock. She jiggled the clip for a few seconds. Ben heard a tiny clicking noise. Christina withdrew the paper clip and the drawer popped open.

''Not really designed to hold state secrets,'' she said.

''Lucky for us.'' Ben examined the top row of files. ''True to the man's word, here's what we're looking for.'' He pulled three thick files out of the drawer, then closed it.

Ben perused the files for a few moments. ''These are exactly what we need. They explain how much money Lombardi got from ADC, with names, dates, and places. Have you got that copier?''

''You bet.'' Christina withdrew a black hand-size device from inside her jacket.

"That's a copier?"

"The *crème de la crème*. It can scan four by eight inches at a time, and it's very quiet."

"What did that set you back?"

"Only twenty bucks. I got it from Burris. Secondhand."

"At least." Ben handed her the documents. Christina turned on her machine. There was a soft purring noise, then a red light flashed.

"Watch this." She pulled the scanner down the first column of the top document, then pressed a button. A printed strip of paper emerged from the back of the scanner, but after a second or two, the paper became tangled and snarled. The paper backed up, clogging the machine. The scanner began to vibrate, then emitted a high-pitched squealing noise.

"Shut it off!" Ben said. Christina pressed the power button. The squealing gradually subsided.

Ben sighed. "So much for the *crème de la crème*. Get your money back."

"Can't. Burris doesn't give guarantees."

"With good reason. Where's the firm's copy machine?"

Christina led the way. At the end of the hall, they turned left into the central supply room. A large wall-to-wall window admitted faint illumination into the room. Ben saw paper cutters, typing paper, printers, a computer terminal, and in one corner, wedged between a tiny supply closet and the wall, a large photocopier.

"Stay away from the window," Ben whispered. "We don't want to be seen from the street." He scrutinized the front panel of the copier. "I can't tell which button turns this machine on. Have you still got that flashlight?"

"Yeah." Christina withdrew a small plastic flashlight. A weak beam shone across the room for a few seconds, flickered, then died.

"D'you get that from Burris, too?"

"As a matter of fact, yes."

"Just a lucky guess. Next time, Christina, you might try testing these things first. Or better yet, shop at Wal-Mart."

"Easy to say in hindsight."

"Help me pull this monster into the light." Ben gripped the photocopier. Although the machine was on wheels, it was extremely heavy. After a few moments, it began to budge. Ben and Christina wheeled it out of its niche beside the closet into the faint light.

Ben squinted at the control panel. There were at least a hundred buttons, in different sizes and shapes, some red, some green, some labeled, some not. He didn't know where to begin.

"Allow a bona fide document handler to assist," Christina said, pushing him aside. She punched a large green button. The lights came on and a low humming sound emerged. It was alive.

"Look at all these buttons," Ben exclaimed. "This machine collates, staples, enlarges, reduces, copies on both sides, and copies in color."

Christina frowned. "Boys and their toys. Stop drooling and get to work."

Half an hour later, the documents were almost copied. Ben nudged Christina's shoulder.

"Did you hear something?"

"Oh, please don't start that again."

"I'm serious. Listen."

Christina listened. After a few seconds, they both heard it. The sound of footsteps. And voices. Coming closer.

"Is it the guard from downstairs?"

Ben shook his head no. "Maybe an employee, maybe a real cop, or—it could be Reynolds! Quick, hide!" Ben grabbed the documents, originals and copies, and ran into the supply closet behind the copier. Christina followed.

They closed the door quietly. The closet was pitchblack. There was barely enough room for its top-to-bottom supply shelves, much less two adult bodies. They crouched down and listened.

"I could've sworn I heard something, Joe," said a voice on the other side of the door.

"You're losing your mind," a second voice growled. "This Reynolds clown is never here after five-fifteen, much less this late."

"Which is all the more reason we should check it out. Oooof!"

Ben heard a sharp grunt followed by mild swearing, then the sound of something clattering to the floor. Ben saw the beam of a flashlight, one that worked, crisscross the room.

"Look at this," the first voice said. "The goddamn Xerox machine is in the middle of the room. I could've killed myself."

"That would be embarrassing," his companion said. "Imagine the obituary. Frank Kellerman, security guard. Killed by a Xerox machine."

"Don't be a jerk. Help me push this back against the wall."

Ben and Christina held their breath and tried to be as quiet as possible. Two seconds later, Ben felt something bang against the closet door.

"Much better," the first voice said. "Jesus, isn't that just like an attorney to turn his office into a goddamn deathtrap? Probably hoping for a slip-and-fall case."

"Sure, Frank. Now, if you're done redecorating the supply room, let's find this intruder of yours."

Ben listened as the footsteps receded.

"Think they'll talk to the guard downstairs?" Christina whispered.

"Possibly. And he'll tell them we're supposed to be here, and those clowns'll assume we left by the back door and they just missed us. We're okay." Ben released a sigh of relief and tried to open the closet door.

It wouldn't budge.

"I may have spoken prematurely."

"That's not funny, Ben."

"You'll get no argument from me." He pressed against the door again; it wouldn't open, not even a crack. He leaned forward and pressed his shoulder, with all his weight behind it, against the door. He felt a slight give, then the door slipped back into its groove.

"Ohmigod," Christina said. "They pushed the copy machine back against the closet door, didn't they?"

"Kind of looks that way." Ben twisted the doorknob both directions, without results. "What's more, I think the top of the machine is wedged under the doorknob. Even though it's on wheels, it's holding tight. We're stuck."

"Ohmigod, ohmigod, ohmigod," Christina said. "What are we going to do?"

"Not a hell of a lot, I think, since we can barely move."

"What will we do in the morning when everyone comes in and finds us trapped in the closet?"

"I suppose we'll find that out when it happens."

"Isn't there something you can do?"

"Like what? I left my acetylene blowtorch at home, Christina. Ditto on the sonic screwdriver. You might as well try to get comfortable." He fell back against the side wall, stretching his legs out as much as possible, which wasn't much.

He heard a muffled sputter from the darkness on the other side of the closet. "Ben, are those your feet?"

"Yeah. Why, do they smell?"

"Not really. But I still don't want them in my mouth."

"Sorry." He folded his legs back into the cannonball position. "Know any good jokes?"

"Sorry. Haven't been in much of a joking mood lately."

"Nor I." Ben tried to make out her face in the darkness, but it was impossible. "For what it's worth, Christina, you were a good sport at the Lamaze class. Pretending to be pregnant. That probably wasn't pleasant."

"I didn't mind. I enjoyed it, actually. I once mentioned to

you that I . . . had a chance to be a mother. I let that slip away, for reasons that seem trivial now. The way my life is shaping up, that pillow stuffed under my blouse is probably as close to motherhood as I'll ever get." She paused. "Thanks for letting me pretend."

Ben sat silently on his side of the closet. Christina could still surprise him, it seemed.

"So, since we're having a little *tête-à-tête*," Christina said, "may I ask a personal question?"

"Such as?"

"Why won't you take any money from your mother?"

"What makes you think she's offered any?"

"Common sense. If you can raise fifty grand at the drop of a hat for me, I suspect you could get enough to find yourself a decent office."

"I prefer to take care of my business on my own."

"Of course. Ben Kincaid, the eternal lone wolf. He's not going to let other people intrude in his life. He can do everything by himself."

"I didn't say that."

"But it's what you meant. Ben, maybe you've been burned a few times, but that's no reason to isolate yourself from the rest of the world. Let other people help you."

"Other people confuse me. I'm better off keeping to myself."

"Is that what your shrink told you?"

Ben fell silent. How did she know these things?

"There's nothing wrong with that," Christina continued. "I saw a psychiatrist once. After my divorce. I was pretty strung out. Spent an hour lying on a sofa spilling my guts to this guy with a beard and a steno pad, but it didn't help. I never went back."

"That must be rough," Ben said. "Divorce."

"Yeah. It was." She inhaled sharply. "Good grief, Ben,

you're thirty years old. Reasonably attractive. I'm surprised you've never been married."

Ben bit down on his lower lip. Not here. Not in front of Christina.

"Ben?" She leaned forward and touched him on the shoulder. "I didn't mean to pry. I'm sorry if—"

"It's all right," Ben said quickly.

"I don't think I've properly thanked you for taking my case. I realize I've kept you from accepting other cases that would be more profitable."

"Yeah, those corporate giants have been banging down my door."

"Still, *merci*." She settled back into her corner. "Think we'll ever get out of here?"

"Not till morning."

"Without getting caught?"

"Seems unlikely."

"You'll think of something. You always do." Ben felt her reposition herself. "I suppose we ought to try to sleep."

"I haven't been sleeping very well lately at home. My chances for a good night's sleep in a closet are not good."

She yawned. "I'm sleepy already. Mind if I catch forty winks?"

"Be my guest."

"Thanks. Feel free to sing me a lullaby."

"The only song I know the words to is 'Oklahoma.' "

"Maybe in the morning." She snuggled in closer.

Ben listened to the sound of her breathing, inhaling, exhaling, gradually falling into a slow, easy rhythm.

In a few minutes, she was asleep.

"Christina?"

She didn't stir. He nudged her gently. "Christina? Christina, wake up. I hear movement outside."

"What—where—*Ben*?" After a moment, she regained her bearings. "We're still in this closet, aren't we?"

"I'm afraid so."

"Was I asleep?"

"Yes. Very soundly. All night."

"Oh, God. I didn't snore, did I?"

Ben smiled. He wasn't about to tell. "You were fine."

"Ugh." She tried to straighten herself out. "My legs feel like lead." She reached down and yanked off her shoes.

"Yeah, I'm pretty stiff, too."

"Did you sleep?"

"Not really, but I tried not to move too much. Didn't want to wake you."

"You sweetie."

"Shhhh! Footsteps."

They listened to the clicking of little heels down the hallway. The footsteps turned into the supply room, then they heard a woman's voice: "What in the—" The footsteps returned to the hallway. "Cliff, can you come here?"

Another pair of footsteps, softer and squeakier (sneakers, Ben guessed) bounded down the hallway. "What's up, Marjorie?"

"Would you look at the copy machine? How did it get out in the middle of the room?"

"Beats me."

"Were you and the other clerks playing around last night?"

"No way, Marjorie. Honest."

"Making goofy faces? Xeroxing your hairy buns?"

"I promise, no."

"Well, help me get it back where it belongs. Mr. Reynolds will pitch a fit."

Ben listened to the grunting on the other side of the door. "Look, it's wedged under the doorknob," Marjorie said. He heard some more heaving and straining, then the door popped free. Ben could see it slacken in the jamb. "Got it. Now let's wheel this behemoth back where it belongs."

A minute later, the squeaking of wheels came to an end. "That about right?" Cliff asked.

"Close enough," Marjorie said. "Thanks. Now go back to sorting the mail. Mr. Reynolds gets grumpy if it's not set out neatly on his desk when he arrives."

Ben waited until they both left the room. Slowly, he opened the door, just a crack. The coast was clear.

Ben and Christina crawled out of the closet. Their joints cracked and popped as they pulled themselves erect for the first time in hours.

"My legs are asleep," Christina whispered.

"Mine, too."

"I hate this. Tingles and pinpricks." She shook her legs until the sensation subsided. "How do we get out of here? Marjorie's probably sitting by the front door. Even assuming we could explain our presence here, I can't let Marjorie see me without my pillow."

"I know." Ben spotted a telephone on the other side of the room. "I have an idea." He glanced at the extension numbers on the card beside the phone, then dialed the operator.

"Hello, operator, can you help me? I can't seem to get an outside line. Thanks." He covered the receiver and whispered to Christina. "I don't want Marjorie to be able to tell the call is coming from inside the office." After he heard the dial tone, he punched in the front desk number.

"Hello?" Marjorie said.

Ben affected a fake nasal tone. "Lady, we got a package down here for you."

"Are you the one who left all these document boxes on the dolly outside the front door?"

"Uhh, yeah. That's right, ma'm. Any problems?"

"The boxes are all filled with blank paper."

"Really. The things people do. Look, lady, we just ship 'em. But you need to get this package."

"Send it up."

"No can do. You have to come down and sign for it."

"Mister, I'm eight months pregnant. I don't make trips for no good reason."

"Sorry, lady. Regulations. Must be really confidential information."

"Very well. I'll be there in a few minutes. Assuming I don't give birth on the way."

As soon as they heard her leave, Ben and Christina tiptoed out of the supply room. Ben dropped the originals of the financial documents back into Reynolds's credenza, more or less as he found them. Careful to avoid the clerk, they sidled out the front door. They had rounded the corner and almost made it to the stairwell . . . when Quinn Reynolds stepped out of the elevator.

"Mr. Kincaid," he said, aghast.

Ben realized he must look awful. He ran his fingers through his oily, matted hair and felt his stubbled chin. "Decided to grow a beard," he mumbled.

"I see." Reynolds glanced briefly at Christina, then returned his attention to Ben. "I thought I made it clear to you we had nothing further to discuss."

"We didn't come here to see you."

"Oh?"

Ben saw Reynolds's eyes roam to the documents he was cradling. He held them upright so Reynolds couldn't see what they were. He hoped. "We were visiting my broker in another office."

"Indeed," Reynolds said dryly. "Rather early to be checking your investments. Your financial status must have improved markedly."

"As a matter of fact, it has," Ben said.

"No doubt. Well . . . if you'll excuse me."

Ben stepped aside and let him pass. As soon as Reynolds was out of sight, they ducked into the stairwell. Ben closed the door behind him just as he saw Marjorie step out of the elevator, an extremely irritated expression on her face.

"We made it," Ben whispered, wiping his forehead. "Assuming Reynolds didn't suspect."

"I think he suspected you were a king-size slob." Christina started down the stairwell. "Now his suspicions are confirmed."

* 28 *

Ben strolled toward his office feeling renewed and invigorated. It was amazing what a difference a shower and a shave could make. Especially when you've spent the night in a closet.

He grabbed a copy of the *World* on his way in. Naturally, the impending trial of the so-called Drug Princess was the page-one story. How could any juror claim to be unbiased, he wondered, after reading a daily deluge of articles characterizing this case as "instrumental to the federal government's quest to shut down the Cali drug cartel"?

He stepped into his office and stared at the floor. "Jones," he asked, "what is this?" He pointed at several plastic margarine tubs filled with gray pellets.

"That's Barbara's feed bowl."

"Okay, I'll play along. Who's Barbara, and why are we feeding her?"

"Barbara is the chicken you just scared away."

"I suspected as much."

"And we're feeding her because she was hungry. And because you told me to."

"I did not—" But why bother? He tried a different tack. "Why do you call her Barbara?"

"Because that's her name."

"Barbara is a name for a human being, Jones, not a chicken."

"Is that a rule? What would *you* call her, Chicken Little? Foghorn Leghorn?"

"I told you to get rid of the chickens, Jones, not adopt them. I thought you were going to build a coop out back."

"I did. They hated it. All twelve of them, confined in a tiny area, staring at the world through chicken wire. How would you like to live like that? Sorry, Boss, but until we find them a nice home, they're staying right here."

Ben realized it would be pointless to argue. "Any luck getting the trial postponed?"

"None. I'm facing a brick wall. Derek's clerk keeps pleading the Speedy Trial Act."

"That's ironic. The Speedy Trial Act was supposed to benefit the accused. Instead, it's become a tool prosecutors use to hang them. The U.S. Attorneys can take their time, wait until they have all the evidence they need, then file charges whenever it suits them. And the hapless defendant has perhaps as few as thirty days to prepare his defense." Ben noticed something new on Jones's table. "What's with the TV and VCR?"

"I rented them from Burris. He's charging me by the minute, by the way, since I work for you. I wanted to show you something." Jones turned on the television and pushed the play button on the VCR. It creaked and groaned into action. "Not exactly quality equipment."

"Feel fortunate if it works at all."

The picture flashed on and Ben saw himself, gritting his

teeth and shaking the lapels of a decidedly intimidated blond reporter.

"Oh God."

"I figured you wouldn't want to miss this," Jones said, grinning.

Ben watched himself lecture the reporter on the evils of tainting the jury pool. His face was flush red; veins throbbed across his temples.

"I look like a maniac," Ben said. "I'll probably be tossed out of the bar for this."

"I don't think so." Jones reached under his table and withdrew a thick rubber-banded stack of mail and phone messages. "All this came for you after that clip was broadcast. They're congratulating you for standing up to that obnoxious reporter."

Ben ran his fingers through the mail. "All this?"

"Yes. Read it for yourself—they love you. Letters from lawyers, private citizens, bar committees. Two of them are from judges."

"You're kidding!"

"Face it, Boss. You're a folk hero. A new urban legend."

"Unbelievable."

"Now, remember, when you sell the TV-movie rights to your story, I want to be played by—" He froze, then completed the sentence in a whisper: "Kevin Costner."

"What's the problem?" Ben asked. "Jones?" He turned to face the door.

He immediately realized what the problem was. It was Loving, the disgruntled divorcé.

Ben dove behind Jones's table. "Call the police!" he shouted. Jones started dialing.

"Wait a minute," Loving said. "I ain't here to hurt nobody." He opened his windbreaker. "Look. I ain't carryin'. Not even a pop gun."

Ben poked his head out from behind Jones's chair. "Then why are you here?"

"I just wanted . . ." He looked embarrassed, shuffled his feet. "I just wanted to say thank you."

Ben slowly crawled out from behind the table, an inch at a time. "You wanted to thank me? For what?"

"For not pressin' charges. After that little pop gun incident."

"Oh. *That.*"

"I don't know what got into me. I'd had a little too much to drink, tell you the truth. I had all this mad inside of me, beggin' to get out. So I let it out on you."

"Well," Ben said slowly, "it could happen to anyone."

"Aww, you're just bein' nice. You had every right to send me to the slammer. And with my record, I would've been there a good long while. But you didn't. 'Cause you're a nice guy."

Actually, Ben thought, it was because I was too embarrassed to tell anyone what happened.

"I admire that," Loving continued. "Especially in a bigshot like you."

Jones gave Ben a seriously arched eyebrow.

"Bottom line is, I owe ya," Loving continued, "and I know it. And Frank Loving doesn't let a debt stand unpaid. So you just tell me what I can do for you, and I'll do it."

"Well," Ben said, "that's very kind of you, but . . ."

"You need any heads busted?"

"Uh, not today, thank you."

"How about women? I could fix you up with a babe so hot she'll put you in traction."

"Really, no . . ."

"Identical twins. Blondes."

"I'm terribly busy right now."

Loving folded his arms across his chest. His frustration was evident—and scary. "Busy with *what*?"

"Well . . . my secretary is trying without much success to interpret some financial information."

"Some deadbeats holdin' out on ya, huh? Just give me the names. I'll soften 'em up for ya."

"Not deadbeats. These are business records of transactions between Tony Lombardi—"

"I don't know him."

"And Albert DeCarlo."

"Whooooee!" Loving whistled. "Him I know. You really play with the big boys, don'tcha, Skipper?"

"Skipper?"

"I got a few pals who work for DeCarlo. I'll set the ball in motion, see if I can shake anything loose for you."

"I can't ask you to go to the trouble—"

"It's no trouble." He thwacked Ben on the back. "If I find out something, who should I call?"

"Jones here takes my calls. He's my secretary."

A furrowed ridge formed over Loving's eyes. "This *guy's* your secretary?"

"That's right."

"Hey, you two ain't, like, dating or something?"

"Definitely not," Jones said. "He's not my type."

"I'm gettin' out of here," Loving said. "I'll call you when I've got something." He exited through the front door.

"Very funny there, Jones," Ben said.

"I try to amuse, Boss. I mean, Skipper."

"By the way, if anyone from the police department inquires, we did *not* ask Loving to investigate for us, and he is not our employee. In fact, we don't know who he is."

"Got it."

Ben picked up his briefcase. "I'm out of here."

Jones shook his head and pointed.

"What now?" Ben swung around and found himself staring at orange hair and a cookie dough nose. Clayton Langdell. That cinches it, Ben thought; I'm going to put a bell on that door.

"Mr. Kincaid," Langdell said, "may I have a few moments of your time? I want to hire you."

Ben's eyebrows floated to his forehead. A client? A client who wasn't wearing handcuffs? A client dressed in a suit? That hadn't happened in a good long time. "Step into my office."

Ben ushered Langdell from the lobby into his office. Ben sat behind his desk and let Langdell take the sofa.

"How can I help you?"

"Mr. Kincaid, I'm inviting you to act as legal counsel for the Society. We've needed ongoing representation for some time, but I've been stalling, hoping to find a suitable person. I think you're our man."

Ben stifled his grin. Acting as legal counsel for a high-profile charitable organization would definitely be a step up in the world. "What would my duties entail?"

"You would advise us on legal matters. Review our publications to keep us out of unnecessary trouble. File lawsuits to enjoin activities that are harmful to our other-than-human brethren. Help organize our lobbying efforts. For instance, I'd like you to be involved in our cockfighting campaign."

"Cockfighting? Isn't that illegal?"

"Not in Oklahoma, or five other states, for that matter. And in some states like Texas, it's illegal, but only a misdemeanor. Oklahoma does have a statute prohibiting animal fights, but in a notorious case, *Lock* versus *Falkenstein*, the Oklahoma Supreme Court ruled that, although the chicken was an animal, people of ordinary intelligence were incapable of understanding that. Since those people wouldn't know they were breaking the law when they fought chickens, to try them for that offense would be an unconstitutional denial of due process."

"That's ridiculous."

"I knew you'd be outraged," Langdell said. "I saw your pet chickens in the lobby."

"Those aren't—oh, never mind." Ben pulled a legal pad out of his desk and started making notes. "Who runs these cockfights?"

"Professionals, mostly. Each season, October through June, breeders bring their birds to game clubs and set up fights. We're talking about birds that for centuries have been selectively bred for aggression. Plus the owners equip their birds with ice-pick gaffs or razor-sharp knives, just to make the birds tougher and the fight bloodier."

"That's grotesque," Ben said quietly.

"Precisely. And a lawyer like you should be able to turn some heads down at the capitol. I saw you on television the other day. I figure if you can push around reporters like that, you can arrange to be heard by the state legislators, too."

"I'd be happy to work on this," Ben said. "As you know, I'm neck-deep in a murder case at present, but as soon as that's concluded . . ."

"I understand. Fit us in as soon as you can. Cockfighting is just the tip of the iceberg. After that, we'll go after the puppy mills."

Ben felt a hollow in his heart. "Puppy mills?"

"Puppies confined to filthy mesh cages, forced to stand on chicken wire, day in, day out. Bred like rabbits, without regard to congenital defects or disease, then shipped off to pet stores and sold at exorbitant prices. Again, Oklahoma has many of the prime offenders."

"Clayton, I don't want to seem rude, but this conversation is depressing the hell out of me."

"Believe me, I know. I live with it every day."

"Why don't I give you a ring as soon as I get free of the McCall case? We can develop a systematic plan of action."

"Sounds dandy to me." Langdell rose and shook Ben's hand. "So, does this mean you're my lawyer now?"

"Well, it means I'm the Society's lawyer. Why do you ask?"

Langdell laughed, a bit too heartily. "I just like to know who is and isn't on my side." He winked and left the office.

Leaving Ben to wonder exactly what that meant.

* 29 *

"Come on, Giselle. Eat!"

It was a fair compromise. He'd filled her bowl with one-fourth Feline's Fancy and three-fourths regular Cat Chow. He figured it would smell enough like what she preferred to get her started, till she developed a taste for the other. Eventually, he would wean her off the expensive brand altogether. He thought.

Apparently, Giselle didn't see it that way. She circled the food bowl a few times. Her face crinkled; her whiskers shook. She stared at Ben with what he could have sworn were eyes of betrayal. Then she curled up in his easy chair, now covered with black cat hair, and acted as if he didn't exist.

"Look, Giselle. I just can't afford to feed you that ridiculously overpriced gourmet cat food every single day!"

She licked her paws idly, entirely oblivious to him.

"I repeat—"

He was interrupted by a knock at the door. He opened it to find Mrs. Marmelstein standing in the hallway.

"Is something wrong?" Ben asked.

"I didn't want you to take this case in the first place," she said emphatically. "I knew what would happen. Policemen waving their guns around, chasing crazed drug pushers, tramping through my garden. . . ."

Ben's eyebrows rose. "There was a police officer here?"

"Yes." She gave him an accusatory look. "Looking for you, of course."

"Did you get a name?"

"No. But he left a note."

Ben took the note from Mrs. Marmelstein and unfolded it. It said: *Third base—8:00.* He checked his watch. It was already 8:30.

"Gotta go," Ben murmured. "I may be late tonight."

"I wouldn't be surprised. Socializing with police hooligans. You'll probably go to the pool halls. Visit some ladies of loose morals."

Ben smiled. "I'll leave before the loose morals get out of control. Did he really tramp through your garden?"

Mrs. Marmelstein sniffed. "Well, no. But only because I stopped him."

Ben hadn't been to a Tulsa Drillers game in years.

Not that he was a jock, but he did enjoy watching the Drillers play when he could. Actually, his favorite part was the hot dogs. They were awful, but that was part of the charm. He'd bought two at the stand downstairs and was carrying them, the foil wrappings sweating in his hands.

The game was already into the top of the sixth inning when he arrived. The Shreveport Captains were four runs ahead of the Drillers. A Shreveport victory seemed inevitable, and the crowd was thinning. It didn't take Ben long to find Mike up in the cheap seats on the third baseline.

"I was beginning to think you weren't coming," Mike said.

"I didn't get home till late." Ben took the empty seat

beside Mike and handed him a hot dog. "Got your note and came straight out here."

Mike nodded. "I didn't want to leave a message on your machine. I wanted to meet somewhere we could talk. Freely. Privately."

"So you set up a meeting at a baseball stadium?"

"Sure. Buried in a crowd. Didn't you ever read *The Purloined Letter*? The best hiding place is out in the open." He paused to watch the shortstop trigger a magnificent double play. "Besides, I wanted to see the ball game."

"What if Abshire sees you out here with me?"

"No chance. He's back at FBI headquarters burning the midnight oil. He works on this case night and day."

That was reassuring. "What did you want?"

Mike's eyes didn't waver from the ball game. "Ben, I don't like what's happening any more than you do. There's nothing I can do about it, but I am . . . sorry."

"Got any specifics?"

"Well, I find it tough to believe Christina stuffed a cache of drugs in a Betty Boop doll."

"Then who did?"

"That's the problem. I know both of the investigating officers who accompanied me to her apartment, and I'd swear they're clean. No way they'd plant false evidence."

"Someone did."

Mike shrugged.

"What about the other evidence? What's Abshire holding back?"

"As far as exculpatory evidence goes, nothing. I would've raised holy hell if he hadn't shown you that paraffin report, though."

Ben hoped that was right. But as he recalled, Mike was pretty tranquil at the time.

"Virtually all the evidence they've found goes against

Christina. I gotta tell you, Ben, they're building an airtight case. If this were in my jurisdiction, I'd ask the D.A. to press charges, too.''

"Even though you know Christina wouldn't shoot anyone? Much less four times in the head?''

Mike didn't say anything.

"Is there anything you can do to loosen up Abshire? Make him more reasonable?''

Mike laughed. "He doesn't listen to me. He doesn't listen to anyone, except maybe Stanford. Officially, he can't go to the bathroom without Stanford's okay. But a mere local cop like me he can blow off with impunity. Hell, I tried to get him to have the goddamn drug test done on Christina the day they brought her in. But he didn't. He didn't have to, so he didn't.''

There was a sudden burst of shouting and applause. The Drillers batter had knocked the ball high and far. It flew into the outfield, soared and . . . *yes!* Over the fence for a grand slam. The crowd leaped to its feet, yelling, tooting horns, ringing cowbells. The batter nonchalantly floated around the bases. In the space of seconds, a hopeless defeat became a tie game. Things weren't always what they seemed.

"You're not exactly a fount of information tonight, Mike.''

"If you expected me to slide you some secret file that would break the case wide open—sorry. I couldn't do that, even if such a file existed. Which it doesn't.''

"If some new evidence comes to light, will you give me another call?''

"You know I can't, Ben. I've got to play this by the book.''

Ben could not mask his disappointment.

"I took an oath to serve and protect the City of Tulsa and the United States of America. I'm on the prosecution side, and any act in opposition to them would be a betrayal of my oath.''

"Oh,'' Ben said, blinking rapidly.

"Ben, you remember what I said about watching your backside? Well, it goes double now. There's some serious trouble getting ready to go down—involving the mob, the South Americans, the FBI, everybody. And you're right in the middle of it.''

''Thanks for the warning. It was good of you to meet me like this. I know you're running some . . . career risks.''

Mike shrugged again. He was still looking away, but not at the ball game. His gaze seemed to be much further. ''It was the least I could do.''

Ben had to agree. The least.

They sat together in silence. Ben felt almost invisible. Incorporeal. He snarfed down his hot dog and tried to focus on the game, without success. He just wasn't interested; his attention kept drifting back to the gray void beside him that used to be his friend.

He slipped away during the seventh-inning stretch.

* 30 *

Ben surveyed the courtroom with disgust. You'd think they were trying Lizzie Borden again.

The courtroom was loud, crowded, and chaotic. Reporters flanked the aisle; spectators packed every available seat. Everyone was talking at once, pointing out the players, shouting questions at Ben or Moltke, demanding answers. And this was just a pretrial hearing.

A camera bulb flashed in Ben's face, momentarily blinding him. Derek had issued a minute order permitting photography in the courtroom prior to and after the actual proceedings; the reporters were busily getting their money's worth while they could. They were turning the courtroom into a carnival, and Moltke was playing it to the hilt—smiling, posing, pontificating about law and order and his personal crusade for justice. It was exactly what Moltke wanted: maximum exposure, minimum attention to detail.

Early that morning, Ben had received a phone message from Myra. Moltke was offering what he called his first and final offer to plea bargain: Christina pleads guilty and the government promises not to ask for the death penalty. Christina would most likely get a life sentence—long enough that no one could be critical of Moltke, but Moltke didn't run whatever tiny risk he perceived that he might actually lose the case. And Christina? Well, of course, a huge chunk of her life would be wasted in prison. But she would live.

Ben turned it down. "No deals," he had said.

He watched Moltke now, sitting at the other table with his flunkies. Moltke seemed supremely confident. He hadn't mentioned the rejected plea bargain; he just kept babbling in his TV anchorman voice about "liberal criminal-coddling judges who care more about supposed civil rights than human beings." Ben wondered if he had done the right thing. What did Moltke know that made him so damned self-assured?

After the bailiff intoned his *oyez oyez* routine, Derek strode into the courtroom. "Approach the bench," he grumbled.

Ben and Moltke hurried to the judge's platform.

Derek pulled out a white handkerchief and wiped his nose and eyes. His face seemed red and puffy. "Damned hay fever," he said. "Pollen count in Tulsa must be over a hundred today. I'm miserable." He looked down from the bench, directly into Ben's eyes. "So let's not make this too unpleasant, shall we?"

Ben tried to nod reassuringly, with little success.

"I assume you have some motions to present, Mr. Kincaid, although God knows I can't imagine what motion you haven't already made three or four times.''

"I have new ones, your honor.''

"Oh goody.'' Derek rubbed his hands together in an exaggerated expression of delight. "Can you give me a hint as to the general nature?''

"Trying to thwart the government's effort to cover their own butt by railroading my client.''

"God.'' Derek pressed his fingers against his temples. "This isn't going to be another of your grand conspiracy theories, is it?''

"I don't know what you mean.''

"We both know exactly what I mean. I'm referring to your tendency to take a simple litigation matter and turn it into an episode of *Perry Mason.*''

"If I may proceed with my motions, your honor . . .''

Derek wheezed heavily. "Very well, counsel. You can make them at the bench.''

Ben hesitated. "I would prefer to make them in open court.''

"Aren't you the one who urged privacy when last we met? These motions are apparently of a sensitive nature. I'm sure you don't want to publicly defame government officials unnecessarily.''

"I want the motions heard formally,'' Ben insisted. "I want the court reporter to make a record.''

Derek peered through his handkerchief. Ben's meaning had not escaped him. Ben wanted the court reporter to make a record—for the appellate court to review.

"I don't suppose I can deny your request, can I?''

"Not unless you want to give me grounds for an immediate interlocutory appeal, your honor.''

Derek's teeth ground together. "Proceed with your first motion, counsel.''

Ben returned to counsel table. Moltke did the same, with

exaggerated shoulder shrugging and head shaking. Part of his routine: the noble civil servant, exasperated by the devious machinations of defense counsel.

"First motion," Ben said. He could sense the reporters leaning forward, scribbling away. "We move to exclude the alleged evidence found by law enforcement officers during their improper search of the defendant's apartment."

"I'm familiar with the circumstances," Derek said. "What was wrong with the search?"

"No warrant."

Derek opened the file before him and scanned it for a few moments. "Yes, that's as I remembered it. Your client invited the police into her apartment."

"She invited them to investigate a breaking and entering incident, your honor. She did not invite them to start searching for evidence to use against her in a pending murder case."

"She invited them into her home. She waived her right to privacy. They saw what they saw."

"They did not just *see* the alleged narcotics, your honor. They were not in plain sight; they were inside a stuffed doll. In order to find them, the police had to actively reach in and withdraw the evidence. In so doing, they went well beyond the scope of their invitation."

Derek did not seem impressed. "Any response, Mr. Prosecutor?"

"Yes, your honor." Moltke rose. "The alleged burglars caused the, er, injury to the stuffed dolls. It occurred before the police officers arrived. It was only natural for the officers, in the course of the investigation they were invited by the defendant to conduct, to try to discover what the burglars were looking for. In so doing, they discovered the incriminating evidence."

"That's how I see it also," Derek said. "I rule—"

"Your honor," Ben said. "May I rebut?"

"I think I've heard enough."

"Your honor, the legal question is whether Ms. McCall had a reasonable expectation of privacy regarding the inner contents of the dolls. She clearly did, and she did nothing to waive that constitutionally protected—"

"Counsel!" Derek's voice boomed through the courtroom. "I would have thought you'd learned in your first year of law school that when the judge says he's ready to rule it's time to shut up."

"But, your honor, I haven't—"

"Mr. Kincaid! You are not doing your client any favors."

"I'm sorry, your honor."

"The motion is denied. Anything else?"

Ben tried to calm himself. "Yes, your honor. A motion to suppress."

Derek sneezed, then wiped his nose. "And what is it you want to keep out this time, counsel?"

"Testimony by prosecution witness James Abshire regarding an alleged confessional statement made by the defendant at the time of her arrest."

"Ah, yes," Derek said. "I'm familiar with that, also. I've read the magistrate's report."

"Your honor, this statement is grossly prejudicial and not probative in any meaningful way of any issue to be tried." Ben noticed an odd expression on Derek's face. "Is something wrong, your honor?"

"No, no," he said, chuckling, "I was just trying to imagine the appeal brief in which you try to explain why the statement 'I killed him' is not probative in any meaningful way of any issues in this case."

"Your honor, the evidence at trial will show that the defendant was dazed, confused, and unaware of what she was saying. There's a strong possibility she was drugged."

"Then you may present that evidence at trial, Mr. Kincaid, and the jury will decide whether it is trustworthy. Your problem is you don't have enough faith in the jury." He looked out toward the gallery. "You keep wanting to protect the jurors of this district from any evidence that goes against your client."

Playing for the morning edition, Derek? Ben began to realize why Derek had been so liberal about allowing press coverage. "There's a Miranda problem, your honor."

Moltke evidently decided it was time to make some of his arguments for himself. "The defendant was properly Mirandized. She signed an acknowledgment."

"*After* she made the statement in question," Ben added.

Derek leaned back in his chair and stroked his chin. Ben took this as a sign of encouragement. At least he was going to ponder this motion before he denied it. "She was in custody at the time she made the statement, wasn't she, Mr. Moltke?"

"Yes," he admitted. "They had slipped the cuffs on her and finished the frisk."

"Still, there was no actual custodial *interrogation*, was there?"

Moltke brightened. At least when you led this dog to water he was smart enough to drink. "No, your honor, not at all. No questions were asked."

"You don't need a question to start an interrogation," Ben said, "as we all know. The Christian burial case, in this very state, proved that point."

"As far as I can see, there was no provocation or inducement of any kind," Derek said. "Mr. Abshire made a simple declarative statement, and your client was unwise enough to start babbling."

"That's what Abshire says," Ben replied. "He's hopelessly biased, your honor. He's the instigator of the investigation from which this case arises. He considers the whole affair a career move. He has a personal stake in seeing that the government obtains a conviction."

"All of which I'm sure you will draw out on cross-examination ad nauseum,'' Derek said. His eyelids fluttered; he was beginning to look bored. ''We'll let the jury decide.''

''That would be fine if the jury could hear the actual conversation, your honor. But all they'll hear is Abshire's slanted retelling—''

''I've ruled, Mr. Kincaid.''

''Not very well,'' Ben muttered.

Derek's eyes flared. ''What did you say?''

''I said, I can tell.'' He flipped a page on his legal pad. ''I move the court to permit an interlocutory appeal to the Tenth Circuit on this issue.''

''Waste of time. Denied.''

''Your honor, after this evidence is presented, the jury will be hopelessly tainted—''

''By unfavorable evidence!'' Derek shouted. He half rose from his chair, leaning across the bench. ''That's the way it works, counsel. If all the evidence is against you, as it seems to be in this case, you *lose*. You don't try to hide the evidence from the jury. You take your lumps and move on.''

Ben couldn't tell if Derek was truly angry or simply playing for the indignant Republicans in the audience. ''But your honor—''

''Mr. Kincaid! I've spoken to you in a prior context about your tendency toward whining. I expect more professional behavior from an officer of the court. Even if you do not possess the requisite maturity, for your client's sake—and this court's—I will expect you to feign maturity during this trial. If you do not, you may find yourself the subject of a legal competence proceeding.''

Ben braced himself and pushed ahead. ''Your honor, I renew our motion for a continuance.''

Steam seemed to rise from Derek's brow. ''Denied.''

''May I know the grounds?''

''No.''

"Not even a hint? Just to make life easier for the appellate court?"

Derek drew himself up in his chair. "Mr. Kincaid, the only reason you are not currently in jail on contempt charges is that your client would be forced to obtain new counsel. While that undoubtedly would inure to her benefit, it would also delay the start of this trial, and I am determined to see that speedy justice, as dictated by the United States Constitution, is done in this case." He raised his gavel. "I may reconsider contempt charges, however, when the trial is over. This hearing is adjourned."

With the bang of the gavel, the reporters leaped to their feet. Flashbulbs flared and a thousand voices filled the courtroom. Ben heard only one. As he passed the defendant's table, Alexander Moltke smiled a sickening smile and said in a singsong voice, "You should have taken the deee-al."

Ben wondered if he was right.

* 31 *

"Here's your fourteenth motion for a continuance," Jones said, as he tossed the pleading to Ben. "Shall I draft the judge's denial also?"

"What a wisenheimer." Ben scanned the brief, then passed it back to Jones. "What about our petition to the Tenth Circuit for emergency relief?"

"Denied. Premature."

Ben sighed. It was hardly surprising news, but he couldn't

help but hope. "I'm about at the end of my rope. Is there anything else we can try that I haven't thought of yet?"

"I don't think so, Boss. That trial is gonna start Tuesday morning whether you want it to or not. What about hiring a shadow jury?"

"Shadow juries are for big firms with lots of money to spend and a client to impress. No shadow jury could ever duplicate the thought processes of a real jury, no matter how many demographic studies are conducted. You just have to pay attention during the trial and do the best you can with the jury you draw." He ticked through his mental checklist. "Have you made any progress with the business records we got from Reynolds's office?"

"Yeah." Jones pointed to a tall stack of papers. "These are my notes and work papers. I've been backward and forward over these records a dozen times. I can tell you what they *say*, but not what they *mean*. I need something to compare and contrast these figures with."

"Something like Albert DeCarlo's business records of the same transactions."

"Exactly. Then I could put the two together, see what matches and what doesn't. And if there were discrepancies, say, large infusions of cash that appeared in one set of records but not in the other—"

"We'd be onto something. I know. Have you heard from Loving by any chance?"

"Not since he took off the other day."

"I was afraid of that. I hope he's not in trouble. Why don't you see if you can find him?"

"Why me? You're the Skipper."

"Yeah, yeah, just do it. Seen Christina this morning yet?"

"She called."

"Did you tell her about the pretrial hearing?"

Jones nodded.

"How did she take it?"

"Very calmly. But Boss," he added, "you know she's scared to death."

"I know," Ben said quietly.

The phone rang; Jones picked it up. He appeared puzzled for a moment, then he passed the receiver to Ben. "I think this is for you."

Ben took the phone. "Ben Kincaid here."

"Yeah? This is Lennie. We gotta talk. Fast."

"When I needed to talk to you, you ran me off with a gun."

"You was buttin' in where you had no business, but screw that anyhow."

"Is this about the Lombardi case?"

"Of course it's about the fuckin' Lombardi case," Lennie shouted. "Why the hell else would I be callin' you?"

"Look, I'm very busy—"

"No, you look, you little shit. This is life and death I'm talking about here." Despite his belligerence, his voice was trembling. "We're all in danger. Including that bimbo client of yours."

"What do you mean?"

"I mean we're all dead men, you asshole! Fuckin' dead men!"

"Lennie, calm down and tell me what you're babbling about. Why is Christina in danger?"

"I can't tell you over the phone, man. It's too dangerous."

"Are you still at the Cowpoke Motor Inn? Room 13?"

"You got it."

"Fine. I'm leaving now."

The motel hadn't changed, except perhaps that it seemed even more deserted than before. The occupancy level was down; business wouldn't pick up again until nightfall, Ben supposed, when the hourly clients started dropping in.

Ben swerved into the parking lot. He was grateful to have

made it; his Accord stalled twice on the drive over. He jumped out of his car, rushed to room 13, and pounded on the door. "Lennie! It's Ben Kincaid!"

There was no answer. Dead silence.

Ben pounded and yelled, but there was no response. *Oh God*—please don't let anything bad happen. Don't let it be my fault again. Let him be out for coffee, or Twinkies, or the *Sports Illustrated* swimsuit issue. Anything but—

He smelled something. Even through the door. Something disturbingly familiar.

He considered running for the front desk clerk, but he knew that would take too long—the clerk wouldn't want to come and wouldn't open the door for a stranger if he did. Motel owners couldn't legally force their way into leased premises without a compelling reason, and an officer of the court such as Ben couldn't incite someone to break the law. Not in front of witnesses, anyway.

He ran back to his car and took the pocket knife out of his glove compartment. He extended the blade and wedged it into the space between the door and the jamb, just beneath the bolt of the lock. The lock was old, and not much of a lock in the first place. After a few moments, the door sprung free.

Ben pushed the door open. The smell hit him like a wall. He inhaled deeply, clearing his lungs, then scanned the room. The decor was much as before—dirty clothes, fast food, porn magazines. And as before, Lennie was lying on the bed. But this time, Lennie wasn't moving. His body was contorted in a painfully unnatural position; there was an ice blue pallor about his skin.

And a huge, bleeding, star-shaped hole where the left side of his head should have been.

Ben held the handkerchief over his nose and mouth, trying to keep the odor out and his lunch in. This was a smell he would never get used to. Never.

"Well," Mike said, "the plot thickens. The cemetery plot, that is."

"Spare me the Halloween humor," Ben replied. "What killed him?"

"Four bullets to the head. Just like before."

Four bullets. To the head. What was left of it.

"Look at the blood color," Mike added. "This happened recently. Couldn't have been more than ten minutes before you arrived."

Ten minutes. Ten goddamned minutes. If only his stupid car hadn't stalled. If only he hadn't gotten caught in traffic on the Beeline. If only he had been smarter.

"Any idea what he wanted?"

"Not really. He said he had some important information. He said we were all in danger."

"It seems he was right. At least about himself."

"Yeah."

"And if he was right about himself . . ."

"Thanks. I grasped your point."

Ben tried not to watch as the paramedics lifted Lennie onto the stretcher. The body sagged; bloodied brain tissue fell out of the exposed cranium. "You think this was a mob killing?"

Mike considered the question. "A possibility. Given this chump's occupation. But there's nothing about this murder that screams out gangland execution."

"What about the four shots to the head? Surely one would have been sufficient for any normal murderer."

"Well . . ." Mike said hesitantly. "Of course, that factor doesn't make the killing resemble a mob execution. That factor makes the killing resemble the murder your client is going on trial for Tuesday."

Ben's face and neck muscles tightened. "What are you saying, Mike?"

"Where was Christina twenty, thirty minutes ago, Ben?"

"How should I know?"

"I think you'd better find out."

"Are you telling me she needs an alibi?"

"You're the one who told me Lennie was snitching to the FBI. That he might have been planning to testify against her." He fumbled through his coat pockets for his pipe. "You could hardly blame her for becoming desperate, under the circumstances."

"Just spit it out, Mike. What's your goddamn point?"

Mike matched his volume. "I'm saying your case just got about one hundred thousand times worse, Ben. And it wasn't great in the first place."

"I can't believe you would even consider bringing charges against Christina for this weasel's murder!"

"I'm a cop, Ben! I catch bad guys; I don't bring charges. But I can sure as hell tell you what's going to happen. Moltke and his buddies will view this development as proof of the pudding."

"And let me guess," Ben said bitterly. "There's nothing you can do to help."

Mike jammed the pipe stem between his teeth and turned away.

"As I suspected. Thanks for nothing."

Ben stormed out of the room. The blood was racing to his head. And the words, the words kept racing through his brain, filling him with dread.

Your case just got about one hundred thousand times worse, said Mike, a man in a position to know.

And it wasn't great in the first place.

* 32 *

Ben drew in the sweet smell of damp pine needles. It felt good coursing through his lungs, but it didn't dispel his intuitive feeling that he shouldn't have come, shouldn't have brought Christina, should've stayed home and locked the doors. *We're all in danger,* Lennie had said. *We're all dead men.*

The night wind whistled through the trees, bringing a sharp chill. Ben watched Christina draw her arms tighter around herself. "Told you to bring a coat."

"All my coats are neon colors," Christina replied. "Not really appropriate for this line of work."

"That's true." He glanced at his watch. Almost two in the morning. According to Wolf, the plane was overdue. Was it coming? Or had he been totally mistaken? The only way to find out was to wait and watch and listen. All night, if necessary.

Wolf began pacing in a small circle. He'd been antsy all night, not that Ben could blame him. It had been a long stakeout, and so far, entirely unproductive. Ben had been trying to get him to go home for hours; this was much too dangerous for a boy his age. And what did Wolf's parents think about him being out all hours of the night? Wolf refused to leave; and he wouldn't discuss the subject of parents at all.

"I gotta take care of something," Wolf said abruptly.

Ben nodded. "Don't be gone long."

"I won't. If I see anything, I'll call for you. Like this."
Wolf placed both hands over his mouth and released a long,

eerie hooting noise. It was some kind of bird call—an owl, perhaps? It sounded authentic, whatever it was.

"Nothing in this forest makes that noise," Wolf explained. "So if you hear it, you'll know it's me."

"All right," Ben said. "I'll be listening."

"And if something happens, or you need me in a hurry, you make the same call."

"Me? I couldn't make that noise if I practiced a million years. I can't even whistle."

"What noises *can* you make?"

"I can do excellent armpit-farts." He cupped his hand under his armpit and brought his arm down over it. "I learned that in college."

Wolf wasn't impressed. "What about you?" he asked Christina.

"Sorry," she said. "I didn't go to college."

"Maybe you should just yell, 'Hey Wolf.' "

"That I can handle," Ben said. "And when I do, what course of action does a twelve-year-old boy plan with regard to these professional criminals?"

"I can handle myself." Wolf reached into his jacket and withdrew a small wooden slingshot. "I'm a crack shot."

Ben smiled. "Just stay out of trouble. Hurry back."

Wolf plunged into the dark thicket and within seconds Ben couldn't see him at all. He couldn't hear any movement, either. The boy was almost as much a part of the forest as the trees.

A few moments later, Ben's ears pricked up. "Did you hear something?"

"Oh God, it's Mr. Paranoid again—"

"This is serious, Christina. I heard some leaves crunching."

"It must've been Wolf."

"No, it was over there. The other direction."

"Ben, if you see something, fine—let me know. Until then, stop giving me the creeps."

"Have it your way." He crouched down beside her. "You never actually told me what you were doing this afternoon."

"What does it matter? I can't believe anyone would suggest I killed this Lennie creep. I didn't even know him."

"He knew you. And unfortunately, he may have been planning to testify against you."

"How could he know anything about me?"

"Who says he did? He was in trouble, and he was planning to turn informant to get out of that trouble. He wouldn't be the first crook who invented some testimony to buy himself immunity."

"That really stinks."

"I agree, but nevertheless, having a witness for the prosecution offed on the eve of trial doesn't augur well. So where were you this afternoon?"

"I was at home. Alone. Watching television."

No chance of an alibi, then. Nothing to protect her from another murder charge but her word—the word of the accused.

Ben heard a low rumbling noise on the opposite side of the clearing. The noise grew stronger, and a few seconds later, Ben could see the outline of a small plane flying low, just above the treetops. It was painted black; but for the noise, it would be almost invisible. He watched the plane circle the clearing a few times, then approach.

"Stay low," Ben whispered. "Don't let him see you."

Christina obeyed.

The plane swept in for a perfect landing. Shortly after the engines died, a man in a dark leather jacket and blue jeans crawled out of the cockpit. He looked like the pilot Wolf had described before. Instead of waiting by the plane, he walked briskly across the clearing. He entered the forest about a hundred feet north of Ben and Christina.

After Ben was certain the man was far enough ahead, they started after him. They couldn't see the pilot, but they could hear him—the soft, steady sound of his boots bearing down on branches and leaves.

They followed him for almost ten minutes. At last, the pilot arrived at the wooden shack Ben and Christina had discovered during their previous visit—Wolf's animal sanctuary. The pilot paused, apparently trying to read the notice on the door. Then he examined the lock; it was already open. He stepped inside.

Ben heard a sudden commotion—some scuffling, a muffled yell. Could Wolf be in there?

Ben crept forward, but almost instantly shrunk back into the shadows. On the far side, a silhouetted figure moved toward the shack. Ben could barely make out any detail; it seemed to be a man, a tall man, on the thin side. The moonlight caught the side of his face—and his long flowing blond hair. It was Vinny, DeCarlo's so-called executive officer.

Vinny pushed the door of the shack open and strode inside. Ben heard another burst of scuffling, and a sudden, sharp sound—a slap? a blow to the head?—then silence.

"I think Wolf may be in there," Ben whispered to Christina.

Her eyes widened. "No!"

"He probably went in to check on his birds, only to get caught by these goons. Perhaps they were scared by all the recent FBI activity and decided to make the exchange somewhere more secluded than the clearing."

"What are we going to do? We can't just leave him in there."

"Agreed." Before Ben had a chance to suggest a course of action, he heard a violent crashing noise from inside the shack, followed by muted angry shouts.

"I'm going in," Ben muttered.

"And what are you going to do once you're in?"

"I'll figure that out when I get there." He started to rise, pushing forward on the balls of his feet, but almost instantly felt an arm wrap around his neck and jerk him onto his back.

"What the—"

Before Ben could finish, two more hands pulled a gag tightly between his teeth. Another hand wrapped heavy duct tape across his mouth, plugging the gag into place.

He coughed, choking, and squirmed helplessly on the ground. He saw Christina, just a few feet away, getting the same treatment. Men in dark clothing were holding her in place, one gripping her arms, the other yanking her head back by her hair. Ben pushed toward her, then felt someone twist his arms painfully behind his back and snap a pair of handcuffs over his wrists.

An electric bullhorn blared in the darkness. "This is the FBI. Your current location is surrounded by FBI and DEA agents. We have impounded your airplane and your motorcycle. There is no escape. Come out with your hands up."

What the hell was going on here? Ben tried to twist free, to no avail. How did the FBI find this drug drop, and why would the FBI treat him and Christina like criminals? He tried to shout, but couldn't—just trying made him choke and gag. Where was Christina? He couldn't see her now at all. By God, if they hurt her—

"You have sixty seconds to come out on your own," the bullhorn voice said. "If you do not, we will be forced to fire tear gas grenades which may be hazardous to your health. I repeat: you are surrounded. There is no escape."

Unless the smugglers have a hostage. Ben heard another crashing noise inside the shack, followed by more scuffling and banging, more muffled shouts. A struggle was taking place. Ben tried to say something, tried to tell them Wolf was in there, but it was impossible.

"Don't shoot!" a voice inside the shack shouted. The voice was frightened, panicked. "No gas. *Please.*"

Someone darted out of the shack. Ben couldn't see the face, but he knew from the height, or lack thereof, who it must be.

"Stop where you are," the bullhorn demanded. "Hands in the air. If you do not cooperate, we will be forced to fire."

The figure paused, bouncing from one foot to the other. He was obviously frightened, uncertain what to do. He kept looking back over his shoulder.

The bullhorn crackled to life. "I repeat, put your hands in the air." The shadowed figure continued to deliberate. "Gentlemen, prepare your gas grenades."

"No!" The figure outside the shack screamed, terror-stricken. "You'll kill them!" Ben saw his hand dart inside his jacket.

He never had a chance. The assault rifles fired at once, splitting the night with their thunderous booms and flashes of light. The first shot sent him careening backward. The second shot knocked him against a tree. He fell slowly down the side, leaving a grotesque red smear on the bark.

The figure hit bottom and fell forward slightly. His eyes closed. Blood dripped out of his mouth onto the ground beside his hand, still tightly clutching a small wooden slingshot.

PART THREE

*　　*

The Show of Evil

* 33 *

Ben willed his eyelids to remain open. He would've slapped himself if there hadn't been a couple hundred people watching. He had to bring himself around, and quickly. It was the first day of the trial—and he was barely able to stay awake.

By the time the federal agents had hauled him back to their headquarters, it was four in the morning; it was six-thirty before he was released. Ben was certain they were aware he had an early court date. They probably considered it an interdepartmental favor to assure that defense counsel and defendant would be operating under extreme sleep deprivation.

He hadn't heard a word about the two men they arrested. Or Wolf.

Ben watched Christina at counsel table, her hands folded neatly in her lap. She was trying to remain placid, as Ben had instructed her, but he knew it was a struggle. She was just as worried as he was, with better reason, and she had been out just as late. Despite her valiant effort with cosmetics she customarily never used, the dark half moons under her eyes were plainly visible.

She was wearing a simple blue print dress with a lace collar. It was unlike anything to be found in Christina's clothes closet; Ben bought it himself at the secondhand store down the street from his office. He was taking no chances; he even bought the shoes and accessories. He thought he had the look right—reasonably attractive, in a simple, understated fashion. Not at all upper class. Someone the jury could sympathize with.

The courtroom, as expected, was packed. A special row in the front of the gallery had been cordoned off for members of the press. The remaining six rows on both sides were jam packed with curious people who wanted to see the notorious Drug Princess for themselves. There were even two standing rows in the back of the courtroom, for those who were willing to remain on their feet all day long. In fact, there were still more would-be spectators outside waiting for a seat to open up in the gallery. The security guard told Ben some of them had been there since six in the morning. Ben couldn't believe it—this was a murder trial, for God's sake, not *Phantom of the Opera*. But *Phantom* wasn't in Tulsa this week, Ben realized, and everybody loves a good trial.

Ben scanned the sea of faces in the courtroom. He saw few he considered friendly. Ben had forced Jones, against his wishes, to stay at the office, monitoring the telephone and poring over the records from Reynolds's office. Loving still had not resurfaced. Ben just hoped he wasn't found at the bottom of the Arkansas River in cement galoshes.

There was one face in the gallery Ben recognized: Margot Lombardi. He realized he shouldn't be surprised; she was the victim's widow, after all. She was sitting in the front, wearing dark sunglasses. Didn't want to be recognized, he supposed. He could hardly blame her.

He leaned over the rail separating the gallery from the courtroom. "Mrs. Lombardi?"

She seemed startled. "Y-yes?"

"It's not my job to advise you, but you know, if you're in the courtroom, you could be called to testify." And remind the jury that Lombardi was married, Ben thought. Wouldn't that be great?

"Mr. Moltke assured me that wouldn't happen."

Ben leaned in closer. "Ma'am, your attorney, Quinn Reynolds, has been withholding documents I believe may be crucial to Christina's defense."

"Oh . . . my. Have you talked to him about this?"

"Yes. Repeatedly. And he's refused to produce the documents. I was required to obtain them from . . . uh, an independent source. As a result, I don't have a witness who can act as custodian of the documents and testify as to their authenticity."

"How can I help?"

"I know Reynolds would refuse if I asked him to authenticate the documents. But you're his client; if you ask, he'll have little choice."

"Oh. I . . . see."

"Will you do it? My client's life may be at stake."

Margot hesitated. Her finger stroked her chin. "If my attorney didn't want you to see the documents, he must have a reason."

Ben's jaw clenched.

"My financial situation is quite precarious at the moment. . . . If my attorney believes this is not in my best interest, I must trust his judgment."

It was a familiar Catch-22: the lawyer blames the client and the client blames the lawyer. Disgusted, Ben returned to defendant's table.

Moltke, of course, was playing the publicity to the hilt. He seemed ebullient; he clearly thought he had a win. He could already taste the victory, and the Senate seat beyond. And why not? Ben thought. A criminal jury trial was the prosecutor's playpen. All that television hype about judges and lawyers making it impossible to lock up criminals was absurd. The reality was they could convict almost anyone if they wanted. Prosecutors, cops, forensic scientists—they were all players on the same team, and they all liked to win. Juries were the prosecutor's Play-Doh. The hallowed principle of *presumed innocent* was a joke; most jurors presumed that if the defendant wasn't guilty of something, he wouldn't be sitting at defendant's table.

Ben checked his watch; Derek was late again. Probably reading the eleventh-hour motions Ben had filed, trying to contrive reasonable excuses to deny them all. Ben hoped Derek would make a final pronouncement on his motion in limine to exclude any evidence relating to Lennie's murder. Although Moltke insisted he had substantial evidence against Christina and expected to be filing charges against her on that murder soon, he hadn't done so yet. And as long as no charges were filed, Ben insisted evidence of Lennie's death didn't help prove who killed Lombardi, so the matter shouldn't be discussed. Derek, in a typical display of judicial cowardice, decided to reserve his ruling "until the issue was raised at trial."

Ben nudged Christina and tried to sound jovial. "Too bad you don't have a handsome, supportive husband in the first row. Juries eat that up."

"Pardonnez-moi," Christina said. "Would you like me to rent one? I think Burris stocks those."

Ben smiled, but the smile was forced. Would this trial never begin?

At last, he saw some movement behind the bench. The bailiff called everyone to order and Judge Derek entered. He seemed healthy, well-scrubbed, unusually buoyant. Probably the thrill of displaying his vast judicial prowess to the packed gallery. Ben had always suspected the man was a ham actor at heart.

Derek popped a tablet out of a small box and tossed it into his mouth. "I've been thinking about your most recent spate of motions, Mr. Kincaid."

This was about as welcome as an announcement that Herod had been thinking about babies. "Yes, your honor?"

"As far as I can tell, they're just revamps of your prior motions. Consider them all denied."

"Thank you, your honor."

"Any other preliminary matters before we select a jury, gentlemen?"

"Yes, your honor," Ben said. "I have a new motion."

"You've got to be kidding," Derek said. "Can there possibly be one you haven't already made?"

"Yes, your honor. We move for a change of venue."

"Based on what?"

"Based on the adverse pretrial publicity that has undeniably tainted the jury pool."

Derek popped another tablet into his mouth and chewed it vigorously. "Care to elaborate, counsel?"

"Your honor, this trial has been discussed on all three local TV news programs and in both Tulsa newspapers every day for the past month. Usually as the lead feature or headline story. Furthermore, the reports are clearly slanted in favor of the prosecution—"

"Could that perhaps be because the *evidence* is slanted in favor of the prosecution, counsel?"

"It doesn't matter, your honor. Criminal cases should be tried in the courtroom, not on TV or in newspapers. Even this morning, in this very courtroom, reporters were shouting statements that suggested my client must be guilty. Prospective jurors were likely within hearing range."

Moltke rose to his feet. "May I respond, your honor?"

"I don't think that's necessary, Mr. Prosecutor. Counsel, can you show me a newspaper article that has unequivocally announced your client's guilt?"

"No, of course not. That would set them up for a lawsuit."

"Can you present any evidence specifically indicating that any of the citizens on today's jury roll are biased?"

"No."

"Well, that's the standard, isn't it? Convincing evidence of prejudice to prospective jurors?"

"This court has the discretion to do what it thinks is right."

"And I shall, counsel," Derek said, "believe me. But if I took your lamebrained recommendation, I'd have to transfer every noteworthy case that ever comes before my court. Motion denied. You, of course, may explore any potential prejudices during voir dire. Within reason."

"Very well, your honor."

Derek's voice increased in volume. "And counsel, let me add that this court is weary of your relentless efforts to delay this trial and prevent justice from being done. I reiterate that any further frivolous motions may be considered grounds for contempt."

Grandstanding for the press again? "Understood, your honor."

"I hope so, counsel. For your sake. Now let's proceed."

Prior to trial, Derek had announced that due to the seriousness of the charges presented, contrary to the usual practice in federal court, he would permit the attorneys to directly question the prospective jurors. Ben wasn't about to complain—he could learn a good deal more about the jurors than he would if Derek were asking the questions.

The bailiff called the first nineteen names on his list into the jury box. On cue, each of them introduced themselves and briefly described their occupations and marital statuses. Ben saw Myra furiously trying to scribble down each biographical detail. The jury pool appeared to be largely lower middle class, not well educated. The usual. Too often, people in the upper strata of society have means of avoiding jury duty, leaving it to those workaday sorts who are grateful to have a day off with pay. The same folks demographics indicated could be influenced by tabloid journalism and prosecution pleas for justice.

There were twelve women, seven men—a devastatingly unfavorable imbalance. Conventional wisdom dictated that Ben try to get rid of as many women as possible; women tended to be much harder on other women than men, particularly when sexual impropriety was involved. Unfortunately, the remaining jury pool was over two-thirds female; even if Ben used all twenty peremptory challenges, this jury was going to have a disproportionate share of women.

Derek introduced all the lawyers and asked if any of the jurors knew them. No one did. When he asked the same question about Christina, every hand in the box shot up. As became clear, most of the jurors either read the papers or watched the TV news, and many considered themselves very well informed about Tulsa's Drug Princess. Then Derek asked the ultimate questions—whether they had already formed an opinion about the case, and whether they believed they could still evaluate the evidence fairly and without prejudice. Not surprisingly, they all did. Ben knew without a confession of prejudice he had virtually no hope of removing a juror for cause. That left him with a limited number of peremptories. Of course, even if he could remove more jurors, with whom would he replace them? The jury remainders sitting outside would be no different.

After Derek finished his preliminary questions, Moltke strolled to the podium. He made a little speech about the role of the prosecutor in protecting the commonwealth from lawlessness and anarchy. "But you jurors have one of the most important jobs in the entire world," he said. "A job upon which the very fabric of our society is dependent."

After he finished flattering them, Moltke began the voir dire. His first few questions were all softballs designed to continue cozying up to the jurors, and to suggest that he was a good ol' hometown boy, just like them. After that, Moltke asked the usual questions, totally irrelevant to the legitimate purposes of voir dire, designed to preview the prosecution theory of the case and prejudice the jury in his favor. Finally, he made the jurors promise they would evaluate the evidence fairly, but not shy away from a conviction if the evidence convinced them the defendant was guilty.

"Now, let me ask you a question, Mrs. McKenzie."

The elderly woman looked up, startled. Another venerable trial lawyer trick: memorize while the jurors are called, so later you can address them by name. Jurors tended to be impressed by this showy display of attorney acumen.

"I believe you said you were married."

"T-that's right," Mrs. McKenzie answered.

"You probably wouldn't think very highly of it if your husband went off and had an affair, would you?"

"I should say not."

"Adultery is a bad thing, wouldn't you agree?"

"Well, of course I would."

"And you probably wouldn't think very much of the floozy he was with either."

"I'd probably wring her neck," Mrs. McKenzie said. The rest of the jury chuckled.

"And if this floozy got your husband involved in criminal activity, oh, let's say drugs for instance, you probably wouldn't be happy about that."

Her neck stiffened. "No, I certainly wouldn't."

"And if that floozy actually *killed* your husband—"

"*Objection*, your honor," Ben said. "This has gone far beyond the bounds of permissible voir dire."

Derek nodded. "I'm afraid I have to agree. Mr. Moltke, please confine yourself to rooting out areas of possible prejudice, without creating any yourself."

"Yes, your honor," Moltke said, seemingly chastised. "I certainly don't want to prejudice anyone. And speaking of that, there's some evidence I want to ask you jurors about, just to make sure you won't be unfairly prejudiced by it."

Very smooth segue, Ben thought. Under the cloak of obedience he's going to do exactly what the judge told him not to do.

"Unfortunately, ladies and gentlemen, you're going to hear some evidence in this trial of . . . well . . ." He paused and acted embarrassed. "Of a . . . sexual nature."

Well, they're all wide awake now, Moltke. Good technique. Trial by titillation.

"As I'm sure you all know, some people . . . well, darn it all, some people just don't conduct themselves like you and me. I'm not saying their morals are worse than ours—"

The hell you aren't.

"—but they are certainly . . . different. Now, Mrs. Applebury, you wouldn't hold a grudge against a woman just because she was having, um, relations without benefit of marriage, would you?"

There was nothing Ben could do. If he objected because there was no evidence of any, um, relations between the defendant and the victim, he would only appear defensive, which would ensure the jury would assume that there were some, um, relations. . .

Mrs. Applebury placed her hand against her chest. "I-I would try not to."

"And how about you, Mrs. Bernstein?"

"Well, I always try to keep an open mind."

"And you, Mr. Svenson? You wouldn't assume a woman was guilty just because she engaged in sexual practices you don't consider . . . normal."

"Your honor!" Ben said. "This is outrageous. This is totally irrelevant to this case."

"Well," Derek said, "if it's totally irrelevant, it can't do your client any harm, can it?"

Ben had to hand it to him; Derek was pretty quick on his feet.

"That's all right, your honor," Moltke said. "I'm ready to move on. I have one last subject to discuss, again, with considerable regret. This case will touch upon the subject of illegal narcotics. I'm sure each of you knows what a serious problem this is in the United States today, with drugs available on every street corner, even in decent, God-fearing neighborhoods. Even on grade-school playgrounds—"

"Objection, your honor."

"Sustained."

Moltke continued unperturbed. "I'm sure each of you knows there's a war on—a war against drugs. Many of us in the government consider ourselves foot soldiers in that war. Perhaps many of you do, too. But I must remind you that this is a trial for murder in the first degree. Even though you may find the defendant was in possession of sizable quantities of illegal narcotics, you must not let that prejudice your decision on the larger issue. I'd like each of you to promise me you will view the evidence fairly, and that if you bring back a conviction against the defendant, it will be based upon the considerable evidence proving she committed murder, and not simply an understandable, if misguided effort to sever this link in the virulent chain that is destroying our fine nation—"

"*Objection*, your honor!" Ben said, practically screaming. "This is grossly prejudicial. Counsel is practically testifying."

Derek nodded calmly. "The objection is sustained."

"I also move to strike the prosecutor's improper remarks from the record, and that the jury be instructed to disregard."

"If you insist."

Well, at least he didn't say: Why bother?

Derek gazed impassively at the jury. "You are instructed to disregard any remarks of counsel that may have suggested criminal activity as yet unproven." He peered down at Moltke. "Anything else, or are you about done?"

Moltke could take a hint. "I'm done, your honor."

"Good. Counsel for the defense?"

Ben went to the podium and began running through the

list of questions he had prepared in advance. He did it like they taught him in law school; he avoided questions intended to tarnish opposition witnesses, questions designed to preview opening statement, and questions designed to predispose the jury in his favor. The point of voir dire was to determine whether the jurors could be fair and impartial, and he stuck to it. That was the way it was supposed to work. Right?

Ben was barely halfway through his questions when he sensed the jury's attention was beginning to wane. They kept peering over his shoulder, trying to size up Christina. The sad fact was that half of them would probably be more influenced by her personal appearance than any evidence they heard at trial.

"I noted that opposing counsel required you to make all kinds of promises during his voir dire examination," Ben said in conclusion. "I'm only going to ask you to make one. Later in this trial, you will hear the judge use the phrases *presumed innocent*, and *beyond a reasonable doubt*, and he will instruct you on the meaning of those phrases. Please listen carefully to what the judge tells you, and bear in mind at all times that Christina McCall is presumed innocent, and that the burden of proving her guilt beyond a reasonable doubt is entirely on the prosecution. All I ask is that you hold them to that legal standard. Will each of you promise to do that?"

There was a general, unenthusiastic nodding of heads.

"What about you, Mrs. McKenzie? Will you make that promise?"

It was a mistake, Ben realized almost immediately. He just didn't have Moltke's finesse. She looked stricken, embarrassed to be singled out. "I—why, yes, I suppose," she said, flustered. She covered the side of her face with her hand.

"Thank you." He decided not to compound the error by trying anyone else.

"And thank you, counsel," Derek said. "Both sides will take ten minutes to deliberate, then I want to see counsel in chambers to make their initial challenges."

All in all, it could have been worse. Ben took off three older women, including Mrs. McKenzie, the one he had mortified. Moltke took off three men, all for reasons that eluded Ben. Perhaps they weren't responding properly to his charismatic feints.

Derek called for opening statements. Moltke strode up to the jury box and smiled. Derek cleared his throat and pointed at the podium.

"Oh, of course, your honor. I forgot where I was." He retreated to the podium.

Just another tactic from Moltke's bottomless bag of tricks. He went up front and close to the jury, to remind them he was one of them, one of the gang. Ben knew he would never have an opportunity to get that close. They would always perceive him as being more distant.

"It was a dark, moonless night," Moltke began, setting the mood. "Most law-abiding Tulsans were still asleep in bed. All was calm, silent, still. Until suddenly, the night was shattered"—he pounded on the podium, startling the jurors—"by a sudden act of grisly violence."

Ben tried to refrain from rolling his eyes. He hated attorneys who thought they were Edgar frigging Allan Poe. He hated seeing what should be a cold, unemotional recitation of the facts turned into "The Fall of the House of Usher."

"Ladies and gentlemen, the overwhelming evidence will show that on that moonless morning, the defendant, Christina McCall, took her lover's gun and shot him, at point-blank range, four times in the head. As you might imagine, one such shot would easily have killed him. What kind of woman would stand there and shoot, not once, but four times? The same woman, as the evidence will show, who was found by FBI agents hovering over the body, her finger-prints still fresh on the gun. The same woman whose only statement to the arresting officer was, 'I killed him.' "

There was no point in objecting. It was argumentative, but Moltke was carefully couching his statements in terms of what "the evidence will show," which theoretically kept him within the scope of opening statement. Derek would simply rule that the jury could listen to the testimony for itself and decide whether the opening remarks were accurate. Then Derek would sneer and make it clear to the jury that he held Ben in complete contempt. No, Ben was going to save his objections for when he needed them.

Moltke continued for about twenty minutes, painting Christina as a spiteful tramp, linking the murder to drug smuggling and organized crime, and evoking sympathy for the bereaved widow, the betrayed woman. He gestured to Margot, now without her sunglasses, poised in the front of the gallery with a stricken expression on her face. Had he arranged for her to get a front-row seat? Probably.

Moltke seemed to go back and forth on motive, sometimes suggesting the killing was the product of a lover's spat, some-times suggesting Christina was after Lombardi's drug stash. It didn't really matter. The motives weren't entirely contra-dictory. Besides, this was a jury trial, not Logic 101. Ben watched the jurors follow Moltke's words, gestures, and fa-cial expressions. He held them spellbound throughout his presentation.

When Moltke was finished, Ben took the podium. He would be the voice of reason, he thought, presenting the hard facts in a calm, even-handed manner, without Moltke's ma-nipulative gimmicks. "Ladies and gentlemen of the jury," Ben began. "Everything counsel for the prosecution has just told you is disputed. You will hear evidence refuting every fact of importance in their case. And the judge will instruct you to make your ultimate decision based upon the evidence, not the things attorneys tell you. I merely ask that you listen carefully to the evidence presented, and that you remember the promise you made to me earlier.''

He saw a puzzled expression on Mr. Svenson's face. Promise? Oh yes, you had one, too, didn't you? What was it about? Ben could tell he didn't remember. He wondered if any of them did.

Ben carefully sorted through the facts previewed in Moltke's opening, presenting Christina's denial, or refutation, or explanation. He covered the forensic evidence, the medical evidence, the ballistics evidence, and the inconclusive drug analysis. All the hard-core facts. All the nitty-gritty detail that Moltke left out of his opening.

For good reason. Again, Ben could feel the jury's attention drifting. He was boring them. It was hard to believe a drug-related homicide could be boring, but he was making it so. Of course they loved Moltke. He fulfilled their expectations; he made the lugubrious trial process almost as compelling as it was on television. Ben turned it into algebra in a courtroom.

Ben saw them stretch, twist, and glance at the clock on the wall, but there was nothing he could do. He stuck to the script he had prepared in advance; he couldn't improvise a Stephen King subplot just to grab the jury's attention. He finished his preview of the evidence and began identifying the anticipated defense witnesses.

"Excuse me, counsel."

Ben glanced back at Derek. He was yawning. Thanks, Judge, very subtle.

"I believe your time has expired."

"Time?" Ben said. "I wasn't aware the court was imposing time restraints on opening statement."

"Well, normally I wouldn't, but . . ." His voice trailed off. Several of the jurors smiled. "Try to wrap it up, okay?"

Ben could argue, but it would be pointless. The jury clearly sympathized with Derek. He listed his witnesses quickly and returned to defendant's table.

Christina was still focusing straight ahead, looking alert, but not otherwise displaying emotion, just as he had told her to do. But Ben could see past that. He could see the tiny crinkles encircling her eyes, the near invisible trembling of her hands. She'd been in the courtroom many times before—more times than Ben for that matter. She knew who was winning. And who wasn't.

"Splendid," Derek said, popping another tablet. "Let's move right along. Mr. Prosecutor, call your first witness."

* 34 *

"The United States calls James Abshire to the stand."

Ben was surprised. They were foregoing the usual slow buildup and leading with a heavy hitter first out of the box.

Abshire was wearing a blue sports jacket, khaki pants, and a dark tie—standard government witness costuming. In solemn sonorous tones, he repeated his oath to tell the whole truth. Moltke ran through Abshire's résumé, eliciting a laundry list of qualifications and experience that made Abshire sound like the J. Edgar Hoover of the 1990s. *Summa cum laude* from Georgetown, top of his trainee class at Quantico, junior agent on several important investigations. Then Moltke traced the history of the Lombardi investigation, beginning with an account of how the FBI first obtained evidence of the so-called Tulsa connection, the purported narcotics pipeline flowing from South America to Oklahoma via small planes and smuggled goods.

"Do you know a man named Tony Lombardi?" Moltke asked.

"Yes," Abshire replied. He was restraining himself, maintaining a flat, even tone. He gave no indication that he might have a personal stake in the success of the investigation. "Mr. Lombardi was engaged in the importation of parrots and other rare birds from South and Central America."

"And why did that interest you?"

"Drug smugglers often use legitimate importation avenues to cover the movement of illegal goods. We suspected Mr. Lombardi was using his parrot network to bring cocaine and other narcotics into this country. Mr. Lombardi transferred his imported goods to another company for distribution in the United States." He paused and made eye contact with the jurors. "A company owned by a man named Albert DeCarlo."

Ben watched the jurors' eyes widen. There was no misunderstanding the point of that little exercise in guilt by association.

"And do you know the defendant, Miss Christina McCall?"

"Yes I do."

"How did you first come to know her?"

"During the course of our investigation of Mr. Lombardi. Miss McCall was his . . ." Abshire paused, allowing the jury to run all the possible synonyms through their minds. By the time he finished his sentence, it didn't matter what word he used. "His special friend."

"Was this friendship romantic in nature?"

"We believe it was, yes. They met as a result of her work for a local law firm, but the relationship became more than simply professional."

Ben watched the jurors' gazes shift to Christina, the scarlet woman. Well, thank God he got Mrs. McKenzie off the jury.

"Please tell us what happened on the night of Monday, April first."

"The evidence we'd gathered indicated that major drug shipments were made on Monday nights, about every other week, and we were expecting one that night. We had been unable to determine the drop site—that is, the place where the drugs were delivered. We hoped to follow Lombardi to the site, or at least to witness an intermediate exchange."

"What did you do?"

"We watched Mr. Lombardi. Unfortunately, he remained at his office, apparently alone, until after midnight. When he finally left, we followed him directly to his apartment. He went inside"—another meaningful glance at the jury—"and never came out. Not alive, anyway."

"Did you hear a gunshot?"

"No. After Lombardi went inside, we returned to headquarters and tried to obtain a search warrant. From one to two, the apparent time of death, none of our agents were—"

"Objection," Ben said. "Lack of personal knowledge regarding apparent time of death. He's not the coroner."

"That objection will be sustained," Derek said with an air that clearly suggested that he considered the matter trivial and that Ben was a petty pain in the butt for mentioning it.

"What happened next?" Moltke asked.

"No disrespect for the court intended, but the wheels of justice sometimes move rather slowly. About two A.M., we returned to the apartment building with a warrant and moved in."

"Were you personally involved in the raid on Lombardi's apartment?"

"I was. In fact, I had what police officers call the death seat. I led the way."

How heroic. J. Edgar Hoover becomes Teddy Roosevelt. Ben tried not to gag.

"What did you find in the apartment?"

Several jurors, ever so imperceptibly, leaned forward. They knew they were coming to the juicy part.

"The front living room was dark, except for the blue glow of a television set. I turned on the lights and saw the defendant, Christina McCall, hovering over the body of Tony Lombardi. The gun was lying on the floor, just a few inches from her right foot. When she saw us, she screamed, panicked. As if she'd been caught in the act."

"Objection," Ben said. "Move to strike."

"Sustained and granted," Derek said. "The witness will stick to the facts." As usual, it was barely a hand slap. Derek was keeping a clean record, ruling against the prosecution when he knew he had to, but all the while sending the jury a clear indication of his disdain for everyone at the defense table.

"Mr. Stanford and I examined Lombardi's body. It was immediately clear he was dead—a huge section of his head was blown off; the entire cranium appeared shattered—"

"Objection—"

"Yes, yes," Derek said. "We know. Not the coroner. Sustained. Let's move along, gentlemen."

"What did you do?"

"I proceeded to take the defendant into custody."

"Did she resist?"

"Well . . ." A slight smile. "She didn't exactly cooperate. Of course, we're trained to handle that."

Of course, Ben thought. And you never actually answered the question, did you? Although you left a clear, negative impression that she resisted arrest.

"I searched her, then handcuffed her. That's when she made the statement."

Moltke's eyebrows rose, feigning surprise for the jury. "Statement? What statement was that?"

"She said, and these are her exact words, 'I killed him.' "

"Are you sure that's what she said?"

"Absolutely positive."

"And did you provoke or elicit this statement in any way?"

"No, I did not." He faced the jury. "I had no reason to. Frankly, it was perfectly obvious she had killed him. I didn't need a confession. She volunteered it."

"Objection, your honor!"

"That's all right, your honor," Moltke said. "We'll strike the last remark. Are you aware of any other evidence indicating Ms. McCall's guilt?"

"Yes. Just last week—"

"Again I object," Ben said. "Your honor, this touches upon my motion in limine. Regarding the events of last week."

"Well," Derek said, "was Mr. Abshire personally involved in the investigation of last week's incident?"

"No," Moltke admitted, "he wasn't."

"Well . . . then we'd better not have him testifying about it," Derek said grudgingly. *It was always a struggle to do the right thing, huh, Dick?*

"Very well," Moltke said. "Nothing more at this time, your honor."

"Excellent," Derek said. "And let me commend you, Mr. Prosecutor, for your succinct, straight-to-the-point examination." He glanced at Ben. "I only hope defense counsel has been paying attention."

Ben repeated all the points he'd made at the preliminary examination—that Abshire didn't see Christina holding the gun, that he found no drugs on her (at that time) or elsewhere in the apartment, and that he found no weapon on her person. Ben decided not to pursue the theory that Abshire's zeal for conviction biased his testimony. He could tell the jury liked

Abshire, and they would probably find his zeal admirable, not impeaching. No, he would have to see what he could do with the gun. . . .

"You found no gun of any kind on Christina's person, right?" Ben's job was to humanize his client, to make her seem like a real person to the jury. Therefore, he would always call her by her first name (and refer to prosecution witnesses by their last).

"True," Abshire said. "We found the gun on the floor beside her."

"You don't know that she actually used that gun, right?"

"Of course we do. There were clear latent fingerprints on the gun. The prints belonged to Christina McCall."

Ben could object to this evidentiary harpoon—Abshire was not the forensics expert. But the evidence would come out eventually, and he had a different plan of attack in mind.

"Well, let's talk about that, Mr. Abshire. You say Christina's prints were on the gun."

"That's right."

"But—didn't the FBI also perform a paraffin test?"

"Objection, your honor," Moltke said. "We have an expert who will testify about that."

"This witness opened the door," Ben insisted. "He inserted the fingerprint evidence into his testimony. Now I'm permitted to cross-examine him about his statement."

Derek sighed. "I will allow limited cross-examination regarding the testimony given by the witness. Don't exceed that scope."

"Thank you, your honor." Ben turned back to Abshire. "Was a paraffin test performed on Christina?"

"I believe so."

"Can you explain what a paraffin test is to the jury?"

Reluctantly, Abshire did so.

"And did the paraffin test reveal any nitrous traces on Christina's skin?"

"No, it did not."

"Well, doesn't that prove she didn't kill Lombardi?"

Abshire made a snorting noise. "Obviously, she wore gloves."

"Really." Ben leaned forward against the podium. "Tell me, Mr. Abshire. If she wore gloves, why were her fingerprints on the gun?"

Abshire stuttered for a moment. "I . . . I suppose she must've taken the gloves off later."

"I see," Ben said. "Although she was smart enough to wear gloves when she fired the gun, she later removed the gloves and rubbed her prints all over it."

"Something like that."

"Mr. Abshire, does that make any sense to you?"

It was the classic one question too many. "Cards-on-the-table time? Murder often doesn't make sense, Mr. Kincaid. Especially a crime of passion like this. Only in the movies do you find cold-blooded killers who do everything right. Ms. McCall was angry with Lombardi, emotionally distraught. She wasn't thinking clearly. She could easily have absentmindedly taken some action that seems illogical in retrospect."

Ben saw a slight nodding of several jurors' heads. Made sense to them. Made sufficient sense to support their predisposition to convict, anyway.

"Did you in fact find any gloves on Christina's person?"

"No. I found some in Lombardi's clothes closet, though."

"So your testimony is that, after shooting him, this emotionally distraught woman removed the gloves, put them neatly back in the clothes closet, and pawed the gun?"

"I don't know that she used those gloves. I'm just saying it's possible. She may have flushed the gloves she used down the toilet. It's been done before."

More nodding in the jury box. Ben knew it was time to move on.

"Mr. Abshire, you mentioned an alleged confessional statement made by Christina."

"That's correct."

"Do you recall when we discussed this matter at the preliminary hearing?"

"Yes."

"And at that time, you testified that you said something that provoked Christina's statement."

"I said I might have said something," Abshire replied. "I was confused. Frankly, you caught me by surprise with that one; I didn't really remember. But since that time, I've had a chance to think about it, and to talk to my superior, Mr. Stanford, who was also present. I'm certain now. I didn't say a word to her. Her statement was completely voluntary."

As it would have to be, Ben noted, to get around your enormous Miranda problem. "So you're changing your testimony in the courtroom today."

Abshire gave the jury a gosh-shucks grin. "I'm not changing anything, sir. Before, I didn't remember clearly. Now I do. Her statement was unprovoked."

And there's nothing you can do to prove otherwise, Abshire said but did not say, unless you put the defendant on the stand, something no defense attorney ever wants to do. Having smoked out Ben's Miranda argument during the preliminary hearing, Abshire and Moltke had put their heads together and figured out a clever way to salvage the evidence.

"No more questions, your honor," Ben said regretfully. He returned to defendant's table.

"Any redirect?"

"I don't see the need," Moltke said. Derek smiled back, obviously in agreement.

"Very well. Mr. Abshire, I thank you for your testimony.

You may step down. Mr. Prosecutor, call your next witness.''

* 35 *

"The United States calls Officer John Tompkins."

Tompkins, the surprise witness from the preliminary hearing, took the stand in full uniform. If the jury had liked Abshire, Ben thought, they were going to love this guy. It would be difficult to imagine a straighter arrow.

Moltke introduced Tompkins and ran through his background, before and after he joined the police force. Eventually, they discussed the day Tompkins went to Christina's apartment to assist the follow-up investigation of the breaking and entering. He described his initial conversation with Christina, the search of her apartment, and the discovery of cocaine in the Betty Boop doll.

"Was there any identification or marking on the drugs?"

"Yes. The top plastic Baggie contained a strip of paper with the word *Lombardi* written on it."

"Officer Tompkins, based on your years of experience in matters of this sort, can you draw any conclusion from that strip of paper?"

"Well, the obvious conclusion is that these drugs were part of a shipment received by or intended for a man named Lombardi."

"Do you have any idea how Ms. McCall might have obtained the drugs?"

"Objection," Ben said. "Calls for speculation."

"That's all right," Moltke said. "I'll withdraw the question. I believe the jury is capable of putting two and two together."

Yeah, Ben thought. Especially if you do the math for them.

"Now, how many days after Lombardi's murder was this?"

"Just three, sir."

"So three days after Lombardi was killed, Ms. McCall had the drugs that were probably delivered to him the night of the murder." *Good grief, Moltke, why don't you just draw a diagram on the chalkboard for them?* "Based upon your years of experience, Officer, would a person of average intelligence be able to dispose of these drugs?"

"Easily," Tompkins replied. "I hate to admit it, but there are well-known drug drops all over Tulsa. We can't possibly police them all. Anyone who wants to score some drugs could do so."

"And would this cocaine be valuable?"

"Extremely so."

"Now, you were in Ms. McCall's apartment, Officer. Would you say she is a wealthy person?"

"Objection!" Ben said.

"Overruled." Derek motioned to the witness. "Proceed."

"No, I would not. All indications were of a relatively low income level."

"Do you think a quantity of cocaine such as you discovered could significantly improve such a person's lifestyle?"

"Again, your honor, I object!"

"I think you've made your point, Mr. Prosecutor," Derek said.

"Very well, your honor. No more questions."

Ben positioned himself for cross-examination. He knew he had to be careful. The jury didn't want to see Tompkins taken apart; after all, he was just doing his job. Ben would have to impeach him without casting any aspersions on his character or competence.

"Officer Tompkins, you testified that the packet of drugs you allegedly found in Christina's apartment bore a label with the word *Lombardi* written upon it, right?"

"That is correct."

"Isn't that rather unusual?"

"I don't know what you mean."

"Well, drug smuggling is a criminal activity, isn't it?"

"Yes."

"People don't normally go around posting signs saying THIS IS MY STASH OF ILLEGAL DRUGS, do they?"

"The label was probably affixed by the supplier."

"And why would the supplier want to create identifying labels? Isn't he just as subject to criminal liability?"

"Probably more so."

"And if Lombardi gets caught, the supplier is likely to go down next, isn't he?"

"It does often happen that way. But the fact that an activity might not be prudent doesn't mean it didn't happen. You have to realize we're not discussing rocket scientists here. These are drug smugglers."

Score one for Officer Tompkins. "Nonetheless, Officer, before this incident, had you ever seen a similar label?"

"No," Tompkins admitted.

Hallelujah. "Now let's talk about this cocaine in the stuffed doll. The doll was not intact when you found it, was it?"

"No. All of the dolls were damaged. A chunk of their midsections had been removed."

"That's strange. Why would anyone tear up a bunch of stuffed animals?"

"Possibly a rival member of Lombardi's organization was searching for the stolen drugs."

"And somehow that rival member knew to look for the drugs in the stuffed animals?"

"The entire apartment appeared to have been ransacked."

"Tell me, Officer, if this rival knew to look for the drugs in the dolls, and ripped open the dolls while looking, why didn't he find and *take* the drugs?"

There was a short pause. A line appeared between Tompkins's brows. This question obviously had occurred to him before, and it troubled him.

Suddenly, Derek broke the silence. "Counsel, I think that question calls for speculation. Let's move on."

Ben turned slowly toward the bench. "Excuse me, your honor. Was there an objection?"

"No," Derek said, casting a quick look at Moltke, "although the need was obvious. I'm sure the prosecutor was just being polite. The court, of course, has the inherent discretion to limit speculative testimony. Move on."

Ben stared at him, speechless. Ben was finally making some headway, and Derek was shutting him down.

"I said, *move on*, counsel."

Ben closed his trial notebook. "I have no more questions, your honor. Other than those the court has just forbidden."

Derek looked at him sharply, but let it pass. Since there was no redirect, the witness stepped down.

"It's been a long day," Derek said, "and I don't want to inundate the jury with too much information at once. We'll resume tomorrow morning at nine o'clock with the prosecution's next witness."

He banged his gavel against the bench. "Court is adjourned."

* 36 *

Ben waited until everyone but the security guards had left. He was overdue at the office. He needed to prepare for the next day's trial, he needed to see how Christina was holding up, and he needed to contact Wolf's parents. But he was determined to talk to Derek first.

Derek was still puttering around in chambers—making phone calls and attending to administrative matters. Ben decided to give him time to unwind, take care of his business, and have a quick snort from the bottle of Scotch he'd removed from his bottom desk drawer.

Ben stood just outside the doorway and listened while Derek dialed the phone. "Hello, Louise? . . . Yeah, I'm still here. . . . I don't know, I'll probably be home in an hour or so. . . . Of course I'm working, I started a trial today, for God's sake. Where else would I be? . . . Look, Louise, I don't give a good goddamn what you suspect. I've been in court all day, and you can take it or leave it. . . . Yeah, well, the hell with you, too.''

Derek slammed the receiver back into its cradle. Ben heard an undercurrent of indistinct muttering. He decided to give Derek a few more moments to cool off.

After he'd clocked a full minute on his watch, Ben stepped inside. Derek's chambers seemed sparsely decorated, but to be fair, he'd only been in them about eight months. Ben did see Derek's Harvard law diploma, squarely placed where it couldn't be missed, just beneath Derek's pride and joy, a large stuffed bobcat, poised forever in mid-spring.

He knocked on the open door. "Excuse me, Judge."

He caught Derek in the middle of chewing another tablet. "Kincaid? What the hell are you doing here?"

"If I may have a minute of your time . . ."

"Is Moltke outside?"

"No, he left. Press conference, probably."

Derek drew himself erect. "You want to have an *ex parte* conversation? Without the presence of opposing counsel? Do you know how improper that is?"

Ben stared at a safe point in the middle of Derek's desk. "This isn't about the case. Well, it is, but not about the substance of the evidence or legal issues."

Derek took another swig from the Scotch bottle and washed down the remains of the tablet. "Then what is it you want?"

"I want to ask you . . . to *plead* with you, really . . . to stop taking your hatred of me out on my client. In the courtroom. If it were just me on the firing line, I wouldn't complain. But someone else's head is in the noose, and it isn't fair that she get a bad shake just because you're holding a grudge against me."

Derek stared back at Ben, his mouth slightly agape. "I cannot *believe* . . . Are you actually suggesting I am biased in my deliberations?"

"Let's not play games. You've ruled against me at every important juncture. Even when you occasionally toss me a bone, you make it clear to the jury that you do so grudgingly. Juries are very good at picking up messages from the judge, and yours are going to be translated into a conviction if you don't ease off."

"I do not believe my ears. Bad enough that you barge in here demanding an unethical *ex parte* conversation. But then you use that time to accuse me of judicial impropriety of the worst order.''

"The pattern of your rulings is clear—''

"Did it ever occur to you that my rulings might be against you because you have a lousy case!" Derek shouted. "Correction. A combination of the fact that you have a lousy case and that you are a lousy attorney.''

"That's uncalled for.''

"That's the goddamned truth, you miserable wimp.'' He reached into his desk and brought out what Ben now could see was a box of Tums. "I've had the worst heartburn all week long. I shouldn't be surprised. In the world of indigestion, you're a frigging carrier.''

"Derek, listen—''

"No, you listen to me, Kincaid.'' He crunched another tablet. "I tried to work with you back at Raven. With God as my witness, I did. But I could see then you'd never cut it as a litigator, and I was right. You just haven't got the cajones for it. I said you had to learn to work, not whine. And what is this whole conversation but proof of my point?''

"That's not fair—''

"Just shut up and listen. You were a whiner then, and you're a whiner now. Okay, you took some knocks in the courtroom today. Tough, it happens. You should be back at the office working, trying to figure out a way to make the next day go better. Instead, you're in the judge's chambers, trying to get an edge on the competition by complaining to the judge when they're not around!''

"That's not justified—''

"This whole conversation is not justified, Kincaid! You've violated every rule of ethics I know.''

"Which one would that be?''

Derek's teeth clenched tightly together. "They never should have let you pass the bar. I was right about you back at Raven, and I'm still right.''

"That's what this is all about, isn't it?"

"What do you mean?"

"I mean Raven, Tucker & Tubb. A year ago. The Sanguine Enterprises fiasco."

Derek didn't say anything.

"You lost a big client so, in your infinite pettiness, you got me fired."

Derek made a *pfui* sound.

"Haven't you hurt me enough already? I lost the job with the big firm. I've been scrabbling along on my own, one day at a time, barely getting by, for over a year now. Haven't you exacted your revenge? Isn't that enough punishment for one lousy client?"

Derek was silent for a long, dreadful time. He placed his palms against his desk, fingers spread wide. "There's more to it than that," he said finally.

"In what way?"

"In the first place, I lost more than a client. I lost a hell of a lot of money." He patted himself down, searching for cigarettes, but didn't find any. "That Sanguine business was just the first event in a miserable chain reaction. I imagine you know, even from your brief tenure at Raven, that I was not exactly the most popular shareholder in the firm." He laughed. "Hell, when you're good, when you're the best there is, you're not going to be popular."

Ben could think of other possible explanations for his lack of popularity.

"But they couldn't touch me, because I had a great client base. Until you came blundering along. I'd lost a few clients in recent years, nothing major, but they stung a bit. When Sanguine pulled out and took his business to Conner & Winters—well, it was the beginning of the end. Other clients heard about what happened; they pulled out, too. It's a bad scenario for a lawyer—more clients going out than coming in. Before long, my client base was so low the controlling shareholders at Raven could justify giving me the heave ho. Bastards.''

"I'm . . . sorry," Ben said haltingly. "I never suspected—"

"I wanted to go back to Philadelphia, but of course, Louise said no. Can't uproot our children and all that crap. What the fuck does she care about my problems? As long as someone pays the Visa bill every month, she's happy." He slammed his top desk drawer shut. "I need a cigarette. I don't suppose you'd lend me one?"

"I don't smoke."

"No, of course not. Still campaigning for sainthood." He inhaled sharply, then continued. "The firm gave me four months to find a position somewhere else. Shit, when you've already worked for the best firm in town, where are you supposed to go?"

"I know exactly what you mean," Ben said quietly.

"A judicial position opened up in the Northern District, so, what the hell, I took it."

Ben could not conceal his amazement. "You mean you're *disappointed* about an appointment to the federal judiciary? Most people would kill to be where you are!"

Derek made a snorting noise. "Do you know what I make here?"

Ben shook his head.

"Less than half what I used to pull down at Raven. Less than *half*!" He leaned across his desk. "And the worst part is, I have to sit around and listen to a bunch of inferior, incompetent pseudo-litigators argue day in, day out, none of them one-*tenth* as good as I was. But I've been taken out of the game, Kincaid. I've been put on the sidelines, and in my personal opinion, it's all because of *you*, you miserable little turd!" Spittle flew into Ben's face. "It's all your fucking fault!"

Ben was dumbfounded. It was worse than he had imagined. Incredibly, devastatingly worse. "I-I still hope you'll be fair to my client—"

Derek threw a pencil across the room. "Stop whining and get the hell out of my chambers!"

"I think she's innocent, I really do—"

"I said get *out*!"

"But—"

"Shall I call my bailiff? Would you enjoy spending the night in jail?"

Ben hated to leave on that note, but he had no choice. He departed, knowing full well he had not accomplished any of his goals. On the contrary, he'd only managed to bring all Derek's hatred bubbling to the surface. Christina's case already looked grim, and now he'd made it worse.

And the prospect for tomorrow was no better.

* 37 *

The next morning passed tediously. The forensics testimony was no more interesting at trial than it had been at the preliminary hearing. The dactylogram expert confirmed that Christina's prints were found on the gun and elsewhere throughout Lombardi's apartment. Ben reminded the jury during cross that the paraffin test had been absolutely negative. All hair and fiber analysis apparently had proved inconclusive; the prosecution didn't call their designated witness.

The ballistics expert testified that the shots that destroyed Lombardi's cranium came from the gun bearing Christina's prints, fired at point-blank range. Moltke, of course, suggested that the proximity to the victim proved the assailant was a friend . . . or lover. Ben proposed a few other possibilities during cross-examination ("If someone's pointing a gun at your head, he can probably get as close to you as he wants, huh?").

Ben did his best to avoid any contact with Derek, even eye contact. Derek never addressed him directly, but it was clear he had not forgotten their conversation the night before. Every time he looked at Ben, his face was stone cold.

In the early afternoon, Moltke called the coroner, Dr. Koregai. Ben remembered Koregai from their previous encounter during the Adams case; he hadn't warmed up any during the intervening year. In a curt, clipped voice, Koregai declared that Lombardi died where he was found, between one and two A.M., of gunshot wounds to the head. Irreparable fractures of the occipital bone. In all likelihood, he testified, the first shot killed Lombardi.

As far as Ben knew, that was the end of the prosecution's case. They had covered all the bases, and Moltke had the jury eating out of his hands, nodding their heads almost every time he pontificated. To Ben's surprise, however, Moltke stood and called an additional witness.

"Your honor, the United States calls Holden Hatfield."

Spud? The security guard from Lombardi's building? But of course. To establish that Christina was in the apartment well before Lombardi, and hadn't left before he was killed.

After the preliminaries, Moltke asked, "What do you do for a living, Mr. Hatfield?"

"Call me Spud," Spud said. "Everyone does."

Moltke smiled. "All right, Spud. Tell us about your job."

Spud ran through a general description of his duties as security guard, making his duties sound as glamorous as possible. He explained in detail the system of doors and elevators he controlled, how a visitor could only enter through the front door, could only ride the elevator if Spud triggered it, and could only open the stairwell doors from the outside. Spud explained that, as a result, he could state positively that only four people went up to Lombardi's apartment the night of the murder before Lombardi himself.

"And who are those four people, Spud?"

"Well, there's the defendant, of course. Miss McCall."

"Who else?"

"That would be Quinn Reynolds, Clayton Langdell"—he drew in his breath—"and Albert DeCarlo."

As before, the mention of the mobster's name had an electrifying effect on the jury. This time, however, Ben saw several jurors nudging one another, pointing toward the gallery. Sure enough, DeCarlo himself was sitting in the back of the gallery, wearing his scarf and white overcoat, dark sunglasses hiding his eyes, even while he was inside. Pretty damn gutsy, showing up here at the same time federal agents were trying to use Vinny and the other drug runner they picked up Tuesday morning to build a case against him. DeCarlo must've realized his name would come up during the trial. Why else would he be here?

Moltke continued his direct. "And you don't know when those people left Lombardi's apartment. Correct?"

"That's right. The back door to the parking lot can be opened from the inside, and most people go out that way. I know when Miss McCall left, though."

"And why is that?"

" 'Cause I went upstairs with the FBI agents and watched them haul her out of Lombardi's apartment. I am the security guard, after all."

"I see. So to summarize, you know the defendant went up to his apartment around ten, before Lombardi arrived, and that she was still there at two, when Lombardi was found dead."

"That's about the size of it."

"Just a few more questions, Spud. Could you describe the defendant's demeanor when she came in that evening?"

"Oh, she was pissed." He looked quickly at the judge. "I mean she was real angrylike. 'Scuse my French."

"I think we all catch your meaning, Spud," Moltke said, with a quick wink to the jury. "Any idea what she might've been angry about?"

"I think so."

"Please tell us."

"Well, Mr. Lombardi called that afternoon and told me—"

"Objection," Ben said. "Hearsay."

Moltke raised a finger. "This is not being offered to prove the truth of the matter asserted, your honor. Goes to show the defendant's state of mind at the time of the murder."

"I believe that's correct," Derek said. "Overruled. You may answer the question."

"I don't remember the exact words," Spud continued. "Mr. Lombardi called and instructed me to let this woman up when she arrived. I kind of teased him about having a new girlfriend, and he said, 'I don't think you'll be seeing much of her after tonight.' " He chuckled. "I guess she was about to get the big brush-off."

Ben glanced at the jury box and saw Mrs. Applebury cast a meaningful look at another woman in the jury. Yes, they knew what that meant. Hell hath no fury. "Move to strike, your honor. The witness is speculating."

"I think he's simply characterizing his observations in a colorful manner," Derek said. "Overruled."

"So when the defendant went up to Lombardi's apartment," Moltke said, "she was furious because she either had been dumped, or knew she was about to be dumped. Is that correct?"

"Objection," Ben said. "Leading."

"That's all right," Moltke said. "I'll withdraw the question.'' Why not? He'd already made his point. ''Nothing more, your honor.''

''Cross-examination?'' Derek asked, in a tone of voice that clearly implied he thought it inadvisable.

Ben couldn't think of a single question worth asking. Spud was wrong, and Ben knew it, but there was nothing malicious about his testimony. Right or wrong, he wasn't lying; he was telling the jury what he honestly believed. And Ben knew if he tried to get tough with Spud, Derek would shut him down in a heartbeat. For that matter, regardless of what Ben tried, Derek would be sure to turn it against him.

''No questions,'' Ben said reluctantly. He felt the eyes of the courtroom—the reporters, the jury, even Christina—bearing down on him.

''Anything more from the prosecution?'' Derek asked.

''No, your honor,'' Moltke said. ''The prosecution rests.''

''Very good,'' Derek said. ''I think that's enough for today. Tomorrow morning, at nine o'clock sharp, the defense will begin presenting . . . whatever case they may have.'' He banged his gavel. ''Court is adjourned.''

The courtroom came alive. Reporters sprang into the aisles, blocking the way. Flashbulbs and minicam lights illuminated the room. Moltke strolled back to give his daily press statement about his triumphs on behalf of the cause of the justice everywhere. A few reporters yelled questions at Ben, but he ignored them.

He felt Christina's eyes burning down on him. She didn't understand; how could she? She hadn't been there last night. All she knew was the conventional wisdom—a criminal defendant wins by breaking down the prosecution's case. If the defense attorneys haven't made their mark by the time they call their own witnesses, turning the jury around is almost impossible. And she knew what they had lined up in the way of defense testimony to turn that jury around. Not much.

"We need to discuss . . . our case strategy," Christina said haltingly.

Ben nodded. They started toward the door, plunging into the throng of reporters. "Who are you going to call?" "Do you think you have a chance?" "Was this a revenge killing by a jilted lover?" Ignoring the questions, avoiding the blinding lights and the sense of impending doom tightening its grip around them, Ben and Christina pushed their way out of the courtroom.

* 38 *

Ben stomped into his office, sending chickens flying in all directions.

"How goes the war?" Jones asked.

"Not well at all. We start putting on our case tomorrow morning, assuming we have a case tomorrow morning." He noticed a brown lumpish thing on Jones's table. "What in the world is that?"

"Mrs. Marmelstein sent you a fruitcake. She's been watching the TV coverage; she thought you needed it."

Ben scrutinized the alleged edible. "I hate fruitcake."

"Doesn't everyone? Still, it's the thought that counts."

"You're right, of course. Get rid of it, okay?"

"Will do, Boss." He thought for a moment. "I wonder if chickens like fruitcake?"

"I wouldn't be surprised."

"Hey, Skipper!"

Ben whirled around and saw Loving sitting in the lobby.

"Hi ya, Skipper. How's the big trial going?"

"Let me see," Ben said. "The judge hates my guts, the jury is convinced Christina is guilty, and we haven't got a shred of defense evidence."

"Things could be worse."

"How can you possibly say that?"

"Because he hit the jackpot," Jones explained.

Ben planted himself beside Loving, who appeared to be wearing the same stained T-shirt he'd worn every time Ben had seen him. Was that the only shirt he owned, Ben wondered, or did he have several of them, just alike? "You got the DeCarlo documents?"

"Guess so," Loving said nonchalantly. "I dinnt really know what was important, so I grabbed everything. Yer secretary pulled out what he wanted."

"That's wonderful! How did you do it?"

"Oh hell, it weren't nuttin'. Some of the boys put me on to DeCarlo's head bean counter. A CPA. Very soft. I waited for him in his car last night. He was kinda startled to see me."

I'll just bet. "You didn't do anything improper, did you?"

"I just suggested in a nice way that it would be bad for his health if I didn't see DeCarlo's business records."

"It wouldn't be ideal for his health if DeCarlo found out he showed them to you."

"His point exactly. So I described the various ways I could rearrange his face without even working up a sweat. Real friendlylike, you know. He said he thought maybe he could lay his hands on the documents. I promised I'd get them back to him in twenty-four hours. DeCarlo's all wrapped up in this trial business, so he's not likely to miss them."

"Jones," Ben said, "get everything you need copied, pronto."

"Already done, Boss. I've begun comparing DeCarlo's records with Lombardi's. There are several discrepancies, and numerous unexplained financial contributions from DeCarlo to Lombardi. I think you'll find that DeCarlo had a definite motive for offing Lombardi. If Lombardi went down, so would DeCarlo.''

"That might work," Ben said, thinking aloud. "Even if we can't absolutely prove that DeCarlo killed him or hired out the job, the mere suggestion of motive and involvement by such a notoriously shady figure might create reasonable doubt about Christina's guilt.''

"Can we subpoena DeCarlo?" Jones asked.

"Probably not at this late date," Ben said. "Especially since he doubtless has a battalion of lawyers who would try to quash it. But he was in the courtroom today. Maybe he'll be foolish enough to show up again tomorrow. Draft a subpoena dated tomorrow, Jones. Just in case.''

"Will do, Boss.''

"Loving, I can't tell you how grateful I am. This is the first piece of solid evidence we've turned up. You may have helped save a woman's life. Consider us even. Square.''

Loving batted his eyes. "Gosh," he said softly. "I never really done anything, you know, *good* before." Ben could see his throat constricting. "I'm never gonna forget this. You're the best, Skipper. The abso-goddamn-lutely best.''

Ben moved away before Loving tried to hug him. "Jones, I'm going to be in my office, planning strategy for tomorrow. I don't want to be bothered.''

Jones nodded. "Give 'em hell, Boss. Pull a Perry Mason.''

"Oh *yeah*!" Loving said enthusiastically. "I love that show. I watch the reruns all the time. I love the way he makes the killer break down right there on the witness stand. I bet you watch it too, huh, Skipper?''

"No," Ben said. "I can't stand it. It's not remotely realistic. That never happens in real trials.''

Loving looked crushed.

"Too bad," Jones said. "We could use a little Raymond Burr pizzazz right now."

"Mind if I use the phone, Skipper?"

"Of course not. Help yourself." Ben started once again for his office.

Jones piped up. "Boss?"

"Yessss?"

"Since the trial isn't really going so hot, and we're, well, we're basically desperate, how about I do a little investigating of my own at the scene of the crime?"

"Absolutely not. I need you right here comparing those records."

"What if I finish early?"

"You'll be lucky if you finish before dawn. And the trial resumes at nine A.M."

"You sure are tough sometimes."

"These are tough times." Ben started again for his office.

"Uhh, Skipper?"

"I have *work* to do, people!"

Loving stared at the floor. "Gee, sorry."

"Total stress-out," Jones muttered under his breath.

"What is it, Loving?" Ben asked.

"It's your phone." He put down the receiver. "There's something wrong."

"Tell Jones. He's in charge of office maintenance."

"You don't understand. I was calling that CPA guy to let him know I'd be back with the records soon."

"Yeah, so?"

"So, listen." He picked up the receiver. Ben heard a quiet but distinct click, followed by the dial tone.

"Okay," Ben said. "So what?"

Loving looked at him earnestly. "Maybe you don't know what that means, Skipper, but I sure do." He picked up the receiver again and let them both listen to the quiet click. "Someone's tapped your phone."

* * *

Ben sat at his desk trying to rethink the case from every possible angle. What had he missed? What brilliant question had he failed to ask? He tried to read his trial notes, but it was virtually impossible; you can't take notes and try a case at the same time. Normally, a legal assistant would take notes, but he didn't have one, unless he counted Christina, and he couldn't have the defendant scribbling away during the trial. His mind kept drifting off, thinking about all the victims this case had created. Christina. Margot. And Wolf.

He forced himself to focus on his trial plans for the next day. As far as he could tell, he'd punched every hole he could find in the prosecution's story, and it still hung together. The testimony was all circumstantial, but overwhelmingly so. None of the evidence was absolutely conclusive, but the cumulative effect would weigh heavily on the jurors' minds. No one wanted to be responsible for letting a murderer go free; and Moltke would make the jury feel that, unless they returned a guilty verdict, they were co-murderers themselves. Conviction by guilt complex, a tried-and-true prosecution technique.

Ben heard a timid knock on the door.

"Who is it?"

"It's me. Christina." She opened the door and poked her head through. "May I come in?"

"I'm preparing for tomorrow."

"Jones told me you've been in here for hours. Maybe you should take a break." She gave him the once-over. "Boy, do you look wrecked."

"Thanks bunches."

"You need a serious pick-me-up, Ben. Something to pull you out of the doldrums."

"I agree, but I think a trip to Hawaii would be inappropriate at the moment."

She shook her head. "Nothing that elaborate. Just a little

something to remind you what's important in life. You need some tall, seductive blonde to plant a cool wet smoocher on you. Square on the lips.''

He shivered in mock revulsion. "Brrrr. Don't you know lawyers never kiss on the lips? It would destroy our image.''

"Maybe that's your problem.''

Ben averted his eyes to his notes. "I'm afraid I haven't come up with much for tomorrow.''

"You'll think of something. I know you will.''

"I'm just trying to be realistic, Christina. Our prospects are bleak.''

"Nonsense. Things could be worse.''

"Now you're saying it. Why does everyone keep telling me that?''

"Because it's true. You'll pull something out of your hat.''

"I'm not a magician, Christina. I'm not even a very good lawyer.''

"I disagree.''

"I feel like I'm trying to be the White Queen. You know, in *Through the Looking Glass*. She believed six impossible things every day. Before breakfast.''

"I thought you displayed great *panache* in the courtroom today.'' She fidgeted with her hands. "Ben, I told you earlier I wanted to discuss strategy. I think you should put me on the stand.''

"Absolutely not.''

"Why?''

"As far as I'm concerned, the Fifth Amendment is there for a reason, and it's a good one. I'm not going to put you through that.''

"Oh, Ben. What's the use of protecting me from cross-examination if the end result is a life sentence? Or worse?''

"Most criminal attorneys never let the defendant testify. It rarely helps and always hurts.''

"You haven't any choice!'' Christina's voice trembled.

"Look, Ben, I'm an experienced legal assistant. I've been down this road before, and I know where we stand. We need an impeccable defense witness, and I'm all we've got. So use me."

"Not a chance."

"Ben, just this once, don't try to do everything by yourself. Let me help."

"Christina, I—"

"Ben!" Her eyes went straight to his heart. "Who's the client here?"

Ben bit down on his lower lip. "You are."

"Who calls the shots?"

"Unless he or she is requesting something unethical, the client."

"Fine. I'm glad we got that settled." She stood up and smoothed the wrinkles out of her dress. "Tomorrow morning, I expect to be called to the witness stand. Understand?"

Ben nodded.

"Don't stay up too late. I don't want the jury thinking my attorney is a zombie. And don't forget to feed your cat."

"I'll feed her," Ben said. "But that doesn't mean she'll eat."

Christina left the office. Ben tried to concentrate on his notes, but insistent questions in the back of his mind kept distracting him. Who would bug his phone? The same person who killed Lennie? The same person who'd been following him? Why was DeCarlo in the courtroom today? And a million other enigmas that had little or nothing to do with the trial. Or perhaps they did, and he was just too stupid to realize it.

He forced the questions out of his mind. He had to concentrate. He had to cover everything, and cover it again and again and again, until it made sense. Until he spotted whatever he had been missing.

The moment of truth was less than twelve hours away.

* 39 *

The courtroom, as before, was packed. The reporters maintained their front-row flank. Ben spotted DeCarlo taking a seat in the back, a few rows behind Margot Lombardi. Spud was still around, too—probably standing by in case the prosecution wanted to recall him on rebuttal. On the same row, Ben saw Quinn Reynolds. What was he doing here? And behind him, Clayton Langdell. Behind Langdell, Stanford and Abshire sat on the back row, far corner. Abshire made eye contact with Ben and winked. Smug son of a bitch. He thought they had it in the bag.

And he was very possibly right. Ben had stayed at the office as long as he could, well past midnight. Even after he went home, he found he couldn't sleep, couldn't even come close, so he opened his briefcase (to the delight of Giselle, who thought it was great fun to play in) and continued looking for the magic answer. After he awoke that morning he went straight to the courtroom, still mentally searching for the elusive detail he had overlooked, the crucial clue that explained everything and proved Christina's innocence.

He never found it.

Ben walked down the aisle and planted himself in front of DeCarlo. "Have you got someone following me?"

"Why, Ben! The questions you ask. Have you seen someone following you?"

"Maybe. I'm not sure. I think so."

"Does that necessarily mean I'm responsible?"

"You're the most likely candidate. So how about it?"

"Would you believe me if I denied your accusation?"

"Probably not."

"Well, I deny it."

"You're a prince."

The bailiff stepped out of chambers and, a few steps behind him, Judge Derek. Ben felt a helpless, hollow feeling inside. It was happening—the trial was going forward. There was nothing he could do to stop the inevitable course of events, to prevent the conspiracy of circumstances from condemning Christina and destroying her life.

Derek brought the court to order and made his usual opening remarks and instructions to the jury. Preliminaries out of the way, he asked, "Are you ready to proceed, counselor?"

Ben rose slowly to his feet. He could feel his knees wobbling. He felt sick. "Yes, your honor."

"Call your first witness."

Ben saw Christina pull herself erect. He tried to speak, but he could not make the name come out.

"Mr. Kincaid?" Derek repeated.

Ben felt a wave of embarrassment cross his face. Here he was, making a fool of himself in the courtroom once again.

"Mr. Kincaid. Please."

But wait a minute. Derek wasn't even looking at him; his eyes were focused on the rear of the courtroom. Now that Ben noticed, most of the jurors were looking back that way, too. What in the—?

"Mr. Kincaid. I believe there's a member of your staff attempting to direct traffic in the back of the courtroom."

What? Ben whipped around and saw Jones waving his arms wildly in the air, trying to get his attention. And he was holding . . . a pair of sunglasses?

"Your honor, may I have five minutes to confer with my colleague before calling my first witness?"

"You really like to build up the suspense, don't you, Kincaid? Very well. Five minutes."

Ben bolted to the back of the courtroom before the reporters had a chance to block his way.

"Jones, what is going on?"

"I expected you to stop by the office!"

"Sorry. I was running late, so I came straight to the courthouse. So?"

"So? Boss, I've been up all night! Guess why."

Ben was gone almost fifteen minutes, but he had to make sure he understood everything Jones told him and had considered all the ramifications. And he had to grab a magazine from the law library.

"Mr. Kincaid," Derek said upon his return. "We were afraid you had gotten lost in the hallway."

Ben raced up the aisle. "Sorry, your honor. It won't happen again."

"Of that I am certain," Derek said menacingly. "Are you at last ready to call your first witness?"

"I am, your honor." He saw Christina again draw herself up. "The defense calls Holden Hatfield."

Ben saw Christina give him the most clearly expressed what-the-hell look he had ever seen in his life.

Moltke rose to his feet. "Your honor, this witness has already testified. Learned counsel had the opportunity to cross-examine. Why do we need to hear from him again?"

"An astute question," Derek said. "Learned counsel?"

"Your honor, the testimony I anticipate goes outside the scope of the prior direct."

Moltke interrupted. "But your honor—"

"The man is listed on the prosecution's own witness list," Ben insisted. "They can hardly claim prejudice."

"But your *honor*—"

"I'm sympathetic, Mr. Prosecutor, but if I don't let him

call this witness it will be reversible error, and we both know it. Take the stand again, Mr. Hatfield.''

Spud leaned against the pew, a stricken expression on his face. "Do I have to, Judge?"

"I'm afraid so, sir."

Spud crawled down the aisle and into the witness box, looking as unhappy as any man who ever lived.

Ben went to the podium. "Spud, I apologize for hauling you back up here, but I had no choice. I promise I won't make this take any longer than necessary. You testified before that you saw four people go to Lombardi's apartment on the night of the murder, right?" Sure, he was leading, but he figured Moltke wouldn't object. He wanted this to be over, too.

"That's right."

"And those four people were Christina, Clayton Langdell, and Quinn Reynolds."

"And Albert DeCarlo," Spud added.

"Yes. That's the one I want to discuss. Are you *sure* it was Mr. DeCarlo?"

"Course I'm sure. What kinda fool question is that? I've seen him a dozen times before. In person and on the TV. I know what he looks like."

"I'm certain you do. Are you aware that Mr. DeCarlo denies going to Lombardi's apartment that night?"

Spud grinned. "Well, he would, wouldn't he?" There was a mild tittering of laughter.

"Spud, what was your vision like that night?"

"What was my—I don't get it."

"I'm asking about your eyesight."

"What about it?"

"What was the quality of your vision?"

"I don't see why that's any of your business."

Ben glanced at Derek. "Permission to treat Mr. Hatfield as a hostile witness."

Derek deferred to Moltke. "Any objections?"

"If it will get this over with sooner, I'm all for it."

Derek granted the motion.

"Now Spud," Ben continued, "don't get me wrong. I'm not trying to get you in trouble, but you have a certain fondness for a good stiff belt, don't you?"

"I take a drink every now and again. What of it?"

"And sometimes you drink on the job, don't you?"

"What are you saying, son? Are you trying to get me fired?"

"Please answer the question."

"My answer is no."

"Spud." Ben looked down at the floor regretfully. "The morning after Lombardi died you were on the job, weren't you? And didn't you offer me a shot of Jack Daniel's from a silver flask strapped to your leg?"

Spud didn't answer.

"I wonder, Spud, if I asked the bailiff to take a look, would he find that same flask strapped to your leg right now?"

Spud steadied himself on the bar beside the witness stand. "Sometimes I work as much as twelve- or eighteen-hour shifts," he said. "That's a long haul for a man my age."

"I know that," Ben said. "And no one's condemning you. But, in fact, you'd been drinking the night Lombardi was killed, hadn't you?"

"Maybe a little," he mumbled.

"And drinking can make your vision blurry, can't it?"

"Objection," Moltke said. "Ambiguous. Is he asking if it can or if it did?"

"I'm asking if it can, your honor. Theoretically."

Derek nodded. "The witness will answer the question."

"I suppose it's possible."

"So it's possible your vision was blurry the night of the murder. And the fact of the matter is, your vision isn't so hot in the first place. Is it, Spud?"

Spud's face was cold as ice. "I don't know what you're talking about."

"Spud, aren't you nearsighted?"

Spud didn't answer.

"I understand your reluctance, Spud. I realize that if you admit your vision is failing, you may lose your job, maybe even your permit. But this is very important. And I keep remembering when we talked before, at the lodge, and how you had to practically press the clipboard against your nose to be able to read it. Isn't it true you're nearsighted?"

"No."

"Well, let's have a little test then." Ben walked back to counsel table and tore a picture out of *Time* magazine, careful to hide it from Spud. "How close to you was the person you identified as DeCarlo on the night of the murder?"

Spud thought for a moment. "Oh, maybe ten feet away when he came through the door, maybe five feet away when I activated the elevator."

"Okay." Ben walked back about ten feet from the witness stand, then held a full-page, glossy photo of George Bush over his face. "Spud, I'm holding a large photograph of a well-known person. Someone who's on television frequently. Can you tell the jury who it is?"

"I'm not that quick with names," he grumbled.

"Oh, I bet you'll know this person, Spud. If you can see the photo clearly. Who is it?"

Spud squinted at the photograph, his eyes obviously straining. "Elizabeth Taylor?" he guessed.

Mrs. Applebury covered her mouth with her hand. Smiles appeared on the faces of other jurors.

"I'm afraid not." Ben walked about five feet closer to the stand. "Now I'm moving to about where the visitor would have been while you were activating the elevator. Can you tell the jury who this is now?"

Spud hesitated a long time. "Paul Newman?" he said at last.

"Well, you're getting warmer. Take one more shot at it."

Spud appealed to the judge. "Do I have to play this fool game?"

Derek stifled a smile. "Answer the question."

Spud leaned against the front of the witness box. Technically, that was cheating, but Ben had a hunch it wouldn't matter. "What about that fool reporter? Geraldo Whatever-it-is."

"I'm afraid not," Ben said. "But tell me this. Why did you guess the people you guessed?"

" 'Cuz I thought that's who it was, obviously!"

"But I mean *why*." Ben explained himself slowly, making sure the jury could absorb every word. "Wasn't it because, although you couldn't make out the details of the face, you had a general impression of the hair color, the clothing, and the shape of the head?"

Spud shrugged. "I suppose so."

"Good. Now, Spud, I want you to think back to the night of the murder. When you saw that person you called De-Carlo, what did you actually *see*?"

"I saw what I always see when I see DeCarlo. Dark sunglasses. Dark muffler. Black hair slicked back in a ponytail. That white overcoat."

"Thank you," Ben said. "That's exactly what I thought. No more questions, your honor."

The judge looked at Moltke. "Any cross-examination?"

"No, sir. On the contrary, I move to strike the entire examination for lack of relevance."

"Oh, give me a break," Ben said. "You usually make Myra make motions of this ilk, don't you?"

"I'm serious," Moltke insisted. "What does it matter who else might've been in Lombardi's apartment? We know for a fact that the defendant was, and she's the one who's on trial."

Ben stared at Derek. "Do I even need to respond to this lame motion?"

Derek frowned. "Regrettably, no. The motion is overruled. Call your next witness, Mr. Kincaid."

Ben scanned the rows of spectators, all waiting for his next sentence. He saw DeCarlo look away, apparently hoping Ben wouldn't notice him. Reynolds and Langdell also seemed to be avoiding his glance. And at counsel table, he again saw Christina correct her posture. *Pardonnez, mon cheri.* Always a bridesmaid, never a bride.

"Get on with it," Derek said.

"Yes, your honor. The defense calls . . ." He peered into the gallery. "Margot Lombardi."

* 40 *

Ben heard the sudden silence, the suspension of breath, the tangible surprise. Half the gallery turned to scrutinize Margot.

Her lips parted slightly; her eyes widened. She obviously was not prepared for this development.

"I object, your honor," Moltke said.

"Again?" Ben replied, an eyebrow arched.

"Your honor, we've had no advance notice."

"How could he?" Ben asked. "I didn't know I needed to call her until this morning."

"Your honor, this court should not make excuses for counsel's sloppy preparation and eleventh-hour discovery."

Ben stepped closer to the bench. "Judge, my client is on trial for her life. I ask for the widest possible latitude."

Derek's lips were pursed. "You are pressing this court's patience to the outermost limit, counsel. The days of trial by ambush are long past."

Ben stepped even closer to the bench and said in a soft voice the reporters couldn't hear: "If you don't let this witness testify, I'll make an offer of proof on the record indicating that this witness could have exonerated my client. You'll not only be reversed; the Tenth Circuit opinion will make you look like an idiot."

Ben felt Derek's eyes burning down on him. If he had any recourse against Ben whatsoever, Ben knew he'd take it. But he didn't have any choice. "I'll allow you to call this witness, counsel, subject to a subsequent ruling on the relevance of her testimony. But the court is mindful of the fact that this witness is the victim's widow. You will proceed quickly to the point, and it had better be a relevant point at that. Furthermore, if you harass or mistreat this witness in any way, you will find yourself in a federal jail cell for a period of time longer than your entire previous legal career!"

"I understand, your honor."

Derek cast his eyes into the gallery. "The defense has called Margot Lombardi."

"As a hostile witness," Ben added.

"Whatever." Derek waved her to the front of the courtroom.

She rose slowly, like a wobbly pony just learning to walk. She hovered for a moment, apparently confused. The men on the end of the row slid out, allowing her to pass. She pressed past them and walked to the witness stand.

After she was sworn, Ben said, "Mrs. Lombardi, please excuse my bluntness, but the judge has instructed me to get straight to the point. What was the state of your relationship with your husband at the time of his death?"

"We . . . were separated."

"In the process of becoming divorced?"

"Y-yes."

"How did your husband treat you?"

"I'm not sure what you mean."

"Well, Mrs. Lombardi, I'm referring to what you and I talked about when I visited your home. Your husband was very cruel to you, wasn't he?"

"In . . . in some ways."

"Both mentally and physically."

Her voice became quiet, almost infinitesimal. "I suppose."

"Did you know he was seeing other women?"

"Yes. Lennie—Tony's assistant—told me."

"What did you think about that?"

She considered her answer for an extended period of time. "Not very much," she said finally.

Ben closed his trial notebook and took a step away from the podium. His notes couldn't help him now. "Mrs. Lombardi, what were you doing the night your husband was killed?"

"I was at home."

"Was anyone else there?"

"No, I was alone. I told you that before."

"So you have no witnesses?"

Her fingers were locked together; her arms were pressed tightly to her body. "I suppose not."

"Mrs. Lombardi, you weren't home *all* night, were you?"

"What do you mean?"

"There's something that's been nagging at the back of my brain, Mrs. Lombardi, but I didn't fully realize what it was until this morning. When I first talked to Spud about you, the day after your husband died, he described you as a blonde. But now, as the jury can see, your hair is black—just like Mr. DeCarlo's. Have you dyed it?"

"That's . . . rather personal."

"Mrs. Lombardi, don't make me yank out a strand and show the jury the roots."

Her lips twitched ever so slightly. "So I dyed my hair. It's a woman's prerogative to change her hair color."

"And, I imagine, her hairstyle as well," Ben said. "Tell me, Mrs. Lombardi, have you ever worn your hair in a ponytail?"

Ben felt the activity behind him, the furious notetaking, the quiet whispers.

"I guess. Once or twice."

"And I know you have a pair of dark sunglasses. I saw you wearing them in the courtroom yesterday."

"I hardly see how that proves—"

"And how about a black muffler, Mrs. Lombardi? And a white overcoat. Do you have those, too?"

Her face was becoming blotchy, even more so than before. "Let me ask you again, Mrs. Lombardi. You didn't stay home the entire night your husband was killed, did you?"

She didn't say anything.

"Isn't it true you went to your husband's apartment that night, after altering your appearance sufficiently to fool a nearsighted, blurry-eyed, drunken doorman?"

Tears welled up in her eyes. She moved her mouth wordlessly.

"Isn't it true the doorman let you up to your husband's apartment?"

More movement, no words. The tears streamed down her face.

Ben looked away. He couldn't let it get to him. He had to press forward. "Isn't it true you let yourself in and found another woman, Christina McCall, in the apartment with your husband?"

"I-I—oh God, *no* . . ."

Ben heard the sound of an objection somewhere in the background, and some sharp words from the judge. It didn't matter.

"Isn't it *true*, Mrs. Lombardi?" Ben shouted. "Isn't that exactly what you did?"

"I—*no*, I—"

"Mrs. Lombardi, isn't it true you took your husband's gun and shot him in the head?"

"Oh God, *God*!" she wailed. Her voice was a shriek, a sick, desperate cry.

"Isn't it *true*, Mrs. Lombardi? That you shot your husband?"

"Oh my God," she cried. Her voice was hoarse, broken. "Oh God—*yes* . . . It's true."

* 41 *

Derek banged his gavel, futilely attempting to reassert his control. Almost as one body, the front rows of the gallery raced toward the back door, each reporter hoping to be the first to call in the story. The running, yelling, talking, and crying drowned out the impotent banging of Derek's gavel.

Margot's head drooped forward, her face in her hands.

"I repeat, *objection*, your honor!" It was Moltke, running up to the bench where he could be heard.

"A bit late for that now, isn't it?" Ben asked.

"Your honor, I see no reason to put this poor widow through further ordeal—"

Ben interrupted him. "Are you ready to dismiss the charges against my client?"

"I—why—" Moltke looked sideways toward the gallery, his remaining audience. "Well, I don't know. . . . I think that's premature. Perhaps we could just recess and let everyone take a minute to regroup.''

"No way," Ben said. "If you're dismissing the charges, fine. Otherwise, I'm continuing my examination now, before you can get to her.''

"Your honor," Moltke said, "I think the most charitable course of action would be to allow Mrs. Lombardi a chance to clear her head—''

"Sorry," Derek said. "Much as it grieves me to do so, I agree with Mr. Kincaid. Either you dismiss or the trial goes on.''

Moltke looked imploringly at Derek, then back at the gallery. "I can't do that," he said. He slowly retreated to his table.

Ben returned to the podium and continued his examination. "Mrs. Lombardi, I'm sorry to press you, but if you're able, we need to continue.''

Margot brushed the tears from her eyes and face. She seemed to have collected herself somewhat. "I know," she said. "Go ahead.''

"Mrs. Lombardi, would you tell the jury why you went to your husband's apartment that night?''

"I—" She coughed, cleared her throat. "I told you before Tony called me the night he died, desperate, begging for money. I didn't have nearly enough. But I wanted to comfort him, to help him any way I could. I asked if I could come over to see him." Her face clouded over. "But he said no. He said he was expecting someone. And I knew what that meant." She pulled her head erect. "You see, I still foolishly hoped Tony and I might get back together.''

Ben was stunned. After all the beatings, the cruelty, and the humiliation, she still wanted him back. "And you feared his relationship with Christina would prevent any reconciliation between the two of you.''

"That's right," she said. "Of course, I realized his feelings for me"—her voice dropped—"or lack thereof, would never change. But if he was going to have someone female around, for whatever reason, why shouldn't it be me? I *was* his wife, after all."

"And you intentionally disguised yourself."

"I didn't want anyone to recognize me. I knew Spud had been instructed by Tony not to admit me under any circumstances. So I made Spud think I was someone else. I knew it wouldn't take much to disguise myself. Spud could barely see over his desk and everyone knew he had a, well, predilection for the bottle. I chose Mr. DeCarlo because his trademark apparel was well-known, and I thought Spud was very unlikely to give him any trouble. And I was right. Spud didn't say a word to me."

"And you were willing to let DeCarlo be blamed for the murder?"

"Well, of course, at that time I didn't know . . . ."

"I see. Please continue. What did you do after Spud let you up the elevator?"

"I went to Tony's apartment and knocked on the door. There was no answer, so I let myself in. I found your client sound asleep in the living room chair. I assumed she was dead drunk."

"And that's when you shot him? Because you found him alone with Christina?"

Margot frowned; her eyebrows knitted together. "You just don't get it, do you, Mr. Kincaid? He was *already dead*."

Ben felt as if his head might explode—too much blood to the brain. "But you said—I don't understand—"

"Don't you see? He killed *himself*. Shot himself in the head. I told you before he had a fear of going to prison. Absolutely pathological. Apparently he'd gotten some inside information, found out about the FBI net closing in around him. What's more, someone was demanding money from him and threatening to get him into trouble with DeCarlo if he didn't pay. Tony saw no way out. So he killed himself."

Ben stood sputtering for several seconds, trying to frame a question. Nothing in law school had ever prepared him for an examination like this. "But . . . how can you know why he killed himself?"

"I've still got the suicide note he left," she answered. "It's clearly in his handwriting."

"But . . . you said before that *you* shot him."

"Of course." She almost laughed, seemingly amazed at his stupidity. "How do you think he managed to end up with *four* shots to the head? He only fired the first; he was dead after that. I picked up his gun from where it fell on the floor and, after wrapping my hand in my scarf to avoid leaving fingerprints, supplied the final three shots."

"Why?"

Margot's eyes drifted away from Ben, to a place at the table behind him. "To get . . . *her*."

She was staring at Christina, of course.

"I'd been married to Tony for twelve years, Mr. Kincaid. I had a lot . . . invested in him. For better or worse, he was all I had. I had no desire to be divorced. And I especially had no desire to be the spurned woman. The castaway. Last year's model. The woman who gets shunted aside when a newer, livelier one comes along."

Ben remembered what Spud had told him. She was a madwoman, he'd said. Crazy jealous. The pieces were finally beginning to fall into place. "So you fired the additional shots into your husband's head after he was already dead, and took the suicide note, to make it look like a murder. To frame Christina."

"It was a perfect setup. There she was, lying in the same room with him, sound asleep, and nobody knew I had even been there. I guess I'm weak. It was more than I could resist."

"That would explain why the coroner had so much trouble establishing a time of death," Ben said, thinking aloud. "There were *two* times of death, so to speak. What did you do after you fired the shots?"

"The obvious. I wiped the gun clean and put it on the floor beside her. I considered pressing her fingers against it, but I was afraid that would wake her. I made sure I hadn't touched anything in the apartment, and I left. I expected to be interrogated, if not arrested, but it never happened. No one suspected. Even when the police finally questioned me, it was strictly routine."

That's because they already had their patsy, Ben mused.

"Afterward, I tried to rinse the dye out of my hair but, to my surprise, it wouldn't come out. I must've mixed it wrong—given myself too concentrated a dose. I didn't want to be seen buying any blonde hair color; after Tony's death was announced, that would be likely to arouse suspicions. So I just left it the way it was."

Ben knew he had enough. There was no reason to keep pressing. "Thank you for your candor, Mrs. Lombardi. I know it wasn't easy for you, and that you've put yourself at mercy of possible criminal charges."

"For what?" She laughed quietly. "I told you—he was already dead. What am I going to be charged with? Tampering with a corpse?"

Ben suspected Moltke would be more imaginative than that, but there was no reason to bring it up now. "Your honor," he said, "I have no more questions. And I move for dismissal."

Derek looked sternly at Moltke. "Any objections, Mr. Prosecutor?"

Moltke's dismay was obvious, but under the circumstances, he had no alternative. "No, your honor. We'll consent to dismissal."

"Very well," Derek said. "The charges are hereby dismissed. Miss McCall, you are free to go.'' He banged the gavel. It reverberated through the courtroom like a clap of thunder.

Everyone leaped to their feet at once. The crowd was loud and raucous, cheering and shouting more like the audience for a rock concert than a criminal trial. Ben saw Jones in the back of the courtroom giving him the thumbs-up. He saw Loving pressing his way to the front, yelling something about a ''perfect Perry Mason moment.'' The reporters (the ones who were still there) leaned against the railing, shouting questions at Ben.

He ignored them all and strolled back to counsel table. ''Well, *ma cherie*,'' he said to Christina, ''it looks as if—''

He never managed to finish. Christina threw her arms around his neck and kissed him, right there in front of everybody. A big wet smoocher.

Square on the lips.

PART FOUR

*   *

Six Impossible Things

* 42 *

"Have I told you recently how sick I am of this case?" Mike asked.

"Aw, what a whiner," Ben replied. He glanced at Mike's desk. "At least you're not reading Shakespeare any more. Tell me what you've discovered about the suicide note since the trial."

"No surprises. Our experts are convinced it's genuine. The handwriting matches, plus the note makes reference to financial matters Margot couldn't have known about. Probably no one could have, other than Lombardi. And we've checked with Quinn Reynolds. It's all accurate. Bottom line— it must have happened just as Margot said it did."

"Amazing. How could anyone have guessed?"

"I don't know," Mike said. "How did *you* guess?"

"I didn't. Not really. Jones was the one who had the revelation. Despite my telling him not to on repeated occasions, he snuck out to the scene of the crime, as he likes to say, and visited with Spud while he was on duty. Jones picked up on it pretty quickly—the drinking, the nearsightedness. Maybe it was the stress of the trial, but for whatever reason, Spud was hitting the bottle heavily and couldn't see well at all."

"And that led you to Margot."

"Very good, shamus. You've been back to crime school." Ben stretched out in his chair. "I realized then we were looking for someone Spud *mistook* for one of the three suspects—

but which one? Reynolds and Langdell both admitted they went to Lombardi's apartment; only DeCarlo denied it. That suggested that the person in question had passed him- or herself off as DeCarlo. I saw Margot on my way back into the courtroom and I began to remember—the dark sunglasses, the discrepancy over her hair color. That's when I figured it out.''

''You had a lot of guts, Ben, calling her to the stand on a wild hunch like that. And no hard evidence.''

''Yeah. But, of course, it wasn't as if I had a lot of other alternatives. I was very lucky.''

''Chance favors the prepared mind.''

''Is that Shakespeare?''

''No. But it should be.''

''Have you got everything you need?'' Mike asked.

''I think so.'' Ben scanned the papers spread across the table in Mike's office. ''Requisition forms, invoices, declassified FBI reports, the works.''

''Let's just hope everything goes according to plan.''

''It will,'' Ben said. I hope, he thought silently.

At that moment, Abshire bounced into the office, his thumb tucked behind his suspenders. ''What the hell is this?'' He bent over the table and ran his fingers through Ben's papers. ''These are confidential FBI documents. How did you get this stuff?''

''Through the Freedom of Information Act, mostly,'' Ben said, not looking him in the eye.

''Like hell,'' Abshire replied. ''FIA requests take a month, minimum, even assuming you know what to ask for.'' He whirled around. ''Cards-on-the-table time, boys. You did this, didn't you, Morelli?''

''As a matter of fact,'' Mike said, ''I did.''

Abshire approached him, gritting his teeth. ''When are

you going to figure out which side you're on, Morelli? I specifically said I wanted no cooperation—"

"The case is over, Abshire. You lost. Give it up."

Abshire's fists balled up. "Goddamn it, this benevolent attitude of yours is probably the reason we lost the case. May I remind you that a second murder remains unsolved?"

Mike glanced at Ben out of the corner of his eye. "It won't be unsolved for long."

"Oh, is that right? I guess you and your old college buddy have got that one all worked out too, huh? Goddamn it, when are you going to get it through your thick fucking head that *I'm* in charge of this investigation!"

"You were in charge of the murder case," Mike said. "It's over."

"It's over when I say it's over! Goddamn it, I hate it when you local peons start telling federal officers how the game is played. *I* make the rules, and *I'll* tell you—"

Without saying a word, Mike stepped forward, grabbed Abshire's tie and tightened the Windsor knot until Abshire started to choke. "Let me tell you what the rules are, Mr. Federal Officer. I toed the line when there was a pending investigation and prosecution, because I took an oath to defend, obey, and serve the federal government, even when it's represented by pricks like you. But the trial is over now, and the feds are packing their bags and praise God getting the hell out of Tulsa."

Abshire started to speak, but Mike tightened the knot until the agent's tongue came sputtering out of his mouth. "Now, my friend, Mr. Kincaid, may be an attorney, but regardless of who his client is, he tries very hard to learn the truth and do the right thing, two motivations which you could never be accused of having. Mr. Kincaid needed a few FBI documents to complete his investigation, so I got them for him. And frankly, if you don't like it, we'll see how well trained you federal assholes really are."

Mike loosened his grip just enough that Abshire could speak, barely. "What are you saying?" Abshire whispered hoarsely.

Mike smiled. "Cards-on-the-table time? I'm saying that if I find out you so much as lodged a complaint against me, I'm gonna flatten your miserable little face. Got it?"

Abshire nodded his head.

"Good." Mike dragged him to the door, still gripping his tie. "Be seeing you." He shoved Abshire out the office door and closed it after him.

Ben wagged his head back and forth. "You shouldn't have done that, Mike."

"I know," Mike said. He grinned from ear to ear. "But, *damn*, it felt good."

Mike glanced at his watch. "He's late." He pounded his fists together.

"Keep your machismo in check, pal. He'll be here."

"Then where is he?"

"Maybe he thought we were meeting at the federal building. You know how easily these guys are confused."

"Possible. I'll go next door and take a look around."

With Mike's absence, the office seemed quiet, almost dead. It was way after hours. Everyone else had gone home; the night shift worked out of a different building. Ben looked over his notes, preparing what he would say. He had to get this right. If he made stupid mistakes, he wouldn't accomplish anything.

After two or three minutes passed, Ben heard someone walking down the outside hallway. "So did you find—" He looked up, startled. It wasn't Mike.

"All right," Stanford said. "I'm here. What did Morelli want, anyway?"

"Well . . . actually, I was the one who wanted to talk to you."

Stanford peered through his half glasses. "What about?"

"I . . . think we should wait until Mike gets back."

"Why? Surely you can say whatever you have to say without hiding behind him."

Ben felt the burn creeping up his neck. "We can start now if you like."

"Very good," Stanford said. "Shoot."

"Number one. Someone tapped my phone."

"Indeed? Who would want to do such a thing?"

"You," Ben said simply.

"Is that a fact?" Stanford's eyebrows rose slightly. "What makes you think so?"

"A friend of mine named Loving. He's the one who detected the tap in the first place. He later found the blue box on a transmission pole down the block from my office."

"Oh, well," Stanford chuckled. "That proves I did it."

Ben slid a piece of paper across the table. "This is a copy of your application for a warrant to tap my phone. I gather you tried every judge in the Northern District, and they all said no. You didn't have probable cause, and even if you did, it would've been a clear violation of attorney-client privilege to allow you to tap the opposing attorney's phone while a criminal proceeding was in progress."

"So I got turned down. So what?"

"So you did it anyway. Without authorization."

"Suppose I did. Just speaking hypothetically. What do you care? You got your client off the hook."

"I think the phone tap was just one renegade act in a long-standing renegade operation, orchestrated by you. At first I suspected Abshire, but then I remembered what Mike told me—that Abshire wasn't authorized to go to the bathroom without your okay. You used Abshire, your hotheaded underling, to create a smokescreen, a camouflage. The person really pulling the strings was always you."

"Mr. Kincaid, where do you get these farfetched ideas?"

"I've done some checking, using the Freedom of Information Act and some FBI records Mike managed to obtain. You haven't had authorization for half the things you've done since this operation began."

Ben slid more documents across the table. "You started this investigation almost three years ago, on your own initiative, based upon evidence, flimsy at best, that Tulsa was the drop site for a major drug-smuggling operation. After two years and the expenditure of tons of FBI money, your investigation was getting nowhere. Just when it looked as if the money would dry up and your operation would be shut down by your superiors, some new evidence providentially appeared linking Lombardi and DeCarlo to the Cali drug cartel. Evidence that you obtained from an unnamed informant who was never verified, I might add.

"Even then, the paperwork indicates the FBI denied authorization for some special operation you wanted to mount. I'm reading between the lines a bit here, but it appears you wanted to supply arms and ammunition to certain people in a certain South American country in exchange for information about drug smuggling. The FBI said no, so you borrowed some pals from the Department of Alcohol, Tobacco and Firearms and hired a few soldier-of-fortune types to staff your operation."

"That's an awful lot of reading between the lines," Stanford said, smiling pleasantly.

"Feel free to stop me anytime I go wrong." Ben continued. "During the following year, your little cadre stirred up a lot of dust but precious little hard evidence. Nothing like the bombshell you needed to promote yourself from a mid-level paper-pushing post to a position of senior authority. To your credit, you did eventually turn up a drug-running operation, though rather a small one, which you still haven't managed to link to Lombardi or DeCarlo. And of course, you didn't find that operation through any investigation of your own. You found it by tapping my phone and having someone follow me around. Christina and I led you to the drop site in the Creek forest; you nabbed the bad guys and took all the credit. And shot a little boy in the process." He glanced at Stanford. "How am I doing?"

Stanford leaned back, his arms folded across his chest. "Go on."

"Of course, you totally blew it the night Lombardi died—you missed the delivery. You raced to Lombardi's apartment, warrant in hand, hoping to find some drugs. They were never delivered. I don't know why—maybe the supplier got wind that the FBI was in town, or maybe Lombardi died before he completed some essential prerequisite. You saved your butt by arresting Christina for murder. The evidence was slim, but you worked double-time making it stick, all to lend some validity to your precious investigation. You even resorted to breaking into her apartment. You, or your accomplice, must've been there before DeCarlo's blond goon showed up. But he was looking for information, and Christina and I arrived before he had a chance to find anything. You were there to hide a packet of cocaine where you knew she wouldn't find it, but the police would."

Stanford's eyes became dark. "You can't prove any of this."

"You might be surprised."

"And suppose it's true. What's the charge going to be? Overzealous performance of my job? They'll probably give me a good-conduct medal."

"There's more. There was a reason Lombardi was so scared, so convinced the FBI was closing in on him. Someone was blackmailing him."

"And I suppose you're going to blame that on me, too?"

Ben pushed another document across the table. "We subpoenaed the MUD phone records for Lombardi's apartment. It appears someone from your office called him twice the night he died. Shortly after the last phone call, he killed himself."

Stanford's upper lip curled. "That doesn't prove anything," he snapped.

"It doesn't have to. Lombardi explains it all in his suicide note. During the first phone call the blackmailer told him the FBI had all the evidence they needed, and that he'd be locked away in prison till he was an old man if he didn't come across with half a million bucks. Problem was, Lombardi didn't have that much money; in fact, he didn't have a tenth that much money, and he was heavily in debt to DeCarlo. Too many generous contributions from the boss at usurious interest rates.

"During the second phone call, the blackmailer pushed even harder; he said if Lombardi couldn't pay, he'd have to provide him with information, which of course was what the blackmailer really wanted all along. He demanded evidence linking DeCarlo to the drug cartel, not realizing Lombardi was even more afraid of DeCarlo than he was of prison. No wonder Lombardi seemed tense the last day of the Simmons trial—his entire world was crumbling all around him. He was trapped, poor schmuck. He had a choice between his two worst fears, prison or DeCarlo, and he saw no escape. So he killed himself."

"I don't have to listen to this work of fiction," Stanford said.

"It wasn't a coincidence that the blackmailer called that night. He wanted to get to Lombardi before he was taken into custody, before he was surrounded by lawyers and judges or eliminated by a DeCarlo hit man. It was the blackmailer's last chance to extort information."

"I'm leaving." Stanford pushed himself out of his chair.

"I think you'd better stay," Ben said. "You see, Lombardi killed himself, but before he did, he told someone he was being blackmailed. His associate—Lennie."

"So?"

"After Lennie read about Lombardi's death in the newspapers, he realized he had some hot information on his hands. He didn't know who the blackmailer was, but he knew his identity could be traced through the phone records for Lombardi's apartment. So he used his information in the natural way—for Lennie. He tried to sell it. Unfortunately, he tried to sell it to the FBI, which unbeknownst to him was the home of the blackmailer himself."

Stanford's eyes narrowed. He eased himself back into his chair, not saying a word.

"When you found out Lennie was offering information about Lombardi's death, you knew you had to shut him up but quick. Problem was, you didn't know where he was." Ben's voice softened. "But you eventually found him. By listening in on my phone conversation with him. And then you went to his motel room and killed him. Of course, you shot him four times in the head, just to confuse things and to cast additional suspicion on Christina."

"Do you have any idea what you're accusing me of?" Stanford said. "Do you have any idea what this . . . *crap* could do to my career? And you haven't even got any proof!"

"Wrong," Ben said. "Lombardi identified you in his suicide note. By name."

It started before Ben knew what was happening. Stanford threw himself across the table. He hit Ben mid-chest, tipping him backward. His chair crashed down on the floor, dropping Ben and Stanford with a thud.

Ben felt the impact of Stanford's elbows jabbing into his ribs. He tried to pull away, but Stanford was squarely on top of him. Stanford raised his fist and brought it down hard. It caught Ben on the side of his face, jarring his teeth together, making him bite his tongue. A sickening queasiness spread through his body.

Stanford raised his fist again. Before he connected, Ben

shoved him backward as hard as he could. Stanford teetered, just enough to allow Ben to squirm out from under him. Ben rolled under the table and scrambled out the other side. Stanford leaped over the table and positioned himself between Ben and the door, blocking his exit.

"Help!" Ben shouted. "Somebody get in here!"

Stanford smiled malevolently. "That's the down side of working after hours. You're on your own, Kincaid."

Ben grabbed a chair and held it between them like a lion tamer.

"That's pathetic," Stanford said. He jabbed his thumb against his chest. "I'm FBI, man. I'm a trained killer. Do you really think you're going to stop me with a chair?"

He knocked the chair away with a single swipe of his arm. Ben's wrists twisted painfully; he had to drop it. As soon as the chair fell, Stanford tackled him, knocking him to the floor. In the space of a second, Ben tried to remember something Christina had told him once: use your hands to break the fall, roll on your arms, don't hurt your back. He tried to cushion his fall, but after he landed, Stanford fell on top of him, crushing the breath from his lungs. Ben felt sick, disoriented; his vision was obscured by flashing white lights.

For a moment, the pressure eased. Ben gasped, trying to catch his breath. Suddenly, he felt a sharp pain in his side. He opened his eyes, tried to focus. Stanford was standing over him, kicking him in the ribs.

"Take this, you sorry bleeding-heart sack of shit. Christ, even Lennie put up more of a fight." He pulled his boot back and kicked Ben again, this time even harder.

Ben cried out in pain. He felt something inside his chest snap. His ribs felt as if they were on fire.

He clutched his side, but it didn't help. He was breathing rapidly; he couldn't catch his breath. He could taste blood trickling into his mouth. Another moment passed, then he felt the boot slam into his ribs again, in the same soft spot as before.

Ben screamed in agony. The pain was excruciating, blinding. He tried to move, to think, to do something—but he couldn't. He was absolutely helpless. Tears flooded his eyes. He saw a blurred image of Stanford, pulling his foot back for another killing blow.

Then he heard a blessed sound outside the door. *"What the hell?"*

It was Mike. Ben had a vague impression of Mike running down the hallway and throwing himself against Stanford. They began to struggle.

Ben clenched his teeth and tried to push himself up. He pressed against Mike's desk, pulling himself up the side by inches.

Stanford and Mike rolled on the floor, exchanging blows. Ben saw several sharp punches fall into Mike's stomach, then several more into Mike's jaw. Mike pushed Stanford back, and they both went careening into the wooden coat rack. The rack tumbled over, spilling Mike's suit jacket, his overcoat . . . and his gun holster, gun intact.

Stanford and Mike both saw it at the same time. Mike reached out, but Stanford jabbed him in the solar plexus. Mike winced, retracted involuntarily. Stanford got the gun.

Stanford pulled himself onto his knees, pointing the gun at Mike's heart. "Thought you could take me, huh?" Stanford said, breathing heavily. "Thought you were going to nail me to your self-righteous cross. Well, think again." He stretched out his arm and aimed. Mike closed his eyes.

Ben grabbed the book on Mike's desk and slammed it against the side of Stanford's head. Before Stanford could regain his balance, Ben hit him again, this time in his face. Mike sprang forward and grabbed Stanford's wrist, pounding it against the desk, loosening his grip on the gun. Mike kicked the gun away, then brought his fist directly into

Stanford's face. Stanford fell backward onto the carpet, unconscious.

Mike slowly pulled himself to his feet. A steady flow of blood trickled from the side of his mouth. "What the hell did you hit him with?"

Ben looked. *"The Complete Works of William Shakespeare,"* he said, gasping.

"Another triumph for the Bard," Mike announced jubilantly.

It was the last sound Ben heard before he passed out.

* 43 *

"Oww!" Ben cried. "Be careful!"

The nurse frowned and plunged ahead, winding the stiff tape around Ben's rib cage. Clearly, she had no patience for wimps.

"Where did this woman take her training?" Ben asked Mike. "Belsen-Belsen?"

"Yeah, that's where we get all our nurses. Helps prepare them for life with the force."

"No doubt. *Ouch!*"

The nurse wound the tape around Ben's chest a final time, then cut it off with a small pair of scissors. "There," she said. "You'll be fine."

"Really?" Ben rubbed his sore arm, the one on the side Stanford had kicked repeatedly. "I guess that explains why I feel like I've been hit by a tank."

"Just take the medicine the doctor prescribed," she said brusquely. "The cracks are small. You'll heal." She turned and left the infirmary.

"A doting mother," Ben murmured.

"She works the police department and both jailhouses," Mike said. "She has to be tough."

"I suppose. How are you feeling?"

"All right. I can't believe I let that goddamn old white shirt get the drop on me."

"Don't keep riding yourself. He was desperate."

Mike shook his head in self-disgust. "I just lay there like a pansy while Stanford tried out his recipe for face pudding."

"I thought you handled yourself okay. At least you didn't get totally walloped, like yours truly."

"Yeah, well. Things could be worse."

"Now you're doing it! Everyone keeps telling me that, but somehow, I've yet to be convinced."

"What the hell did you say to Stanford, anyway? To get him so rattled?"

"I told him we had the goods on him. Described his entire scheme. And I mentioned that Lombardi had identified him by name in his suicide note."

"But Lombardi didn't identify Stanford in his suicide note. He didn't identify anyone."

Ben looked away. "Gosh, I guess I misspoke myself."

"You sly dog, you. You set him up."

"The least I could do. Considering what he did to Christina."

"Understood. By the by, Ben Kincaid, consulting detective, I have one final question. Something that occurred to me while I was running around like an idiot."

"Okay. What's your question?"

"Are you going to tell her?"

Ben laid back on the examining table, taking some of the pressure off his bruised and aching ribs. "Care to explain that?"

"Surely you're not going to make me outline the entire line of reasoning."

"Well, I've always wondered if you're really any good at this detective stuff. Now's my chance to find out."

"All right. It goes like this. It occurred to me, that between what you'd told me, what we found out, and what we'd deduced, there was still one detail unexplained."

"Which was?"

"Who drugged Christina? I'm assuming she was drugged. There's just no other explanation for the fact that she dozed through four rounds of a gun with no silencer." He took his pipe out of his pocket, blissfully ignoring the sign on the wall that thanked him for not smoking. "The rosé she drank must have been doctored. But by whom? And why?

"Given what we know, there's only one person who had a realistic opportunity to violate the vino. Lombardi. He could get the drug easily enough from DeCarlo, or perhaps Lennie, and of course he had access to his own booze. But why would he do such a thing? Obviously, because he knew Christina would drink it when she came over that night. In fact, he invited her to do just that when he left the message asking her to come to his apartment. And that deduction leads to the big question. Why did he want to drug Christina?"

"And the answer is?"

"He was planning to let Christina take the fall for him. As we've established, even before Stanford called to blackmail him, Lombardi knew the FBI was closing in. Whether the FBI ever proves it or not, I've no doubt Lombardi was using his parrot operation to run drugs, especially after he started doing business with DeCarlo. And now he knew they were on to him. He panicked. He had to think of some scheme to prevent himself from going to prison. He was still expecting a big drug shipment. DeCarlo probably got wind of the FBI investigation and and called it off, but Lombardi didn't know that. So he planned to leave Christina in his apartment that night, sound asleep with a large stash of cocaine, while he was somewhere miles away with an unbreakable alibi. He thought the FBI would come charging in, as in fact they did, and they'd find her with all the illegal narcotics.

"Lombardi's theory was, let Christina fill the FBI quota; at the very least, it would temporarily take some of the heat off him. The fact that she was in his apartment might be somewhat incriminating, but there would be no hard evidence against him—since Christina didn't know anything about his drug-running activities. She'd just plead innocence, and no one would believe her, and she'd be put away for a long haul. And if he got lucky, the FBI would call their investigation a success and close it down before they got to him."

Ben nodded. "But something went wrong."

"Yeah. Stanford. After Lombardi's telephone conversations with him, he knew it was hopeless; he couldn't divert suspicion from himself just by planting the drugs on someone else. Christina had already drunk the rosé; it was too late to stop that part of the plan. But it was not too late to save himself from his worst nightmare—a long stretch in prison and the wrath of Albert DeCarlo. So he killed himself."

Ben tried to roll over onto his side, but the pressure on his sore arm was too great. "I remember what Margot said when she was testifying. Something like, 'I don't know why Lombardi wanted Christina around, but it wasn't for the reason everyone assumes.' I thought that was chilling at the time. Now I realize it was chillingly true."

"Which brings us back to my original question. Are you going to tell Christina?"

"She may have already figured it out," Ben said. "And if not, well . . . I think she's been through enough pain and disappointment these past few weeks."

"I concur." Mike started out the door, then stopped, as if something were holding him back.

"Ben," he said, after a long moment.

"Yeah?"

"I just wanted . . . well . . . to discuss the way I've been behaving—"

"You were on the other side, Mike. I understand."

"Let me finish, will you?" He walked closer to Ben and leaned against the examining table. "When I took this job, I swore an oath."

"I know. To defend the United States and the Constitution, etc."

"More than that. To obey the rules and procedures of the state and federal law enforcement agencies. To be a good cop. To play it by the book. And that meant something to me, Ben. It really did." He exhaled slowly. "Well, I've learned something from all this."

"Yeah?"

"I've learned that *by the book* isn't good enough anymore." His eyes became hooded. "That following the rules isn't always sufficient. Oh, I'm not talking about becoming a vigilante or anything. I'm just saying . . . I think sometimes we hide behind our professionalism, our badges, our licenses, our procedures—"

"Our Rules of Professional Conduct," Ben added.

"Yeah. Maybe. We hide behind those things because they protect us from moral debate, from the really tough questions. It's easier to read a rule than to consider individual cases—specific people in specific situations.

"But that's wrong," Mike said firmly. "People are more important than rules. I won't make that mistake again." He half smiled. "You think you can forgive me?"

"Mike, pals are for thick and thin—no matter what happens. That's why they're called pals."

Mike clasped Ben's arm firmly. "Thanks, pal."

"Don't mention it. Incidentally, pal, you're hurting my arm."

* 44 *

Ben slipped into the Oneok Building at about 7:45 and rode the elevator to the tenth floor. He might be slow, but he wasn't stupid; if the security guard didn't take names until eight, the intelligent burglar slipped in just before. He ducked into the bathroom, hid in a stall and read back issues of *Stereo Review* for two hours. He had a story planned out in the event someone came in to clean the bathroom, but the contingency never arose.

At eleven o'clock, when he was reasonably certain everyone was gone, Ben slipped out of the men's room and crossed the hallway to Swayze & Reynolds. Keeping an eye out for security, he used his copied key to open the front door. He passed through the ornate lobby and into Reynolds's office.

He found Polly in her usual place, trapped in a cage much too small, barely alive. Her coat had lost its sheen; the colors of her wings and the brightness of her eyes had faded. Worst of all, the pile of feathers at the bottom of the cage had doubled in size. Ben could see exposed patches of flesh where the feathers had been yanked out.

As quietly as possible, Ben removed the cage from the stand and carried it out of the office. He rode the elevator to the ground floor.

He stopped at the security guard's station. "I've got a medical emergency," he said. "This parrot's dying."

The security guard scrutinized him with evident suspicion.

"I was working in Reynolds's office," Ben added, "when she started croaking."

"Working this late?" the guard asked.

"Of course. Why else would I be up there? Look, if Mr. Reynolds's prize parrot dies, he is not going to be happy."

The guard shrugged. "So what do you want me to do, call an ambulance or something?"

"Never mind," Ben said. "I've got a car." He brushed past the guard and walked out onto the street.

Whew! Managed to bluff his way through that one. Reynolds, of course, would be furious the next morning when he found his parrot missing. Even if he thought to ask the night security guard, though, Ben didn't think the guy could describe him well enough for Reynolds to make an ID. And if he did, that was fine, too. Ben would sic Clayton Langdell and his entire organization on Reynolds. Maybe the ASPCA and a few others, too, just for good measure.

Ben crossed the street and walked about halfway down Fifth Street. After a few seconds, he heard the low plaintive wail of a hoot owl. He walked toward the sound.

"Pssst." Ben followed the voice into a side alley.

In the soft moonlight, he could just make out Wolf's face. He looked good; his appearance had improved a hundred percent since he had been released from St. John's. His right arm, the one that caught the first bullet, was still in a sling, but otherwise he almost seemed like his former self.

"Here," Ben said, passing him the cage. "Take care of her."

"Sure." With his free arm, Wolf opened the cage and gently drew Polly out. Polly cooed quietly, then nestled against his shoulder. "Ma says I have to spend less time in the forest and more time in school."

"I'm sorry to hear that."

"It's okay. She says I can still search for traps, and I can start keeping my birds at home. I'm building a shed in the backyard. The landlord doesn't like it, but he hasn't said anything. Everyone seems to be bending over backward to be nice to me. Since I got shot and all.''

"Milk it for all it's worth,'' Ben advised. "It won't last forever.''

"Yeah, I 'spect you're right.''

"And pay attention in school. You need to make good grades so you can grow up to be the world's greatest veterinarian.''

"Aw, I hate school. The other kids never like me.''

"Nonsense. You should be very popular. How many kids can brag about being shot by the FBI?''

"Hmmm.'' This was apparently a prospect Wolf hadn't contemplated. "Well, I'd better go.''

"Okay. See you around.''

Wolf started out of the alley.

"Oh—*Wolf*!''

Wolf turned. "Yeah?''

"I've been meaning to ask you. Do you know anything about chickens?''

* 45 *

There was something wrong with Ben's office, but he couldn't quite put his finger on what. For starters, Jones's card table had been replaced by a desk, a real *desk*, with drawers and everything. What's more, there were two other real desks, one on either side of Jones's.

That was different, sure, but Ben sensed there was more. He stood in the middle of the lobby trying to figure out what had changed.

And then he realized.

"What's wrong, Boss?" Jones asked.

Ben frowned. "I hate to admit it," he said, "but I miss the chickens."

Jones sighed. "Yeah. Me, too. Especially Barbara."

"Well, I'm sure Wolf will provide them with a loving home."

"Yeah, I guess. Hey, what's in the sack?"

"Sack?" Ben held his groceries away from Jones's eyesight. "Oh, nothing in particular."

"Uh-huh." Jones pulled down the side of the sack. It contained a large quantity of Feline's Fancy. "Giving in, are we?"

Ben yanked the sack away and put it in a closet. "I just thought I should have a little on hand. For special occasions."

"Right. That's why you bought the king-size twelve-pack. Don't feel bad, Boss. Cats have broken better men than you. Oh, that reminds me. Clayton Langdell called. He wants to set up a meeting."

"He still wants me to represent him?"

"Apparently so."

The light dawned: Langdell wasn't a suspect trying to buy him off. He really *did* want to hire Ben because he thought he was a decent lawyer. "Did he mention anything in particular?"

"He said he checked you out during the trial and was very impressed. Oh, he also said he liked the way you handled that reporter on television. He wants to consult you regarding their new public relations campaign."

"Oh, swell. A new career teaching lobbyists how to bully reporters."

"At least it's work, Boss. Things could be—"

"Don't say it!" Ben said, cutting him off. He glanced at the pleading Jones was typing. He had the carbon in backward; the second copy was a blue smear. Oh, well. If this Langdell business paid off, maybe he could spring for a photocopier. "By the way, Jones, I've been meaning to thank you for all the work you put in on the Lombardi financial records."

"Oh, yeah. And that was so helpful, too."

"No, really. It was. I also want to thank you for your first-rate fieldwork. You got a lot more out of Spud than I ever did. I won't forget it."

Jones leaned forward eagerly. "Does that mean you'll let me do more investigating in the future?"

Ben cleared his throat. "Well . . . we'll see." He turned and almost smacked into Loving, who was carrying a tall stack of file folders. Loving veered away at the last moment before impact, plopping the folders down on one of the new desks.

"Loving!" Ben said. "What are you doing here?"

Loving looked back at him, puzzled. "Didn't she tell you? Christina hired me."

"*Christina* hired you? To do what?"

"To be your investigator, of course. Nuttin' personal, Skipper, but you've really been lettin' the work pile up around here."

"I've been kind of busy. . . ."

"Anyway, I went through all your active files, and figured out where I could lend a hand. I've already started working on several of these cases."

"You have?"

"Yeah. It's going pretty well. I may have to rough some people up, but I'll get the dope you need."

Rough some people up? "Wait a minute—"

"Hi, everyone."

Ben whirled around and saw Christina come through the front door. "Just who I've been wanting to see," he muttered.

"It's Ben Kincaid!" she cried out. "My hero!" She batted her eyelashes.

"Yeah, yeah, yeah. Look, Christina—"

"Do you like my new desk?" she asked.

"Yeah. That's what I wanted to discuss with you."

"Guess what! I figured it out."

Ben knitted his eyebrows. He had the distinct impression this conversation was getting away from him. "Figured out what?"

"My dream, silly. Frosty the Snowman and the tremendous explosions."

"It was just a dream, Christina. It doesn't have to mean anything—"

"But it wasn't just a dream. I was fighting the drug, trying to shrug off its influence and see what was going on in Tony's apartment. I saw a blurred image of Margot with coal black eyes, wearing a big white overcoat and a black scarf. She fired a gun three times. Hence, in my drugged-up state, Frosty the Snowman and the tremendous explosions."

"Pity you didn't think of this sooner."

"True. *Comme çi, comme ça.*"

"I guess so," Ben concurred. "Anyway, what's with the new desks?"

"That's my handiwork. Consider it a down payment on legal fees owed."

"That's not necess—"

"My thinking is, if you're going to be a big-time lawyer, you're going to have to start upgrading your appearance."

"Oh yeah?"

"Yeah. And your staff. So I hired Loving to handle your investigations. And," she said, pulling some files out of her briefcase, "I'm going to be your new full-time legal assistant."

"Christina, I can't afford to pay him. Or you."

"Oh, Ben, don't be such a spoilsport. Look how happy he is over there, playing with his little files, threatening to punch people's lights out. He really wants to be part of our little family."

"Family?"

"Besides, he's already gotten more work done in a day than you've done in two weeks. He'll generate his own salary."

"Let's hope so."

"And don't worry about me. I realize this will mean a serious cut in my usual paycheck, but I'll live. I think it's clear you need me here. Where I can keep an eye on you."

Ben felt a familiar burning sensation creeping up his neck. "There's not going to be much money here for anyone," he said. "At least not at first."

"Don't worry about it. After all you've done for me, I owe you."

"That's nonsense. You don't owe me anything. I was just lucky, that's all. I made a thousand mistakes."

Christina swiveled around in her chair and grabbed Ben by his shoulders. "I can't *believe* you would say that. After all you've accomplished. Listen to me, Ben. You are a miracle worker. You're like the White Queen. You've accomplished *at least* six impossible things."

"Such as?"

"Such as, getting me off the hook against incredible odds—*numéro un. Deux*, nailing Stanford for killing Lennie. *Trois*, convincing the U.S. Attorney's Office that Margot should get counseling, rather than a jail sentence. *Quatre*, finding Spud a nice job at the file desk in the downtown police station."

"Mike had something to do with that."

"*Cinq*, saving Polly from Reynolds and finding her a good home with Wolf, whom you also managed to keep out of

J.D. court. *Six*, um—" Her eyes darted from side to side. She stalled for time. "Er, getting rid of those chickens."

"Stretching it a bit, aren't we?"

"Well, okay, number five was really two impossible things. The point is, Ben, you're a winner and everyone knows it but you. Now if you'll excuse me, I'm rather busy. I've got a lot of work to do if I'm going to whip this Popsicle joint into shape."

She closed her briefcase, put it away, and opened her top desk drawer. "Oh!" She gasped. "Ben!" She removed her small French porcelain pig, *cochon* emblazoned on the side. The cracks showed where it had been broken, but it was more or less intact. "You put my French piggy back together! And put it in my—" She looked up at him. "Then you must have known!"

"Well, I suspected."

"But this is so—oh, *Ben*!" She placed the pig atop her desk and looked up at Ben with sparkling eyes. "I'm going to keep my piggy right there, always. And whenever I look at it, I'll think of you."

How flattering.

Ben surveyed his new office, marveling at the changes. No toilet paper, no chickens. Loving was growling into his phone, threatening to "make someone's life a misery." Jones was banging away at the typewriter, still typing on the wrong side of the carbon. And Christina was right beside him. Safe.

Ben smiled. Things could be worse.

Acknowledgments

I want to thank Kathy Mozingo and Deborah Loss for their assistance in the preparation of the manuscript; Arlene Joplin and Kindy Jones for their assistance with the intricacies of federal criminal law; countless volunteers at the Oklahoma offices of the American Humane Society; and my wife Kirsten, for the closet bit.

Ben Kincaid was late getting to his office the next morning, not that that was unusual. What was unusual was that his entire office staff—Christina, Jones, and Loving—were standing shoulder to shoulder just inside the front door waiting for him.

"Let me guess," Ben said. "You're on strike. Look, I don't blame you, but until some of our clients pay their bills—"

He stopped. The huge ear-to-ear grins on their faces told him that wasn't it. "Okay, what, then? Is today my birthday or something?"

"Where have you been?" Christina said, wrapping her arm around his shoulder and pulling him into the office.

"At Forestview. I had to take Joey to school, and then there was this big sign-up for the spring bake sale—"

"Never mind that." Christina pushed him into a chair while

the other two huddled around. "We've been trying to get hold of you all morning."

"Why?"

Jones leaned forward. "I got a call the minute I came into the office, Boss."

"And?"

"The mayor wants you!"

Ben fell deep into thought. Was this about that incident with his daughter at Forestview last Friday? It was just a little bump. And she ran into him...

"Can you believe it, Skipper?" Loving grabbed him by the shoulders and shook him. "The mayor wants you!"

"That's nice...I guess."

Christina cut in. "Ben, do you even know what we're talking about?"

"Well, actually...no."

"The biggest cause célèbre to hit Tulsa in years, and you're totally clueless. What were you doing last night?"

"Well, let me see. I had soup for dinner, then I read *Goodnight Moon* to Joey about eight thousand times..."

She slapped her forehead. "I can't believe it. Everyone in the state watched the chase last night. Except, of course, you."

"Chase? What are you talking about?"

"Ben, the mayor has been charged with murder."

"Murder!" The light slowly dawned. "And he wants me to get him off?"

Christina and Jones and Loving all exchanged a glance. "Well," Christina said, "he wants you to represent him, anyway. *Entre nous*, I wouldn't get your hopes up too high on the outcome."

"What do you mean?"

Christina grabbed his arm. "I'll brief you while we drive to the jailhouse."

Because Mayor Barrett had specified that he wanted to see Ben alone, Christina (after considerable protest) agreed to cool her heels outside while Ben went into his cell to talk to him.

"Don't worry about me, Christina," he told her. "I'll be fine."

"I'm not worried about you. I'm worried about us."

"Come again?"

"I'm afraid you'll do something idiotic like not agree to represent him."

"In fact, I do have some reservations..."

"See! It's starting already. You're going to veer off on some wacky ethical tangent, and we're going to go hungry."

"Just let me talk to him. Then we'll see."

She grabbed him by the lapels. "Ben, promise me you'll take this case."

"We'll see."

"Ben!"

"We'll see."

Ben allowed the guard to lead him down the long metallic corridor. Mayor Barrett had the cell at the far end, a private suite, such as it was. A five-by-seven cell, with a bunk bed, a sink, and an open-faced toilet. Not exactly the mayor's mansion.

He was lying on the bottom bunk, his hands covering his face. When he moved them, Ben saw black and red lacerations on his face, and a bandage wrapped around his jaw and the back of his head.

The guard let Ben into the cell, locked the door behind him, then disappeared.

"How do you feel?" Ben asked.

"Better than I have a right to feel."

"My legal assistant told me you were in a traffic accident."

Barrett tried to smile, although between the bruises and the bandages, his face didn't have much give in it. "I crashed into a brick building with four cop cars, two television helicopters, and about half the world watching. Like I said, I'm better off than I have a right to be."

"Jeez. What were you doing?"

"Trying to kill myself," he said, with a matter-of-fact air that caught Ben unaware. "As it was, I didn't even break a bone. Goddamn air bags."

Ben paced nervously around the tiny cell. There was nowhere to sit, so he stood awkwardly by the cell door and contemplated the dominant question.

This was a part of criminal defense work that Ben particularly hated. Most criminal defense lawyers never asked the question. Since defending a client you knew was guilty raised a million ethical difficulties, most lawyers preferred not to inquire.

Ben, however, wanted to know the truth. He wanted to know where he stood. If he was going to put his name and reputation on the line, particularly in what was certain to be a high-profile case, he wanted to know he was doing the right thing. As his old mentor Jack Bullock used to say, he wanted to be on the side of the angels. But with such a horrible, heinous crime, how could he possibly ask?

Barrett sat up suddenly, hands on his knees. "Ben, I want you to know something up front. I didn't do it."

Ben gazed at him, his face, his eyes.

"I did not kill my wife. I did not kill my two precious daughters. How could I?" His eyes began to water, but he fought it back. "I couldn't do anything like that." He stared down at his hands. "I couldn't."

"I've read the preliminary police report. Neighbors say you and your wife had a disagreement yesterday afternoon."

Barrett nodded. "That's right. We did. I'm not going to pretend we didn't." He spread his arms wide. "It was that kind of marriage. We fought sometimes, like cats and dogs. But we still loved each other."

"What was the fight about?"

Barrett shrugged. "I hardly remember."

"The prosecutor will want to know."

"It was something about the kids. She thought I was spoiling them, giving them everything they wanted. Undermining her authority. And not paying enough attention to her. We'd had this argument before."

"How many times?"

He shrugged again. "I don't know. Many."

"Were these fights...violent?"

He twisted his head around. "Violent? You mean, did I hit her? Absolutely not."

"Well, I had to ask."

"Look, I don't know what people are saying about me now, but I would never hurt my wife. Or my girls. They're the most precious things in the world to me." His voice choked. "Were. I couldn't hurt them. Don't you think that if the mayor of the city was a wife beater, it would've come out before now?"

"I suppose." Ben pulled a small notebook out of his jacket pocket and began taking notes. "So you had an argument. Then what?"

"I can barely remember. It's all such a blur. And smashing into a brick wall didn't help."

"Just tell me what you recall. We don't have to get everything today."

"Well, I got mad. That doesn't happen often; most times I can just laugh it off. But this time she really got my goat, suggesting that I was hurting the girls and all. So I stomped out of the house."

"You left?"

"Right. Got in my car and drove away."

"How long were you gone?"

"I don't know exactly. Not long. Maybe an hour. I got a Coke at a Sonic—you can check that if you want—and I started to feel bad. So what if we disagreed on a few minor points. I loved my wife, and I loved my family. I didn't have any business running out like that. A strong man stands up straight and faces the music. So I headed back home."

"What happened when you got there?"

"I was in such a hurry, I left my car on the street and ran into the house. And—"

"Yes?"

He hesitated. "And then...I found...them. What was left of them."

"They were already dead?"

"Oh, yeah." His eyes became wide and fixed. "My wife was spread out like...like some sick human sacrifice. And my little girls..." Tears rushed to his eyes. His hands covered his face.

"I'm sorry," Ben said quietly. "I know this is hard for you."

Barrett continued to cry. His whole upper body trembled.

Ben took a deep breath. He hated this. He felt like a vulture of the worst order, intruding on this man's grief with these incessant questions. Guilty or not, Barrett was clearly grief-stricken.

NAKED JUSTICE
by William Bernhardt
Published by The Ballantine Publishing Group.
Available in bookstores everywhere.

William Bernhardt made his debut as a novelist with *Primary Justice*. His subsequent novels include *Blind Justice, Deadly Justice, Perfect Justice*—which won the Oklahoma Book Award and led the *Vancouver Sun* to dub the author "the American equivalent of P. G. Wodehouse or John Mortimer"—*Double Jeopardy, Cruel Justice, Naked Justice, Extreme Justice, The Midnight Before Christmas*, and his newest: *Dark Justice*.

As an attorney, Bernhardt has received several awards for his public service, and in 1993 he was named one of the top twenty-five young lawyers in the nation. He lives in Tulsa with his wife, Kirsten, and their children, Harry and Alice.